FIRST COMES LOATHE

Lilly Atlas

ISBN: 978-1-946068-37-8

Other books by Lilly Atlas

No Prisoners MC

Hook: A No Prisoners Novella
Striker
Jester
Acer
Lucky
Snake

Trident Ink

Escapades

Hell's Handlers MC

Zach
Maverick
Jigsaw
Copper
Rocket
Little Jack
Joy
Screw
Viper
Thunder

* * *

Audiobooks

Audio

Join Lilly's mailing list for a **FREE** No Prisoners short story.

www.lillyatlas.com

Facebook

Instagram

TikTok

Twitter

To Sam.

First book of each series goes to you. There wouldn't have been a single book without you.

<3

Table Of Contents

Prologue

Michaela figured she would either vomit or pass out cold on the floor.

It was a toss-up which of the mortifying acts would happen first, putting a quick and final end to her dreams.

She shifted back and forth as she stood there gnawing her lower lip. No one had said anything yet and she'd been standing there at least a full minute. Every person in the room seemed busy with whatever tasks they had to complete.

Should she start? Launch into the scene? Or was she supposed to wait for instructions? Maybe she should have asked one of the other girls sitting in the long line outside the audition room for some advice, but she'd been going for confident and experienced, not the unsophisticated noob that she was.

"Name?" A man had a placard in front of him with the words *Casting Director* on it. He didn't even look up from a clipboard. The man looked like he walked straight off the cover of GQ in trendy black jeans, a metallic button-up with rolled sleeves. Black nail polish, an eyebrow ring, and perfectly gelled hair completed the look.

"M-Michaela." She cleared her throat. "Michaela Hudson," she amended in as strong a voice as she could muster with her legs shaking and insides bubbling with anxiety. Standing in an audition room at a real Hollywood studio for the first time made her high school audition nerves laughable.

A bright light flashed and she blinked and jumped back. "Wh-uh…" She ran a damp palm over her shoulder-length and newly blond hair. The hair she'd spent more time perfecting that morning than ever before.

"Sorry, casting photo," a tall, thin woman said from behind a camera.

"Oh, uh, sure." Michaela blinked a few more times to get the spots in her eyes to disappear.

Stand tall, look them in the eye, and be the star I know you were born to be.

Her mother's words rang loudly in her ears as the urge to shrink in on herself and curl into a ball grew with each passing second. Her very first memory was standing on a chair in her mother's kitchen around age four, holding a bottle of Mrs. Butterworth's syrup and thanking the stuffed animal Academy for the award.

All through Michaela's childhood, her romantic of a mother had been in awe of Hollywood. The glitz, the glam, the magic of being loved by the entire world. Michaela had fallen hard for the allure of movie star life as well. Acting was the only thing she'd ever wanted to do. Not just acting but excelling at it. Becoming a star. Living in one of those jaw-dropping mansions in the Hollywood hills where she'd never have to wonder where her next meal would come from or how her mother was going to pay her medical bills. They'd live the ultimate life without any cares, concerns, or hardships. How could anyone have a moment of unhappiness when they had the entire world at their feet?

Even before her mother had passed away six months ago, Michaela decided their dream would live on, so she'd done it a few weeks ago. Moved from a tiny spec of a town in West Virginia to big-city Hollywood to begin her career as a starlet.

"You waiting for an engraved invitation?" the casting director barked, again not so much as glancing her way. "You may have all day, but I don't. Get started."

"Yes, sir." Michaela closed her eyes, inhaled a shuttered breath, and launched into the short scene the talent agent instructed her to memorize. The one she'd practiced no less than eight hundred times over the past four days—in front of the mirror, while eating, sitting on the toilet, when she should have been sleeping, and even while waiting tables at the coffee shop. She'd kill to have the opportunity to act this captivating scene on a real set.

Three lines in and one heartfelt attempt at sophistication, the casting director dropped his pen and finally gave her his eyes. His gaze stayed focused on her as she ran through the scene, pouring every ounce of her soul into the cheesy dialogue. From the same table as the director, another man without hair and skinny as a rail with thick, square glasses read the male parts in a bored tone.

Michaela gasped and pressed a hand to her chest in response to rejection from her fictitious love. The more he spoke, the more she fell into the character. Before long, she'd fully immersed herself in the role, feeling the character's personality wash over her and chase away the poor, small-town girl, replacing her with the high-maintenance socialite she portrayed.

Her heart soared. The director sat with his chin propped on his hand, watching her every move. Sure, he wasn't smiling, but he didn't frown either. That had to be good. Though a minuscule role in a made for television movie, she'd be in a film if she got this part. A real live Hollywood movie. With her name in the credits and face on screen for all the world to see.

"I'm not canceling this trip," she spat out, channeling her inner diva with a flip of her long hair. Hiding her slight southern accent was the hardest part of this process, but she'd been practicing for weeks and thought she had it down pretty well. "Do you have any idea—"

"Cut!"

Huh?

Michaela snapped her mouth closed at once, and her arms slumped limply to her sides. That was it? She'd only made it through half the assigned script.

"What is this shit, Bob?" The casting director stood with a mighty frown and aimed the question at a talent agent seated at the back of the room.

Michaela peeked over her shoulder in time to see Bob shrug. "Don't know. She ain't one of mine."

"Who got you this audition, kid?" the director asked with an expression akin to someone drinking spoiled milk.

"Um, E-Elvira with Star Finder Incorporated." The eclectic agent with snowy white hair and enormous cat-eye glasses had promised Michaela would be *absolutely perfect* for the role.

"SFI." The director snorted. "Figures."

Her face heated under the stare of everyone sitting at the table.

"I-is there a problem, sir?" Trying to speak louder than the pounding of her heart had her nearly yelling.

"Yeah, there's a problem." He slapped his palms down on the table as he rose. "There's a huge fucking problem. Have you even looked in a mirror today?"

Michaela blinked as every person in the room abandoned their tasks and fixed their curious gazes on her. She felt as though she were naked, standing in front of a panel of hypercritical judges all taking pot shots at her in their minds. Though only the casting director slung the insults, agreement with his assessment shone on projected from every other person's face.

The tip of her nose tingled with the urge to burst into tears.

Had she looked in a mirror?

Seriously?

Only the stark fear of disrespecting a man who held her fragile future in his hands kept her from laughing out loud.

She'd spent approximately four hours in front of the mirror, bleaching then styling her hair, giving herself a homemade oatmeal and honey facial, and slapping on more makeup than she'd ever worn. That was after countless hours of YouTube tutorials on how to apply Hollywood-style makeup.

"I'm sorry, sir, is my makeup smudged?" She ran a quick finger under each eye, proud of the way her voice didn't waver. Because inside, she was a quivering mess of fear and anxiety.

He sighed. "No. Look, I'm gonna save you a lot of time, trouble, and heartache, okay, kid?"

The quiet in the room somehow rushed louder than the roar of an angry sea.

Michaela nodded. What else was she supposed to do with the spotlight on her? Argue?

Flee?

Tempting.

"Go to college. Get a degree and a real job. Move on with your life."

What?

Her chest constricted as though a band tightened with each word he spoke. Move on with her life? This was her life. At least, her life's dream.

"I-uh, I'm not interested in college," she said in a small voice. The bleach blond female clones and eclectically dressed men's gazes morphed from interested to pitying, as if they all recognized what the casting director meant while she was still in the dark. "I want to be an actress."

He sighed and ran a hand down his face as though weary from the conversation. "I've sat through thousands of these auditions in my career. And here's the thing, we usually know within five seconds of you walking in the door whether you have it or you don't. And I'm sorry, kid, but you don't. It's a look. A vibe. An attitude. Some girls are Hollywood, and some aren't. You can dress up a turd and all that..." With a shrug, he sat and began shuffling through a stack of papers as though he hadn't destroyed her life. "It's an expression for a reason."

A fat tear wavered in the corner of her eye, blurring her vision and threatening to roll down her face at any second. She blinked rapidly. The man would not get the satisfaction of seeing her crack. He would not go out tonight and laugh with his buddies about how he made the simple country girl cry by wrecking her dreams with a few cutting words.

She was too ugly to be a serious actress. That's what he'd said. Not pretty enough, maybe not skinny enough, or glamorous enough. Regardless, the message was clear.

You're not good enough.

"You may go." He was back to speaking without so much as glancing in her direction.

Dismissed.

Michaela swallowed a painful lump as she turned and began to walk toward the exit with measured steps. The sound of her thrift-store heeled boots clacking on the tile floor rang out like shots of a gun in the silent room.

Her arms hung heavy and lifeless at her sides, not swinging as she strode on stiff legs. She felt like a doll with a plush, vulnerable center and rigid plastic limbs that couldn't bend. She didn't so much as blink as she held the fake smile and focused straight ahead on the door. But with each forward step, she grew closer to losing her composure.

Just a few more feet.

Finally, her hand gripped the door, and she yanked it open with enough force to have it hit the wall with a loud bang. Her heart was too heavy to cringe at the unexpected clamor. Michaela walked down the long hallway past the line of girls with nerves in their bellies and hope in their eyes. Same as she'd had ten minutes ago.

How many of these girls would walk out of that room with shattered dreams and demolished self-esteem? All? Some? Only her?

As she emerged into the heat of the California sun, the weight of despair sat heavily on her chest. The idea of climbing onto a stifling LA city bus and returning to her depressing shoebox of an apartment made her nauseous, so she turned in the opposite direction of the bus stop and walked.

And walked.

And *walked*.

Michaela strolled through the city until her feet blistered and her calves cramped.

What was she supposed to do now? Continue working hours upon hours serving coffee to ungrateful tourists? Tuck her tail between her legs and return to West Virginia? God, the thought of it had her wanting to grip her hair and scream at the top of her lungs. Small-town life wasn't for her. After eighteen years of living it, she could say that with certainty. Her heart wanted more, bigger, grander. She wanted the world to know she was so much more than a penniless girl from West Virginia whose family had never amounted to anything. Not a single person in her family had ever left their town. Every relative as far back as she knew had lived and died in the same town. It hadn't been enough for Michaela's mother, but she'd been too afraid to take a chance. Now she never could. Michaela vowed she wouldn't reach the end of her life with more regrets than accomplishments.

After hours of aimless wandering, she found herself on Hollywood Boulevard surrounded by tourists squatting next to the stars and taking hundreds of selfies. Their smiling faces and undisguised delight reminded her of herself just yesterday. Oddly enough, it seemed like years since she'd shared their wonder and awe though it had been less than twenty-four hours.

With an audible sigh and throbbing feet, Michaela stared down at the ground in front of her.

"Meryl Streep," she whispered aloud as she gazed in reverence at the pink star at her feet.

A laugh bubbled up from her gut, pouring out into the air. A few of the sightseers glanced her way with scrunched brows before returning to their business.

Meryl Streep? Of all the places she could have ended up, Meryl Streep's star it was.

Michaela's lips curled in a genuine smile. This had to be a sign.

Early in her career, many told this multi-award-winning actress she'd never amount to anything in the film world because she wasn't attractive enough. And look at her now. She sure as hell showed all the ignorant chauvinists who judged her.

What's to keep you from doing the same?

Nothing. Not one damned thing.

Michaela straightened her shoulders.

Screw that casting director.

Screw the rest of those uppity jerks peering down their noses at her.

She'd show them. She'd show everyone.

She laughed again, longer and louder this time, drawing the attention of dozens of tourists. Let them look. She'd need to get used to people gawking at her as she walked down the street.

Michaela Hudson was going to be a star.

Chapter One

Ten years later

"SCARLETT, HEY SCARLETT. You gotta get up!" A voice whisper-yelled into the darkness as a hand shook her shoulder, making her brain rattle around painfully in her skull.

Michaela blinked, then groaned. "Fuck, stop!" Even after all these years of going by her stage name, her mind reacted with confusion to being called Scarlett first thing in the morning. The stage name had been her talent agent's idea after a series of crushing rejections early on. A name change and colored contacts, professional hair bleaching, shedding twenty pounds, and speech training to rid herself of the southern accent. He claimed the stage name gave her an allure of mystery.

Or some bullshit like that.

Sprawled on her stomach, Michaela lifted her head. "Becca?" she croaked. God, her throat felt dry as the freakin' Sahara. "Why are you here? Why am I on my couch?"

"Because you needed to be up about twenty minutes ago," her personal assistant whispered.

"The fuck?" she asked. "Why?"

"God, Scarlett, you're really out of it this morning. Today is the first day where you're filming the battle scene through sunrise. Remember? You've got a four thirty call time for the next five days. You're due on set in an hour, and based on the look of things, you're gonna need at least that long in hair and makeup."

"Oh, shit," Michaela said on a long groan. Now that she'd officially been awake for a few moments, unpleasant sensations bombarded her from all angles. Her head throbbed like a bongo drummer was whacking on it, her tongue felt like a dried-out slug, and someone might have actually rubbed her eyeballs with sandpaper before she'd passed out.

Not like she could remember.

What the hell had she gotten up to last night? Probably nothing more than her usual. This sure wasn't the first time Becca had to get her ass out of bed after a night of partying. Hell, she paid her good money to be useful.

"Jesus," she mumbled. She pushed up from the armrest until she was seated. Fuck, her neck hurt. She shoved the rat's nest of hair off her face. "That better be coffee I smell, or you're out of a job."

"Yes. Triple shot." Becca, her assistant of four years, shoved a monster-sized to-go cup in her face. "Want me to turn the light on?"

"Fuck, no." Just the thought of it had her head screaming in protest. "Give me five minutes to throw on my robe and brush my teeth. I'll meet you outside."

"Okay. Do you want me to grab you something to eat?"

The thought of food had her stomach turning. "What time is it?"

"Three-thirty."

Torture. "Ugh. No, coffee is all I want."

Even through the darkness, she saw Becca's mouth turn down. "Are you sure? I don't think you had anything for dinner last night." She still whispered, probably in blessed reverence to Michaela's wicked hangover.

"I had drinks." And Lord knew what else.

"Surprise, surprise," Becca mumbled.

If she'd had more energy, Michaela would have called her out on the snark. Naked as the day she was born, Michela shivered. "Damn, it's cold. Where the fuck's my robe?" Nudity, her own and others, didn't bother her. Hadn't for a long time. Not since that shitty slasher movie she'd done at twenty. It'd been the first she'd starred in to make it to the big screen as well as her first lead. And it'd been shit. Absolute garbage. She'd had a fifteen-minute-long scene where she'd run from the psycho killer in a towel that fell toward the end. After being naked through countless takes, she'd lost any shyness she'd once possessed.

Now she felt nothing, whether clothed or in the nude.

"I think I see it on that chair," Becca said as she maneuvered through the trailer. "Here." She tossed Michaela the silk robe. "I'll wait for you outside, Scarlett."

"Thanks, hon." After donning the robe, Michaela stood and stretched her arms over her head. Her shoulder cracked and her back ached. God, she felt older than her twenty-eight years. Especially this early in the morning.

A few sips of coffee cleared the cobwebs enough to have her stumbling through the dark trailer into the bathroom. She did her business and brushed her teeth by the light of her makeup mirror. No way in hell was she going to flip on the overhead light and rocket her hangover headache into a full-on migraine.

She didn't bother checking her appearance, either. That could wait until hair and makeup performed their magic and made it look like she hadn't spent the majority of the night partying. Or at least that's how she assumed she'd spent the previous night. The details were fuzzy at best.

Which reminded her. Coffee alone wouldn't cut it today.

She opened the mini medicine cabinet in her trailer's bathroom and pulled out the little vial she kept on hand for just this kinda day. Which unfortunately seemed like most days, lately. This would take care of the fact she'd only gone to bed an hour or two ago.

Michaela twisted the cap, pulled out the snuff spoon, then frowned. "Shit," she murmured. "I'm out? How can I be fucking out?" Dammit. A bump of coke would have been perfect. Now she'd have to suffer with nothing more potent than caffeine to get her through the early morning shoot.

It would have been painful with the coke; now it was going to be downright excruciating.

"What fucking choice do I have? I'm the goddammed star," she muttered as she left the bathroom. After shoving her feet in some sandals, she exited the trailer.

Becca waited with her back against the trailer, using two thumbs to type on her phone furiously. "Ready?" she asked without looking up. "We gotta book it. They've been ready for you for twenty minutes."

Michaela snorted then took a long sip of the tepid coffee. "They can fucking wait. Not like they're gonna start shooting without me."

"Yeah, but sunrise is—"

She shook her coffee cup in her assistant's face. "I'm gonna need another one of these as soon as this is empty, which will be in about five seconds."

"Okay, sure." Her assistant fell in step beside her.

"And I need to run an errand after we wrap up for today."

"I'll get you whatever you need." Becca's eager to please eyes came shining through even in the darkness.

"What? No, I said I'd do it." She never had her staff meet with her dealer, well, except for the ones who bought from him too, and Becca was definitely not one of those assistants. She was as gleaming as a recently polished shoe. "God, why the fuck is it so bright out here?" Michaela shielded her eyes as she passed under a lamp in the lot. "Fucking middle of the night."

Becca shot her a side-eyed frown but wisely kept her trap shut. The caffeine hadn't done shit to wake Michaela up, and, frankly, she felt like garbage. The walk to the hair and makeup trailer only took a few moments. Not long enough get her blood flowing and make her feel human.

When she stepped into the well-lit space, she flinched as the shocking bright lights assaulted her senses. "Fuck, can we turn a few of those down?" she asked without greeting anyone.

Ralph, her best friend and long-time stylist gave an elegant snort. "Uh, no, babe. We most certainly cannot." Then he frowned. "With the way you look this morning, I'm gonna need all the tricks in my bag, and I can't work my magic in the dark." Then he winked. "Well not the kinda magic you need, anyway. Sit that skinny ass down in my chair," he said as he spun the salon chair toward her. Then he tilted his head and gave her a long up and down look. "You losing more weight, Mick?" His voice took on a note of concern, matching the frown pulling down his lips. She'd known him since the first week she'd moved to LA. They'd climbed the cinema ladder together, and he refused to call her Scarlett in private.

"What?" She shuffled over to his station in front of the mirror and plopped into the chair. "No. I actually need to drop a few pounds." Someone had commented on a social media post from a few weeks ago that the dress she'd been wearing made her look fat. Last thing she needed was a viral post about how fluffy she'd become.

She leaned forward, examining herself in the mirror. Oh man, Ralph wasn't kidding. She looked rough. "My mane needs some serious help this morning, babe."

Coming to stand behind her, he placed his hands on her shoulders. "Yes, sweetheart. I have eyes. Speaking of eyes, Libby is gonna need to put about a gallon of concealer under yours. Wild night?"

Had it been? She shrugged. Maybe.

Ralph frowned as he switched on a hair straightener. "One of those again, huh? Mick, we've all had 'em, but maybe you could do me a favor and save the extra wild nights for days when you don't have to be on set at the ass crack of dawn, huh? Help a sister out."

"Yes, Daddy. I'll stay in tonight and do my homework."

Ralph laughed, but it didn't hold the normal joy he carried. "Thank you." He grabbed some clips and began sectioning off her hair but stopped after only a few seconds. "You okay, Mickie? For real? Because you've been worrying me a little latel —"

Oh, *hell* no. They were not playing the I'm-worried-about-you game. She was fine. At the top of her game, richer than sin, sought by all for her skills and her appearance. Not a goddamn thing was wrong besides the lack of sleep. "Becca! Where the fuck's my coffee?" she yelled, holding up the empty Venti cup.

Ralph narrowed his eyes at her in the mirror but kept his mouth shut. Thank God.

"On it," her assistant called back.

It was going to be a long-ass morning.

Forty-five minutes later, Ralph had straightened her long, platinum locks into a sleek, silky waterfall, which he then gathered high on her head in a fierce power ponytail. She'd have to keep the look in mind for a future awards show. But for today, the ponytail would be braided with leather ribbons woven through. After snapping the metal cuff which accompanied her ensemble around the pony, his part was complete, and she was well on her way to resembling a movie star again. Libby took over once Ralph departed and used her makeup skills to produce the badass look her tribal warrior princess character required.

And now she was standing in the middle of the California desert at four thirty in the morning waiting for the director to call action. This post-apocalyptic movie had been a surprise offer. Not a typical dramatic role for her. But so far, she'd been enjoying the challenge of stretching her acting skills. Even if Charles Francola, the director, was a bit of a misogynistic asshole. They'd rubbed each other the wrong way from day one when she'd mistaken him for an intern and demanded a coffee.

The man held a grudge like a champ and had been growly with her throughout filming.

"Fucking finally," Francola grumbled from his chair under a tent as he stretched his arms overhead.

At least she wasn't the only one hating the early morning hour.

After a jaw-yawn that stretched out his stubbled face, Francola straightened the ball cap he was never without. "Let's get this fucking show on the road now that our star has decided to grace us with her presence."

Michaela resisted the urge to roll her eyes and flip him off. Damn right, she was a star. One who'd made forty million dollars on her last movie release, which was only one of many chart-topping films she'd starred in. Francola could bitch and moan all he wanted, but he knew his movie would sell on the clout of her name alone.

"*Sunrise Battle,* take one," the clap loader called out the scene name before the familiar snap of the clapperboard indicated the start of filming.

Despite an unyielding headache and increasing nausea—maybe she should have had a bite to eat—Michaela fell into the dynamic character like she was born to it.

And she was. Nothing gave her a thrill like delving inside the skin of a new character. Learning who they were and adopting their personality for a period of time. Especially a character like this one, a warrior who clawed her way to the top for everything she'd earned in life. Though not the commander of a post-apocalyptic army, Michaela understood the struggle and perseverance to be the best.

To be more accurate, nothing *had* given her a thrill like learning a new role. Lately, everything in her life had become muddled. A day-to-day rush of promos, interviews, meetings, stress, and drama.

"Charge!" Michaela shouted an hour and a half later, thrusting her golden sword in the air as she commanded her troops to attack the warring faction of Armageddon survivors. The small army of extras charged around her. Later, in post-production, thousands of additional soldiers would be added via CGI.

"Hold steady!" the director hollered, springing from his chair. He followed next to the camera panning her face, then shouted an irritated, "Cut!"

Michaela's arm dropped to her side. Damn, that blade was heavier than it looked. What the hell was Francola's problem now? This director wasn't satisfied with her scenes if she didn't shoot and reshoot them seventy times.

"Scarlett!" he bellowed as he waved her over. His gaze was fixed on the camera viewer, probably reviewing what she'd just performed.

"What's up?" she asked as she took her time, strolling to him. No way would she hustle just because he snapped his fingers. She hadn't been that actress since she'd made her first ten million. This director needed *her,* and she'd make sure he remembered it. "What has your panties in a twist this morning?"

"You. I'm unhappy with you." He stepped aside and indicated the camera with a snort. "You even bother looking in a mirror this morning, Scarlett?"

Michaela's spine snapped straight. "Excuse me?" Without bothering to peer at the screen, she rounded on the director. His disrespectful question pinged around in her head, dredging up one of the lowest moments in her life.

Francola scoffed. "Scarlett, you look like shit. You're so fucking skinny, you're like a bag of bones. Your hair is limp, and your skin is waxy and pale even with fifty layers of makeup. It's coming across like garbage on camera. You're losing the thing that made you a star, Scarlett."

Her blood ran cold.

Hell fucking no. No one spoke to *her* that way. Not anymore and especially not a man. Men dove in front of her to lay their bodies over puddles so she wouldn't get her designer shoes wet. They jumped to do her bidding with one sultry glance. They showered her with affection and tripped over their tongues to tell her how stunning she was.

And here was this nothing of a man daring to lecture her in the manner she'd been spoken to ten years ago. Back when she'd dumped a nine-dollar box of bleach in her hair and thought drug store makeup would make her magnificent.

Fuck him.

She'd spent fifteen hundred dollars at the spa yesterday on her hair, a facial, and body treatments. And this little elf had the nerve to comment on her *vibe*?

She squared her shoulders and advanced. "How dare you speak to me like that?" With the five-inch heels on her thigh-high boots, she topped out at six feet tall and towered over the little man.

Little in both stature and character. She may have been small once when she was a nobody living in a mining town in West Virginia without two nickels to rub together, but she wasn't now. She'd worked her ass off for a decade to make sure no one would ever look down their nose at her again.

He rolled his eyes.

"Have you forgotten who I am?" Michaela asked with venom dripping from her voice.

They'd drawn a crowd. It seemed the entire cast and crew stopped what they'd been doing to gawk at the escalating argument. Good, it'd be great to have witnesses to Francola's downfall.

No one could accuse her of not appreciating the value of a good audience.

Nostrils flaring and eyes narrowed to deadly slits, he met her head-on. The six inches she had on him forced his head back to meet her gaze, but he wasn't intimidated. "I know exactly who you are, *Scarlett*. A spoiled fucking diva who snorts her meals instead of eating them."

"Be careful, Charles. I'll walk." She smiled the kind of smile victors wore right before delivering the kill shot. The same one she during the last scene they film when her character led her arm to defeat a warring faction. "I'll walk, and this movie will swirl down the toilet where it belongs. The studio probably won't even fine me once they hear how you treated their favorite actress." She tossed the end of her braid over her shoulder for good measure, then took a few steps back to enhance the visual of her walking away from his shitty movie.

Damn, the view from the top of the world was spectacular.

He spread his arms, sneering. "Knock yourself out. You'll be doing me a favor."

"What?" Her heart skipped a beat.

Why wasn't he begging her to stay?

"That's right. Walk, princess." Now it was his turn for a smug, winner's grin. "And guess what? I won't even feel tempted to stare at your boney fucking ass while you go."

No, no, no.

This couldn't be happening. The studio had warned her of how important this movie was for her career. She'd gotten in hot water on the last set for allegedly causing too much drama and unrest among the cast by sleeping with her co-star. How the hell was she supposed to know he'd had a pregnant girlfriend? The chick had never once hung around the set. Besides, he'd come on to her, not the other way around.

Asshole.

Regardless, the studio warned her if she acted out on this set, it'd be the last time they worked with her.

And they were a big fucking deal. As in, career makers or breakers. Even at her level of stardom. In Hollywood, there was always someone above you on the food chain. Few could destroy the life she'd made for herself, but a major studio executive was one of those people.

And with the way his grin curled in sinister delight, Francola knew it.

"Charles..." She'd have died from the flood of panic without years of solid acting experience propping her up. To everyone watching, she stood tall, arrogant, indifferent to his idle threats. But her insides shriveled and died in the same way they'd done at her very first audition. Only then, she had the resiliency of youth to bounce back and charge forward. Now? Now all she wanted was to lock herself in her trailer with a bottle of vodka and some Xanax until the pain subsided.

"Please go, Scarlett. I'd hate to have to call security on you," Charles said, and then that motherfucker turned his back on her.

Fuck the studio and fuck Charles. She was the country's hottest movie star, for fuck's sake.

With the sun barely peeking over the horizon, Michaela let out a harsh laugh. "Enjoy the unemployment line, asshole," she said as she lifted both hands in a double middle-finger salute. "I'm a fucking star known through every household in America. Who the fuck are you?"

With that parting shot, she spun on her heel, making sure to present her widest smile as she sashayed toward her trailer. Despite NDAs, these photos would go viral in minutes. She'd be damned if she didn't look hot as fuck while leaving these losers in the dust. Her PR team would flip their shit, but fuck them, too. They worked for her, not the other way around. She paid them a shit ton of money to make her look fantastic, and they could earn their worth.

By the time her trailer was in sight, Becca had sprinted up next to her. "Okay, will do," she said into her phone before ending a call. Breathless, she nearly jogged her tiny legs to keep up with Michaela's long stride. "Soon as we get in the trailer, we'll call Tatiana and get moving on damage control." Her fingers flew over her phone screen. "Shit. I was hoping we'd a least have a few minutes before the videos started hitting social media, but no luck."

"I want that man ruined," Michaela spat as she marched forward.

Becca didn't respond.

Michaela's headache jacked up in intensity until the rising sun felt as though it were burning her brain. God, was it only just past five in the morning? Seemed as though an entire week had gone by since she'd woken up.

When she reached the trailer, Michaela wrenched the door open so hard it smacked against the outside wall. Of course, Becca followed her inside. Just as she was about to kick her assistant out, Michaela's gaze fell to her bed. She drew up short. "Who the fuck—"

Becca smacked into her back. "Sorry. Who are you talking about—oh."

Michaela gaped at the two men passed out face down on her bed. She turned to her assistant. "Who the fuck are they?" One of the guys slept on his stomach, sheet covering his ass, but fully tattooed back on display. The one next to him had smooth, bare skin, but lay on his back with the sheet covering, well, nothing. "Jesus, are they naked? What the fuck?"

Becca's nose wrinkled as she averted her gaze. Michaela knew that Becca had seen far worse while working for her and shouldn't be afraid of a little male nudity, but still, the sweet girl blushed and stared at the floor. "Um, you don't remember?"

"Obviously, I don't fucking remember. Would I be asking if I did?" She gripped the back of her neck and blew out a breath. The braid in her hair had to go. It pulled her scalp ridiculously taught, exacerbating the pain.

"Uh, they're extras." Becca still kept her gaze on the floor. "You were partying with them last night and, uh, invited them here."

"What?" She whipped her gaze back to the disheveled bed with a scrunched brow. "I did?"

"Yes."

"Shit." Had she slept with them? One? Both? Being that they were naked, and she'd awakened the same way, it wasn't a leap. The coffee soured in her stomach. How the hell could she have fucked two men and not remember it only a few hours later? Rubbing her tender forehead, Michaela fought for an unconcerned tone. "I need to use the bathroom. I want them gone by the time I get out."

"What? Me?" Becca squeaked. "You want me to get rid of them?"

One of the men stirred but didn't wake. If someone had offered her the exorbitant sum she'd earned from her last movie, she couldn't have recalled his name. Or the other one. Had they both touched her, kissed her, been inside her? Jesus, had she taken them into her mouth? She pressed a hand to her rolling stomach. Michaela wasn't shy when it came to sex, and this sure as hell wasn't her first threesome, but not remembering a single detail of the night, including the fact she'd had sex at all, well, that was a new low.

And frankly, it rattled her to her core.

Never let them see your weakness. You're going to be a star.

Her mother's advice rang loud in her ears. Michaela straightened her shoulders as she glared at Becca. "Yes, you. What the fuck do you think I pay you for?" she snapped as she stormed into the bathroom and slammed the door with enough force to shake the entire trailer. There, she'd done her part in waking the guys. All Becca had to do was kick their asses to the parking lot.

She blew out a breath.

Finally, alone.

Michaela rested her hands on the tiny sink and bowed her head. The empty cocaine vial still sat there, mocking her.

So she'd lost a few pounds recently. Since when had anyone in Hollywood complained about women being too skinny?

Fucking Francola.

The growls and curses of displeased men exiting her trailer had relief flooding her. She took a breath, closed her eyes, then raised her head. As she opened them, finding her reflection, Michaela let out a sharp gasp. A sunken-cheeked, sallow-complexioned skeleton with purple smudges under each eye stared back at her. Now that Francola had ripped her blinders off, she barely recognized the shell of a woman in the mirror.

Her hand shook as she lifted it to probe her gaunt face. Cheekbones that used to be the envy of women across the globe now jutted out in harsh lines.

Enjoy being a star, my beautiful girl. Just don't let them take away who you are.

Her eyes closed as she pressed a hand to her heart the way her ailing mother had done all those years ago when Michaela told her she planned to move to Hollywood. They'd both known the end was near for her mother, and Michaela wanted her to pass knowing her daughter would fulfill their dreams. At the time, she'd laughed off the advice, too high on the prospect of fame and fortune to recognize the true warning there.

Now, dozens of movies and millions of dollars later, she used chemicals and sex to chase that high. The one that had long worn off. And to fill the void of living a vapid, superficial life devoid of any meaningful human connection.

Last night she'd been too stoned and wasted to remember fucking two strangers. This morning she lost her coveted role in what was projected to be the next big blockbuster. And right now, images of her flipping off her director and sensationalized accounts of the encounter were popping up on every social media platform available. Stories of the temper-tantrum-throwing starlet would be trending within minutes.

But despite it all, only one problem dominated her mind and demanded immediate action. And that was the empty vial of cocaine. She longed for a hit to pull her from the crushing fatigue assailing her. If she couldn't have that, the half-full bottle of vodka she'd seen on the table in the trailer would do. Though it wouldn't energize her, it'd numb the pain and the voice in her head now screaming she was a failure.

And that was a serious problem.

Who had she become?

No longer able to look at the husk of a woman now crying in the mirror, Michaela jerked back from the sink. She hit the wall hard. The crash seemed to dislodge a sob wedged in her gut. She sank to the floor, weeping as despair washed over her.

She was tired. So tired her bones ached, and her soul held a heaviness that weighed down her entire being.

If she just had something to combat the exhaustion, she could think clearer and find a way out of this mess.

She crawled forward with tear-stained cheeks, opening the small cabinet beneath the sink. She'd often hidden her stash in a tampon box when visitors stopped by. Sure enough, a baggie peeked out from the tampons. "Holy shit. Yes." The relief at knowing she'd feel better had her sighing in pleasure.

It was crystal meth.

She swallowed as she held up the small bag. One of the guys from last night must have put it there. This would take the edge off and allow her to make it through the remainder of this miserable day. But it was one drug she'd never tried.

Growing up, she'd seen one too many toothless tweakers in the crappy apartment complex she'd lived in. She'd sworn to herself, no matter what, this was a line she would never cross.

She stared at the baggie with a sinking heart.

Today would go down as one of the worst days in her professional career. She needed a boost, just this once.

Desperate times called for desperate measures.

After setting up, she snorted a line, then leaned back against the door as the rush of endorphins fired up her blood.

"One more," she whispered, then repeated the process once again.

With her heart now racing, she finally felt alive and not like the zombie who'd woken up and stumbled through the morning.

Fuck, that's better.

She smiled, then eyed the baggie, which still held plenty more meth.

"Fuck it." After snorting two more lines, she was flying high. Now she was ready to talk to her team. To make a plan and fuck Francola good.

As she tried to stand, the room spun, and she stumbled. Giggling, she landed on her ass and hit the door with her back. "Let's try that again." She leaned forward only to have the left side of her chest seize up in a crushing pain that took her breath away.

With a gasp and a garbled shout, she grabbed her chest and slumped against the door. It felt as if the entire trailer had collapsed on top of her chest. Fire shot down her left arm. She tried to yell as panic set in, but it came out as a strangled cry once again.

"Scarlett?" Becca called out as she knocked lightly on the other side of the door. "Are you okay?"

"No," she croaked, throat tight and aching.

"What do you need? What can I get for you?" Even after being snapped at and treated like nothing more than a servant, Becca's sweetness won out.

"Help," Michaela whispered through the agony. "I think I need some help."

The knob jiggled, and pressure hit her back. "Scarlett, I can't get the door open."

"Call…call EMS," she managed as the room began to fade to darkness.

Please don't let me die here.

Chapter Two

The phone rang at the exact second Keith's teeth tore through his Big Mac. "You've gotta be fucking kidding me," he muttered with his mouth full of bread and greasy beef. He dropped the sandwich to the open wrapper on his lap then brushed his hands together, sending crumbs flying through the cab of his tow truck. As owner of his own garage, he typically had someone to do the towing for him, but they'd been out sick, so he gotten stuck with the job he hated for the day.

When he saw his sister's number on the screen, he groaned. "This better be fucking good," he barked into the phone once he'd swallowed.

"Hey, Keith, I love chatting with you too," Veronica quipped.

"What do you need, Ronnie?" He wiped his mouth with the rough napkins the fast-food restaurant provided and rested his head against the back of the seat. It'd been a shit day. If Ronnie needed him to bail her out of a mess, he might cry.

"Got a tow for ya, bro. Oh, I like that." She laughed. "A bro tow."

Keith rolled his eyes. His family was nuts. "Yeah, you're a regular Dr. Seuss. What do you mean you got a tow? Thought you were working at the bar tonight."

"I am. JP had an *appointment* and asked me to keep the garage cell for him. And actually, it's not a tow. Just roadside assistance. Blown tire, but I couldn't pass up the rhyme."

An ache began to form above his eyes. Keith massaged it, but it didn't help. "So he closed the garage? No one's there?" It was nearly eight in the evening. JP couldn't have waited the extra twenty minutes before taking off?

"Guess not." Then Ronnie's tone changed and she said, "That'll be seven even, buddy," presumably to a customer.

"If I wanted to shut down my garage, I'd have taken the phone myself and not asked JP to stick around in case someone came by. What the fuck kind of appointment does he have?"

"Beats me. Chlamydia test?"

Keith snorted. His youngest brother wasn't exactly discerning when it came to who and how many women he fucked around with.

An appointment, my ass.

In JP's world, an appointment most likely meant a booty call. The irresponsible jerk.

"You wanna know where this vehicle is or what?"

"Yeah, gimme a second." He reached for the pen in his center console. "Okay, shoot." As Ronnie rattled off the location of the broken-down vehicle, he scrawled it on the side of his fast-food wrapper. "Got it, thanks. I'll swing by and relieve you of the phone on my way into town."

"Thanks, big bro. See you soon. And hey, it was a woman who called. Try cracking a smile while you're rescuing her. Who knows where it'll lead you?"

She ended the connection before he had a chance to tell her to fuck off. His sister loved nothing more than trying to get him a girlfriend. "Smile at her," he muttered. Just what he was in the mood for, a whiny damsel in distress who couldn't even change a tire.

He drove with one hand while scarfing down the now-cold Big Mac with the other. It didn't take him more than five minutes to pull his truck up behind a broken-down Audi SUV on the side of a quiet one-lane highway. They were only about a mile from where he lived with a few of his siblings.

After parking his rig, he wiped his oily hands on his jeans and then approached the vehicle. Letting out a low whistle, he took in the classy car. The Audi SUV wasn't as flashy as some luxury vehicles, but this baby could run the owner close to a hundred Gs. It was the kind of car one bought when financially loaded but not wanting to flaunt themselves as a rich prick.

The dome light was on, giving him a clear view of the woman sitting in the driver's seat with her head on the headrest and eyes closed. Keith would be lying if he didn't admit part of him relished the idea of scaring her out of her wits for the inconvenience of sucking up his time. Maybe it'd motivate her to learn to change her own damn tires. Of course, if everyone did that, he'd be out a substantial portion of his business. But his Friday nights would be a whole lot more relaxing.

He rapped his knuckles against the window with a little more force than necessary.

With a high-pitched yelp, the woman sprang forward. Her hand hit the horn which blared into the quiet night and made her squeal again. With a mumbled curse, she pressed a hand to her heaving chest.

"Keith Benson, ma'am. I'm here to change your tire," he said through the closed window as he fought a laugh.

She glared at him through the window as she grabbed the door handle. "Back up."

He did, which allowed her to shove the door open. When she stepped out, still breathing heavily, she scowled a perfectly made-up face at him. "Jesus, would a gentle tap on the window have killed you?"

"Didn't think you'd hear it. Seemed like you were out cold."

She sniffed, one of those rich-lady, patronizing sniffs. "I was resting my eyes."

"Whatever. You got a spare?" In less than five seconds, he'd sized up her type. Wealthy. Snobby. Judgmental. Frigid in bed.

Hard pass, despite the fact she was objectively beautiful. Slender without being stick skinny, though she did have some meat to her ass, she probably topped out at about five-eight. Her light brown hair was styled in a chic, chin-length bob that made her beautiful face stand out. He'd always been a sucker for a lady with glasses, and she had black-rimmed ones that made her look like she walked out of a fantasy role play video. Especially when combined with skinny jeans, a fitted gray sweater, and knee-high boots. The prim and proper, conservative stick-in-the-mud look he loved to mess up.

Too bad those types tended to be bitches who looked down their surgery-perfected noses at his less than glamorous lifestyle.

"Hello? Did you hear me?" she asked, head tilted. Now it was her turn to inspect him, and her assessing expression didn't morph into an impressed one. Big surprise there: woman in her ninety-thousand-dollar car isn't instantly smitten with the dirty, tattooed mechanic who stopped to help her change her tire. Someone better alert the porn writers they were way off base.

"What?" he said, though to her it probably sounded more like an animal grunting.

"I said it's in the trunk."

Damn, the woman had some smooth, full, kissable lips.

"The spare?" One of her perfect eyebrows arched.

Shit. She was too distracting. He needed to get laid. How fucking long had it been?

Way too long if it took more than ten seconds to remember. Well, it wasn't gonna happen now, so he might as well get on with changing the tire.

"Got it. This'll be quick," he said as he strode to her trunk. "I don't have these fancy tires in stock, but I can get them from the dealership. Tomorrow, next day at the latest. You shouldn't do too much driving on the donut."

She sighed. "Thank you."

With a nod, he opened the trunk then worked out the spare tire. She stood on the side of the road, watching every move he made with calculating, judging eyes. Neither spoke while he went to work on the tire. Within minutes he had the car jacked up, the busted tire off, and was tightening the lugs on the spare.

Of course, being a man whose cock hadn't had any action beyond his own hand in a scary amount of time, he couldn't help but sneak glances at her every few seconds. At one point, a bird squawked high above them. The woman turned and glanced up, putting her backside right in his line of sight. And day-um, he'd be dreaming about that lush ass for days to come. High, tight, round, fuck, it was a thing of beauty. Whether those expensive jeans gave the illusion of a perfect ass or she spent hours doing squats, he didn't care. The visual worked.

He shifted as the crotch of his pants grew tight. From the corner of his eye, he caught the woman shivering. "Cold?" he asked.

Jesus, why was he initiating conversation? No one would accuse him of being chatty. In fact, most considered him standoffish. It was something his siblings loved to rub in his face.

She spun his way. "Yeah, I'm not used to this Vermont weather. I'm, uh, from California."

Ahh, that explained quite a bit. Probably some rich housewife like the ones on those ridiculous reality TV shows. "This isn't even close to cold yet, but I'll be done in a minute, and you can get back to your seat warmers."

"It's okay." She walked closer, those long legs eating up the distance between them until she practically loomed over him, where he was crouched next to her rear passenger wheel. "I actually like it. It's refreshing."

A hint of something sweet, but not overly so wafted his way. Shit, she even smelled expensive. He glanced up at her, and this time, her eyes widened, and she took a step back.

Seriously? What did she think, he was gonna lunge for her there on the side of the road? He wouldn't be in business long if he attacked random female motorists instead of fixing their cars.

The thick silence wormed its way under his skin until he couldn't stand it. He swore he could feel the discomfort and fear coming off her in waves. Leave it to the classy woman to judge him for his tattoos, beard, and profession.

"You staying nearby?" Shit, that sounded too much like a come-on. Like he was feeling her out, seeing if she'd be willing to invite him to her hotel room.

That snooty eyebrow rose again, this time accompanied by a haughty glare. Clearly, she'd interpreted it as a poorly executed pickup line. This was why he didn't make small talk. He sucked at it.

"I'm staying at my house," she said in a tone that indicated she found him far beneath her on the social scale.

Let's face it, he was.

"All right," he said, as he straightened. "You're good to go." He lifted the blown tire, tucking it under his arm.

He caught her eyes widen as his biceps bulged against his Henley and couldn't help his smirk. Looked like the lady wasn't a complete stone.

"Thank you," she said, voice clipped. "I appreciate you coming out so quickly. How do I pay you?"

He fished a crinkled business card out of his pocket. "You can pay when you come in for the new tire. Give that number a call tomorrow afternoon to see if we got it in yet. Unless you want to take it directly to the dealership, but it's a hike from here." Taking her card now would only prolong the interaction. If he were lucky, JP would deal with her when the tire came in and he'd never have to see her again.

"No, uh, this is fine." She took the card with two perfectly manicured fingers, turning it back and forth in her hand as though inspecting dirty underwear instead of a piece of paper with a slight grease smudge.

"Won't kill you," he muttered as he hauled her tire to his truck.

"Excuse me?"

The innocent way she'd asked had his blood boiling. What a bitch. He couldn't stand fakes or liars, and this woman was the worst kind. The ones who pretended to be kind and unprejudiced while judging and mistrusting him behind plastered-on smiles with a safe distance between them.

"I said, getting a little grease on those fancy fucking fingers won't kill you," he said. "Neither will I. Won't try to fuck you either."

She frowned. "Wha—"

"Not my type, lady."

With a snort, she squared her shoulders. "And you think you're mine?"

It amazed him how a woman six inches shorter than him could look so far down at him, but this one managed to do it just fine.

"Nope, could tell in the first five seconds of meeting you that you're a rich prude who cringes at a little ink or grease. Or anyone beneath your station in life, for that matter."

She shook her head. "I—no—I…"

Christ, was it his imagination, or were her eyes fucking welling? Goddammit, this woman could put on a show. "Look," he said as he ran a grubby hand through his hair. "I'm as eager to get out of your company as you are of mine, so get in your fucking car. I may be an asshole, but I'm not enough of one to leave a woman on the side of the road by herself while it's getting dark."

Her face fell, and he had the flash of a puppy who'd been scolded for chewing a shoe.

Whatever. This woman would forget him two minutes after she got in her Audi and headed to her house, which was probably one of the fancy mansions at the base of the mountain.

Worse, she'd most likely end up taking her car to the dealership, stiffing him on his fee.

"I'll call the shop tomorrow," she muttered before scurrying to her car. When he heard the click of the locks engaging, he climbed into the truck, fired it up, and drove off. A glance in his mirror showed her pulling that wealth-mobile onto the road behind him.

About a mile down the road, she turned left, and he frowned into the mirror. The house he shared with his siblings was on that very road. The only reason he'd been able to afford the modest home on the quiet street was that it'd been a fucking disaster when he'd purchased it. A fire had ripped through it coming up on ten years ago. Keith was able to grab it up for next to nothing and, with the help of his contractor brother, did all the repair work himself.

He loved the place, loved the entire neighborhood, but it certainly wasn't opulent.

As he turned right onto the road to make his way toward the bar his sister worked at, his cell rang. Without checking the screen, he lifted it to his ear. "Hello?"

"Keith?" a familiar woman's voice asked. It had the rasp of a life-long smoker.

Fuck.

His night just got about a hundred times shittier. "Hey, Brenda," he said, as the weight of the world settled on his chest. "I'm on my way."

She sighed. "I'm so sorry to call you again, honey, but it's this or I have to call the cops."

He blew out a breath as he swung a left instead of the right that would have taken him where he wanted to go. "It's not a problem," he lied. "Be there in five."

"You're a good son, Keith," she said before disconnecting the call.

He grunted into the quiet phone. A good son.

Right.

As promised, five minutes later, he stepped out of his truck and made his way into the run-down bar outside of town that his father preferred. Probably because it was one of the few that still allowed him through the doors. Brenda had known the old man since they were kids, which was why she had a soft spot for him. However, it was more pity than a friendship.

When he stepped into the building, Keith sure as hell didn't need anyone to point him in the direction of his father. Drunk off his ass, as was his typical state, the old man was stumbling from table to table, making Brenda's patrons as uncomfortable as possible. He looked like he hadn't bothered to run a brush through his short gray hair in weeks, and his tattered clothes hung off his body.

Keith caught Brenda's eye, giving her a lifted hand in greeting. He swore the woman's entire body sagged in relief at the sight of him. With a large inhale, he steeled himself for the unpleasantness to come.

He strode over to his father. "Come on, Pop," he said, clapping a hand on his father's shoulder. They were similar in height, but the once-strong man had wasted away to practically nothing after subsisting on a diet of alcohol and pills for so many years. "Sorry for the trouble, ladies," he said with a nod to the table of frowning women. "Next round's on me."

"Get your fucking hands off me, boy," his father spat out, wrenching out of Keith's grip.

The burn of shame and humiliation accompanying these public displays had long since faded. In its place, a hatred so deep it stemmed from his core was the only emotion Keith felt toward his father.

"Time to go, old man," he said, somehow keeping that hatred from bleeding into his words. The women sitting at the table didn't bother to hide their curiosity or pity as they openly observed the scene.

"Not going anywhere with you. Fucking loser," his father said as he faced the women at the table. "Calls himself my son but he ain't done shit to take care of me."

The women averted their gazes to their half-finished drinks.

His father stumbled toward the bar. "Brenda, get me another whiskey."

As she wiped a glass with a bar towel, the gray-haired owner shook her head. "Sorry, Earl. You're done here for tonight. Let your boy take you home to sleep it off."

Earl snorted and nearly fell over as he tried to walk backward away from the bar. "Ain't no son of mine."

Through the years, Keith had wondered if that could be true. He'd heard it enough as a child, but the physical similarities between him and his father were too striking to ignore. Or at least they had been before a lifetime of drinking, shooting up, snorting, and swallowing any pill he could get his hands on aged Earl before his time.

"You hear that?" his father yelled to the room of patrons who wanted nothing to do with him. They all knew him and tried not to engage with him when he got like this. Which was often. "No son of mine would abandon his fucking father." He got right up in Keith's face. The stench of booze and stale cigarettes nearly knocked him out. Smelled like it'd been weeks since his dad had stuck a toothbrush in his mouth.

"Yep, heard this all before, Pop. Come on. Brenda doesn't want you chasing away her paying customers."

"Don't give me a damn penny. I put a roof over your head your whole fucking childhood. Now you show up when you want to embarrass me. Told that goddamned woman she shoulda let me use the goddammed coat hanger on her."

Hatred boiled in Keith's gut, bubbling until it nearly spewed out the top of his head. Only two things kept him from wrapping his hands around his father's throat and dragging his limp body to the car.

The first was a promise he'd made to his mother in the last seconds of her life. And the other was his younger siblings. At eighteen, Keith joined the military. He'd never planned on college and needed money and to learn a sustainable skill. He'd been an Army mechanic, trained on all types of ground vehicles from Humvees to tanks to basic trucks. Every spare penny went to a house fund and when he left at twenty-two, he purchased the home he shared with some of his siblings now.

But enlisting meant he'd left his siblings and mother to deal with their father's bullshit and abuse on their own for four years. Since then, he'd worked his ass off to make sure none of them ever had to deal with the man again. It was the only way to assuage his guilt over abandoning them for four years. They didn't need this garbage tainting their lives. As long as Keith dealt with it as quietly and efficiently as possible like he always did, the toxicity wouldn't touch them.

For their sake, he resisted the urge to turn and storm out, and tried yet again to get his father to leave.

"Let's go. Car's warm, and we'll swing by a drive-thru before I drop you home. Get you something solid to put in your stomach." At least he'd have something in his gut to soak up the liquor.

Earl swayed on his feet. "Don't need your fucking charity, boy. Can get my own damn food."

Sure he could, if he didn't blow his government checks on his flavor-of-the-month drug. First, it was Keith never helping his father, then it was not wanting to take charity from him. No matter what he did, Keith couldn't win with the man. Not that he wanted to gain any ground. What he wanted was never to see the bastard again.

Unfortunately, his luck didn't run that way. No wonder the wealthy Audi owner looked down at him. He sure lived fucking beneath someone like her.

Earl spun toward the bar once again. "You call him?" he asked Brenda. "Always fucking selling me out."

Having owned this bar her entire adult life, Brenda wasn't fazed by drunken assholes anymore. Apparently, the pathetic relationships between father and son got to her, though. She shot Keith a pitying look before nodding. "I did, Earl. It was him or the cops. You were making a scene. Bothering my customers. Figured leaving with your boy and sleeping in your own bed was better than spending another night drying out in a cell."

Some shred of rationality must have still lingered somewhere in Earl's booze-soaked mind because he grunted then trudged past Keith toward the door without a word. Guess a ten-minute ride in the car with a son he hated won out over trying to sleep on a concrete bench in a jail cell.

How flattering.

"Sorry, Brenda," he said with a nod to the older woman.

"Don't worry about it, honey."

He tossed two twenties down on the bar. "Please buy those ladies a round on me. Keep the rest for yourself."

"Will do."

With a final nod, he followed his father out the door, pretending the stares from Brenda's customers didn't burn his back like lasers. The second his ass hit the seat, his father turned to him.

"Waste of fucking space. That's what you are. Poisoning your siblings against me. Letting me lose my job."

Same song, different day. As though Keith had anything to do with his father being fired from the logging mill two years ago.

He bit the inside of his cheek to keep from firing back. It was fucking late, and he still had to swing by Ronnie's bar to grab the garage's phone so she wouldn't have to keep it for her entire shift. Last thing he wanted was a screaming match with his sloshed father.

"I want a fucking burger," his father said. "Swing by McDonalds and buy me a fucking burger. Do something for me for once in your life."

After making that polite request, Earl promptly passed out with his head on the window. It bounced against the glass with every bump in the road.

Keith could have shifted his father's head to the seat's headrest, but fuck that.

Least of what the old man deserved was to wake up to a nasty bruise on his temple.

With bitterness churning in his gut, Keith pulled into the drive-in line at Quick Eats. How the fuck had this become his life? Babysitting an ungrateful, drunk asshole multiple nights per week.

The woman who's tire he changed probably never had a shitty day like this in her life. Hell, the blown tire mostly likely was the worst thing to happen to her in years and she hadn't even had to fix the problem. Money had a way of making troubles disappear.

Must be nice.

At least with the burden of managing Earl sitting on Keith's shoulders, those troubles stayed far away from the rest of his family.

Chapter Three

"Thank you, ma'am. You've been a pleasure to work with." The head mover of the four-person team who'd delivered her household items tipped his baseball cap in Michaela's direction. "You enjoy your new home, ma'am."

With a good seven hours sleep under her and two cups of coffee she'd had an entirely more pleasant encounter with the movers than she had with the man from roadside assistance. Not that his opinion of her should matter, but for some reason, she hadn't been able to shake his instant dislike of her.

"No, thank you," she said with a smile from her open doorway. She handed over a thick envelope with a hefty tip. "You guys have made this process a breeze. Have a safe trip back."

Despite the chilly air, she remained propped against the door frame, watching until the enormous truck disappeared down the road. Then Michaela shut the door and leaned against it with a cleansing sigh.

Alone in her new home and ready to begin a fresh chapter of life as a sober, responsible, and hopefully kind adult. A jobless and purposeless adult, but that was okay for now. She planned to change both those facts once she figured out what fulfilled her and gave her a sense of happiness. She wouldn't blow this second chance at life.

Not like she'd done with the first one.

With a shake of her head, she pulled her phone from the back pocket of her jeans and called one of the two people from Hollywood she'd kept in contact with since entering rehab and the only person who knew her exact location. When she'd told her manager she was done and wanted to disappear, she'd meant it. Remaining off the press and paparazzi's radar was priority number one. Well, number two. The first priority had been getting healthy and clean, but now that she'd accomplished that mission, anonymity rose to the top of the list.

But she wasn't stupid. *Someone* needed to know how to find her in case…whatever happened. Plus, she couldn't live without her bestie, even if she could kiss the rest of Hollywood goodbye without so much as a flicker of regret.

"Mickie," Ralph said as he answered the phone. "How are you, gorgeous? Survive your first night in the boonies?"

A smile curled her lips. It was impossible not to light up at the sound of her best friend and long-time stylist's voice. She could picture him standing around his luxurious condo in his fuzzy slippers with his sleep-mask propped on his forehead and the first of many coffees in his hand. "I did. However, I'm happy to have a bed tonight. Been a long time since I've slept on an air mattress, and I'm not nearly as young as I was then. Overall, I'm doing great."

"Hmm."

She could practically hear his frown through the phone.

"What?"

"You know this is me, right? The one who sat by your bed in the hospital, and who drove you to rehab, and who picked you up from rehab, and who found you this little hole-in-the-wall town to disappear your fabulous self. You know it's me, who has never and would never judge you. Who loves you more than anyone in the world, and who wants you to be happy even if you have to move to Podunkville, USA to do so?"

Chuckling, she circumvented a pile of boxes to make her way to her kitchen. "All right, guilt trip received. I'm scared and lonely, but I feel okay physically and emotionally. Don't worry, I have a virtual appointment with my therapist in a few hours. Ralphie, I'm excited to rediscover who Michaela Hudson is and what makes her happy." She grabbed the teakettle and moved to the sink, where a large window revealed the view of her picturesque backyard and Vermont's mountains in the distance. Just one glance had a sense of peace settling over her.

"Well, she is fabulous, and you will love her."

Her heart clenched. God, she hoped so. She sure couldn't hate herself more than she did seven months ago at the lowest point in her life, lying in a hospital bed after having a heart attack at the age of twenty-eight. "Thank you, Ralph. Hey, can I ask you something?"

"Of course. Anything. I can draw pictures for you if you need visuals."

She chuckled. Talking to Ralph always boosted her mood. Without their weekly chats, she wouldn't have survived six grueling months of drug rehab and intense therapy. After evaluation, the director of the program recommended three months for her. She'd decided on her own she needed more and doubled her stay. The extra months of introspection and healing had served her well. "On a scale of one to ten, how much of a judgmental bitch am I?"

Ralph's laughter had her rolling her eyes. After about thirty seconds of listening to him cackle, she'd had enough.

"I'm glad you find my insecurities so entertaining, but could you maybe stop laughing at me for one minute?"

"Oh, honey, no I don't think I can. You are too funny."

"I'm going to hang up," she said as she set the full tea kettle on the stove.

"No, no, no don't. I'm done. Okay." He took a deep breath, which had her rolling her eyes again, but her lips quirked. "Okay, I'm ready to be serious. You, Michaela Hudson, are neither judgmental nor a bitch. Not one single morsel of either. And you know me, I'd tell you."

A rabbit hopped across the grassy backyard. Nothing special; a simple act of nature that probably happened a dozen times per day, but it was something she wouldn't have noticed *before*.

That was how she'd begun thinking about her life, in terms of before and after the spectacular public meltdown that ruined her reputation and woke her up to the reality of her dangerous downward spiral.

For the past ten years, her life had been go, go, go. She'd always been striving for more, bigger, better. There was never any downtime to enjoy the simple pleasures in life. Even if she had noticed something like the small rabbit hopping through her yard she'd wouldn't have cared enough to stop and watch. Her mind had been filled with selfish nonsense and frivolity. Now, sober, jobless, and on the other side of addiction, she wanted to appreciate everything life had to offer, from the mundane to the small wonders to the grand surprises.

"I'm pretty sure most of the world disagrees with you," she said to Ralph as she scanned the backyard for more gifts from nature.

"Sweetie, what's bringing this on?"

"I got a flat tire on the way into town. When roadside assistance showed up, I panicked a little."

"Did he say something to make you uncomfortable? Was he inappropriate?" No one would believe the fun, flirty, and playful Ralph had a protective lion buried in him, but he sure as hell did. His tone grew fierce. The mechanic from the night before could have snapped Ralph in half like a toothpick, but that wouldn't have kept Ralph from defending her honor should she have needed it. A girl couldn't ask for a better friend in her corner.

"No! Nothing like that at all. I just, well, I didn't know how to talk to him, so I think I was a little short and unfriendly which made him act all prickly. It was completely my fault. I'm all up in my head and afraid of being perceived as I was before." She sighed as her genuine fears began tumbling out of her mouth. "Somewhere along the way to becoming Scarlett, I completely lost Michaela. I feel like I've been acting so long, even in my personal life, I don't know how to be around normal people anymore. People who aren't trying to kiss my ass. People who aren't trying to use my name to advance their social status. People who think I'm just Michaela. I had no idea how to talk to the man because I have no idea who I am. He interpreted my standoffishness as me judging him for his casual appearance and job. I believe he called me a 'rich prude who cringes at the sight of a little ink and grease.'"

"Ink and grease?" Ralph whistled. "He sounds hot."

Despite her pity party, she laughed as an image of the mechanic popped into her mind. "He was hot." Was he ever. Muscles galore, tattoos running up and down his arms, a thick beard that made her shiver to think about it brushing her skin. Yeah, he'd been hot. So hot, in fact, she'd had a wild sex dream about the man bending her over the hood of her car and showing her exactly what he could do with all those work-hardened muscles.

Shit. She fanned her face only to hear Ralph snickering. "What?"

"You're thinking about him naked, aren't you?"

"No!" Like he'd buy that. Ralph knew her too well. Seven months of sobriety and abstinence, of course she was thinking about the sexy man naked. Too bad she'd lit that bridge on fire.

He let out an inelegant snort. "We'll come back to that. I'm gonna get real with you, sweetie. You ready?"

All she'd done over the past months was *get real* with herself. How could she still be without all the answers after such exhaustive work? Why didn't she have her shit sorted yet?

Though happier than she'd been in ages, every day took a conscious effort to keep from backsliding. Not because she craved the drugs or alcohol that had been her companions for so long, but because falling back on old patterns was so much easier than fighting to become a better version of herself. She'd used substances to dilute the crushing pressure of always being the best and to numb the pain when all the money and fame in the world still left her empty inside.

"Lay it on me. Let's see if you come up with something I haven't heard from the shrinks yet."

Ralph huffed. "You, Michaela Hudson, are not a bitch, you're not judgmental, and you're definitely not a prude. Hello? Public sex at that club in Vegas."

Michaela cringed. Yeah, that was one of the nights she was trying to forget, not dredge up. She'd been coked out of her mind and let some guy fuck her in the bathroom of a swanky Vegas club. Of course, there'd been a mob of paparazzi there to gobble up and sensationalize the story. By the time she'd read about it online, the story had grown to an epic tale of her having sex out on the dancefloor with a stripper from the club. One of her many less-than-stellar moments.

"Is there a point here?" she asked through clenched teeth.

"Yes. The point is that Michaela Hudson is a sweet, loving, completely non-judgmental, a little bit kinky, kind, and generous woman who is not a bitch. But all those wonderful traits left Michaela vulnerable to being used and hurt. Hollywood tossed her around, chewed her up, and spit out Scarlett."

She sighed. "And Scarlett *is* a bitch. She pretty much destroyed Michaela."

"No, she isn't, and she didn't. Scarlett built up a very thick coat of armor and a personality to match what was expected of her. She tried her damnedest to run Michaela out of town, but Michaela has another trait I haven't mentioned yet. She is strong as fuck. So much stronger than you give her credit for. She fought back, kicked Scarlett's ass, and has taken back over."

"Ralph," she whispered, as his words soothed her battered soul. She had a deep-seated fear no one would ever see her as anything more than the drugged-out Hollywood starlet who'd fucked up her life and driven away anyone who once cared about her. Because of her drama on set, friends in the business had begun to steer clear of her near the end. She'd destroyed a marriage by sleeping with a co-star about two years ago. The worst part of that entire situation was that she'd been so stoned, she barely remembered. The list of transgressions went on from there. But he was right, she'd owned her mistakes and indiscretions and worked her ass off to atone for those mistakes.

"Thank you. I miss you so much," she said with a sigh as she turned to survey the disastrous kitchen. At least unpacking would keep her mind occupied for a while and off her problems.

"Same, sweetie. Not the same without you stealing my Twizzlers and letting me play with your hair."

That had her smiling. Ralph was rarely without his beloved candy, and she'd become somewhat infamous for swiping them every chance she got. Next time she went to the store, she'd have to buy some and ship them to him with a few of his other favorite goodies.

"Ralph, I'm so worried about sliding backward. I didn't treat people well at the end, and probably not in the middle either. I know I'm sober now, but what if that's what my personality has become? What if I—"

"It's not. Have you listened to a word I've said?" He was in full-on bitchy mode now.

"Yes. I think I've just lost trust in myself."

"Oh, sweetie, that breaks my heart. But you want to know what makes it whole again?"

"What?" Phone at her ear, she walked into the half bathroom and stood in front of the oval mirror. The woman staring back at her was barely recognizable. Twenty-five pounds heavier—all in a healthy way, she looked like a woman instead of a skeleton. After trading in her platinum blond hair extensions for her actual brunette color, she chopped the locks into a sleek, angled bob as well. With glasses over her chocolatey eyes instead of the shocking blue contacts, which everyone thought was an enviable gift from nature, she didn't even resemble Scarlett any longer.

"What makes me happy is knowing how much you are going to fall in love with Michaela once you remember all there is to love about her. Because she is in you, and she is just about the best thing since Twizzlers. You need to breathe, stop overthinking, and act in a way that comes naturally. Don't second guess yourself. All these life improvements don't mean you can't get mad, can't be sassy, or funny. None of those are bad things. Stop doubting Michaela and just let her out."

"When did you get so wise, Ralph?"

"Girl, you don't get to be this fabulous without reading a few self-help books along the way. Feel better?"

With a laugh, she left the bathroom. She'd certainly read her fair share over the past six months. "Yes, actually, I do. Thank you. Seriously."

"Anytime, my love. And, I'm guessing I'm going to have to be the one to come to you, huh?"

Michaela blew out a breath. "Yes. I'm not going back to LA for a very long time." If ever. Her lips twitched. "Besides, a trip to the country now and then will be good for your soul. Your lungs, too. It'll keep you grounded and remembering your roots."

His pained whimper had her chuckling. He'd grown up in a town similar to hers. So small it didn't register as a blip on a map. His had been a coal-mining town in Ohio that wasn't exactly LGBTQ+ friendly, whereas she'd been from a floundering farming community, but the end result had been the same. Two dirt-poor teens with stars in their eyes and dreams of fame and fortune. They'd been beyond naïve, a true stereotype of small-town kids in the big city. Together, they'd climbed the ranks of Hollywood, yet only one of them managed to keep their grip on reality.

Hint: it hadn't been her.

Heavy thoughts.

A knock on the door had her shaking off the gloom. Had the movers left something behind? "Ralph, someone's at my door. I gotta go."

"Oooh." He clapped his hands. "Maybe it's the mechanic come to ravage you."

She snorted. "You watch too much porn. I'm hanging up. Love you."

"Love you too, sweetie. Kisses! And there's no such thing as too much porn," he shouted before she disconnected.

The doorbell rang this time. "Coming!" she called out as she hustled to the door.

An odd thrill ran through her. Opening the door to a surprise visitor hadn't been a thing in her life for nearly ten years. In LA, she'd had a gate, security guards, personal assistant, and checkpoint guests had to navigate through before making it to the door. The staff always informed her of who stood outside before they'd rung the bell. Popping over for a surprise visit wasn't a thing. Too risky with the hordes of paparazzi that seemed to live on the street outside her ten-bedroom home.

A twinge of unease twisted her stomach. What if they'd found her? What if she opened that door only to have a camera flash blind her?

No. Chill out, Mickie.

She'd taken hundreds of precautions, leaked fake stories of where she might have landed, and with the changes to her appearance, she wouldn't be recognized by Ralph, let alone a reporter.

You're fine. A normal person. Peek out the window and see who it is.

Her hand trembled as she reached for the curtain on the window next to the door. With a deep breath, she pulled the fabric over an inch. If the twenty-something woman standing on the other side noticed her, she had the decency to pretend otherwise.

There didn't seem to be a camera, wasn't a news van in sight, and she wasn't holding a phone. Crossing her fingers, Mickie released the curtain then opened the door.

Standing there in distressed jeans and a faded Pearl Jam T-shirt, the long-haired woman offered a genuine smile. "Hi!"

"Hi," Michaela said. Hopefully she sounded friendly and welcoming, and not like a *rich prude.* "Can I help you?"

She had long, dark, pin-straight hair, striking green eyes, and a flawless complexion without a stitch of noticeable makeup. The kind of skin women like Michaela and all in LA paid big bucks to achieve.

Lucky bitch.

"Hi, I'm Ronnie!" The woman stuck out a chipped-nailed hand.

As Michaela shook her hand, Ronnie glanced back over her shoulder and pointed. "I live right there," she said, indicating the house across the street and one over to the right. "I saw the moving trucks and figured I'd come to introduce myself and see if you wanted to take a break from the unpacking and have some cookies."

Though the welcoming smile and offer had her wanting to say yes, years of programing had Michaela's insides recoiling at the idea of cookies.

That's not you anymore.

If she wanted a cookie in the middle of the day without plans to exercise it away, she could damn well eat a cookie. Hell, she could have ten of them, and no one would say a word. Nobody would be seeing her on Instagram and judging every inch of her within seconds of the treat hitting her tongue. She wouldn't have to read dozens of critical comments which would make her drink the self-loathing away.

The same panic that had gripped her last night threatened to return, but she recalled Ralphs's words.

Don't second guess yourself.

Easier said than done, but she'd give it her best. Making friends and being neighborly was part of her new life now. She needed to remember Ronnie didn't know she was Scarlett, and embrace the chance to make a friend. To chase away some of that loneliness she'd mentioned to Ralph.

"Uh, I'm Michaela, but feel free to call me Mickie, or even Mick."

The woman's jaw dropped. "Seriously? Your name is Mick?"

The unease returned. Had she inadvertently outted herself? As far as she was aware, her actual name had never been made public. She'd gone to great lengths to keep it that way. "Y-yes."

"Holy shit, that is so perfect." Ronnie's head fell back, and she let out a joyful laugh. "Priceless."

"Uh, okay. Why?"

Ronnie waved her hand. "I'll explain another time. You game to hang for a bit?"

"Yeah. That sounds great, thanks." She almost turned to grab her phone and purse but stopped herself. There was no need to check social media, and no one would be calling.

Huh, that was kind of freeing.

"Awesome. Follow me," Ronnie said before turning and leading the way across the street. "You don't need to lock up. We can see the house from my porch."

As Michaela stepped out of her house into the crisp early September air, she swallowed her nerves. What the hell was she supposed to talk about with Ronnie? Her house? The fact she had no job? The weather?

Ridiculous.

Who would have believed a near thirty-year-old woman worth millions of dollars who'd charmed the entire world for a decade would be terrified to spend an hour making small talk with her neighbor?

Chapter Four

Keith dragged his tired ass into the kitchen sometime shortly after noon. He hadn't slept this late since he'd been in his early twenties. And, Christ, that was a decade and change ago.

Damn, when had he gotten so old?

Scrubbing a hand down his stubbled face, he veered straight for the coffee pot. Thank God, one of his siblings took pity on him and left a full pot hot and ready to go. He was tempted to drink it straight from the pot since one or two cups wasn't going to cut it.

Gonna be one of those days.

Even if it was already half over.

Oversleeping tended to happen when a man worked a fourteen-hour day then spent the night dragging his belligerent, drunk-ass of a father out of a bar. He'd had hopes of dumping the old man in his trailer and making it back home before midnight, but the trailer had been in such a disgusting state he'd had no choice but to spend a few hours cleaning while his father slept off his sixth binge in as many days. It was either that or he'd be getting a call from the board of health condemning the place. Food wrappers, weeks' worth of unwashed dishes, piles of trash, and a few unidentifiable items littered every spare inch of space in the mobile home, turning Keith's stomach.

Fuck.

Every time he left the toxic shithole, he swore he'd never be back. Never clean up after a man who wouldn't piss on Keith or any of his siblings if they were burning. But inevitably, he'd walk out of the trailer and his mom's weakened voice would sound in his ear.

"Please just don't let him die alone in there," she'd whispered after she'd awakened from the surgery to repair the ruptured aneurysm she'd suffered. But that hadn't been all. She'd gone on, pleading her case for a man who'd treated her almost as poorly as he'd treated his kids. "I know he's not perfect," she'd continued. "But I love him, Keith. I've always loved him." She hadn't lasted long after that. Not even a full day following surgery, she had a stroke. The surgeon had warned them it was a possibility. Something about the blood vessels in her brain constricting and spasming following the rupture. He still didn't fully understand. But back then, all he'd known was that his mother was dead, and she spent her last hours worrying about his jerk of a father.

Her plea haunted him to this day.

His mother had her own set of problems, but she'd tried to make a loving home for her children. She'd grown up in an abusive home and had wretched self-worth. At seventeen, she'd latched onto Earl hoping for a way out of her unsafe home. The sad thing was, by any other woman's standards, Earl would've been considered a verbally and emotionally abusive son of a bitch, but to his mother, he was some kind of fucked-up savior.

Having never graduated high school and having six children, she had difficulty finding work. His father sure as hell never brought home much money. What little he made went toward booze and drugs before feeding his offspring. Still, his mother found creative ways to provide for her children, form traditions they upheld to this day, and to deliver glimmers of sunshine in an otherwise gloomy homelife.

So ever since that damned aneurysm had robbed her of her life way too early, Keith had been cleaning up his father's messes despite a profound hatred for the man and despite keeping his actions a secret from his siblings. If they found out, they'd tell him to throw the man to the wolves. To let him rot in a cesspool of his own making. But they hadn't been there. Hadn't seen their mother begging for her husband as the life drained from her eyes.

Shit.

All he'd wanted was dark coffee, not dark thoughts.

As he poured the liquid gold into one of Ronnie's oversized mugs—the one he always teased her about because it had her name spelled wrong on the side—the woman in question came through the front door.

"Take a seat on the porch," she called through the window that opened to a view of their front porch. With his back to her, Keith wasn't sure who she was talking to. "I'll be right out with some cookies and coffee."

"Thanks, Ronnie. This is really sweet of you," a woman's voice responded back.

Keith frowned. The voice rang familiar, but he couldn't place which of Veronica's friends was out there.

He cleared his throat and he turned to face her back. Ronnie spun around. "Oh, hey, big bro." She smiled but the gesture slipped off her face as she took in the sight of him. "You look like shit. Why'd it take you so long to come pick up the cell for the garage?"

By the time he made it to the bar last night, it was late. Ronnie had been swamped serving customers, so he just grabbed the cell from behind the bar and taken off without talking with her. After taking a sip of his coffee he shrugged. "I'm fine. Leave it alone."

But of course, she didn't. She always worried about her big brothers. How she managed to keep from growing up with a chip on her shoulder as the rest of them had, always baffled him.

Not that she was soft. Veronica Benson was an independent badass, she just did it with a smile. Growing up with five older brothers ensured the tough skin; her sweetness she must have come by honestly. A genetic gift from their mother.

"Was it your mysterious nighttime caller?" With a mischievous grin, she walked to him and grabbed his free hand. "Come on, tell me who she is."

That's right. He led his siblings to believe his frequent nocturnal absences were the result of a repeated booty call instead of trips to bail out their drunk father. How noble of him. "Leave it, Ronnie."

She huffed. "I don't understand the secrecy. We all have sex, Keith. There's nothing to be ashamed of." Then one eyebrow raised. "Unless there is. Are you sleeping with Mrs. Lary?" she asked of their eighty-five-year-old neighbor.

Annoyance hardened Keith's spine. "I said leave it," he barked with more bite than he'd meant. It wasn't the teasing, but her digging forced him to prolong the lie and twisted the guilt a little harder.

Ronnie lifted her hands in surrender as she took a step back. "All right, I'll drop it."

Thank Christ.

"For now."

Figures.

"Though you'd think you'd be a little less of a grump with the amount of sex you're supposedly having," she muttered in way that he was definitely meant to hear.

He watched as his sister grabbed a Tupperware of peanut butter chocolate chip cookies she'd made the day before, then pulled two matching mugs from the cabinet.

"Oh good, you left some coffee."

Only because he hadn't had enough time to polish it off yet. "Who's out there? I couldn't place the voice."

"That would be our new neighbor." Glee made her squeak higher than usual.

Lifting his mug to his lips he asked, "Oh, someone finally moved into the Neely's place?" then took a sip.

"Yep." Ronnie turned around, eyes sparkling. "And she's gorgeous. Just your type."

He almost choked on the mouthful of coffee. "My type? I don't have a fucking type."

"Oh yes, big brother, you sure do."

With a snort, he rested his ass against the large kitchen island, set the mug down, then motioned for her to keep talking. "Okay, what's my type?"

"Short haired brunettes who are fit but not skinny, especially in the ass. You like some you some booty."

He rolled his eyes.

"Oh, and glasses. You're a sucker for a girl in glasses."

Damn, she had him pegged, and the smug gleam in her eye said she knew it. His stomach sank.

"Not even close," he said, though his mind had already conjured the snobby woman from last night who'd had the look but not the personality to match.

"Whatever," Ronnie said with an inelegant snort. "Come on out and meet her." She shoved the container of cookies at him before he had a chance to turn her down. Then she grabbed the mugs. "Come on."

Guess he was meeting the new neighbor.

Keith trudged after his sister. Hopefully, he didn't look too much like a hobo who hadn't slept or showered in a week. At least he'd tugged some jeans over his boxer briefs and tossed on a shirt. Given that his little sister lived in his house, he rarely paraded around in underwear, but he forgot the shirt often enough.

After Ronnie stepped through the swinging screen door, he caught it with his ass and managed to keep the cookies and his coffee upright.

"Mickie, this is my one of my brothers—a much, much older brother, Keith. Keith, this is Mickie, our new neighbor."

"Hey," he said as he turned in her direction. When his gaze landed on the woman from last night before, he said, "Oh fuck." He set the coffee down on the small table. It was either that or drop it in shock.

"I…uh…nice to meet you." Mickie lifted a hand in a weak wave. Her eyes reflected as much surprise as he imagined his did. And not happy surprise.

Ronnie smacked his arm with a horrified gasp. "Keith! What the hell is wrong with you? I'm sorry," she said, turning her attention toward their red-cheeked guest. "He had a late night and clearly it's made him rude. And stupid." Without looking at him, she punched his arm again. Damn, the woman might be small, but she had some force to her. Came from surviving five older brothers. He rubbed his shoulder. Perhaps they taught her to defend herself a little too well.

"No, uh, it's okay," Mickie said, gaze firmly on his sister as though avoiding him at all costs. "It's my fault. I had a flat tire last night and he rescued me. After such a long drive, I was a little snippy, so we didn't get off on the right foot."

Well, now she'd made him feel like an asshole for getting on her case.

"I'd like to start over," she said with a smile as she stepped forward and extended a perfectly manicured hand.

"Forget about it. I have."

His statement made her face light up behind those sexy glasses. "Great. I'm Michaela, your new neighbor."

As he slid his palm across hers, electricity popped and sizzled, sending a spark straight up his arm. Finally, years of suppressing his feelings came in handy as he kept his face neutral. Christ, those were some soft fucking hands. That shit would feel incredible sliding up and down his—

Fuck.

Hell no. Not going there. He had no problem jerking his shaft while picturing her bent over the hood of that fancy SUV of hers, but he damn well wasn't going to daydream about her soft fucking hands running all over him.

He released her without so much as a one pump to her hand.

She stepped back with a slight frown while Ronnie screwed her face up at him. A small V formed between Michaela's neatly shaped eyebrows. Even standing there in olive-green sweatpants and a light gray T-shirt, the woman looked like she walked off the page of a high fashion catalogue. Or out of some fancy boutique or whatever the hell those rich women shops were called. For Christ's sake, her shirt said *I can't please everyone, I'm not an avocado.* What the hell did that even mean?

Avocados were gross.

And could she stop staring at her fingers like one touch of his working man's hands had ruined her for life.

"Feel free to use the sink inside," he said. Though he worked to keep his voice level, annoyance bled through.

"Excuse me?" she asked at the same time Ronnie said, "Huh?"

"To wash your hands. I mean, I'm pretty sure I got all the grease off, but you never know. Wouldn't want to make you uncomfortable." That time he didn't even bother to stem his sarcasm. Irritation grew by the second.

"Jesus," Ronnie said with a shocked gasp as she stared with appalled eyes. "What the hell is wrong with you?" She faced Miss Rich whose eyes had narrowed with displeasure. "Mickie, I'm so sorry. He clearly doesn't know how to act around people." Then she turned back to him. "You can go now. Remind me to never introduce you to another human being ever again." Rolling her eyes, she yanked the container of cookies from him and turned back to Michaela.

"No, uh, that was my fault. I'm so sorry," Michaela said, as she opened and closed her fist. "It's been a really long few days —months really," she muttered. "I'm off my game."

"Seriously." Ronnie said as she slid an arm around Michaela's shoulders then guided her new BFF to the bench swing that hung on their porch. Scowling in his direction, she opened the cookies then set them on the wicker table. "It's Keith's fault. Trust me. He's like an untrained dog."

He folded his arms across his chest and raised an eyebrow at his sister. "I'm standing right here."

Ronnie gave him a sugary smile. "I know. What I don't know is why because I told you to go."

Her voice dripped with sweetness, but he knew better than to fall for that garbage. The moment he or any of his brothers let their guard down around Ronnie was when she struck. They'd all had their balls nailed enough by their loving little sister to have that lesson drilled into them.

Turning back to Michaela, Ronnie said, "Here, have a cookie."

"Thanks." Michaela grabbed one with her left hand. The one he'd shaken rested on her lap, still balled in a loose fist as though she didn't want to use it.

Shit.

Keith rubbed his chin. Damn, his beard had grown more than he realized. When the hell had he trimmed it last? He glanced at Michaela to find her studying him. The moment their gazes met, she averted hers.

Suddenly he was hit with the insane desire to rub his beard along her smooth cheek. Would she like it? He sure as fuck would. Maybe she'd like it brushing across other parts of her body as well.

What the hell was he thinking?

Didn't matter. What mattered was that Michaela was not from his world and he had no intention of getting close to her.

Last thing he needed or wanted was some rich priss sniffing his way. He'd been there and had the internal scars to prove it only ended in disaster.

He watched as she lifted the cookie to her plump lips, parted them, and took a bite.

"Oh, my God," she, eyes rolling upward. "This is so good. Oops!" she said with a giggle as a crumb fell from her mouth. The laugh turned into a moan that was practically obscene. Her tongue peeked out, swiping a dot of chocolate from her lower lip, and fucking hell, Keith's cock jerked.

Prissy woman like her probably shuddered at the idea of giving head. Hell, she probably couldn't fathom getting on her knees on the ground. Though, damn, she'd look hot down there, big eyes canted up his way, pupils blown, mouth stuffed full of his cock—

Jesus, he needed to get the fuck outta here before his dick got any harder and he sent the woman running in horror.

But first, he reached out toward the tub of cookies. Those babies were damn good. Nothing like a little sugar with his coffee to get his motor revving.

Ronnie smacked his hand so fast she might as well have cracked him with a whip. "Fuck! Ouch! Damnit!" he yelled, yanking his hand back as Ronnie went to slap it a second time. "Jesus, woman, what the hell?" He glowered at her smirk.

"Sorry, Keith. The cookies are for the boys who are nice," she said with an evil glint in her gaze.

Fucking sisters. "Cut the shit, Ronnie." He reached for the tub again only to have it snatched out of reach before he could snag a cookie. "Seriously?"

Michaela watched them with wide eyes as though she'd never seen siblings needle each other before.

Ronnie smiled at him from her seat on the swing with the cookies protectively hugged to her chest. "Weren't you leaving?" she asked, back to false sweetness though her eyes shot fire.

Fuck, she was pissed, and he'd be paying for it later.

With a grunt, he turned from them. Fuck it, he'd just dump a half cup of sugar in his next cup of coffee.

"Sorry, I'd say he's not normally such a neanderthal, but I'd be lying," Ronnie whispered as he stepped into the house.

Both women dissolved into a fit of giggles as though they weren't twenty-six and…however old Michaela was. Probably around the same as Ronnie.

Keith's lips twitched even as he tried to keep the scowl in place. But then Michaela's collided with his once again and her laughter dried up.

Fucking rich women.

Damn, he couldn't stand them. He'd dated one once. Back in his last year of high school. She'd been with another guy since they were freshmen, but they broke up at the start of senior year, or so he'd been told. Her name was Della and, man, he'd had a thing for her since the first time his dick began noticing girls. When she expressed interest in him, he'd jumped on the chance to be with him faster than Ronnie had just slapped his hand. For three months they'd been inseparable despite the extreme differences in their social status. Her family lived in a fucking mansion at the base of the mountain and his in a double wide near the dump.

For a horny seventeen-year-old who'd grown up with nothing his entire life, Della and her world fascinated him. At the time, he'd been convinced he loved her, and they'd get fucking married after high school. Instead, before Christmas break, she'd dumped him out of nowhere and gotten back together with her old boyfriend. Turned out he'd just been a way to get back get back the guy for cheating on her. He'd never forget the expression on her face when she told him it was over.

"Come on, Keith," she'd said, staring at him like he was shit on her shoe. "How could you not see this coming? Why on earth would someone like me be with someone like you?"

"What does that mean?" he'd asked as his young heart broke.

She'd laughed and given him a haughty smirk. "Ever heard the expression trailer trash, Keith?" she'd asked, before turning on her heel and jogging to where her ex was waiting to rekindle their relationship.

They'd married a year later and divorced five years after that.

Recalling the event through the eyes of an adult, he realized what he'd felt wasn't love, just teenage infatuation. But the sting of humiliation had stuck with him and soured him on the wealthy. To this day his hackles rose whenever someone so much as glanced at him as though he was beneath them.

Yeah, rich people could shove their entitlement up their collective asses.

Chapter Five

Michaela stepped into the lobby of KB's Garage around eleven the following morning. An hour ago, someone from the garage, not Keith thankfully, had called to let her know the tire was in and she could swing by at any time to have it put on. As attractive as he was, she'd embarrassed herself in front of the man enough for one lifetime.

The click of her heels across the short distance to the desk alerted the man behind the counter to her presence. He glanced up from the computer, eyes widening as he took in the sight of her.

Her steps faltered as a quick flash of panic rushed her. Oh, my God, had he recognized her? She reached up and fingered the ends of her short, brown hair.

The man gave her a wide grin as he folded his arms across his chest. "Well," he said, raising an eyebrow. "You are either new to town or just passing through."

What? How did he know?

She froze, midway to the counter. Only her heart still moved, slamming against the wall of her chest.

Oblivious to her internal freak out, the man behind the counter kept on grinning. "There is no way I'd have missed taking out a woman as hot as you. So, which is it?"

Stagnant air left her lungs in a rush of relief. Of course he would wonder about her. This was a small town, and he was being friendly. Flirting, even. Had she become so paranoid she could no longer pick up on flirty banter and a welcoming smile?

Clearing her throat, she pasted on what hopefully was an approachable a grin. "Brand new in town as of two days ago."

"And car trouble already? That sucks."

"Just a blown tire. Nothing major."

"Ahh, you must be the Audi owner I spoke with this morning. Michaela, right?"

"That's me." There, she could be friendly too.

He rested his lean but toned and very tattooed forearms on the top of the high counter. Something about his eyes seemed familiar to her. "So, did your boyfriend or husband move here with you?"

Michaela couldn't help it. She laughed out loud. "That was the most blatant fishing I think I've ever heard." The man was handsome for sure, though a little less bulky than she typically went for. With very dark hair in a pompadour style and deep blue eyes, he certainly had that tall, dark, and handsome thing going on only with an edge due to the tattoos, a few rings, and gauges in his ears.

Without an ounce of repentance, he shrugged and laughed along with her. "Hey, I had to check if there was competition before I ask you ou—"

The door between the garage bays and the lobby swung open at that moment and in walked none other than Keith with his focus on the paper he was holding. Instantly her gut tightened at the sight of him. The man was too sexy for his own good. Maybe she still needed more therapy if the first man she felt an attraction to in months was also the one who couldn't stand the sight of her.

"Seriously, JP, could you maybe let one female customer walk out of here without hitting on her." His head popped up. "Oh, Michaela. Hey."

The way his face went from teasing to flat so fast would have been funny if she wasn't the cause. The playful atmosphere deflated faster than a balloon pricked by a pin.

"Jesus, bro, you sure know how to suck the fun out of a room." The resemblance was obvious to her now, and JP rolled his eyes. He must have gotten Keith's share of the sociable genes. "Think you could you scowl any harder?"

Keith's lips compressed even thinner.

"Guess you can," JP mumbled. They did look a lot alike. Black hair, startling blue eyes, olive complexion. JP wasn't as tall or nearly as built, but he was certainly no slouch.

"Think you could actually do some work to earn your paycheck instead of flirting with the neighbor?"

JP's eyes lit as they shifted back to her. "No shit," he said, happy once again. "You bought the place across the street?"

"I did." His jovial personality made it easy to feel comfortable despite the cold waves wafting off Keith.

"Well, welcome to the neighborhood." JP snickered. "I feel like this could be really good for me. And for you, if you know what I mean." He waggled his eyebrows.

Had anyone else spoken to her with such blatant innuendo, she might have bristled, but as it was, he seemed like so much fun she couldn't help but laugh at his antics. Like Ronnie, she could envision him becoming a friend.

Now his growly brother on the other hand…

Keith rolled his very nice eyes and shoulder-bumped his brother out of the way. "When you're done making an ass of yourself, JP, I need you to pull her car into bay three." He held his hand out and stared at her.

"Um…" Was he waiting for something?

JP snorted. "The keys, hon. Sorry, he's a bit of a caveman but we love him anyway. He's gonna need your keys." With a glower of his own, he elbowed his brother. "Keith, next time try saying something like, 'May I please have your keys so we can move your car.' You'll find life so much easier if you use polite words."

Keith just glared at him with a look that had Mickie cringing. Her intention hadn't been to cause any sibling strife, but JP seemed unaffected by Keith's demeanor.

She shook her head, "Of course. Sorry, I should have realized." As she dropped them on Keith's upturned palm, her fingers brushed his skin and the same goddammed zing that shocked her yesterday rocked her again.

A buzz of electricity shot up her arm, traveled down her spine, and settled low in her belly, turning into an inconvenient flutter. "Sorry," she whispered as she snatched her hand back to her side.

"Here." Keith tossed the keys over his shoulder without so much as a glance in JP's direction. "Make yourself useful. I'll take care of Michaela."

"Mmm, I bet you will," JP said with a wink before he snagged the keys out of midair, then disappeared through the same door Keith used. Only he was laughing whereas Keith still hadn't managed to erase the scowl from his face.

The man hated her. It shouldn't be getting under her skin. He was nothing to her. A neighbor she'd met three times and exchanged twenty words with, max. So why the hell was his undisguised disdain grating on her like an itchy mosquito bite?

Because he woke up her neglected libido?

She sighed.

He sure as hell made for some delicious eye candy, but his appearance wasn't why she'd spent two hours the previous night frowning at her television while trying to figure out how to get on his good side.

In her new life, she'd vowed to be different. To be better than she'd been the past ten years. To be someone kind and likable from the first meeting. Scarlett had a reputation as a high-maintenance bitch—admittedly well-deserved, but it was a status she now felt ashamed of. Michaela, on the other hand, was a blank slate. No one had preconceived opinions about her personality, and she'd planned to capitalize on that professionally and personally. Offending the first man she encountered in her new town because he thought she was a cold-hearted, unapproachable snob wasn't exactly the vibe she was going for.

"Fucking child," Keith muttered under his breath.

Hopefully he was referring to his brother and not her. It was difficult to tell since he wouldn't give her his eyes.

"Got some papers for you to sign," he said, gaze still anywhere but on her.

Repressing another sigh, she stepped up to the counter. If aloof was how he wanted to play it, that was his right. The urge to demand he look at her and tell her straight to her face what his problem with her was grew strong, but she suppressed it. "Sure, whatever you need," she said instead.

He grunted in response and thrust a stack of papers her way. "Third page and last page need a signature. The last page is an itemized invoice for the tire and the roadside."

"Got it." She handed over her credit card, then moved on to the paperwork. After signing the third page, she flipped to the end and scrawled her name across the line without bothering to check the bill total.

Keith scoffed.

She lifted her head to find the man finally staring at her with a cross between disbelief and disgust on his face. "What?" she asked, forehead scrunching.

Had she messed up? Signed the wrong spot?

And why the hell did his pissed off face have to make him look even hotter? He was all smoldering eyes, sexy beard, and rugged male.

"Must be nice," he said as he slid the card through the machine.

Okay, enough was enough. She could manage to remain polite and find out what his problem with her was. "What must be nice?"

He set the card on the counter then pushed it her way. "Having so much money you don't even need to check the bill." With that parting shot he turned his back on her. "It'll be ready in fifteen minutes, max," he called before walking into the garage bay.

"It is nice," she grumbled under her breath. Being financially well-off was something she refused to apologize for. No, she didn't plan to flaunt her status and wealth as she'd done while embodying Scarlett. It was tacky. She knew it now and had known it then, but in Hollywood acting as though you could purchase the world was not only admired, it was necessary to maintain her brand as a diva.

It was also exhausting.

She liked nice things. Now away from the spotlight, she no longer wanted over the top extravagant or flashy, but she appreciated quality. Clothes, car, home items. Sue her. And it wasn't like she lived in a mansion, drove a Bentley, and wore dresses made of diamonds. She'd purchased a modest house with plans to renovate it to her personal style.

While not busting her butt at a typical nine to five job, she'd worked damn over the past decade. For years she'd had no privacy. She had to be *on* every single waking second of every day. So, no she wouldn't apologize or be ashamed of her wealth.

No matter what Keith thought of her.

He could go screw himself.

Not that she'd voice those words out loud. Didn't vibe with the new image she was trying to project.

Ugh, there she was overthinking again.

As she turned to wait in the uninviting plastic chairs in the lobby, the door opened and two men, probably in their mid to late thirties walked—no, swaggered in. The stench of cigarettes and cheap cologne immediately filled the space.

When both their gazes landed on her, she gave a polite nod while simultaneously working to keep her nose from wrinkling as she sat. Damn, there probably wasn't a drop left in the bottle of cologne.

One of the guys was short for a man, probably about five foot seven and stocky. The other had a few extra inches though she guessed he didn't quite reach six feet. He was thick as well, but more muscular than his buddy. Or maybe brother. There seemed to be some family resemblance. Both had curly, light brown hair and matching eyes.

The shorter one snorted. "No one in here to greet customers. Why am I not surprised at Benson's shitty service?"

The taller one walked up to the counter and turned screen toward himself as though he owned the place. He let out an exaggerated gasp of surprise. "Keith giving bad service?" The gasp turned into laughter. "You expecting anything different from that trash?"

Michaela's spine straightened. Damn, she hated that word. No one, especially not a man who owned a business and worked hard deserved judgment like that. Having spent the past decade being criticized by others every day, she'd lost any tolerance for people who thought they had the right to comment on someone else's life.

Now they were both laughing. "No, guess not." The shorter one said. "That whole family's a bunch of dirty fucking hillbillies."

Seriously? This from the man with an unlit cigarette dangling from his lips and open flannel over his white wife beater? She shifted in her chair as the need to defend people she barely knew bubbled in her gut.

"Seriously," the guy closer to the counter replied. "Wouldn't keep me from doing Ronnie, though."

"Damn straight. That one always did have a tight little ass. Though that may be all that's tight on that slu—"

Okay, that's enough.

Michaela cleared her throat.

Tweedle Dumb and Tweedle Dee swiveled their heads her way. "Shit," the tall one said. "Forgot there was a lady in the room. How long you been sitting here? Customer service is worse than I thought if they make a gorgeous thing like you wait."

Thing? Did he just call her a thing?

All her self-important Scarlett hackles rose. Actually, screw that. Michaela didn't need to be a Hollywood diva to have a huge problem with this asshole as well. "I've been helped," she said, channeling the snarkiest tone she could muster. "So, I'm all set, but I was hoping to pass that time without having to hear a vulgar conversation about a friend of mine."

The short one barked out a laugh. "Well, you're a bitchy little thing, ain't ya?"

Michaela's eyes narrowed. What was with these morons calling her a thing? "Sorry," she said with false sincerity. "Sometimes I just can't help it. Especially when I'm around idiots."

The big one frowned. "Hey! Watch your—"

"I like it," the short guy went on, folding his arms across his wide chest. "Makes me want to tame you."

The big one grunted. "And now that you know she's friends with Ronnie, you know she'll be easy, huh cuz?"

Cousins. That explained the shared stupidity.

"Damn straight." The short one waggled his eyebrows at her suggestively.

"Well, too bad for you," she said, mimicking his pose. "I don't fuck men with only two brain cells. Just a quirk of mine."

The way his face turned a deep shade of red was a hundred times more satisfying than sex with either of those morons would be. That was for sure.

His cousin laughed as though she'd told the funniest joke on earth, then he tilted his head. "You look familiar. Do I know you from somewhere?"

Only years of acting experience kept her from showing the panic on the outside she felt on the inside. "No," she said in a flat voice. "Pretty sure I'd remember meeting an ass like you."

His smile made her skin crawl. "Hmm," he said, narrowing his eyes as he studied her.

Despite all the physical changes she'd made since leaving California, she could almost see inside his brain to a picture of herself with long bleached hair, ice-blue eyes, and minus twenty or so pounds.

"Can't place it," he said, making her sag with relief. He tapped the side of his head. "It'll come to me."

Just as she was about to unleash a comment about there being nothing but air in his skull, the door open and Keith strode in with his customary scowl in place. "Bud, Chuck, to what do I owe the displeasure of your visit?"

Was it her imagination or was his frown more pronounced than usual?

"'Bout fucking time," short stuff said. "Been waiting here so long I'm gonna need Viagra by the time we get outta here."

"Pretty sure you need it now," Michaela muttered at the same time Keith said, "I'm sure your cousin here can manage to get you hard, Bud."

Michaela snorted out a laugh which had Keith glancing her way with something other than annoyance, but the look disappeared so fast she couldn't decipher it.

So, shorty was Bud, which left Chuck for the big guy.

"Fuck you, asshole," Bud shot back at Keith.

Chuck slapped his palms on the counter. "You think you're something now that you got this shop? You ain't. You're nothing more than the garbage you came from." His lips curled into an evil grin. "Everyone in town knows your daddy's a junkie piece of shit, but they don't all remember your sweet mamma, do they? But I remember her. That woman would have done anything for a few bucks." He laughed. "Hell, she did do just about anything."

The hairs on the back of Michaela's neck rose and her stomach twisted. This conversation hit a little too close to home. She'd been well on her way to being known as the "junkie piece of shit" of Hollywood. It was mere luck she'd survived hitting rock bottom. And what was the reference to his mother?

Her heart ached knowing Keith and his siblings might have had a challenging childhood.

For his part, Keith managed to stay calm. Only the pulsing of his jaw let Michaela know he wasn't okay. "Miss Hudson, your car is finished. JP's pulling it around front and keys will be in it."

If there'd ever been a polite way to say *get the hell out*, that was it. But this time it seemed to be his way of saving her from the ugly scene, not because of his beef with her. Huh, look at that, she wasn't the most hated person in the room.

The desire to jump to his defense clawed at her insides. He'd probably hate having a woman fight his battles. Still, she couldn't resist one jab before she left.

"Thank you, Keith," she said. "Appreciate the fast work and excellent service. Also appreciate how you don't stink like shitty cologne and a carton of cigarettes. Too bad the same can't be said of your customers."

With that she spun on her heel and walked out with a grin on her face, one the muttered "bitch" couldn't erase. Especially when she heard a low chuckle that could have only come from Keith.

Small victory, perhaps, but she'd take it.

Chapter Six

Ronnie set a frosty pint down on a cardboard coaster in front of Keith. "Dude, you still look like shit. What the hell is going on with you?"

That was a younger sister for you. Didn't pull a single punch. Ever. In fact, Ronnie packed a wallop stronger than most men he knew. "Long few days," he said, before saluting her with the pint. "Thanks."

Her expression turned serious. "Is everything all right?"

"Yeah, just tired. Go serve your customers before you lose your tips."

A couple had seated themselves at the opposite end of the bar. For seven p.m. on a Saturday night, the small sports bar, Batter's Up, was as crowded as it typically got. About a third of the tables were full, and a few stools at the bar, too. In a few hours, business would pick up, but the place never packed out, which was why Keith enjoyed it. Crowds of drunk townspeople who looked down on his family and thought them trash weren't his thing.

"You know, I might have believed you were just tired if you weren't scowling like you want to smash the bar in half," Ronnie said as she leaned her forearms on the counter. "What's going on, big brother?"

What was going on?

Well, for the second night in a row, he'd been called to pick up their wasted-off-his-ass father. This time he had to drag the old man out of the world's seediest strip club twenty minutes outside of town.

Yesterday he'd had to deal with Bud and Chuck's shit at work. They'd come in for a simple battery replacement and oil change, but the cousins were some of the nastiest assholes to ever live, so of course they couldn't leave without hurling slews of insults his way. He'd have loved to kick them the fuck out of his shop with a few black eyes, but the HVAC in the shop was on the fritz, and he needed every penny coming in to fix the damn thing before winter hit.

Then there was Michaela. The woman who rubbed him the wrong way from the get-go was the same woman he wanted to rub him in all the right ways. Why the hell she'd gotten so far under his skin, he couldn't say, but he simultaneously wanted to throttle her and fuck her stupid. After practically freezing him with her frigid attitude, why the hell had she stood up for his shop when Bud and Chuck were hurling their customary insults?

"Just got a lot on my mind, Ronnie."

"You know, you could share some of it. Just because you're the oldest doesn't mean you need to take on the world's problems by yourself." Another customer sidled up to the bar, flagging her down. Ronnie sighed. "I'll be right back. Hold that thought," she said as she strode down to greet the thirsty man.

There weren't any thoughts to hold. He'd die before burdening his siblings with their father's bullshit. None of them had any idea that when he left in the middle of the night a few times per week, it was to rescue the old man from himself. Ronnie had convinced the rest of their siblings Keith was getting laid regularly.

If she only knew it'd been a solid nine months since anything besides his own hand had come within ten yards of his naked cock. Fuck, he missed pussy. And tits. In his old age and wisdom, he'd become much more discerning with his fuck buddies. Back in the day, he'd hop on any female who looked his way—not quite as many as JP, but close. Maybe he needed to lower his standards for a night or a few hours to scratch this itch. Though, at thirty-eight, he found he was just too old to bed a woman he couldn't hold a conversation with. If it could get Michaela out of his brain, it might be worth it.

By the time Ronnie returned, he'd nearly finished his beer.

"Okay, I'm back." She shoved a lock of hair that had escaped her high ponytail behind her ear. Like the rest of the place, her black T-shirt and black pants uniform was as casual as it got, which suited his low-maintenance sister just fine. "I've got like two minutes before that guy down there needs a refill, so spill."

With a laugh, he rolled his eyes. "What were we talking about?" he asked before swallowing the last of his beer.

She narrowed her eyes, snatching his glass. "You're not funny." As she refilled the glass under the tap, she shrugged. "Fine, be that way. See if I care if you have a heart attack at forty from internalizing all your stress. Just remember when you're lying in the ICU that I offered."

"Well, maybe I'll have a hot nurse, so it just might be worth it." An image of Michaela wearing one of those sexy nurse costumes college girls wore for Halloween popped into his mind. Okay, that was the last straw. After this beer he was officially looking for someone to hook-up with before he lost his mind.

Ronnie wrinkled her nose. "Now you sound like JP." With a perky smile, she handed over his beer.

"Thanks. You're a gem. You'll make some man very ha—"

"Hey, Mickie, over here!" Ronnie called out, waving her hand.

Keith froze. Christ, had he conjured her with his damn thoughts? So much for stopping by the bar to have a few drinks and relax.

"Hey, Ronnie! Figured I'd come to check out where you worked." Michaela's voice had a sunny, bubbly quality he sure as hell hadn't heard any time she'd spoken to him. Granted, he had zero interest in buddying up to his wealthy neighbor, whereas Ronnie seemed to want to be her best friend.

Someone hollered Ronnie's name. "Shit," she said as she glanced down the bar. "Come sit, Mickie. Let me take care of him, and I'll be right back." Then she was buzzing off to serve the client flagging her down, a man named Jack who lived on the other side of town.

He knew each and every person in the bar by name. Most had looked down on his family his entire life. It was only now that he and his siblings had shown themselves to be productive members of society that some of the whispered insults had stopped. Some, but not all. Many were just waiting for the day they followed in their father's footsteps and became true losers.

With each passing second, he felt Michaela moving closer, and his shoulders stiffened further. By the time she sat on the stool next to him, he was barely breathing and mentally kicking his own ass. What the fuck did he care if she sat beside him? He'd polish off his second beer and leave. No biggie.

With the smile she'd gifted Ronnie still on her face, she turned his way. The way her spine straightened and the grin flipped to a frown should have been comical, but he wasn't in a laughing mood.

No, his mood was growing darker by the second.

"Hello, Keith," she said, giving him a polite smile that didn't reach her eyes. Gone was the happiness in her voice, replaced by a cold formality.

He didn't do formality. Especially not today. "Hey."

Christ, did she look out of place in the forty-year-old sports bar that hadn't been updated in over two decades. Wearing a simple fitted black sweater that looked soft as fuck with seriously tight jeans he tried not to stare at, she didn't stand out for being flashy with her wealth, but it was very clear the clothes cost more than his first car. Hell, just the little black bootie things on her small feet probably ran as much as his mortgage. The woman had money, class, and did not fit in with their small-town, blue-collar vibe.

Which begged the question, what the fuck was the well-off woman doing all alone in their itty-bitty town? She didn't appear to have a job and hadn't had visitors since she moved in —not that he'd been keeping tabs on her house.

Was she avoiding an ex?

Rebelling from an overbearing family who controlled her trust fund?

Witness protection?

The ideas only got more outrageous from there.

Dammit, he needed to stop giving brain power to this woman.

The silence that settled between them was thick with tension and discomfort.

Hurry the fuck up, Ronnie.

Michaela cleared her throat. "So, uh, my tire's working, uh… great. Thank you."

He grunted. Awkward silence was better than this meaningless small talk. "Here." He slid a half-full bowl of bite-sized pretzels in front of her. Maybe if she stuffed something in her mouth, she'd shut up again.

As she glanced in the tan plastic bowl, her perfect nose wrinkled.

"What's wrong, princess? Too many carbs?" Back when he'd date Della in high school, she'd been head cheerleader and scoffed at any food with more than one gram of carbohydrates.

Now Michaela's forehead was wrinkled, and her lips pressed into a thin, glossy line.

Keith had the insane urge to lick the seam of her mouth and watch that lower lip puff back up as she parted her mouth in surprise. Then he'd suck it into his own mouth and watch her eyes widen in shock.

And probably disgust.

That thought doused his plumping dick like a bucket of ice.

"No," she said, staring at the pretzels as though they were worms instead of a snack. "Just not a fan of eating from a bowl that a hundred people might have put their hands in."

Christ, she was a fucking princess.

Rolling his eyes, he dragged the bowl back in front of himself with one finger. "More for me," he said before popping a pretzel in his mouth. He couldn't keep from winking as she glared at him. "Mmm, crunchy."

She pressed her lips together again in what he was coming to learn was her disapproval face. Of course, Miss Fancy Pants wouldn't tell him off. He almost laughed out loud. That'd be something to see, but it would never happen. Wasn't proper enough. Instead, she'd just sit there and let the steam rise to a boil with no escape. Maybe she screamed into her pillow at night or something. Wasn't healthy to keep that shit bottled inside. Might give her gas.

But it was kinda fun to watch and beat the tense quiet.

There was another way to work off stress. Even though he could certainly imagine her in a fuck-the-frustration away scenario, in reality, he had a hard time picturing the stiff woman letting go enough to enjoy sex.

"Okay, I'm back, sorry," Ronnie said as she stood on the opposite side of the bar. "You two making nice?"

"Yes, of course," Michaela said. "We're good."

Keith just snorted, which made Ronnie cast him some serious side-eye.

"Mmm," she said. "Well, what can I get you, Michaela? Not sure you seem like a beer drinker or whiskey shooter, but I gotta tell you what little wine we do offer here totally sucks."

Across the room, a table full of guys Keith went to high school with started cheering. Michaela jumped and glanced over her shoulder.

"Baseball playoffs," Ronnie said, as though the woman had any idea about sports.

"Fun," she said, totally unconvincingly. "I'll just have a diet soda, please."

"No way," Ronnie said, shaking her head. She had the same black hair all of the Benson kids did, only about a hundred times more of it. When working, she kept it up in a long ponytail. His sister was pretty, though she'd never seemed to recognize it in herself. "You need a real drink to celebrate your first few days in town."

"Thanks, but I'll stick to soda if you don't mind. I, uh, have had some issues with—" She cleared her throat as though the words stuck.

Christ, don't say it.

"Just, issues with it. So, I steer clear these days. Just wanted to stop by and see where Ronnie worked."

"Good for you," Ronnie said with a smile. "That's not an easy battle to fight. Diet Coke it is." She grabbed a clean glass and filled it with ice.

Just what he needed, another fucking addict in his life. "Typical," he muttered under his breath. Rich woman with no job probably spent her days drinking her boredom away. Bet she was someone's trophy wife. Probably took some shmuck to the cleaners with complaints about infidelity while she was frigid as an iceberg in bed.

"Keith! Jesus, you're an ass." Ronnie tossed him a scathing look before focusing on Michaela. "How about food, hon? You hungry? I can get you a menu."

She'd gone pale, but Keith refused to feel guilty. Maybe having someone not fawn all over her would keep her from falling off the wagon as they all seemed to do.

"Uh, yeah, I'll take a menu," she said in a measured tone. "But first, can you point me toward the restroom?"

She stood, and Keith chose to ignore the slight tremor in her hand.

"Back right corner," Ronnie said, pointing.

"Thanks," Michaela whispered.

As she walked away, Ronnie seared him with a death glare. The second Michela was out of earshot, his sister let loose. "What the fuck is wrong with you? Seriously, why are you such an asshole to her?"

"Hey!" He set his beer down. Ronnie didn't understand. She was younger, less jaded by the world. "I'm not an asshole. Just telling it like it is. She's a cliché. A rich woman with a drinking problem. I give her a month before she's in here tossing 'em back. But don't worry, she won't be eating the pretzels. Too many cooties for her sterile hands."

Ronnie's mouth hung open and she shook her head. "You're right, Keith. You're not an asshole. You're a fucking asshole." She leaned over the bar. "You know, no one makes it through life without some struggles. And not everyone with a drinking problem is like our father. Some people work hard to overcome their demons." She lifted her hands and took two steps back. "But I guess we can't all be as perfect as you without any vices, huh?" She turned to storm away then spun back. "And you know what? I wouldn't eat from that goddammed cesspool of a bowl either," she almost yelled, pointing to the pretzels. "And not just because I saw Bud scratch his ass then eat one."

Anger rose swift and sharp. "I don't need this shit. Not after the shit I've had to deal with the past few days." The stool scraped across the floor with a cringe-worthy screech as he shoved to his feet.

The place had gone quiet. All the patrons stared at the low-class Bensons making a scene. Surprise, surprise. Fuck, he should have left this goddammed town years ago.

Ronnie's shoulders sagged as she stepped against the bar. "One of these days, you're going to realize you have five siblings who love you and would help you any time you asked, Keith. Dad is not a problem you should have to deal with alone."

He stilled.

What the fuck?

She knew?

All the secrets and lies to keep them from realizing what havoc their father still caused had been for nothing? Guilt ate at him. He should have done better. Should have devised a stronger cover story.

Standing with her arms folded across her chest, Ronnie nodded. "Yes, big brother. It's a small town. I know. We all know. And I'm tired of tiptoeing around the issue. It's turning you into a bitter, angry jerk and I'm sick of it. So the cat's out of the bag now, and we can all freaking deal with it."

Her eyes shifted to his right then back to his face. "Mickie is coming back. We'll talk about this at home."

"Fuck," he spat out. "This is none of your business, Veronica."

The glare she gave him let him know she thought he was the dumbest person in the room.

"Goddammit." He yanked out his wallet, tossed a twenty on the bar, and spun only to slam straight into Michaela.

"Sorry!" she yelped as she clutched his arms for support.

Damn, her tits were soft where they'd mashed into his chest. That meant they were probably real. Huh, he hadn't been expecting anything on the woman to be real.

"I was, uh, looking at the screen and I didn't see you," she said with a wince. "I accidentally fell asleep midway through last night's game." Gone was the shaken woman from a few moments ago. Whatever she'd done to calm herself had worked because the air of superior confidence was back.

"It's fine. I'm on my way out and was rushing. See ya."

"Oh, uh, bye Keith." He was helpless to do anything but stare at her ass as she walked back to the bar where her soda waited for her.

Her soda, because she was an alcoholic.

But she liked baseball. And her tits were real.

"Whatever," he grumbled to himself. "I'm leaving."

Fuck this day.

Chapter Seven

Four days later, Michaela was clawing the walls of her new house. She'd spent the majority of her time working on plans for some home renovations and unpacking. The house had four bedrooms, a decent sized basement, and a kitchen that would be a chef's dream with a little updating. In truth, the house was too big for one person, but about a third of the size of the Hollywood Hills monstrosity she was selling in California. Her goal was to modernize the place and create a home she could live in for a long time.

Forever, maybe.

But for the moment, she needed out. For years, she'd barely had a moment alone, and now all she had was solo time especially since she'd been avoiding her neighbors. Ronnie had apologized for Keith after the embarrassing scene at the bar, but she'd felt it best to keep from crossing paths with him for a while. At least until her ego wasn't as fragile. Unfortunately, that meant staying off Ronnie's radar as well.

And since they were the only people she'd met in town, she was becoming pretty damn lonely. A side effect she'd expected to enjoy but may not be all she'd envisioned. At least she had an appointment to keep her occupied for a few hours that morning. Pretty soon, she'd be running out of streaming shows to binge.

The sun shone brightly through the windshield as she pulled the SUV into the parking lot outside a local construction company. LA was almost always bright, with photo-worthy sunsets she'd neglected to enjoy. Now away from it, she found herself enjoying the cool, crisp bite of late summer air that countered the heat of the sun. She also sat on her back porch every night watching the sun dip below the mountains.

Breathtaking in its beautiful simplicity.

The heeled ankle boots she'd chosen might not have been the wisest choice. Teetering across the gravel lot turned out to be a precarious operation. As she was halfway to the entrance, the door swung open, and a handsome man jogged toward her. "Let me help you there, ma'am," he said, shooting her a charming smile complete with the most adorable dimples. He had a smooth-shaven face, but longer hair in a man bun at the back of his head.

"Oh, thank you," she said, looping her arm through his. "I hadn't budgeted an ambulance ride into my time today."

The man laughed, making her frown. Something about him rang familiar. "Always happy to help a damsel in distress. That and to avoid being sued when someone breaks an ankle on my property." He pulled the door open for her. "Ladies first."

"Thank you," she said with a smile. How come she could be relaxed and chatty with this guy while continually putting her foot in her mouth Keith?

And, ugh, why was she thinking about him?

Again.

She cleared her throat. "You said, you're the owner? Then you must be who I have an appointment with."

"Yes, ma'am, Jagger Benson at your service." He gripped her hand in a firm hold, giving a solid shake, which she reciprocated even as her stomach plummeted.

"Benson?" The name croaked out of her throat as though stuck with glue.

His mouth turned down into a familiar frown, but this one didn't have hatred or disgust behind it. "Uh oh, why do you ask that like my last name tastes nasty? Please tell me you haven't *dated* JP."

"Do you Bensons own every freakin' business in town?" she mumbled.

Oh, for crying out loud. Did she really just ask the man that? So much for not shoving her foot in her mouth, boot and all.

Except instead of taking offense to the insult, he let out an infectious, boisterous laugh. "Feels like it sometimes. You've met some of my siblings, I take it?"

Chuckling along with him, she nodded. "Yes. I've met Ronnie, JP, and Keith. I'm Michaela Hudson, your new neighbor, unless you don't live with the others. Then I'm just their neighbor."

She internally rolled her eyes. Why did this family make her stumble over her words like a bumbling idiot?

"Oh, no shit? You're the one who moved in last week? The one who Keith—oh." His smile turned impish. "You've made quite an impression on my brother."

She grimaced. "Yeah, I'm not his favorite person." Understatement of the year. At some point, they were going to have to make nice. They lived too close, and she liked the rest of his family too much to avoid contact with him.

The door closed behind them, leaving them standing in the lobby with a receptionist eyeing them from behind a desk.

She wrung her hands. Just the mention of Keith had thrown her off her game. Before rehab, she could talk to anyone about anything no matter the circumstances. She'd done countless interviews where she spoke eloquently on any topic and answered difficult, sometimes absurd questions on the fly. Her publicist had seen to it with hundreds of hours of coaching. Now, one mention of a man who didn't like her, and she could barely string two words together without making a fool of herself. Had sobriety stolen her personality?

His receptionist wasn't even pretending to mind her own business. She stared at them with rapt attention. Michaela could hear her brain whirring.

What did she do to Keith?

Who is she?

Jagger must have noticed as well, because he placed a large hand on her lower back and nudged her toward an open door left of the reception desk. "Here, come on in my office, and we'll chat about your vision for the house. Rachel, hold my calls until we're done."

The receptionist nodded. "You know, you look familiar," she said, gaze on Mickie's face.

With a nervous laugh, Mickie tried to keep from vomiting. "Huh, I don't think we've met before."

"No, it's not that." Rachel studied her for a moment longer then snapped her fingers. "I know it! You're probably gonna think I'm crazy, but you look a little like that actress, Scarlett. You know, the one who had the huge meltdown and disappeared off the face of the planet."

Michaela couldn't breathe, let alone answer the woman. Everything inside her screamed at her to turn and flee, but that'd give her away for sure. Instead, she made a squeaking noise she hoped sounded like one of disagreement.

Jagger tilted his head. "What? You're crazy, Rach. I don't see it at all. Scarlett has super long bleached hair, weighs about seventy pounds, and has a totally different eye color. You're way off base."

With a chuckle, Rachel shrugged. "Yeah, I guess you're right. Don't know what it was. Just a flash of familiarity or something." She waved a hand in front of her face. "Ignore me. I'll hold the calls, Jagger."

Breathe.

With a nod for his receptionist, he said, "After you," to Mickie.

"Thanks." She followed the larger man into his office. Hopefully he didn't notice the tremor in her voice and the way her hands shook.

"Have a seat. Sorry, it's a bit of a mess."

A mess? The place was a downright disaster. File folders were scattered all over the top of the wooden desk in the center of the room. Three takeout coffee cups, which she hoped were empty, rested on the file folders. One poorly placed elbow would ruin a whole lotta work. Tools, samples of tile, cabinet doors, and a startling amount of sawdust littered the floor and every corner of the room.

Jagger laughed. "Okay fine, it's more than a mess. You don't have to look so frightened."

Mickie jolted and took the seat he'd indicated on the opposite side of his desk. "Sorry. I didn't mean to insult you." At least the mess distracted her from the near freak out in the lobby.

Again, he laughed. "If you think that's insulting, clearly you didn't grow up with five of the most annoying siblings in the world."

Mickie found herself smiling. His easy personality drew her in and set her at ease. "Guilty. Only child."

"Ahh. Well, I'll tell you this. Keith's a good guy, but he's..." Jagger scratched his chin as he turned and stared out a window to his right. Then he focused back on her.

Mickie practically sat on the edge of her seat. She was so eager to learn more about Keith, she nearly lunged across the desk to grab the man and shake the words out of him.

"He's a tough nut to crack. The oldest and most responsible of us. We had a fairly shitty time as far as childhoods go, and Keith took the brunt of it." He gave her a wry grin. "He's pretty much a jaded bastard, but not a hopeless case. Don't give up on him."

"Oh." She shook her head as Jagger's words processed. He was right, she had absolutely no experience growing up with siblings. What little she knew about Keith led her to believe he was the type of man to take his role as oldest seriously. She imagined him always working to protect his siblings from whatever made their childhood shitty as Jagger had said. And just like that, her heart softened a little more toward the man who was beginning to intrigue her more than was wise. "It's okay if he doesn't like me. I'm happy to stay out of his way."

Liar.

"Anyway, I'm about the most chill person you'll ever meet, so don't feel like you have to walk on eggshells around me because Keith can be a growly bear." He leaned back in his chair and laced his fingers behind his head. As his already broad chest stretched even wider, a button on his flannel shirt gapped, giving her a peek of dark chest hair.

The Benson parents sure grew some nice-looking men.

Was Keith's chest furry like that too? Or did a smooth expanse of skin cover his muscles, which were even more pronounced than Jagger's from what she could tell?

Stop thinking about him like that. The man hates you.

Besides, she had enough on her plate with sobriety and figuring out what she wanted to do for a job. Throwing a man in the mix would be a recipe for disaster.

"Now that we got that out of the way, and we're new best friends, why don't you tell me what you're looking to do to the house." Thankfully, the man seemed unaware of her runaway thoughts.

Mickie snorted out a laugh. As with Ronnie, Jagger's personality drew her. The man was good-looking, yes, but the allure she felt toward him wasn't sexual. He attracted her in a platonic way. Maybe they could become good friends. Of course, he'd been joking with the best friend's comment, but between him and Ronnie, she could be on her way to having a small social circle.

The thought had her slightly giddy. It'd been a while since she had a group of genuine friends. Besides Ralph, her friends in LA were there to leech off her name, fame, and money. Any real friendships she might have had, she'd destroyed with her addiction.

"Well," she said as she scooted her chair closer to his desk. "Hope you don't mind that I jotted down some ideas and plans." She placed the portfolio she'd brought right on top of the scattered file folders littering his desk.

"Ooh, you're prepared. Sweet." He rubbed his hands together. "Lemme see." As he flipped the portfolio open, his eyes widened. "Wow, this is more than jotting notes. Looks like you put quite a bit of work into your design ideas. This is fantastic."

His enthusiasm spread to her. It was exciting. In California, she'd hired expensive contractors, decorators, and designers. The team had carte blanche to create something modern, trendy, and enviable. Multiple design and architectural magazines featured her home for its style, which had been incredible, but aside from writing the checks, she'd done nothing to deserve the accolades.

This home, where she hoped to plant her roots, would be her: her style, choices, and sanctuary. She wanted to not only love the place for its design but be proud of it because it came from her. Or as much of her as she was physically capable of completing. Mickie was game for trying new things but demoing and constructing cabinets and countertops was miles above her skill level.

"I'm hoping to completely remodel the kitchen." She pointed out a few images she'd printed and scribbled all over. "Something like this." Her style, as she'd come to discover, was what she what she'd coined "modern cozy." Sleek and current, but without the cold sterility often associated with contemporary style. "I'm also hoping to put an addition on the back. A huge room which will span the length of the house. I'd like it to be all windows so I can see out to the senic backyard. The plan is to use half as a gym and the other half as an office. Then I'd like to add two rooms on the second floor." She placed the final paper down on the desk, a floorplan she'd created with an app. "Oh, and I want to remodel the master bathroom."

His eyes narrowed in concentration as he perused her hard work. Ralph had helped her purchase the house while she'd been in rehab. He'd visited and Face Timed her during multiple walkthroughs. She'd fallen in love with the place, and her vision for it had formed over the final two months in rehab. The hours she'd spent researching, designing, and preparing for this moment were what kept her going on some of the darker days.

With each passing second, the coil of tension in her gut wound tighter. After what had to be a solid three minutes of fidgeting in her chair, she reached to snatch the papers back just as he said, "You have big plans."

"I do." Was that a bad thing? Despite her research, she wasn't sure if all of her ideas were feasible. Contracting was a field she knew nothing about.

"Are you a designer?" he asked, finally leaning back in his plush leather chair.

With a chuckle, she shook her head. "No. Not at all. I just have a clear picture of what I'm hoping for."

His face gave nothing away and she wanted to scream, "Tell me what you're thinking!"

"Well then," he finally admitted, "you've done your homework. These ideas are terrific. It's been a few years, but I've been in that house several times, and if I recall correctly, this will all be fantastic. Especially the kitchen, which is where I'd recommend starting."

"That's where I'd like to start. Kitchen and master bathroom are the priority. I'm in no rush on the rest of the work." She bit her lower lip to keep from grinning like a loon at the thought of having a space designed just for her.

Jagger laughed. "Go ahead and get excited. You have wonderful ideas. I don't know what it is you do for work, but you may have missed your calling as a designer."

Huh. Every heartbeat thudded in her ears like a bass drum.

A designer?

That was...well, that was an idea she'd tuck away and pull back out when she was alone and had time to mull over her future.

"Uh, I'm between jobs right now. Kinda...searching for what's right for me."

"Well, give it some thought. Now, you did your homework on the plans, but did you budget accordingly? I don't want to burst your bubble, but that's something to chat about right upfront before we get into the weeds and start racking up a large bill. And with all this work, it will be costly." He shrugged. "I don't want to discourage you, but I've made a name for myself by being straight with clients. I'll give you a formal estimate, of course, but I don't want you to be shocked and unprepared."

Her face heated, and she cleared her throat. "Budget is, um, budget isn't a concern. I'm good there."

"All right, then. Great," he said without batting an eye. "How about this. I'll get a rough estimate worked up for you by the weekend. Why don't you come for dinner Saturday night, and we can go over it."

Dinner? Her lungs seized. Was he asking her on a date?

With a laugh, he gathered up her papers. "Keith won't be there, don't worry. Ronnie's making fajitas. JP's choice. They'd love to hang with you, and we can chat about the estimate and your plans."

"I don't know..."

"Come on," he said in a cajoling tone. "You're new in town. You need a gang of crazy friends. Fajitas, guac, margaritas." He waggled his eyebrows as he smiled. "And if you drink too many, all you gotta do is stumble your way across the street. No biggie."

"Turn those dimples off," she said with a snort. "They won't work on me."

"I don't buy that." He grinned wide, flashing the dimples. "I'm fully aware of the power of these babies."

She laughed. This mild, harmless banter was fun. She felt no pressure from the man, just a lighthearted, fun vibe she could easily play off.

"Okay, fine. You wore me down." The man didn't need to know she'd be avoiding the margaritas. Last time she brought up her sobriety with a Benson, shit had hit the fan. That was an experience she wasn't eager to repeat. "What can I bring?"

"Hmm," he scratched his rough chin. "A dessert?"

Lord, she couldn't bake to save her life, but it was high on her list of skills to learn, so she might as well give it a whirl. Worse came to worst, the bakery in town would do in a pinch.

"Perfect." She loved that he didn't try to wave her off but suggested she bring dessert. In her Hollywood life, a host would have laughed at her for even offering. Caterers handled dinners, not neighbors and hosts. Of course, that didn't mean one showed up empty-handed. No, an outrageously expensive host or hostess gift was always required. A fun, home-cooked, relaxed dinner with down-to-earth friends would be a novel experience for her.

One she found herself looking forward to as the week progressed.

As long as Jagger was correct, and Keith would be absent.

Chapter Eight

"He owes me eight hundred right now. Rent's due again in two weeks, son. That'll bring it up to twelve hundred."

Keith balled his fist. "Thanks, I can add." He wasn't sure which pissed him off more, the news itself or being called son by the meth-mouthed slumlord who managed the trailer park where his father lived and Keith had grown up. Either way, the man's voice grated like long, pointed nail on a chalkboard.

He massaged the skin above his eyebrows, which now throbbed with the beginnings of a crippling headache. "Pretty sure this has fuck all to do with me, Harvey. Should probably give the old man a call since it's his problem and all."

"Been tryin'. Earl ain't got a phone no more." The hocking sound of Harvey spitting made Keith cringe as he imagined a wad of brown saliva and dip leaving his mouth.

Keith stopped walking midway down the hall to his kitchen. It was way too early in the morning for this shit. "So knock on his fucking door. Kick it in for all I care. His late rent has nothing to do with me."

"Did that. He ain't got the money. Said you'd be good for it."

Of course that fucking piece of shit did. Earl had done nothing but abuse Keith and the rest of his siblings until they left—no escaped—the trailer park. Mentally, verbally, or physically they'd all been scarred in some way by the real evil that inhabited their father's charred soul. To this day, the old man remained the definition of drunken belligerence, and now he expected Keith to pay his trailer's fucking lot rent?

Hell. No.

"Not gonna happen, Harvey." Old Harvey had been managing the trailer park since Keith was a kid living with his five siblings and two addict parents in a dilapidated double wide. Man, those had been some dark days.

"Someone's gotta pay, or he's out on his junkie ass. You gonna take 'im in instead? Bet he'd snuggle real nice with you at night."

Keith grunted. The ground wasn't cold enough yet for Hell to have frozen over. "Gotta go, Harvey. Good luck."

"Sure, yeah. Just one more thing. Your old man said to tell you your momma would roll over if she knew you were turning away from your blood."

Keith pinched the bridge of his nose. There it was. The kill shot. His Achilles fucking heel. Goddam that old man.

Please, Keith. Please promise me you'll help your father. Just don't let him get hurt.

"Give me a few hours, and I'll bring you a check." Resignation set in. At that moment, he hated himself for his weakness. Almost as much as he hated his father. What would his siblings think if they knew how many times he'd bailed the old man out over the years? They'd be disgusted. But then, they were one of the reasons he did this. To keep their father's poison away from his brothers and sister. They didn't deserve his cruelty or the burden of cleaning his messes.

No one did.

But then again, neither had their mother, but she'd been helpless to tear herself away from the venom of Earl Benson. By the time she'd turned twenty, she'd depended on her husband for everything. Especially feeding her addiction.

"Excellent!" Harvey said, his voice oozing like slime. "I'll be wai—"

Keith ended the call. If Ronnie's bedroom hadn't been on the other side of the wall, he'd have bashed his forehead against it.

Fuck. There went eight hundred dollars he'd set aside for the vintage Harley he had his eye on.

With a growl of frustration, Keith rounded the corner into the kitchen. He bypassed the refrigerator, an open box of donuts on the counter, and the coffee pot. Even the thought of his vital morning caffeine hit had his stomach turning.

Grabbing his sweatshirt off the back of a kitchen chair, he rounded the corner into the family room only to draw up short at the sight of three of his siblings staring at him from the sectional sofa with serious expressions.

No, wait, make that all his siblings. Ronnie's computer sat open on the coffee table with Jimmy and Ian's faces on the split-screen.

"Fuck," he said as he slowly entered the room. "Who died?" Something had to be seriously wrong. They didn't sit around and have family chats with the two members of their family in the military. Ian was a Marine, currently deployed to Afghanistan, and Jimmy lived on the Naval base stationed in Okinawa. It had to be the middle of the fucking night in Japan.

His heart started pounding. "Are one of you sick?" he asked, already mentally planning how to rearrange his schedule and help.

"No," Ronnie said. "None of us are sick, and no one died." She held a full mug of coffee cradled between her palms. "Sorry, we didn't mean to scare you, but we wanted to talk to you about something."

Suddenly feeling the heat of a spotlight on him, he raised an eyebrow. "Okay..."

"Have a seat, man," Jagger said, patting the empty cushion beside him.

"I'm good. Gotta head to work. So do you JP," he said, pinning him with his most fearsome glare. JP had promised to open the shop that morning so Keith could grab an extra hour of sleep, which meant no one was manning the place at the moment. And that meant loss of business. "Just tell me what's up."

Why was it starting to seem like he was the guest of honor at a party he had no desire to attend?

"There weren't any drop-offs overnight, and Benny opened for me," JP said of the young man currently training to be a mechanic. He helped out when his schedule allowed. "We've got time."

"Please, sit," Ronnie said, imploring him with her somber gaze.

"Fine." He dropped into the empty spot next to Jagger, giving him a full view of his brothers on the computer. "How you guys doing?"

"All good," Ian said. He wore his uniform and Kevlar body armor, standard attire on the base in a conflict zone.

"Same," Jimmy quipped. His bedhead stuck out all over, owing to the fact that someone got him out of bed for this conversation.

The room fell silent as his three present siblings cast each other sideways glances.

"Oh, for fuck's sake, someone say something or I'm out."

"I wanted us to talk about this shit with you and Dad," Ronnie blurted. The second the words were out of her mouth, she shot him an apologetic look, and her shoulders slumped.

JP snorted. "Smooth Ron. Surprised you didn't become a psychologist."

A psychologist. What the hell? "What the fuck is this? Some kind of intervention?"

Leaning forward with his hands on his knees, Jagger shook his head. "No, this is us being worried about our brother and wanting to talk about it."

"Uh, that's pretty much the definition of an intervention," JP whisper-yelled to Jagger who sent him a death glare.

"Not helping," Jagger said under his breath.

His gaze shifted from one sibling to another, encountering the same pitying and slightly disapproving expression on each of his siblings' faces.

Christ, he'd failed on all counts. Failed his mother's last request by letting his father come this close to living on the streets. The one stipulation he'd made for himself in all this mess was that his brothers and sister would never find out. Not only would they be horrified to learn the number of times he'd jumped to their father's rescue, but the amount of money he'd wasted on the man would sicken them.

But apparently, he'd fooled no one but himself.

"We know when you leave at night, you're usually going to bail Dad out of some kind of a jam."

"How? Did Dad say something to one of you?" He'd throttle the man if he upset Ronnie.

Ronnie met his gaze then stared down into her mug. "I followed you," she whispered.

"What?" he sprung to his feet. "Why the fuck would you do that, Ron? Jesus!" He stalked across the room, running a hand through his hair as his brain spun. The dives he'd dragged their father out of in neighboring counties weren't exactly the safest. "Do you know what could have happened to you?"

Never one to back down from a fight with one of her brothers, Ronnie shot up as well.

"Me? I was in the safety of my locked car. Do you know what could have happened to you? Why are you doing this? Why are you being so stupid? He doesn't deserve a goddammed thing from you!" Ronnie was screaming now with fists clenched at her sides, face red.

"Shhh." JP tugged on her sleeve. "Sweetie, sit."

Keith panted through the anxiety threatening to choke him. This was exactly what he'd been trying to avoid. The last thing he wanted was Ronnie upset. They deserved to live their lives without the shadow of their father's ugly fuckups looming over them. The walls seemed to close in on him at a rapid clip, threatening to crush him to dust.

"Okay, everyone, calm down," Ian said from the computer. He'd always been the most serious, most reflective, probably smartest of the bunch. "You're both running hot on emotion right now, but your goal is the same. You love each other and want to protect each other. Am I right?"

Fuck, he wasn't in the mood for Ian's rational dissection of their family problems. The man wasn't even on the same side of the planet. What the fuck did he know?

"Look, Dr. Phil," Keith started, but Ronnie's tearful, "Yes," had the rest of his words dying on his tongue. She sat next to JP, who'd tugged her to his side. It wasn't often Ronnie cried, hardly ever, actually. And *never* in front of her brothers. She'd always complained they saw her as a dainty little girl, so she'd tried extra hard to be tough and strong. But the woman had a center as soft and gooey as melted chocolate.

"Fuck," Keith said on a sigh as he dropped back down on the couch.

"Why?" Ronnie sniffed. "Why do you do it? He's been so ugly to you your entire life. To all of us. Why would you want to help him?"

"Seriously," Jagger piped in. He hadn't showered or shaved, and a dark shadow covered his usually smooth jaw. "I was oblivious until Ronnie told me. Has this been going on long?"

Shame washed over Keith as he nodded. "Since Mom's death."

Ronnie gasped.

"What is it exactly that you're doing?" Jimmy asked with a confused voice. Being so far for so long often had him out of the loop with regards to family matters. No one meant to exclude him, but with the time difference and how busy he was, Jimmy often missed out.

Keith had tried for so long to keep it a secret, confessing now felt like he was being carved up with a scalpel. "I mostly drag him home from bars before he can get arrested for anything more than public intoxication." Then he dropped his voice and nearly whispered, "Sometimes bail him out financially."

"Jesus," Jagger ground out. He dropped his face to his hands for a second before spearing Keith with a baffled look. "Why? And why by yourself? There are fucking six of us. You don't need to deal with this shit alone."

Whether it was the ambush or the deep delve into his secret activities making him feel so raw, didn't matter. Keith needed out. He needed air, space, and something to think about besides the man who'd tried so hard to ruin his life and still had a grip on him. The pitying looks on his siblings' faces made him sick. He'd rather they all get pissed off like Ronnie's initial reaction than look at him as though he were pathetic. If he didn't get some air, he was likely to explode, and none deserved it.

"I can't—look, I'll tell you guys everything, but can we do it later? I'm not up for talking about it right now. I need to—I just need to get out of here."

"I hope you know that after today, we aren't going to let you handle it on your own. We're involved now no matter how much you fucking hate it." JP was unusually somber, which told Keith just how serious they were. "So, sure, you can run away for a bit, but you will tell us all of it tonight. And you can't leave until you tell us what that phone call five minutes ago was about."

He flopped back on the couch, staring at the dusty ceiling fan. "Dad's two months delinquent on the trailer's lot rent."

"What? So Harvey called to hit you up for it?" JP asked.

"Yeah. Dad told him I was good for it."

"Fuck that," JP spat out. "You told him no, right?"

He stared at his brother's angry face.

"You were gonna pay?" Ronnie asked. Her voice cracked as though she were heartbroken over the news. "Keith, why? I don't understand. He was an abusive, lazy addict who never even tried to take care of his family. And of all of us, you had it the worst. He was horrible to you."

Throwing his arms up in the air, he shouted, "Because I made a promise to Mom, all right?"

The room fell eerily quiet. The weight of his siblings' stares hurt his heart.

He blew out a breath. Might as well get it the fuck over with. "Right before Mom died, she begged me to promise I'd help the old man. To keep him from getting hurt or dying alone."

"Oh, Keith," Ronnie said. She wrung her hands together in her lap. "We all loved Mom as much as you, but she never should have put that burden on you. She'd just had major brain surgery and wasn't thinking rationally at the end. You should have shared this with us years ago. I'm so sorry you've carried this load all alone."

"Our big brother would never do that," JP said with a lopsided grin. "He'd lie in the street and let a tank run over him to keep the bad shit from reaching us."

Keith's head had been so twisted with guilt, love, responsibility, and that damn promise to his mother for too long. Now that he began to unwind the complicated emotions, it all came spilling out his mouth. "I left," he blurted. "I left you all here to deal with him for four years while I joined the military. Mom died six months after I returned home. I owe it to her, to make up for leaving. And I owe it to you all for the years I wasn't here to shield you from his toxicity."

"Jesus," Jagger said as he rubbed his temples. "You've seriously been carrying this shit for more than fifteen years? Keith, none of us resent you for joining the military. The only reason we were able to afford this house was because of that money. You didn't abandon us. You made a sacrifice for us."

"For real," JP added. "And if you think for one second Mom was upset with your decision, you're crazy. She was proud as fuck of you. For fuck's sake, the military is where you learned to be a damn good mechanic. Keith, it set you up with life skills that ensure you'll never live in a shithole like we did growing up."

"You have got to let this go," Ian said from the computer. "If you really want to help us and protect us, then you need get rid of the unwarranted guilt, Keith."

His shoulders sagged. He'd been carrying this heaviness for so long. How was he supposed to suddenly turn off the instinct to payback four years of absence by making his father his responsibility?

Ronnie stood and walked until she was in front of him. Then she sat on the coffee table and grabbed his hands. "You're the best oldest brother a girl could ever have," she said in a shaky voice, making him grunt out a tiny laugh. "Please don't pay that money," she whispered. "He's a lead weight, and he'll drag you down. Maybe not today, but it will happen."

Keith stared at his baby sister's sorrowful expression. So often, he still thought of her as the six-year-old who annoyed the hell out of the boys by following them everywhere. He remembered defending her from bullies, helping her with homework, and making sure she had enough food to eat when there was none in the house. It was easy to forget she was a grown adult. A strong and independent one.

He squeezed her hands as Jagger piped in. "I'm with Ronnie on this. We need to take a stand as a family. No money and no rescuing from bars. If he's gonna get arrested or beat to shit, let it happen."

From the computer, Jimmy winced but didn't disagree. He was the quietest and most introspective of the siblings. Keith wasn't surprised at all he didn't contribute much to the conversation.

"He doesn't deserve our kindness, but this is more about protecting ourselves from more of his damage. All of us." Jagger narrowed his eyes at Keith.

Still in rare serious mode, JP piped in. "Mom wouldn't have wanted this for you, Keith. You can't possibly believe she would have. I promise you, you aren't betraying her by turning your back on Dad. You need to for your mental health and happiness.

For all of ours. We love you for always wanting to protect us, but Keith, we are all adults just as much as you are. Even me, at times." Leave it to JP to try to lighten the mood.

He nodded. When had all his younger siblings become the reasonable ones who helped him?

"Look, I know your head's probably fried right now, so go to work, and we can talk more later. Just promise us you won't give Harvey a dime. Okay?" Ian said from the computer.

Keith met the gaze of each of his siblings. Not a single doubt shone in their eyes. They were all one hundred percent on board with this plan. "I promise."

"Good." Ronnie stood, kissed the top of his head, then said, "Now get the hell to work. What kind of lazy business owner are you, hanging around at home all morning?"

He laughed out of obligation, but they probably realized it was forced. And the second he left, they'd most likely dissect every word of the conversation. But he needed air, so he stood and headed outside without saying anything else.

The fresh, chilly air helped release some of the heaviness from his chest. A bird squawked somewhere in the distance, and the sun shone at an angle. All in all, it was a beautiful day. His siblings discovered his long-held secret, and the world still turned. The urge to keep the stress of their father from touching them was still there, but once he had a chance to process, hopefully he'd feel lighter.

As he jogged down the walkway toward his car, he inhaled a cleansing breath.

What the…

Did he smell smoke?

He sniffed again. Yes, definitely smoke. A quick glance down the block had him dropping his sweatshirt and sprinting towards Michaela's house. Black smoke poured out of the front window on the right side of her house. With each step, the shrill blare of her smoke alarm grew louder.

Shit!

He picked up his pace, forcing his legs to pump faster than they'd ever moved before. With every pound of his feet on the ground, his mind spun further out of control. Images of Michaela lying passed out on the floor while flames licked at her beautiful skin had him pushing himself until his lungs felt they would burst.

This was what he got for thinking life was getting sweeter.

Keith bounded up the steps leading to Michaela's wraparound porch. He tapped the doorknob, which felt cool as a cucumber, before twisting.

Unlocked.

Thank fuck. He barged into the house and turned toward the kitchen, where it seemed the fire had originated.

"Shit, shit, shit," he heard as he waved his hands in front of his face to clear the air.

The sound of her voice had him sagging in relief.

When he emerged into the kitchen, he stopped dead in his tracks for the second time that morning.

Michaela stood below the smoke detector with a cookie sheet, waving it back and forth like a madwoman. Smoke flowed from the sink where she'd stuck a large frying pan. Flames shot straight up and the black smoke sucked out the open window, hence his race to save her ass.

Which had apparently been totally unnecessary.

He narrowed his eyes. After the morning he'd had, rushing to a fake emergency was the last straw. "What the fuck is wrong with you?" he shouted over the ear-splitting drone of the smoke detector.

Michaela shrieked and stumbled backward, bumping into the kitchen island. "Holy shit, you scared me," she yelled back, pressing a hand to her chest.

He scowled at her as he marched to her sink. "You're not going to get the noise to go away until you put out the fire." He flicked on the faucet and within seconds, had the fire doused.

Michaela resumed her fan imitation. Keith grabbed a cutting board from the counter and began to fan smoke toward the window. A few minutes later, the smoke detector cut off, and blessed silence filled the house, though a singed odor still clung to the air.

"Oh, thank God," she said on an exhale. "Thank you for your help."

"What the fuck happened?" he barked.

She frowned. "Um, Jagger invited me to dinner tomorrow night at your house, and I said I'd bring dessert."

What. The. Fuck.

Jagger invited her? Did he want her? Was he trying to get in her pants? Keith shouldn't give a fuck. If Jagger wanted to waste his energy on a stuck-up woman who nearly burned her house down trying to cook, he was welcomed to it.

The sick twisting in Keith's gut had to do with his anger at wasting more time that morning. Nothing more.

"I'm uh, not the greatest cook, but I'm trying to learn." She spoke fast, wringing her hands together then gave a sheepish shrug. "Anyway, I overflowed the pan, then tried to wipe the side of it with a wad of paper towels, and the whole thing went up in flames. I accidentally dropped the paper towels in the pan, which set everything else in there on fire, so I threw it in the sink." She patted her chest. "Phew, my heart is still racing."

"Christ, woman, do you have rocks in your brain?"

Her eyes widened, and a frown appeared on that kissable mouth. Damn her for looking so cute and vulnerable. She was neither of those things. She was a helpless woman who probably moved there after a divorce and would be looking for sugar daddy number two any time now.

"Put the fucking fire out next time, huh? Actually, put all your money to good use and order takeout, so you don't start a forest fire that takes out the whole neighborhood." He started out of her kitchen, stomping the entire way. "Least you aren't drunk," he muttered under his breath as he made for her front door.

Really, he hadn't meant for her to hear that last part. Actually, he hadn't meant to say it out loud. He realized how cruel and unnecessary it was the moment the words left his lips, but he'd hit his limit. Between sleepless nights imagining her naked and screaming his name, his father's fuck ups, and the mess with his siblings, this was just the wrong time for a fake emergency.

Hopefully, she hadn't heard, he could slip out, and finally get to work.

The ear-shattering slam of her cookie sheet against the counter had him jumping and whirling around.

She heard.

Fuck.

"How dare you!" She seethed, fists clenched, and eyes spitting pure hatred. "Since I've arrived in town, you've been nothing but a judgmental asshole. You know what, *Keith*?" She said as though his name were a curse. "You've taken issue with everything I've done and everything I've said, and I'm fucking sick of it."

Holy shit, Miss Prim and Proper was losing her shit on him.

And it was hot as fuck. Even smelling like a campfire, with mussed hair, soot on her cheek, and without a stitch of makeup, she was the most stunning woman he'd ever seen.

"Yes, *Keith*, I have money. But you know what? I've worked damn hard for every single penny I have, and I won't apologize for it. Especially not to a judgmental prick like you. And, yes, I came here after going to rehab because I have issues with alcohol. But I haven't had a drink in more than half a year." She advanced on him like a striking, pissed off runway model. When she reached him, she jammed her finger in his chest. "I get it, Keith. You don't like me. You can stop beating that dead horse. I. Get. It. But if you're so perfect that you can pass judgment on everyone else, then fuck you! You hear me, Keith? Fuck you!"

As she panted, her eyes flew wide, and her gaze landed on her finger, digging into his chest. With a harsh inhale, she jumped back, removing her hand as though he'd burned her. Her fist curled and dropped to her side while her mouth opened and closed repeatedly.

It was too damn late. He'd grown hard as hell from one angry poke of a single finger.

His lips turned up. He also discovered the woman he'd assumed was a cold fish had hot blood running beneath the surface.

And what the hell was he supposed to do with that?

Chapter Nine

Well, that little outburst was the opposite of everything she'd been trying to achieve in her new life. It was also the antithesis of how she'd told herself to act around Keith. If he'd hated her before, there wasn't a word to describe how he'd feel about her now that she'd screamed and cursed at him. The hissy fit was way too reminiscent of how Scarlett would have behaved. Michaela was supposed to be able to control herself and her temper. At least that's what she'd been working on.

But, man, he'd hit a nerve. She'd woken at five, unable to fall back asleep, so she'd decided to tackle the dessert, an apple pie, for tomorrow night. Fully expecting to screw it up, she'd purchased enough ingredients to make multiple iterations. After hours of chopping, sauteing, and attempting to make freaking crust, she'd nearly burned the house down.

Keith couldn't have picked a worse time to take a little dig at her independence and hard-won sobriety. The man was a master at knowing how to cut her down. Still, she hadn't meant to go all psycho on him.

"I'm sor—"

Wait, why was he smiling?

"It's about damn time," he said.

"Huh?"

Eloquent, Mickie.

Her forehead scrunched. Seriously? The first smile she saw out of the man, and it came after she laid into him? Maybe he was a little tweaked in the head.

"Bet that felt good, huh?" He folded his very thick arms across an equally thick chest, then leaned against her wall. "Ripping me a new one like that?"

"Um, well…" Yes, yes it had. "If I'm being honest…"

He laughed, and she nearly peed herself. Damn, that was a deep, gravelly, sexy sound. The kind that went straight to a woman's panties.

"Don't go back to being all stiff again." The word stiff came out a little strangled as though it caught in his throat.

Her sex-deprived mind went to one thing and one thing only. And, of course, her gaze followed. Holy shit. Was he hard? Did he have some sort of humiliation kink where he got off on being insulted by women?

Wait, he'd called *her* stiff, not himself.

Get your mind out of the gutter, Mickie.

"I'm not stiff," she said, as her shoulders straightened in opposition to her words.

"You are stiff."

God, they needed to stop saying the word stiff. She risked another glance at his crotch before looking back at his face.

"I'm pretty sure that rant was the first time you let your guard down around me and were your true self."

She frowned. "A raging bitch is my true self? Gee, thanks. You sure know how to charm a girl." Oh God, was she flirting with him now? Why did she lose her brain around him?

He laughed again. "Not what I meant. It's not a bad thing—you yelling at me. I was an asshole, and I deserved it. You stood up for yourself instead of pretending everything was fine."

That had her meeting his gaze. "I don't do that." But she did. She so did. In trying to start over again she'd felt the need to continually act okay with everything in her life and always be on an even keel no matter how tumultuous she felt inside.

"I think you do."

"I've been through a lot in the last year." Understatement of the century. She shifted her gaze to the disaster of apple peels, cores, and sugar on her kitchen island. "Moving here…well, I left a lot of toxicity behind. Not a relationship, but a life I was drowning in. Right now, I feel a little like a square peg trying to fit into a round hole. I'm trying to find where I fit in the world. So yes, maybe I pretend everything is fine because I'm trying to make it all be fine."

He pushed off the wall and strode toward her. Helpless to untether herself from his molten gaze, she did nothing but stare with arms limp at her sides.

"We're pretty simple," he said when he was close enough to touch.

And smell. Damn, what was that intoxicating scent? Whatever it was, it trumped the smoke still lingering in the air. She wanted to bathe in it, then maybe spend the rest of the day hiding in her room.

With her vibrator.

He cleared his throat, making her blink.

Busted.

"Uh, yes, simple. I'm listening."

With a chuckle, he nodded. "What I mean is, you don't need to put on any fancy airs with us. If you're a fucking mess right now because you're figuring your shit out, then just be a mess. Fuck up, get mad, cry, bring a shitty dessert to dinner."

Her face heated, and she huffed out a small laugh. "Well, that last one is easy."

He reached out and swiped a finger across her cheek. Soot? Maybe flour?

"I like this chaotic version of you much better than the polished one."

Flaying herself open and leaving her soul vulnerable to him went against everything she'd had drilled into her head for the past decade. Spinning the public's perception to meet her needs became second nature. More than that, it became a vital means of survival as she'd careened farther and farther down a dark path of self-destruction. No one knew the real her, and that'd been both by choice and necessity. Only she'd done such a tremendous job of burying herself, uncovering her real personality was proving harder than she'd thought.

Was that is? Was fear keeping her from being herself?

Yes, partly.

Fear of rejection.

Fear of not fitting in.

Fear of failure.

Fear of never overcoming the label of unstable Hollywood actress and junkie.

So many fears.

If Keith knew who the mess he claimed to like really was, would he take back his words? Would he view her as the rest of the world? A bitch, a slut, a high-maintenance addict?

Her eyes closed.

That isn't you.

Okay, she'd play things his way for a while. Lower her guard. Relax. Be herself. Or try to, anyway.

And if it all blew up in her face, she knew exactly how to handle it. Fall back on years of training and hide her true feelings. Act her ass off.

"Really?" she whispered as her face heated.

"Really," he said. "So, don't be afraid to let us see you, okay?"

She watched his face as he spoke and nothing about him had her thinking he was putting her on or making a joke. No, he meant it. He'd rather see her fall apart than pretend she was perfect. Butterflies fluttered low in her stomach. What a nice feeling. To know someone just wanted to see…her. In all her messy glory.

"Thank you," she whispered. Hopefully the simple phrase conveyed the warmth and acceptance his words filled her with.

He winked. "Now, I'm already hours late for work. What do you say I have JP take over my appointments, and I show you how to make a mean apple pie? Mickie?" He used her nickname for the first time. It sounded nice coming from his gruff voice.

"Uh, sorry, zoned out for a second." She almost told him not to skip work on her behalf, but she bit off the words. For some reason, she had a feeling not many people got to see this softer, more relaxed side of Keith, and curiosity won out over politeness. The idea of being folded into this big crazy family, even as a friendly neighbor, was too tempting to resist. "Um, there's already been one fire in this kitchen today. Maybe we should leave it at that."

He snorted. "Tease all you want, but no matter what I make, it can't be worse than this." He lifted the now-cool pan from the sink. Inside were the remnants of charred apples, but her attention focused on where his bicep flexed, straining the hem of his sleeve. "Besides, I have mad kitchen skills."

"Uh…" She fanned her face. Geez, the kitchen was still too warm from the fire. "You have a point. So, what do we do first, chef?"

"That would be the crust." He shoved aside the floury cookbook and went to work.

Mickie's could barely keep her jaw from hitting the floor as she watched him deftly mixing ingredients. "Where did you learn how to do this?"

He smiled as he worked the dough with his fingers. "My mom. She was a fantastic cook. And as the oldest, I was always asked to help her out in the kitchen. Picked up a few skills."

"Well, I've gotta say, this is a good trick to have up your sleeve when trying to impress a girl."

He arched an eyebrow. "Oh yeah? This impressing you?"

Was it her imagination or had his voice deepened to a husky rasp?

"Well, yeah," she said with a laugh, as she tried to get sex off her mind and keep this interaction friendly. "It's super impressive. So do you still cook with your mom?"

His face hardened. "Uh, no. She died when I was twenty-two. Ruptured brain aneurysm."

Her heart sank for all of the Bensons. "Oh, I'm so sorry." Clearing her throat, she said. "Seventeen for me. Cancer."

His agile fingers stopped working the dough. Their gazes collided and something passed between them. What a sad thing to have in common, but it seemed to form a small bond of understanding. Tragedy had a way of bringing survivors together.

"I'm sorry. It's about the shittiest thing ever, isn't it?" He kept his gaze on her and while her first instinct was to play off her grief, she did as he asked and stayed true to herself.

"Yes. I often wonder if maybe I wouldn't have made so many bad choices had she lived." Mickie cringed. "Wow, sorry. That was way too much info for a baking lesson."

Thankfully, he seemed to understand how difficult it was for her to discuss personal issues, so he saved her by asking her to hand him the pie plate.

He worked in silence, rolling out the dough, then expertly pressing it into the pie plate. Surprisingly enough, she found an odd comfort in the quiet. Before their little clearing of the air, she'd have been analyzing every second ticking by wondering what negative thoughts he was having about her. Then to fill the discomfort of the lack of words, she'd have blathered on until she drove him bonkers. Now, she felt confident he wasn't cursing her out in his brooding brain, so she was able to enjoy watching the man's strong hands mold the crust into her brand-new pie pan.

Once he the crust looking as he wanted, he dumped in the pie weights she almost didn't buy. "So, did you actually use a recipe?" he asked after sliding the crust into her preheated oven to blind bake—whatever the heck that meant.

"Um, kind of?" she said, cheeks heating. "I followed one I found online to make the crust, which I threw out because it fell apart. The apples I figured would be simple enough without a recipe. Chop them up, add sugar, cook them in a pan. Right?"

His lips twitched. The man sucked at hiding his amusement over her failed kitchen experiment.

"Just say it. What?" She folded her arms across her flour-dusted T-shirt. The move plumped her breasts, showing the tiniest hint of cleavage at the V of the neck. Was she mistaken or did his gaze shift to that peek of bare skin before coming back to her face?

And if so, why did the thought of him looking at her in a sexual way have her knees weakening? This man was not for her in any way.

"You don't cook the apples first. They just go in the oven raw."

Her mouth fell open. "Shut up. You're messing with me."

He was laughing now. Full-blown belly laughs that had her scowling. "Dead serious," he managed between guffaws.

"Hey!" She used her fingertips to gather up some flour from the counter then flicked it his way. "It's not nice to make fun of people—oh!" She slapped a hand over her mouth two seconds too late to stop the giggle from bubbling out.

The flour hit its mark. As in bullseye, all over Keith's face.

He coughed once, sending a cloud of white wafting her way.

She giggled again behind her hand, even as her insides tremored in uncertainty over how he'd react.

After three seconds of shock on his part and trepidation on hers, he tilted his head. "So that's how you're gonna play this?" he asked as he took a step forward. Then another.

Her heart rate kicked up. He had the look of a hunter and she had the urge to spread her arms and let him catch her.

"Uh, well, I um…"

His hand went to the counter, gathering up way more flour than she had, and suddenly she felt like a little rabbit in the sights of a hungry panther.

"Now wait a minute," she said as she lifted her hands and took a step back. "We don't need to make this ugly. Let's just call a truce."

"A truce?" he said, still advancing on her with a fist full of flour.

"Yes, a truce. See, I spent a lot of time on my hair this morning."

Lies of course, which he knew by his snort. So much for men being oblivious. Guess even the manliest of them knew a sloppy top knot meant they spent one point five seconds grooming.

"Oh yea, I can see that." He stopped walking about two feet from her. "Well, I'd hate to mess up your hard work."

Huh, maybe she had fooled him. With a sigh of relief, she dropped her arms, and his grin instantly grew evil. He tossed the flour up at her from his side, coating her in a shower of chalky power.

"You bastard," she said, though the words barely made it out of her mouth because she was coughing and laughing so hard, tears streamed down her cheeks. "You fight dirty!" She lunged for the counter at the same time he did.

They spent the next few minutes laughing and making a gigantic mess of themselves and her kitchen. It'd take hours to clean, but it was the most fun she'd had in ages. Lighthearted, without thought of how she'd appear to the outside world. She didn't have to take pictures and post them on Instagram for the public to praise or judge. For the first time in longer than she could remember, she enjoyed a moment for its simplicity and frivolity.

As she reached for the container of flour, a strong, firm hand wrapped around her wrist.

"Don't even think about it," Keith half-growled, half-choked, making her giggle all over again.

White powder coated his lips, cheeks, even eyelashes. "I think you're ready for the oven."

"Funny." He snorted, then coughed out another puff of white. "Shit, that can't be good for the lungs."

Michaela laughed so hard her stomach ached.

Still latched onto her wrist, Keith tugged her close. "You're playing with fire, missy."

Her breath caught. His dusty face was mere inches from hers. All it'd take was a rise to her tiptoes and their lips would be aligned.

He stilled. The rise and falls of their chests was the only movement in the room. That and her heart thudding against her ribs, beating faster with every breath.

His eyes darkened, even deeper than their normal midnight blue. Lust. It had to be lust swirling in those heady depths. She had this insane urge to push her hips forward and find out if their proximity affected his body as much as hers.

The moment stretched on with the two of them staring and standing close but not moving.

Then slowly, ever so goddammed slowly, his mouth began a descent toward hers. She shifted, starting to rise to the balls of her feet to meet him halfway.

He was going to kiss her. He was going to kiss her, and she was going to let him. Because she'd been through so much in the past six months, and human touch had been nearly non-existent. Sexual touch completely absent. And while she'd made horrible choices in the past with regards to men and sexual activity, one thing remained true.

She liked sex. Freaking loved it. And she missed it. So as bad an idea as this was, she'd take it and enjoy every second. Damn the inevitable regrets.

Just as he was about to kiss her, one of their phones chimed with an alert. That was all it took to break the spell. One second of noise.

"So, uh..." Keith cleared his throat as he released her wrist. Taking a step back, he ran the hand through his short hair.

Stupidly, she almost asked if she could be the one to finger the strands.

"Jagger invited you to the house for dinner, huh?" He turned, grabbed a green apple from the bag and the peeler. The man either didn't care or forgot he was wearing a coat of flour. Within seconds, he had the apple peeled and set out on the cutting board.

Fine, it they were going to play it that way, she too could pretend they hadn't had a moment.

Or an almost moment.

Or a...whatever.

She smiled. "He did, yes."

"Hmm."

Slice, slice, slice.

Her brand-new knives slid through the apple with ease. She could have watched his long, calloused fingers work all day, especially if they were working on her body.

Shit! She had to veer her mind down a different track. For example, what he meant with the hummed response. "Is that a problem?"

Slice.

The knife froze on the downstroke, and he turned her way.

A shiver ran up her spine. God, those eyes. Did the man have any idea how sexy it was when he stared at her with that molten intensity? She wanted to lay herself out on the kitchen island and beg him to ravage her.

"A problem?" He grunted. "Course not. Just didn't realize you guys had something going on. Surprised me is all." With a shrug, he resumed chopping.

Something going on? If the cell phone interruption had tamped down her desire, this proclamation doused the lingering want with a bucket of icy water. Did he think she wanted his brother?

With his brow knitted, he grabbed a second apple using more force than the first time. At this rate, he could just peel it, pulverize it with his mitts, then toss it in the bowl without ever needing the knife.

He did think it. The goddammed jerk thought she was starting something up with his brother while nearly kissing him. So much for their budding friendship.

"He didn't tell you?" she said, adopting an innocent tone. "Huh, I figured he'd mentioned it. We are definitely starting something. I'll be keeping him *really* busy over the next few months."

With each word, his jaw tensed further. Michaela couldn't keep the smug grin off her face to save her life.

"I've heard he's really good with his…tools. The best, even. I knew I had to have him as soon as I heard a woman in town talking about the amazing things he did in her bedroom. We'll be starting right here in this kitchen."

The chopping slowed until as he once again turned his head toward her, this time with narrowed eyes and the ever-present scowl she was for some crazy reason beginning to find charming.

She bit her lower lip but couldn't keep the corners of her mouth from quirking upward.

Rolling his eyes, he said, "You're a smartass, you know that?"

She tilted her head and raised an eyebrow.

With a grunt, he shrugged. "And I'm an asshole. Would it surprise you to know you aren't the first to mention it?"

"Well…"

"That was rhetorical." He set down the knife and closed the gap between them. "Okay, I'm officially done." He held out his hand. "No more judgment without facts. Okay?"

Michaela looked him straight in the eye. "I wouldn't—"

"I know." He thrust his hand closer. "Truce?"

She'd been about to say she would never have allowed the moment between them to progress to a near kiss if she'd been interested in her brother. Thankfully, he'd stopped her because the words would have made her wince. She'd done that and worse in the past when drunk and high on illicit substances, fame, and fortune.

"Truce." She slipped her hand in his. This time, she expected the jolt of electricity that shot up her arm, but preparation did nothing to diminish the strength of the shock. The man was like a live wire, and she a can of gasoline. Getting too close was not wise.

Especially while she still had so much work to do on herself. Her therapist had told her countless times over the past six months that she wouldn't make a lick of progress if she couldn't forgive herself for past transgressions. She'd learned a million lessons from her catastrophic mistakes, which was great and would keep her from repeating them but forgiving herself had proven to be a substantial challenge. Her behavior had not only been an embarrassment to herself and others, but she knew for a fact she'd hurt people.

Now, sober and living with her feet planted on the ground, shame and guilt were a daily occurrence. She'd yet to master leaving those negative emotions in the past where they belonged. Apologies had been made where they could be, and true repentance occurred.

Too bad forgiving others was simpler than forgiving oneself.

Chapter Ten

"Oh, my God, stop!" Mickie said as she wiped her eyes. "You guys are killing me."

JP shrugged. "It wasn't my fault she decided to lose her virginity outside in December, in Vermont. If you ask me, I taught them a good lesson about preventing hypothermia."

Ronnie threw a tortilla chip across the table at her smirking brother. "What you did was make my first time a one and done because Donavan Carmichael wouldn't come near me after that."

JP snorted. "Like that asshat was gonna be the love of your life?"

"No." Ronnie huffed, folding her arms across her chest. "But a girl likes to think she's good enough for a boy to hang around for a while. Especially when she's sixteen. Right, Mickie? You know what I'm talking about. You're a woman."

"I was a bit of a late bloomer. Didn't lose my virginity until my twenty-second birthday." But she'd sure as hell made up for it after that. The night she cashed in her V-card also happened to be the night she received her first seven-digit check from a production company. And the first time she'd snorted coke. Not exactly one for the memory books. "But I can honestly say that

I'd have been scarred for life if someone dumped a bucket of snow on me mid-deed."

"Thank you," Ronnie said, sticking her tongue out at her brother.

With a laugh Mickie patted her new friend's hand.

"Yeah, but…" JP leaned across the oval table and jabbed his fork for emphasis. "Wouldn't you have also learned a valuable lesson about when and where to go bare?" He waggled his eyebrows as he sat back in his seat. "See what I did there?"

With a snort, Ronnie shook her head. "What? Made a rhyme? Oh, congrats, you've finally mastered kindergarten."

Coughing to cover her laugh, Michaela could only stare wide-eyed when JP gave her the double finger. Sibling banter was a world she knew nothing about. The closest she had to a relationship like the one these four seemed to share was with Ralph, though they didn't have the benefit of the blood bond.

"You'll get used to the children's behavior," Jagger broke in. "I thought about putting them at a kiddie table, but I figured with you living so close, you'd see their true colors eventually. No point in sugar-coating shit."

"Oh, yeah," Ronnie broke in before taking a sip of her locally brewed IPA. "Because you're the picture of maturity. One time, when he and Keith shared a room, Jagger filled the bottle of lotion Keith used for, uh, personal purposes with icy-hot." She shot her brother a *so there* look and lifted her beer in a toast.

"Holy fucking shit, I forgot about that." JP cracked up, slapping his palm on the table. "Ian called nine-one-one because Keith was writing on the floor, screaming. Damn, that was some funny shit. Remember how he kept crying in the ER because he thought they were going to have to amputate his little wee-wee?"

Mickie's mouth dropped open. This bunch was nuts. "That didn't really happen."

Shrugging, Jagger said, "What can I say? I was fourteen, and he'd been a dick to me. Figured if he was gonna *be* a dick, I'd go after his dick."

"You guys are insane."

"Be glad you're an only child, Mickie. Seriously," Ronnie said. "I'd have paid money to get rid of these guys when I was younger." The words were spoken with humor and so much affection, it was obvious that Ronnie wouldn't trade her brothers for the world. Even if they still made her bonkers.

"Speaking of," JP broke in. "Where the fuck is Keith? Why's he missing this walk down memory lane?"

"Think he's working on his bike," Jagger said. "Told me he wouldn't be back until late."

"Maybe he's finally gonna go out and get laid." Ronnie stabbed the last bite of her pie. "Lord knows he needs it."

For some absolutely ridiculous reason, Mickie's face heated. Why? Who knew? It wasn't like anything, *anything* had happened yesterday between them beyond the agreement not to hate each other. So why the hell was she feeling all under the microscope?

"You guys think he's still mad at us for ambushing him yesterday?" JP asked. As he tipped his chair back on its hind legs, he unbuttoned the top of his jeans.

"Uh, we have company, you pig. Maybe you could keep your pants buttoned for a little longer?" Jagger said, rolling his eyes.

"What?" JP looked at her. "I'm fucking stuffed. My pants are pushing on my stomach. It's not like I'm getting naked. That won't happen until later." He winked. "Mickie doesn't mind. You don't mind, do you, Mickie?"

With a laugh, she raised her hands. "Knock yourself out. If I wasn't a guest, I'd probably do the same. This food was incredible."

Everyone laughed and resumed ribbing each other. The topic of Keith fell by the wayside though Mickie couldn't keep from thinking of him every few minutes. Was her presence the reason for his absence? Or was she selfish in thinking he gave enough of a shit about her to alter his own plans? Though, admittedly after the time the spent baking, she'd been hoping he'd be there for dinner. And what had gone down with his siblings that might have angered him enough to avoid a family dinner?

None of it was any of her business, but she couldn't keep her curiosity at bay.

For the next forty-five minutes, they talked, laughed, and sipped their drinks. None of them had so much as blinked when she'd declined the margaritas and mentioned her recovery. By the time they all rose to carry their plates into the kitchen—something Mickie insisted on doing despite all their protests—she felt they'd crossed the line from causal neighbors to friends.

But what about with Keith? She had to admit the desire to spend time with him again was front and center in her mind. They'd had fun yesterday just as she'd had tonight, though with an undercurrent of something a little more intimate.

It made her giddy.

And a little bit braver than usual.

"You know," she said as Ronnie pressed the top onto a Tupperware she'd filled for her brother. "I'm about to run to the grocery store. Want me to drop that off at the garage for Keith?"

"Oh, God, no, that's totally not necessary." Ronnie shook her head as she opened the fridge. "Keith will be fine to wait until he gets home."

"Actually…" Jagger swiped the container from his sister. "That's a great idea. Pretty sure he skipped lunch today, too, so he's probably starved. He gets like that when he's working on his bike."

"His bike?"

"Yeah, he's building a motorcycle from scratch. A passion project."

Man, it'd been a while since she'd been on a motorcycle, but she'd loved every second of it. A while back, she'd had a brief fling with a popular rocker. The relationship had crashed and burned in a public and unflattering way, but it'd been fun while it lasted. And he'd had a bike they took for drives up the Pacific coast on more than one occasion. Incredible experience.

Maybe Keith would take her on a ride sometime when he'd finished the work. She could nestle in behind him with her legs hugged against his muscular thighs.

Wow.

Mickie tugged at the collar of her shirt. Had Ronnie left the oven on or something? The kitchen felt super warm.

"Well, if you don't mind the trip, then have at it. You're a nicer person than I am," Ronnie said with a chuckle.

"Most people are." Jagger ruffled his sister's hair as if she were six instead of twenty-six. She shrieked and swatted him away.

"See what I have to put up with living here?" Ronnie said as she swatted her brother's hand away. "You looking for a roommate, Mickie?"

"Ha, my place is about to be a construction zone, so you may want to think twice about moving in. But whenever you need a break from all the testosterone, just pop over. You can crash anytime."

"Sweet."

"Thanks for this, guys," Mickie said as she accepted a fork to go along with the container for Keith. "I had a blast. Didn't realize how much I needed a night to chill and laugh."

Ronnie threw an arm around Mickie's shoulders. "Kinda thinking we're gonna be besties."

She smiled. "Me too." Damn, that felt nice. "Tell JP I said bye."

After accepting a hug from both Ronnie and Jagger, she made her way back across the street.

Time to take dinner to Keith. Because she was a kind and friendly neighbor and the poor guy had missed the meal.

It had nothing to do with the way he smelled.

Or his voice.

Or those muscles.

Or tattoos…

She groaned. "I'm an idiot."

HE COULD HAVE gone to dinner. Maybe should have gone to dinner. It was just a meal, after all, with his siblings and the woman who lived across the street. What was the big damn deal?

Good question.

Instead of joining the rest of the crew, he'd gone to his deserted garage and worked on the bike he'd been slowly building over the past few months. His first, and something he'd always dreamed of doing when he was a child. Actually, when he was a kid, he'd wanted to rebuild a car with his old man. But of course they didn't have the money for that kind of thing. Their neighbor had a rusted out old mustang behind his trailer. The outside had gone to shit, but the guts had been salvageable. His neighbor was a grizzly old war vet who used a wheelchair and swore like he knew no other words. He'd also grumbled about having no use for the beater. He'd offered it to a pre-teen Keith for a summer of odd jobs, which Keith had sweated out without complaint.

Now, looking back on it with the eyes of an adult, he realized Mr. Brigg's intentions were more about giving teenaged Keith a way out of his home for the summer rather than needing his trailer washed, painted, and repaired. But back then, Keith had a laser focus on the car. And at the end of the summer, when he'd presented the title to his old man and asked him to help his son rebuild it, his father had surprisingly said yes.

Then, not twelve hours later, he'd had a buddy tow it to the salvage yard. An hour after that, the seventy bucks he'd betrayed his son for was sloshing around in his gut.

Christ, why had that memory risen to the surface? He rubbed the back of his hand across an itch on his cheek. For the past few days, his head had been a jumbled mess of guilt, resolve, and desire.

Guilt because he'd done as his siblings advised and hadn't paid their father's debt, going against the promise he'd made to his mother. Neglecting their father also went against the vow he'd made himself when he left the military. For the past sixteen years, Keith had been working to make up for leaving them without their oldest brother to take the brunt of their father's abuse while he joined the service.

Resolve because they were right. Bailing the fucker out time after time wasn't helping anyone and wouldn't have been what their mother wanted.

And desire. The easiest to explain; all it took was one look at Mickie to get him hard, yet it was the most complicated of what he'd been feeling.

Right at that moment, as he cranked the wrench with more force than necessary, she sat at his dining table with his siblings.

Were they laughing?

Were Jagger and JP flirting with her?

Was she relaxed and not putting on airs the way they'd discussed? Was she the amazing woman he'd spent a few hours baking with? Were his brothers reaping the benefit of her quick wit and the fun personality he'd been privileged to yesterday? And if so, why the hell did it bother him so much?

"Fuck," he growled, tossing the wrench on the ground.

He should have gone to fucking dinner. The mental circus was proving to be more stressful than suffering through the actual meal would have been. He peeked at his watch. Seven thirty. They'd probably moved onto dessert by now. The dessert he'd made with Mickie in the hours where they'd put aside their troubles and he'd almost kissed her. Damn, how he'd wanted to feel her lips against his. Which would have been a terrible idea. But maybe then he'd at least have been at dinner instead of obsessing over the idea of her having fun with his brothers.

If he left now, he could make it home in time to hang out for a bit and prove he wasn't the antisocial asshole Mickie thought he was.

Just as he was about to give up and head to his office to grab his shit, there was a light knocking on the open garage bay door. He swiveled to find Mickie standing in the open bay. Wearing skin-tight jeans and a fitted sweater with her hair in its customary sleek style, she looked elegant, classy, and completely fuckable. Not much revved him more than the idea of messing up a put-together woman. Something about seeing rumpled clothes, swollen lips, mussed hair, and maybe a mark or two and knowing he'd been the cause of all that mess? Especially in someone who *always* appeared perfectly styled? Not every man could make a woman like that lose control.

Yeah, sexy as fuck.

"Uh, hey," she said as she pushed her glasses up her nose.

The move had him shifting to adjust for the sudden tight fit of his jeans. In his mind, all her clothes vanished, and she stood there in nothing but those professional glasses. Okay, maybe some skimpy panties, too. Damn, they'd be fun to tear off in a fit of unrestrained lust.

Fuck. Time to shift gears before he showed his hand. Or his cock.

"Hey." He took a step to the right, positioning himself behind the bike to keep from being outed as a perv. "You can come on in. Dinner go well?"

A smile transformed her face from nervous to plain happy. "Yes." She placed a hand against her shirt over her belly. "I haven't laughed that that much in years. My stomach still aches. You have a wonderful family."

He snorted.

Mickie tilted her head as she watched him, and he had the distinct impression she was trying to peel him like an onion, to see his layers and what lay beneath each one. Too bad he wasn't that damn deep.

"You don't agree?"

"I have great *siblings*," he said. "When they aren't trying to annoy the fuck outta me." The rest of his family, not so much.

With a nod, she continued walking but didn't question his stress of the word siblings. "Well, you are lucky to have them. A built-in support system. At least you were never lonely as a kid."

As she trailed off, he watched a host of emotions play across her face before she had a chance to school them. It seemed as though growing up as an only child had been lonely for her. Probably even worse once her mother passed.

Mickie cleared her throat. "Anyway..." She waved her free hand in front of her face. "I brought you some dinner. Jagger said you probably haven't eaten since breakfast."

Accurate, but Jagger's name on her lips had something dark and ugly twisting in his gut.

"I had some errands to run, so I offered to swing by and drop it off."

Hmm. Interesting. Never once had one of his siblings gone out of their way to bring him food if he missed dinner and no way were they planning to start tonight. And errands at seven thirty on a Saturday night?

Bullshit.

She'd straight-up offered to drive to the garage and bring him dinner.

The coil in his gut unraveled, and warmth spread through his veins. "Shit, thanks. Um..." He glanced around, but there wasn't any place suitable or clean enough to sit. "Come on into my office. Let me just wash up. I'm starved."

"I can't, um..." She thumbed over her shoulder as she looked toward the dimly lit parking lot behind her as though longing to escape. Then she sighed. "Okay, sure. Lead the way."

He did, and he swore he felt her eyes on his ass the entire trip. Maybe it was just wishful thinking or many months without sex making his mind run wild.

And wild was the perfect way to describe his fantasies about Mickie. He grunted. Even though they'd formed a tentative friendship, nothing about Mickie conveyed a wild side. Sure, they claimed the ones you'd never expect were the craziest in bed, but who was he kidding? She was still wealthy, reserved, and slightly stiff. Swinging from the rafters wasn't in her makeup.

"Did you say something?" she asked from a few steps behind.

"Nope. Here we go. Grab a seat." Not that she had many choices. She could take the beat-up leather chair behind his desk or the torn fabric one in front of it. "Be right back."

"Thanks." As she moved around him through the small doorway, her ass brushed his hand where he held the door open.

Keith bit his lip to keep from groaning out loud. The woman had a stellar ass. Plump, round, perfect for filling his hands. Not like the skinny Hollywood idols so many women modeled themselves after these days. No, Mickie had the body of a sexy, tempting, exquisite woman.

Christ, he had a one-track mind.

Internally flipping himself off, he popped in the small bathroom, washed as much of the grease off his hands as humanly possible, then darted back to his office. Mickie sat in front of his desk, gazing around the office at the pictures Ronnie had hung when he bought the place. He cleared his throat as he entered.

She jumped as though caught in the act, but then smiled as he sat. "You look so young there," she said, pointing to a small frame on his desk. His favorite photo, taken about sixteen years ago when he'd purchased the house he lived in now and gave his siblings a place to live far better and safer than where they grew up. It'd been a burned wreck they acquired for a steal at an auction after a fire destroyed the place, but it was theirs. With Jagger at the helm, they'd worked together to make themselves a home. In the photo they stood in front of the house, arms around each other as he held the key to their sanctuary.

"Yeah, wasn't even twenty-five there." He lifted the lid on the Tupperware and immediately, the heavenly scent of Ronnie's fajitas had his mouth watering. After assembling one on a tortilla, he shoved a huge bite in his mouth.

"And how old are you now?" she asked, raising an eyebrow above the frame of her glasses."

"Thirty-eight," he said, mouth full. Damn, it tasted good.

Mickie didn't seem revolted by the fact he'd spoken around his bite of food. In fact, she smirked. "Wow. Old man."

He snorted. "And what are you, twenty-five?"

With a laugh, she shook her head. "Don't you know it's not polite to ask a lady her age?"

"Yep," he said, smiling. "But I've seen you covered in flour, so I think we're past the lady stage."

"I suppose you have a point. I'm twenty-nine. I'll be thirty in four months."

"Well, say goodbye to feeling good. I swear I hit thirty, and my body started to feel like I'm ninety." He shoveled another bite into his mouth.

Mickie gave him a shy smile. "Actually, these days I'm feeling better than I have in years." She shrugged and stared down at her hands. "Guess that's what happens when you finally start taking care of yourself, huh?" The laugh she let out was thick with discomfort, as though she hadn't meant to be so frank with her admission.

He could have taken the opportunity to make a joke and re-lighten the mood, but for some insane reason, the need to validate her struggles hit him hard. Maybe because he'd made light of it the other day.

Whatever her reasoning for changing her life, it was significant. "Yes. It is. And I'm sure it wasn't easy."

She let out a noise of agreement, then a heavy silence settled in the room. "Well…" She finally cleared her throat. "As I said, I have some errands to run, so I should probably head out before the store closes." She stood, so he started to do the same until she waved it off. "Please, sit. Eat. I'm parked right out front."

"You sure you don't want me to walk you out?"

"Absolutely."

He sensed it was important for her to leave on her own to demonstrate her independence, so he sat back down. "Thanks for bringing this," he said, lifting a stuffed tortilla.

"Of course. Can't have you wasting away, now, can we?" Her smile was back, but it didn't quite reach her eyes. Whatever her reason for making drastic life changes, they were more than skin deep. Had she been married? Destroyed a relationship because of her substance abuse? Had her family disowned her? Had she hurt someone? Injured them? So many possibilities, each more painful than the last. But with each glimpse he got of Mickie's psyche, one thing became clearer and clearer.

She wanted this clean, better life for herself. And she was trying hard to learn how to live in it.

Keith respected the hell out of her for that, but he also lived in the real world and knew these things rarely lasted.

"No, we can't," he said.

His natural inclination after a lifetime of negative experiences was to distrust addicts.

And he felt that with Mickie too, even if part of him wanted to believe she wouldn't slip backward. The odds weren't in her favor. It was better she walk out right now before their friendship had the opportunity to deepen. His dick might want her, but that was all.

The woman had disaster written all over her, whether it was from an impending relapse or once she grew tired of hanging out with his blue-collar, barely middle-class family. He'd learned that painful lesson the hard way once before with Della and it didn't need repeating.

Either way, he and his siblings would end up burned, and they'd had enough experiences with fire to last the rest of their lives.

Chapter Eleven

Mickie bit her lower lip and shook her head. Why on earth had she brought up her sobriety? They'd been having a nice time and there she went mentioning how this was the first time in her life she was taking care of herself. That had to be just what the man wanted. A reminder of the fact she was a recovering addict.

As she stepped into the lobby of his shop, she took a breath.

At some point, she needed to learn how to talk about her past without having an internal freak out. While she blamed her avoidance of overly personal subjects on trying to remain anonymous and fly under the radar, that was an excuse. One she could fall back on when ashamed of her mistakes or scared of being judged.

She'd been called it all before, both in whispered words behind her back, to her face, and blasted all over social media.

Slut.

Junkie.

Waste of space.

Fake.

Homewrecker.

Had the insults been justified? Maybe. Probably. Some of them. But the hurtful comments had been easy enough to shrug off when she'd been using. Uncomfortable emotions were easier to process with a fuzzy brain and impaired inhibitions. It was when she was lucid that life became real and challenging.

A few months ago, she'd made the mistake of reading a few social media posts with her name hash tagged. While millions loved her and praised her for her glamorous fashion sense, acting ability, and flashy lifestyle, many others found her to be nothing more than a high-maintenance waste of space. And without the benefit of alcohol to lose herself in, their words had cut her.

Deeply.

Unfortunately, she'd not yet mastered the ability to think of her sobriety without recalling every embarrassing and hurtful mistake she'd made to get her to the point of requiring rehab. Somehow, she needed to find a way, though. Leaving the room every time the subject came up would get old fast.

Shaking her head at her foolishness, Mickie stepped out into the quiet night. Thankfully, one garage bay was still open and well lit. Without the light flooding into the parking lot, she'd have been tempted to run back in and ask Keith to escort her to her car, which went against her need to prove she could tackle life on her own.

Alone and sober.

Her new reality.

With a sigh, she dug her keys out of her purse.

"'S he in there?"

Mickie shrieked and jumped so hard she wrenched her neck. The keys tumbled from her hand to the asphalt with a clatter. Standing three feet to her left was a scruffy man in his mid-fifties, maybe sixty. "Shit, you scared me," she said, pressing a hand to her heart. "I'm sorry, sir, I don't have any cash on me."

As she spoke, she scanned the ground for her keys, but it was too damn dark to see much.

The man laughed. "That's too bad. Could sure use some cash. But I wanna know if my piece-of-shit son is here."

He stumbled a bit as he stepped closer. On instinct, Mickie backed away. Now that he'd mentioned it, she noticed the resemblance to Keith. The height, the strong stature, same nose and face shape. This man was once handsome, she could tell, but years of poisoning his body had taken their toll. Hair that had probably been the same near black as Keith's was gray and thinning. He had the same gray across his unshaven cheeks, but in a patchy, unkempt manner.

Suddenly, Mickie understood Keith's initial adverse reaction to the news of her substance issues. The pungent odor of booze wafted off the man. She'd often feared the smell of alcohol would send her running for the nearest bottle with an intense craving. Not the case here. Her stomach lurched, and she took another step back.

He followed.

"I'm sorry, sir," she said, trying to inch toward her car. "I don't know who you're talking about. Just picking up my car. Have a nice evening."

Fuck, I hope I left the car unlocked.

At the very least, she could lock herself inside the vehicle until he left, then come back out and search for the keys.

He snorted, wavering side to side as he walked. "I know my boy. Fancy little slut like you is just his type. Gotta say, the boy's got taste." He licked his lips, sending a wave of revulsion through her.

Oh, God.

Mickie gave up trying to be subtle, spun, and dashed for her car. She yanked on the handle only to have her heart sink to the ground.

No. No. No.

The one time she remembered to lock the damn thing.

She twisted around only to encounter Keith's father right up in her personal space. "Back up," she said as panic began to set in.

Screw independence. Why the hell hadn't she taken Keith up on his offer to walk her to the damn car?

He raised his hands in surrender but didn't move away. Instead, he smirked. "I know who you are."

Holy shit, that could not be true. Mickie stopped breathing.

"You hear me?" he asked, so close his putrid breath hit her face.

She tried to speak, but nothing came out. All she could think of was this hateful man knowing her secret and outing her to the world. Paparazzi would be camping on her lawn before she had a chance to shut the blinds.

"You're the rich piece of ass who moved across the street from my fucking kids. You ain't the first rich bitch he's gone after." The man laughed. "That blew up in his fucking face."

She sucked in air so fast her head spun. He had no clue about her real identity. He was just a drunk jerk spouting off his mouth. The relief came on so strong her knees almost buckled, and with it came her voice.

"Back. Up," she said, with far more force this time.

He smirked but took two long steps away from her.

Mickie blew out a shaky exhale as she drew her purse up. At least she didn't have his putrid breath wafting over her anymore. "H-how about I call him?" She didn't want to send Keith's father into the garage without warning. Too many tools could be used as weapons and, even wasted and with the element of surprise, the large man could do some serious damage. Thankfully, she kept nothing more than a small wallet, keys, and phone with her these days. Within seconds, she had the phone out. Since the garage had been one of the most recent numbers to call her, she'd be able to find it fast.

"Don't you fucking dare," he roared as he slapped the phone out of her hands. It clattered to the ground and skittered across the asphalt way too far out of reach. As she swiveled her head from watching her last hope fly across the parking lot back toward Keith's father, a fiery explosion of pain bloomed across her face.

He'd slapped her so hard, he unbalanced himself, stumbling to the side and nearly falling on his ass.

Mickie half gasped and half screamed as she cradled her cheek. He recovered way faster than he should have, considering his intoxicated state. Before the shock of the pain and fact she'd been assaulted registered, he was back on her, shoving her against the car with a forearm across her chest.

He grabbed her face so hard her lips pouched out, and her jaw felt as though it would shatter in his grip. The cheek he'd smacked burned as though she'd been bitten by hundreds of fire ants.

She whimpered as tears sprung to her eyes.

"Bet he won't want to fuck you anymore if I mess up this pretty face." He spoke so close to her she could easily see the unfocused glassiness to his eyes. The same damn eyes Keith had, only these held sickness and hate. "That'll teach him to abandon his fucking father." His lips curled up in a sinister grin. "Yeah. I think I'll do that. Leave you out here bleeding and sniveling while I go in and have a chat with my son."

Despite the pain and near paralyzing fear, her brain scrambled, trying to come up with a way to keep him from harming Keith or destroying the shop.

His grip grew tighter as his arm released her chest, but she felt no reprieve because that hand was going to be used to hit her again. Or worse.

"S'not alone," she managed to squeeze out through her sore mouth.

"The fuck you say?" He released her mouth, instead, grabbing her hair and yanking her head back with a rough jerk.

She yelped and clawed at his arm to no avail.

"What the fuck did you say?" he growled, yanking her head back and forth until her brain rattled.

"I s-said he's not a-alone. J-Jagger and JP." It was the best she could do. Maybe he'd think twice about charging in there if he was outnumbered.

"You're lying." Spit hit her cheek and she cringed.

As disgusting as it was, the urge to wipe it away was overshadowed by fear of what was to come.

"N-no. I'm not. T-they're all i-in there. G-guys' night."

Please buy it. Please buy it.

He twisted his hand until it felt like he'd rip her scalp right off. She cried out. "I'm not lying!"

"He owes me." His bloated face hovered inches above her, wafting her with the disgusting stench of body odor and booze. "That no-good, worthless, piece-of-shit—"

Chuck-chick.

"I'm right fucking here," a deadly voice rang out from nearby.

Keith.

Her eyes fell closed as relief washed over her. But it only lasted a second. His father was drunk, erratic, and nasty. Who the hell knew what he was capable of?

"Why don't you let my customer go and talk to me?"

Mickie held her breath, not even daring to blink.

His father laughed without turning away from her. "Why would I want to talk to a piece of shit like you when I got such a pretty friend right here?" He gave her head a shake. The pain had tears leaking from the corners of her eyes.

"Because I'm the one who's gonna blow a fucking hole through you if you don't." Keith's lethal tone had her trembling inside. He'd do it. In that moment she had no doubt he'd shoot his father if the man didn't walk away from her.

Maybe it was the gun or perhaps the way Keith spoke the threat, but something penetrated the man's sloshy brain, and his hand disappeared from her head. The urge to reach up and rub her sore scalp hit strong, but she stayed frozen against her car.

Keith's father laughed as he spun toward his son. No surprise, he overshot the mark and stumbled forward. "You don't got the balls to shoot me." His tone held a mocking hatred that a parent should never feel for their son. Despite her fear, pain, and panic, Mickie was profoundly sad about what Keith and the rest of the Benson kids must have experienced growing up.

His staggered as he walked toward Keith.

Mickie's hands started to tremble. Then her legs. Soon her entire body was shaking. Even her teeth chattered as a cold wave washed over her.

What the hell was happening?

Keith kept his frigid gaze on his father. He didn't so much as glance in her direction. "Trust me, old man, I've got the balls. In fact, I'd take pleasure in watching you bleed right now. But I'll give you one chance to get the fuck off my property."

"I ain't leavin' until I get my fuckin' rent money."

Keith snorted. "Unbelievable," he muttered under his breath. Then he lifted the shotgun so it was level with his father's head instead of his chest.

Mickie held her breath as she stared at Keith's face, looking for any sign that he about to pull the trigger.

The man stopped advancing. "You owe me, boy. I raised you and your ungrateful sib—"

"We owe you nothing. You aren't getting the rent money or another cent from me. Now, you have ten seconds to get the fuck outta here before I shoot you and leave you here to bleed out and die alone in the cold like you deserve."

If she'd thought his voice poisonous before, she'd been wrong. Now, Keith's tone held the promise of death, and she had no doubt he'd pull that trigger if his father didn't leave. Though she could only see the back of his father's head now, something in Keith's words or demeanor must have registered through the booze-soaked haze because his father raised his hands in surrender.

"This ain't over, boy," he said as he started to back away. The man didn't seem to have arrived in a vehicle, so at least they didn't need to worry about him getting behind the wheel and killing someone.

Keith waited until his father had teetered far enough down the road he was nearly out of sight before lowering the weapon and turning his flat gaze on Mickie.

She ran her trembling fingers through her hair.

"Are you—"

"I, uh, I need to find my keys." The phone too, but that was probably a loss as there was no way the screen survived the ordeal. She pushed off the car then scooped up the phone, which had landed a few feet away. Sure enough, the entire screen looked like a spiderweb pattern of cracks.

"Mickie," Keith started.

She continued scanning the ground. If she looked at him, she'd lose it entirely. The man barely tolerated her as it was. The last thing he'd want was his neighbor breaking down in front of him. "It'll just take a minute then I'll be out of your hair." Her limbs still shook, and her insides felt like they'd been zapped with a live wire.

Keith needed to walk away and leave her to her task. If she didn't find her keys and get out of there in the next few seconds, it was going to happen. The major freak out she'd tamped down was going to spew out her eyes, giving Keith another reason to find her weak and unable to handle life.

"Where the fuck are they?" she mumbled.

She must look like a total idiot searching the dark ground for the dropped keys.

"Mickie," he said again, with bite this time.

God, if he made a comment about how she better not go home and drink she'd snatch the shotgun and shoot him.

"Y-yes?" Oh fuck, her voice shook with impending tears and her breath started to come in pants. Years of public attention had taught her to suppress her emotions in front of crowds and cameras, and for the first time ever, while sober, she was about to fail miserably.

"Michaela!"

Her head shot up and she stared at Keith who held her keys out by the generic ring. Fire shot from his eyes. He reminded her of a dangerous caged animal, itching to be freed. She wasn't sure it would be wise to be present when he broke free.

"Thank you." She reached out for the keys. "I'll g-get out of your, uh, h-hair."

He pulled they keys just out of her reach. "Go in the lobby. I need to check you out."

She blinked, arm still outstretched. "What? No. I'm fine. Just give me the keys. I need to get going."

"Michaela. Get in the lobby." His eyes fell closed as though he was praying for patience.

Well, too bad. She was about to lose her shit and needed, *needed* to leave. "No, Keith, really. I'm fine and I just want to go home."

Opening his eyes, he walked toward her. "Michaela," he said as he cupped her sore cheek. "Please go in the lobby so I can make sure you aren't hurt. If you won't do it for you, do it for me. I'll never sleep tonight if I don't make sure you're okay."

Her eyes widened and she sucked in a breath. A second ago, she'd have thought nothing could have convinced her to stay. But the genuine concern in Keith's voice and the gentle touch of his hand to her face had her agreeing. "O-okay," she whispered then hurried toward the dimly lit lobby. She swallowed as his footsteps fell in line behind her.

A volcano was about to blow, but one question still remained. Would it be him or her who erupted first?

Chapter Twelve

Keith had never experienced an immediate surge of incendiary anger like he did the second he spotted his father accosting Mickie. And he'd spent the better part of his life angry at someone or something.

Christ, if he'd been seconds later, what would have happened?

After she walked out of his office, guilt had eaten at him. He should have insisted on walking Mickie to her car and would have if she didn't have his head so scrambled. He'd gotten up to check the lot and make sure she got off all right. The second he heard her sharp cry of distress, he knew in his gut something had gone seriously wrong. Thank fuck he kept a shotgun stashed on a ledge under the reception desk.

He followed behind her as she walked unsteadily into his shop. Suppressing his murderous rage wasn't easy. Part of him, hell, most of him wanted to sprint down the road after the old man and beat his ass for putting his hands on Michaela.

Yes, his siblings were right, and he needed to end any and all involvement with the man, but the knowledge that they could have avoided this entire scene if he'd just paid the rent had guilt tearing at his insides like a ravenous beast. He was to blame for Mickie's near miss.

Fuck.

He'd expected some sort of escalation from his father when the rent wasn't paid. But something of this magnitude hadn't entered his consciousness. As far as Keith knew, his father had kept any violence behind his trailer walls and the occasional bar fights. What happened there tonight wasn't something he could hide from his siblings, either. They'd need to be vigilant in case he went after them for the cash as well.

Fuck!

He followed Mickie into the lobby. The lights were off, but the room was bright enough to see her face.

They stood about four feet apart, staring at each other. Mickie had a pale, shocked look to her, so he moved to the waiting area coffeepot and poured her a steaming cup. It'd been sitting on the warmer for hours and probably tasted like tar, but it'd do the trick. After adding about six tablespoons of sugar, he returned to her.

"Drink," he said.

Without a word, she took the half-full Styrofoam cup and lifted it to her lips. Her hands shook in a way that made his stomach roll with shame. After she swallowed a few sips, she set the Styrofoam cup on the counter and nodded.

She must be feeling off if she didn't even react to the shitty taste.

"What did he do to you?" Christ, he sucked at compassion. He could probably do better, be sweeter or softer, but the rage flowing through veins had full control of his mouth.

"Oh." She touched her face, and he swore she held back a wince. "He s-slapped my face, pulled my hair, made some th-threats."

Clearly, she was working overtime to come across unaffected, but like him, the dam was perilously close to breaking. Only instead of lashing out with violent rage, she seemed seconds from bursting into tears.

"I'm sorry," he said, moving closer. The need to be closer, to have his hands on her swamped him. How else could he assure himself she was unharmed if he didn't feel it? With a uncharacteristically gentle touch, he cupped her chin and turned her face. The cheek was red, angry, and turning slightly purple over the cheekbone, but the skin remained intact.

"I'm okay, Keith," she said, voice breathy. "Shaken up, but not really hurt. Nothing an Advil and a good night's sleep won't fix."

When he released her face, she met his gaze with her troubled one then stared at something over his shoulder.

"I'm not gonna go home and drink…in case that's why you wanted me to stay." A flush rose over her other cheek, and he imagined she was feeling the hot burn of shame. "Worked too hard to blow it on your dad."

If she'd been trying for humor, it fell flat. He'd been a dick for throwing her sobriety in her face the other day. Mickie was strong. He realized that now. No one deserved to have their greatest struggle minimized. "The thought hadn't crossed my mind."

She huffed.

Lifting his hands, he nodded. "Swear it. I'm too busy feeling guilty."

With a shake of her head, she whispered, "Don't."

Now it was his turn to grunt out a noise of disbelief. "I'd been bailing him out when he needed money." With a shrug, he stared just to the left of her so he wouldn't have to see the disappointment in her eyes. "Before my mom died, she asked me to make sure he was taken care of so…" He shrugged. "Anyway, this was retaliating for finally cutting him off."

She grabbed his forearm, and he swore her touch nearly burned him. "I'm serious. You are not responsible for anyone else's poor behavior. Especially not when they are drunk. Trust me. I've had to own plenty of things I'd have loved to pawn off on someone else."

Asking for more details sat on the tip of his tongue. He wanted to know more about her, to understand what had happened when she hit rock bottom and realized she needed to turn her life around. It'd been something significant, that much was clear. Something so big she'd physically moved away from her home to start fresh. For his father, there never seemed to be a level low enough to be called rock bottom. Every time he thought the man hit an all-time low, he went and added to his pile of sins.

Like tonight.

"Obviously, I didn't know your mother, but from what I've heard, she was wonderful. I can't imagine she'd have wanted you to sacrifice your happiness for him."

Mickie had good instincts.

Their gazes met again and held. As they stared at each other, the hot rush of anger flowing through him morphed into one of molten desire. Even upset, the woman was one of the sexiest he'd ever seen.

Electricity crackled between them.

Whether it was their close proximity, the way she smelled of apple pie and something fancy, the dim lighting in the lobby, or the adrenalin, the catalyst didn't matter. Want swelled in him, swift and sharp, demanding action.

Having her was all that mattered.

Her chest rose and fell as her breathing accelerated. Before his eyes, Mickie's pupils expanded until they nearly swallowed up the deep caramel of her irises. She licked her lower lip, drawing his attention and hardening his dick to an indestructible spike.

All the fear, anger, guilt, and tension swirling around the room combined until nothing was recognizable but the want.

The need.

The desire.

He didn't know who moved first, or if they pounced at the same time, but he lunged forward, meeting her in a crush of his lips against hers.

Goddamn, the woman tasted like fire and sass and sweetness all rolled into one. She moaned and attacked his greedy mouth with equal fervor.

Somewhere in the back of his mind, he remembered her sore cheek and managed not to squeeze her face as he plundered her mouth. Instead, he grabbed handfuls of her plump ass, yanking her against his erection.

If she was shocked by the aggressive move, she didn't show it. Just ground her pussy against his throbbing length. There was no exploring, no learning what the other liked, or tenderness. This was an adrenalin-fueled fuck to flood their bodies with something other than fear or fury.

Something fucking fantastic, if he had any say.

A little growl of frustration left Mickie as she hiked her leg up around his hip. Taking the hint, he lifted her and walked her backward until she hit the front window with a thunk.

"Yes," she hissed, clearly enjoying the leverage. With a groan, she bit at his jaw and rubbed herself all over his hard-on which nearly made him blow his load right then and there. Never in his wildest imagination—and he had a damn good one—would he have imagined Mickie meeting him at his level sexually.

He'd assumed she'd want sweet, tender, loving, vanilla.

That'd teach him to make snap judgments.

The woman he'd called a prude dropped her legs to the ground and attacked the button on his filthy jeans. "Off," she said with a sexy little growl.

He batted her hands. She had no idea what a hair trigger he was riding. If she so much as grazed his cock, he'd shoot off like a fourth of July fireworks display.

Without his pants to destroy, she went to work on her own, ripping the button open and shoving them over her curvy hips. The little wiggle she did as she shimmied them down had him biting off a groan.

He grabbed a condom out of his wallet and suited up before pushing his jeans down further.

She got one pant leg off around the time he'd shoved his jeans to his ankles and realized he still had his shoes on. "Fuck," he spat out.

Mickie stared, open-mouthed. "God, I want that in me."

He straightened to find her neatly manicured fingers reaching for his erection where it jutted from his body.

"You're so thick." She licked her lips.

The cock in question jerked at the compliment.

"Fuck it." He could work just fine with his pants at his ankles. Catching her hand one second before it wrapped around him, he slammed it against the window over her head. Then he grabbed her ass with his other hand and hoisted her back up.

His cock went right to her soaked entrance as though guided by a map. He slammed her against the window and then they both froze in place.

Hair mussed, cheeks flushed, and pupils blown, she looked needy and wanton and absolutely perfect.

"Keith," she whispered in some kind of half plea, half wonder.

If anyone could make him forget his head and fall for a rich woman again, it would be Mickie. She drew him like no other woman ever had.

But it was just lust. It could only be lust.

With that thought and the demanding ache in his balls, he squeezed her ass and thrust to the hilt in one smooth motion.

"Fuck, yes!" Mickie cried out as she locked her ankles behind his back.

He paused, buried to the hilt. "Good?" The single word was all he coul manage.

"Yes, yes, so good." She practically panted. "More, Keith. I want more."

After that, he didn't check if she wanted more. Didn't think about anything but the searing heat and eye-crossing clench of her pussy. Possessed by the driving need to come, he fucked her with an enthusiasm he hadn't had since his twenties.

With one hand, he held her wrist anchored to the window and with the other he controlled the movement of her hips, ramming their bodies together again and again.

Within minutes, his balls ached with the need to come, to empty inside this woman, and for the first time in his life, he regretted the use of a condom. He wanted to mark her from the inside out.

"Fuck, fuck, yes, fuck me," Mickie chanted. Her fingers curled into the back of his neck, scoring his skin with the nails. The bite of discomfort had him growling and attacking her neck. As he pounded her pussy with his cock, he sucked the soft skin of her neck between his lips. Mickie moaned and tilted her head away, baring her throat to him. He nipped and sucked until she was bucking in his arms and babbling nonsense.

"Close, close," she said, gasping as she tightened her legs around his back. Her heels dug into his ass giving him the impression she was beyond desperate to keep him inside.

He'd be lucky if he wasn't bruised to shit and unable to sit tomorrow.

Damn, he hoped that was true.

"Oh, my God, I'm coming," she shouted.

One flutter of her pussy was all it took to blow his top. "Fuck," he hollered as they writhed and jerked against each other. For long seconds, she bucked in his arms, holding him with a punishing grip. He prolonged her orgasm with tiny thrust, and her continued clenching milked him completely dry while drawing out his own climax until his dick felt so sensitive, he flinched as her pussy continued gripping him. But damn, he didn't want to leave the tight heat of her body.

Eventually, Mickie sagged between him and the wall as if completely depleted. He understood the feeling as his own body felt worn out in the best way. In all the times he'd run into her, he'd yet to see a single strand of her hair out of place. Now, some stuck to her cheek and neck, plastered by sweat while the rest of her head looked as though birds had tried to make a nest. She also had a post-fucked tilt to her swollen lips and suddenly he couldn't resist one last taste.

With a much gentler touch than he'd handled her seconds ago, he smoothed the damp hair back from her face. Her eyes popped open, sleepy and sated but showing her shock at the tender move. He kissed her hard, in contrast to his light hold. Though they'd kissed before, he'd been in such a frenzy to fuck, he hadn't taken the chance to savor her flavor. Or the bold way her tongue met his and her fists curled into his shirt to hold him in place.

This woman like to fuck. Maybe as much as he did.

Reluctantly, he drew back to replenish his oxygen.

Red flushed her cheeks, which was a huge improvement over the ashy gray she'd turned after the encounter with his father.

His father.

Fuck.

The catalyst to all of this.

Christ, she'd been hurt and scared, and he'd attacked her like some savage animal.

The mood in the room plummeted as Mickie seemed to realize at the same moment that what they'd done was madness.

Not meeting his gaze any longer, she cleared her throat. "Can you let me down?"

"Oh yeah, shit. Sorry." He released her, stepping back only after certain she was steady on her feet.

One of her shoes lay on its side a foot away while the other held her jeans around one ankle.

"Mickie that was..." Words failed him. Nothing seemed strong enough to describe what had just occurred between them.

Any lingering pleasure from the monster orgasms they'd shared vanished as horror crossed her features. "So, uh, I need to get going." She scrambled to get into the other pant leg. At one point, she almost tipped over.

Keith reached out to steady her, but she lifted a hand and held him off as though his touch was no longer welcome.

"I got it." Still moving with urgency, she shoved her foot halfway in the shoe, grabbed her keys and phone from the ground, and limped toward the exit. As her hand gripped the rail, she turned. "I'm sorry," she said. "I don't...I mean for losing control and attacking you like that. That's not me." She shook her head. "That's not who I want to be. I didn't mean to. It won't happen again. I'm really sorry. That's not me anymore." Then she shoved the door open and was gone in a blink.

Keith stood there with his jaw hanging open and dick flapping in the breeze as he watched her run to her car. She'd stunned him to immobility.

The woman apologized for being too aggressive with *him*?

That's not me anymore.

What the hell had she meant by that? Was that part of the reason she'd moved to Vermont alone? Had she slept with someone she shouldn't have? Had she cheated or been party to someone else cheating? The more snippets of Michaela Hudson he glimpsed, the more he wanted to know. She was a mystery he wanted to solve.

The woman had burned in his arms. When was the last time he'd let loose like that? Had he ever? For Christ's sake, he fucked her where anyone could have driven by and caught them going at it. It'd been wild and reckless, yes, but hot as fuck.

"Shit," he grumbled as he tossed the condom in the waiting area's trash can. As he did, he made a mental note to take it to the dumpster before he shocked and drove off his customers.

He and Mickie were consenting adults. More than consenting, they'd both been starving for it.

He was single, she was single, and they'd used a condom.

There wasn't anything wrong with what they'd done.

And there wasn't anything wrong with enjoying the fuck outta it.

So why did she think there was?

Chapter Thirteen

Michaela picked up her phone and snorted out a laugh at Ralph's most recent text.

IF YOU DON'T CALL ME IN THE NEXT 5 MINUTES, I'M SENDING THE FBI.

All caps. The man meant business. Dramatic as ever but reaching the end of his patience. And she was a terrible friend. For the past two days, she'd ignored all calls and texts while moping around the house, berating herself for her stupidity. Apparently, Ralph had had enough, and if she didn't want the local SWAT team showing up on her doorstep, she'd better give the man a call.

With a sigh, she picked up her phone and hit the first contact on her favorites list.

"Well, well, well," came his pissy voice. "If it isn't the elusive Michaela Hudson. You better have a damn good reason for ignoring me the past two days. Like *day-um* good. Like, I'll only let it slide if you were locked away in a remote cabin for a sex-fest with the muscly mechanic god. That is literally the only way I'll forgive you for falling off the face of the earth and scaring the shit out of me."

Michaela winced. Whether it was his statement hitting too close to the mark or the guilt of stressing him out, she deserved the lecture even if it was off the charts melodramatic. "Shit, I'm sorry, Ralphie. I didn't think you'd worry so much."

He harumphed. "Didn't think I'd worry about my bestie who recently got out of rehab, moved across the country, and is all alone in a small town? Wow, you think so highly of my friendship skills."

Ouch.

Another bullseye.

"God, Ralph, you know how to lay a good guilt trip. I'm the one with the shitty friendship skills. Something happened the other night, and I've been sort of…processing it."

His tone turned serious. "Mickie, are you okay?"

She could imagine him straightening and clutching the phone tight to his ear with one hand while a Twizzler dangled from the other.

"Yes, yes." She waved her hand even though he couldn't see her. "Seriously, it's nothing like you're thinking. I promise I haven't even been tempted to…fall off the wagon. I promise."

He blew out a breath. "Look, sweetie, I trust you. I don't want you to think I don't. I just, well, I love you and worry about you out there without me. I was seconds away from hopping on a plane, and I'm not sure I have good snowy Vermont attire. It would have been a whole thing."

Oh, the guilt. She truly hadn't considered he'd be imagining her stoned out of her mind and rocking in the corner. "Oh, Ralph, I'm really sorry. I promise no more radio silence."

"Cross your heart?"

She smiled. "Yes."

"Do it for real."

Rolling her eyes, she drew an X over the left side of her chest. "It's done. And by the way, it's September, so not snowing yet."

"Whatever. Now tell Dr. Ralph what you needed a whole forty-eight hours to process. And please let it be hot sex with the even hotter mechanic," he teased.

Staring at the ceiling, Michaela bit her lower lip.

"Sweetie?" he said when she didn't respond. Then he gasped, and she could have sworn she heard him clapping. "Oh my God, you *did* sleep with him! You little hussy, you. So, what are you processing? Was it bad? Oh, please don't let it have been bad. Did he have a tiny dick? Because that would be God's cruel joke. Oooh, was he into something really weird like fucking with his socks on?"

God love the man. Only Ralph could have her busting out laughing about something she'd been ruminating over for days. "Slow down. You're making me dizzy. You're firing questions faster than the paparazzi."

"Oh, you did not just go there."

She laughed again. "His dick was nowhere near small. I have no idea about the sock thing because we really didn't take any clothes off, and no, it certainly was not bad."

It had been the best sex of her life. Hot, dirty, raw. They'd been so desperate for each other that both of them lost their minds right there in the lobby of Keith's shop with windows all around, for crying out loud. And this time, there weren't any substances in her system to blame it on.

"Oooh, tell me more, you dirty girl."

"I'm not giving you any more details, perv."

"Come on, girl," he said with a distinct whine. "I haven't slept with anyone in three weeks."

She gasped around her laugh. "A whole three weeks? How are you still alive?" There'd been a time she'd had more male attention than one woman ever needed. Three weeks of abstinence would have seemed like a lifetime. But not one of those men had meant anything to her and aside from an orgasm —if her partner for the night had known what he was doing— the encounters left her cold, empty, and reaching for a bottle. "Fine, all I will say is that you cannot describe it as *sleeping* with someone. No bed was involved."

"Damn, woman. So this was a down and dirty fuck then?"

"Pretty much," she whispered, rubbing her temples where a headache was forming.

"Ugh, I'm not jealous at all. Not one single bit. I swear it."

She snorted.

"So what's the problem then?" he asked. "Why did you have to disappear for two days to process a hot fuck? You're not exactly a simpering virgin."

What was the problem? What a question. One she'd been obsessing over since the moment her brain returned and the endorphins faded. She'd come to the conclusion that the behavior was way too reminiscent of how she'd have acted in the past and in contrast with how she'd promised to act moving forward as a healthy, sober woman.

"Mickie?" His voice was gentle, inquiring.

"Sorry. It's just…I thought I was done with all that."

"With all what? Sex?" He barked out a laugh. "Please, I hope not. You are way too young to be done with sex, baby doll."

This time she couldn't join in the levity. "No. Not sex, but… Ralph I lost control. Just… poof." She snapped her fingers. "The man touched me, and my brain vanished. I swear a bomb could have gone off, and I wouldn't have noticed it. It was crazy and wild and…well out of control, like I said." She left out the parts about a scary encounter with Keith's father being the catalyst because Ralph would only freak out, and she had a feeling this thing with Keith would have happened eventually regardless. The adrenaline rush from the run-in with his father only sped up the timeline.

"Damn, I'll be right back. I need to stick my head in the freezer."

She groaned. "Ralph, be serious, please. I'm struggling here."

"Well, honey, to be honest, I'm not following what has you so freaked out. To me this just sounds like you're bragging."

She sighed and plopped down on the couch. Resting her head on the back cushions, she said, "I've been working so hard to take control of my life. No drinking, no drugs, owning my mistakes, making sound choices, recognizing my emotions, both positive and negative. It's been months since I've engaged in any destructive behaviors, and I feel incredible. I'm happy here and proud of myself even if the work isn't done. Then here comes one hot man, and I threw out months of emotionally draining work for a shot at his dick."

She closed her eyes and practiced a breathing technique she'd learned in rehab. It helped slow her heart and manage anxiety.

"Sweetie?" Ralph asked.

"I'm here."

"Were you drunk when this happened?"

Her eyes popped open, and her spine snapped straight. "No! You know I wasn't." If anyone else had asked, she'd be offended, but Ralph had seen her at her very worst and stuck by her side when so many disowned her. He was justified in his occasional distrust.

"High?"

"No."

"Was he a nameless, faceless random guy you hooked up with in the back corner of a trendy club only to be splashed all over Insta ten seconds later?"

"No," she whispered. Would she ever completely shake the shame of her past behavior?

"Well then, this sounds to me like an enviable encounter you should be bragging about not beating yourself up over. We all have needs, girl. No one expects you to live like a monk forever."

"But I—"

"Lost control, yes. I heard you. But adults have sex whether they're in or out of relationships. Hot, passionate, wild sex, even. As long as everything was consensual and you were sober, no harm done."

He paused as though understanding she needed a second to absorb his words.

Technically, in rehab, it was recommended to avoid a relationship until one reached a year of sobriety. Now she understood why. There was still a lot of bullshit in her head that needed ironing out. But this wasn't a relationship. And it had been consensual, sober, and exhilarating-as-hell sex.

"Girl, good sex is supposed to make you lose control. That's the kind of fucking we fantasize about. You didn't do anything wrong, unethical, or bad. You're a single woman in your late twenties. This is your prime, sweetie. Getting your shit together and taking control of your life doesn't mean you have to live like a nun and can't have excitement or fun. You need to cut yourself some slack."

Okay, maybe he had a point, but still, it was Keith. She'd let—hell, let wasn't the word, she'd practically demanded—he fuck her stupid at his place of business. "But it shouldn't have happened in the first place. I shouldn't have had sex with *him* at all."

"Why not?"

She grunted. "Because half the time I think he hates me, and I'm not sure if I like him either."

He laughed, and she now had the distinct impression he was having too much fun at her expense. "And the other half? Sweetie, everyone has sex with people they probably shouldn't. If he's single, you're single, and everyone was sober and consenting, there is absolutely nothing wrong with it. It's not a setback. Actually, I think it's a giant step forward."

Hmm, that was an interesting take. "How so?"

"Because it's normal! It's what people do. They date, they hook up, they have fun. It shows you're getting a life—one you choose. One you're working hard to own. One I can tell you're really starting to like. I'm proud of you, Mickie. Hate sex can be fun as hell, girl. It's not like you're out there fucking everything with a dick as a replacement for the drugs."

"No." It was just this one man who she wanted.

Some of the tension she'd been carrying lifted off her shoulders. Ralph was right. The mistakes she'd made in the past needed to stay there. She'd changed so much in the last seven months, mostly due to being sober but also because of the hard work she'd put into therapy. She still checked in with her therapist biweekly via Zoom.

"It's healthy for you to want to avoid repeating the mistakes you've made in the past, but you can't let that take over and become a fear of living your life. Now, I'm going to let you go and *process* all I've said. And you are never going to ignore my texts or calls again."

"Never. I promise and I'm sorry, Ralphie."

"I love you, Mickie."

Her heart clenched with the force of missing him. "And I love you, Ralph. Thank you."

"My pleasure. Oh, by the way, I'm coming for a visit in a few weeks. I need to see this mechanic for myself." He hung up before she had a chance to respond, which was typical of their conversations. Ralph loved to drop little bombs then disappear.

She flopped back against the couch, letting the phone drop on the cushion next to her. She'd been so conflicted that night. Riding high on emotion and adrenalin, she'd lost her head with Keith. It'd been...phenomenal. Had she ever come so hard? Probably not. Ever since, her body had craved more while her mind had run rampant, punishing her for the loss of control.

Ralph's lecture helped quite a bit. He was right. Healthy single adults had sex all the time. And sometimes, it was a one-off with someone who wasn't right for them. Nothing wrong with it. Since she hadn't heard from Keith in two days, he seemed to feel the same way. The encounter had been the product of the unnerving situation with his father combined with their potent chemistry.

Nothing more, nothing less.

Buried deep under all her anxiety the past few days was a smidgen of pride. Not once had she thought of drinking or putting any other substances in her body. She'd allowed the discomfort and dealt with it instead of escaping it. And that was a huge win.

There was a time, not long ago, she'd have spent these past few days numbing herself until the stress passed.

A knock at the door brought her back to the moment. It was high time to stop obsessing and get on with her day. "Coming!" she hollered as she rose from the sofa.

Michaela pulled the door open after the second knock. "Hey, Jagger, come on in," she said to the handsome man standing in her doorway. Even though she'd been expecting him, she had a tiny twinge of disappointment that he wasn't Keith.

Jagger flashed her the charming smile all three Benson brothers she'd met seemed blessed with and stepped into her house. "Man, been a while since I've been over here. Forgot how nice this place is. It's gonna be a stunner once we're done."

A warm sense of pride filled her. "Thanks. I'm really quite smitten with it."

He shifted into work mode as his gaze took in every nook and cranny h. Then he turned to her, and his eyes widened while his lips curled up in a smirk.

No. No, no, no.

Fucking Keith and his should-come-with-a-warning mouth. It'd been three days since the night of insanity, and she'd thought the hickey he'd so generously left on her neck had faded enough to be covered by her makeup alone and not a bulky turtleneck or scarf. Apparently not, since Jagger's gaze zeroed in on it the second he looked at her. At her side, her hand twitched as though ready to slap over the incriminating mark without her brain's approval.

"So, thanks for taking that food for Keith the other night. It was so nice of you to go out of your way like that. Hope it wasn't too much trouble."

Seriously? Could he be more obvious?

She narrowed her eyes and bit off her own laughter to maintain the glare. But it was a wasted effort. Her lips twitched, and the suppressed giggle came out as a snort. "I hope you aren't that terrible at actual fishing." She waved her hands in a come-on motion. "Get it all out now so you can get to work." He was there to take measurements in her kitchen and bathroom.

"Oh, honey," he said, still laughing. "Pretty sure this is gonna take a while to get out of my system. Then once I tell Ronnie and JP, it's gonna start all over again."

Her head dropped back as she groaned. "God, you guys all suck."

"Not as much as Keith, it seems. Just ask your neck."

Her face heated as her jaw dropped. This time she did press her palm to the spot on her neck. "You didn't just say that."

Slinging an arm across her shoulders, Jagger guided her to her kitchen with a chuckle. "Think of it this way, if we Bensons torture you with teasing, it means we like you. Actually, it means we really like you. Teasing is our love language." After winking, he made his way to her cabinets, pulled a tape measure from his back pocket, and got to work.

As he measured, she considered what he'd said. What was probably a throwaway line for him had the warmth of acceptance spreading through her entire body.

They liked her.

Without knowing about her celebrity.

Without her buying them expensive gifts or meals in popular restaurants.

Without the glamorous outfits and perfect hair and makeup she'd relied on in LA.

Without their fifteen seconds of fame from an Instagram selfie with Scarlett.

What they did have, though, was a tiny snippet of insight to her past. They knew she had a messy history with drugs and alcohol and was newly sober.

And they still liked her.

Really liked her.

It had a joyous feeling bubbling up inside her. One she loved and wanted to hold onto for as long as possible.

"So, all joking aside, Keith told me about what happened the other night," Jagger said over his shoulder.

"What?" she squeaked. "He *told* you?" Oh, God, that was a shrill shriek that just came out of her? Well, now she wanted to sink through the floor and die.

"Yeah, about our father hassling you at the garage. Of course he told me."

Oh, he told his siblings about their father. Right, not about the wild monkey sex in the lobby. "Oh, yes. Your father, right. Of course." She shook her head to clear the disturbing image of Keith dishing the dirty details to his siblings.

"Why?" Jagger asked, tossing her a smirk over his shoulder. "Did you think I meant something else?"

Her face burned. Of course, he knew what she'd been thinking. He'd seen the hickey after all. "Nope." Clearing her throat, she said. "I knew you were talking about your father causing trouble."

Jagger's demeanor changed to serious and concerned. "Are you okay after all that? Keith said our father hit you."

"He slapped me, but I'm fine. My cheek was a little sore and red yesterday, but it's barely noticeable today."

"The old man has very few redeeming qualities," he said, shaking his head, "but this is a new low, even for him. I'm sorry you got caught in our family mess."

"Please don't apologize. I'm really fine." She gave him a cheery smile to demonstrate. She'd been shaken of course, but the sex with Keith threw her far more than the frightening moments with his father.

"Hold this for me." He handed her the end of his measuring tape. "Right there on the edge of the island."

She hooked the metal tab over the end of the Formica countertop and held it in place as Jagger stretched the tape the length of the kitchen island. "Is Keith okay?"

He turned to face her with a dark raised eyebrow. "You haven't talked to him?"

Ugh. How embarrassing. "Uh, no, I haven't." There was that disappointment kicking in again.

"Well, this afternoon, Ronnie, JP, and I are dragging him kicking and screaming to pick apples and pumpkins at a farm outside of town. Ever done it?"

"Nope." She laughed. "Back in—" Holy shit! She'd nearly blurted out that back in Hollywood, that wasn't really a thing. "No, I've never done that."

"Well then, you should come with us. I think you'll love it. Fresh air, apple cider donuts, mulled cider. It's all good stuff. Kinda a family tradition we started with my mom when we were kids. We still go every year,"

As an only child whose father left when she was very young and whose mother passed away early, Mickie didn't have a single family tradition to uphold. Sure, she and Ralph spent the holidays together, but those often ended up being sad days where she'd end up wasted and feeling sorry for herself. Apple picking with the Benson crew sounded wonderful. "I don't want to intrude."

He snorted. "Pretty sure Ronnie will love me best when she finds out I got another female to come along. She's always complaining there's too much testosterone in our family. JP bringing his flavor of the week around doesn't count, or so I'm told."

"Yeah, I understand how being the only woman with all you guys would get to a girl." *Say no. Say no.* "Okay, I'll come. It sounds fun. Thanks."

It'd have been an easy yes if Keith wasn't involved. Now she'd have to spend an awkward afternoon tiptoeing around him.

With a hickey on her neck.

But she'd loved dinner with the other Bensons. They lived so close, and she really wanted them to become close friends. She envied their sibling connection but also enjoyed their company individually. She would just have to feel out Keith's mood and if he seemed distressed by her presence, she'd avoid him as much as possible.

"Great! Ronnie and I'll pick you up at three-thirty. Keith and JP are coming straight from the garage, so they'll drive separately. Let's talk about this island. You want to extend it, right?" he asked, as though inviting her to pick apples with him and his family was no big deal, which to him, it probably wasn't. But to her, it was huge.

She'd attended A-list parties on a weekly basis in LA, lunched and brunched with her "friends," and frequented swanky clubs. Now, with that part of her life in the rear-view mirror, she realized none of those events and activities happened because people wanted to hang out with her for her personality or company. It was her status, money, and name that garnered all those invitations. Jagger asked her along for the sole purpose of having fun with him and his family. Because he wanted her around and thought the rest of his family would as well.

She couldn't keep the enormous smile off her face, which probably made her look manic while answering his question about her kitchen. "Yes, I'd like to both widen and extend it. Here's what I'm thinking," she said as she began to walk him through her wish list.

For the next two hours, they worked through her design ideas. He recorded the necessary measurements, shared some recommendations, and together they came up with a plan she couldn't have been more excited to begin. By the time she'd seen him off with a smile and promise of an estimate within a week, she was on cloud nine. Excitement buzzed across her skin at the prospect of having a project to pour herself into. Designing the interior of her home and decorating it was right up her alley and would keep her busy enough her mind wouldn't have as much time to wander to dark places.

Having a renewed sense of purpose was the only reason for the thrill and goofy smile on her face. The only reason. The hum of anticipation and tingle in her fingertips had nothing to do with the afternoon's plans or the guarantee of seeing Keith again.

Nothing.

Chapter Fourteen

"You know, I'm actually at the point now where I'm worried your face will crack if you try to smile," JP said as he reached across the center console and poked Keith's cheek.

"Fuck off," Keith grumbled, swatting his brother's hand away.

"I mean, you scowl so much, your cheeks can't be flexible anymore. Know what I mean?"

If he didn't shut it, Keith was gonna smack that smirk off his brother's mouth. Then they'd see whose face cracked. "I smile."

JP snorted. "Maybe when you're in the shower jerking off or something." He made an obscene gesture, rolling his eyes back and groaning. "Hell, I bet your O-face isn't even happy."

"Knock it off. Are you fucking fifteen?" He risked a glance away from the road to glower at his brother, who sat in the passenger seat without a care in the world. His leather jacket didn't scream apple picking, but JP went with what would attract female attention, not what was practical.

With a laugh, JP just shrugged. "Sorry. Forgot you can't joke around, either."

"I smile, and I fucking laugh, and make jokes, so drop it."

He'd done both with Mickie in the past week, more than once. He'd also come so hard he saw stars. But more than that, he'd had fun with her. Narrowing his eyes, he tried to remember the last time he let go and had fun like he did baking with Mickie. Hell, maybe JP was on to something and he had been on the grumpy side lately. Not that he'd ever give his brother the satisfaction of letting him think he was right.

"Guess I'll take your word for it, 'cause I sure as fuck never see it." JP reached for the adjustment lever on the side of the passenger's seat, cranked it, and reclined halfway back. With a sign of bliss, he closed his eyes and folded his tattooed hands on his stomach. All of them had ink, but JP's body was more of a canvas than all the rest of them combined.

"Sure, have a nap. I'll get us there."

"Thanks, bro. I was up late with Karina."

The man got around more than a fucking germ. "Who's Karina?"

Eyes still shut, JP shrugged. "Met her at the bar. Should have seen the ass on this one, man. Mmm." He lifted his arms and mimicked a squeezing motion with his hands. "Grade fucking A. Swear to Christ, I left teeth marks on that peach."

"You're the reason women think men are pigs. You know that, right?"

The scenery grew more rural the further they drove from town. Usually, a drive like this mellowed Keith, but he'd been antsy as hell since fucking Mickie against the windows in the lobby of his garage. Nothing, not even the decathlon of jerking off he'd engaged in since, had chilled him out. At least six or seven times over the past two days he'd picked up the phone to call her but pussied out. What would be the point? She was rich, classy, way out of his league. The only reason they'd fucked was because of the adrenalin rush and stress of his asshole father scaring her. It's not like they'd be riding off into the sunset together. She'd find a man more suitable. Just as Della had done.

"Not true at all. Women love me. My cards are on the table every time. They know what they're getting from me. Multiple orgasms and a perfect dick."

"Jesus." Keith shook his head as he worked to block out the memory of Mickie coming on his dick. Fuck, she'd been hotter than any one woman should be. The contrast of the classy woman when clothed and the wild one when naked drove him crazy with want.

"Hey, just because you live like a fucking monk doesn't mean the rest of us humans do. Women leave me with a smile on their face and a little hobble in their walk if you know what I mean."

"Yeah, pretty sure I can figure it out. You're about as subtle as a kick to the nuts."

"Good. Then stop whining and let me sleep for the next few minutes before we get to our destination."

"Apple picking. Can't believe I agreed to this shit," Keith grumbled under his breath.

Smirking, JP said, "You'll be glad once we get there. Trust me."

The words trust me coming from JP's mouth were pretty much an order to do the exact opposite. Suspicion slithered up Keith's spine. "Why?" Apple picking was a tradition they'd been upholding since Keith was in his single digits. Even though all six of them didn't usually make it, at least a few of them were there each year to honor something their mother had loved so much.

They'd loved it, too. She'd made everything fun even if they never had enough money to buy mor than a few apples. But no matter what, no matter how bad things got at home or how tight money was, she always made sure her kids had an apple donut and some cider on those chilly fall days.

Those good memories were few and far between but powerful enough they continued the tradition.

"Hmm? No reason." JP was a shit liar, mostly because he couldn't keep a straight face if offered a million bucks.

"Did you guys do something? What did you do?" After a quick glance in the rear-view mirror revealed they were alone on the rural road, Keith braked to a full stop. "I'm turning the fuck around unless you tell me right now what I'm walking into."

"Christ, Dad, you're such a buzz kill." JP finally opened his eyes and glared at Keith with annoyance. "What, are you afraid of? That you might actually have five minutes of fun?"

He'd had five minutes of fun the other night, and now his head was all screwed up, so yeah, that argument wouldn't work.

"John Paul Benson—"

With a groan and a roll of his eyes, JP righted his chair. "Seriously, I pity your future children. Make sure to send them my way often so I can keep them from being boring little robots." He threw his hands up while making a sound of disgust. "Mickie is coming, all right? Chill out."

His stomach flipped, and his grip on the wheel tightened.

Nope. That wasn't a surge of excitement or lust. He wouldn't allow either. Must have just hit a dip in the road or something.

"Cat got your tongue?"

"Huh?" He glanced at JP, whose smug grin had his hackles rising.

"You gonna say anything?"

"'Bout what? Michaela? Glad you guys invited her. She seems like she needs to get out more. Am I supposed to say something else?" Well, he was a shitty actor.

"Oh, for fuck's sake." JP shut his eyes again. "Wake me when we get there, you freakin' android."

Twenty minutes of listening to JP snore later, Keith parked his car on the popular orchard's grassy lot. Families with their kids and even some dogs milled around everywhere he looked.

It only took two seconds for him to zero in on Mickie. The second his gaze landed on her, his gut tightened. She was laughing with Ronnie and the joy on her face had his gut clenching. Damn, she was so beautiful, even more so when she relaxed.

He'd be lying if he didn't admit he got a thrill knowing she enjoyed his family so much.

"We're here. Wake up," he said as he whacked JP on the chest with more force than necessary.

JP gasped and shot to a sitting position, wide-eyed. "What the fuck man? I'm too young to die of a heart attack. Do you know how many women I still have to screw?"

Laughing, Keith rolled his eyes, which was his most common expression when hanging out with JP. The guy was ridiculous on a good day and certifiable on a bad. "There they are, over by the little store thing."

"Sweet." JP opened his door. "Pretty much planning to eat my weight in cider donuts." He was out of the car like a shot and joining the others.

Keith, on the other hand, took his time strolling over to his siblings and Mickie. When JP reached them first, he drew Mickie into a long, tight hug while winking at Keith over her shoulder.

Keith bristled. His fucking brothers were having way too much fun at his expense these days. Rolling his shoulders, he tried to relax and make it seem like the fact JP still had his arms around Mickie wasn't getting to him. When JP kissed her cheek then slung his arm around her shoulders, making himself comfortable, Keith decided all bets were off. He'd be shoving JP out of an apple tree for sure.

At some point, JP must have recognized he was playing with fire and came to his senses. He released Mickie as Keith reached their little group. Maybe it was the less-than-subtle way Jagger cleared his throat as though he had an entire steak lodged in it. Luckily, Mickie seemed oblivious to their exchange.

What she did seem, though, was nervous. Her back stiffened, and she lifted a hand in greeting. "Hey."

She looked striking in a cream-colored turtleneck with a denim jacket and tight black leggings. Some kind of boot with fur around her calf topped off the classy fall outfit.

"Hey." Since JP hugged her, it'd be weird if he didn't, right? Strictly from a social norms standpoint. Not because he was anxious to feel the press of her body against his again, even with multiple layers of clothing and jackets between them.

Not at all.

She returned the hug with wooden limbs and a quick pat to his back before stepping back as though he'd seared her skin through her clothes.

Awkward much?

He had no one to blame but himself for not contacting her the last two days.

As Mickie pulled back, he held her arm above the elbow and examined her cheek. The mark his father had left seemed to have faded and couldn't be seen beneath her makeup. Still, knowing it had been there made his shoulders stiffen.

"It's fine," Mickie whispered. "Not even sore anymore."

As if that was supposed to make it okay.

Ronnie's gaze shifted between the two of them as though they were nuts. "What the hell is up with you two?" Leave it to her to be more blunt than necessary. Keith had told her about the garage incident, but not the fact that they'd had any intimate connection because of it.

Mickie, who was a million times better at disguising her genuine emotions than he was, sent a dazzling smile Ronnie's way. "Nothing's up. I'm just excited to be here. Did you hear the guy say they have a corn maze?" Her eyes sparkled as though she said they had a field of diamonds for her to run through.

"Uh, yeah," Jagger said. "It's huge, and we get lost every time we try it. Hate that fucking thing."

With a laugh, Mickie gently punched his arm. "Big strong guy like you afraid of a little corn?"

JP barked out a laugh. "Damn, I love you woman. Have I invited you to my bed yet?"

Keith stiffened, and not in the way he typically did when Mickie stood so close. Fucking JP was gonna get his balls kicked up to his skull one of these days.

Mickie tilted her head and tapped her lips. "Hmmm, yes, I think six or seven times now. And yes, I'll happily join you in your bed, under one condition."

"Sweet." JP rubbed his hands together. "What is it I can do for you?"

What the fuck?

Hands on her hips, Mickie gave a mischievous grin. "I have this bunny costume I like my partners to wear. Put it on, and I'm all yours."

Keith burst out laughing. The way she'd deadpanned that line was perfect.

"Okay, which of you assholes told her?" JP asked with narrowed eyes. A few years ago, he'd met some chick at a party and headed back to her house for a signature JP one-night stand. When they'd arrived, she pulled a fuzzy pink bunny costume out of her closet and asked him to put it on. JP swore he didn't, but the rest of them never bought it. The guy would do damn near anything, especially in the name of getting laid.

Jagger raised his hand and bounced on the balls of his feet like an excited child. "Me! It was me. I told her."

JP flipped him off with both hands while Mickie snickered. "I'm sorry. I couldn't resist. It was just so perfect." She didn't sound one bit apologetic.

"You, I like," JP said, slinging his arm around Mickie's shoulders. "It's the rest of these jokers who can screw off." He tugged Mickie along with him toward rows and rows of ready-to-pick apple trees. "Come on, I need a donut."

"Let's go, sis," Jagger said. He mimicked JP's move and rested his arm across the back of Ronnie's shoulders as they followed the laughing duo.

That left Keith trudging behind solo, which he didn't mind in the least. Gave him a chance to watch the way Mickie's ass flexed with each step in those skin-tight pants. How women moved in those things, he'd never know, but he was grateful for

it because they made stellar asses like Mickie's look out of his world.

Two hours later, they had bushels of apples, at least ten pumpkins, gourds, hay bales, and plenty of edible goodies packed into the back of Keith's truck. He'd made the mistake of asking why the hell they needed all this crap only to have his head bitten off by both Ronnie and Mickie, who informed him of the importance of something called *seasonal décor*.

After that, he'd shut his mouth and lugged whatever they'd handed to him to the truck. In reality, he'd had a blast. His siblings were goofballs and Mickie fit right in, climbing trees and laughing her ass off when JP accidentally grabbed rotten apple. He'd gotten a gooey mess all over his hands much to the hilarity of the rest of them.

Then there was that moment Mickie had climbed a little higher than she was comfortable with. Suddenly, the rest of his siblings were too busy to help, leaving him to spot her. He'd stood under her, watching her body flex and stretch as she reached for what she'd promised was the perfect apple. On the way down, her foot had slipped on a low branch. With a yelp, she'd half jumped, half fallen into him. He'd caught her with ease, lowering her to her feet. As she slid down his body, her pupils had widened with surprise and awareness. Her breath hitched and she clung to his biceps for support. Her scent, fresh and earthy from the afternoon outside wafted around him making it impossible to keep from getting hard. Luckily, he'd managed to pull his hips back before she got a very detailed demonstration of what being so close to her did. They'd stood, pressed together in their own bubble until Ronnie had yelled, "Hey, jackass, bring me a basket," to JP, breaking the dreamlike spell.

"Thanks," Mickie had whispered as she'd stepped out of his hold.

He'd stood there for a few moments thinking about oil changes and hoping the nippy air would calm his dick.

Now they were tired, stuffed full of sugary donuts, and their faces had numbed from the chill.

As Keith slammed the tailgate closed, Mickie let out a groan.

"Oh no, we forgot to check out the corn maze." Genuine disappointment bled through her voice. She gazed off in the direction of the maze with a crestfallen look. With reddened cheeks from being out so long, she looked fresh and damn adorable. At some point, she'd put on a wool cap, which his siblings had teased her about, but it only added to her fashion magazine style.

"Pfft," Ronnie said with a shake of her head. "I'm out. My legs are shot, and it'll be dark soon. I'm so not in the mood to get lost in the corn. I need a cold beer and a hot soak in the tub."

"Yeah, I'm out too, sorry, Mick. I got a sweet little treat waiting for me at home," JP added.

"What? You just ate like nine hundred donuts. How could you possibly want more?" The wrinkle in her nose had Keith wanting to kiss it smooth.

"He's not referring to food," Ronnie stage whispered. "He means a woman. He's got some date waiting for him to disappoint her."

"Excuse me, I've never disappointed a woman in my life," JP said with a laugh though he made no attempt to deny the fact he was meeting up with someone random for a little naked fun. He made a grab for Ronnie, who laughed as she jumped out of the way.

"Yeah, and I drove you and Ronnie, so…maybe we can come back another time," Jagger added.

"Oh, man. All right, next time." Mickie's shoulders slumped as she started toward Jagger's car.

Don't offer. Don't offer. It's a mistake.

"I've got nothing going on the rest of the evening. Why doesn't JP ride back with Jag and Ronnie, and I'll take you home? We can hit the maze before we leave."

And you did it.

"Really?" Her face lit up, which silenced his inner voice. Who could regret putting that happy sparkle in her eyes?

"Really."

"Oh, thank you!" She launched herself into his arms, and this time, there wasn't a hint of discomfort in the embrace. Hell, she squeezed so hard, she'd have made him yelp if he'd been Ronnie's size. Too bad for all the layers keeping him from experiencing the full press of her tits against him.

Ugh. He was such a perv. Kids mingled all around, and he wanted nothing more than to toss Mickie in the back of his truck and make her scream so loud the apples fell off the trees.

"Why are you so into this anyway?" he asked, hoping to distract himself from the image of her writhing in the bed of his pickup.

Still smiling, she shrugged. "Never done it before. Just excited to collect a new experience."

"Guess we'll see you around midnight after you finally find your way out of that thing," Ronnie said with a snort. She moved in to give Mickie then him a hug, and after saying goodbye to the rest, he was left alone with the woman who'd constantly invaded his mind the past three days.

Their gazes met and the air thickened with tension, even though they stood in the wide-open country. Shit. Maybe this had been a terrible idea. Remembering that they hadn't spoken since the night he fucked her stupid against the window of his shop might have been helpful two minutes ago before he ran his mouth about hanging out.

Alone.

After another thirty seconds of extremely awkward staring, Mickie seemed to shake off her discomfort. Her face brightened, and she held out a hand. "Shall we?"

A challenge. Could he be normal and enjoy their budding friendship or whatever the hell they were to each other without dissecting how they'd pounced on each other three nights ago? Or why she ran out afterward?

Well, far be it from him to turn down a dare. He threaded his fingers through hers and gritted his teeth to ignore the now familiar energy that accompanied her touch. "Lead the way."

Chapter Fifteen

Mickie didn't care about the corn maze. Not one single bit. Sure, she'd been curious when they'd first arrived as she'd never participated in something like this before, but she could have easily hopped in the car and headed back home. In fact, being as cold and tired as she was, she'd have preferred it.

So why was she trekking along on a narrow passageway between stalks of corn?

Well, that would be because of the sexy man with the rough yet gentle hand holding hers. Something had to give between them if she wanted to continue her friendship with his family, and she did. Since she'd moved to town, she'd assumed he couldn't stand her. Then they'd had a semi-bonding morning in her kitchen, then a terrifying encounter with his father resulting in insane sex, after which she'd run like a scared rabbit. So what did that make them now? Friends Neighbors? Acquaintances?

Hopefully, friends. Or if not, maybe spending some non-sexual hang-out time would get them there. She had no intention of delving into the reasons she'd hightailed it out of his garage without even getting her shoes all the way on. They needed to move forward as friends and forget what happened the other night.

That second part was easier said than done with the feel of his rough palm against hers. It only served to remind her of how his hands felt on her skin.

A shiver raced down her spine. Ugh, this had been a mistake. Why couldn't she have just driven home with Jagger?

Well, they were here to make nice; might as well work on it.

"Thanks for doing this with me," she said over her shoulder as the path narrowed. The tight quarters forced her to either release his hand or march on in an uncomfortable position. She missed the warmth as soon as he let go.

"No problem."

Calling the man chatty was like calling Henry Cavill ugly. Just wasn't true.

"I mean, this probably isn't your jam, right? You must have a million places you'd rather be than getting lost in a field of corn." She let out a nervous laugh. "With me."

What the hell was wrong with her? She had years, *years* of media training and could talk to literally anyone about anything. She could answer difficult, embarrassing, or ridiculous questions on the fly and redirect a conversation to any path she chose. Yet here she was, babbling like a moron to fill the heavy silence.

"Seriously, Mickie, it's fine," he said from behind her. "I like being here. Been coming every year since I was a kid."

"Yeah, Jagger mentioned your mom brought you guys here." They came to a fork in the road and stopped walking. Their eyes connected she nearly lost her breath at the intensity in his deep blue gaze. "She sounds wonderful."

With a sigh, he nodded. "She was. Any positive memory from my childhood came from her."

There was something there between them. Some connection that was harder and harder to resist the more she saw him. The draw she felt to him was almost tangible. Like her, he'd been wounded by life. The walls he'd build to keep himself from pain were much stronger than hers. But every time she chipped away even a little bit, she felt like she was flying. Part of her wanted to hold him tight and promise she'd never hurt him while another part of her wanted to spend days in a bed with him naked and hiding from the world.

"Hmm, left or right?" she finally said, turning away from the magnetic tug.

He scratched his beard as he looked left then right. The beard that'd been so soft against her skin a few nights ago when he'd—

Keep your head in the game!

"When in doubt, right it out?" he said with a shrug.

Mickie laughed. "Is that a thing?"

When he chuckled, her heart soared. Making him laugh or smile gave her such a thrill since he didn't seem to do either very often.

"If it gets us out of here, we can trademark it." When smiling, his mouth took on such a tempting shape. Everything about the man drew her. Dressed in an olive-green hoodie, jeans, and work boots, he shouldn't have given off such a sexy vibe, but it was the way he wore the clothes, not what he wore. The denim hugged his thick thighs and incredible ass while the sweatshirt stretched across his broad chest in a way that made her want to shove her hands under it and feel the warmth radiating off all those muscles.

The sun was beginning to set, and tall overhead floodlights came on, illuminating the maze. Many of the patrons had gone, leaving them surprisingly alone in the labyrinth. Along with the dipping sun came a quick drop in temperature.

Mickie shivered.

Keith picked up on it right away. "You too cold? Want my sweatshirt? It might fit under your jacket."

She tried not to look too much into the fact he seemed pretty in tune with her. Did she want to have his scent surrounding her? Hell yes, she did. But it would be a mistake because she'd probably lose her mind, jump him, and ride him like a wild stallion through this cornfield.

"Mickie?"

"What? Oh, uh no, I'm okay." She inhaled a deep breath of the fresh air. "I like it. The cold air here is so clean and invigorating."

He watched her out the side of his eyes. "No fresh air where you were?"

With a laugh, she shook her head. "No, actually. I lived in Southern California. Smog capital of the US." A flutter of nerves charged through her stomach. Though she'd mentioned California, saying Southern California narrowed it down more than she had before. But he seemed utterly oblivious to her actual identity, so she needed to chill out.

Keith shuddered. "Don't know how people live in busy cities. Too many people, buildings, and cars. Mostly people."

She laughed. When the man let down his guard, he made for great company. Sure, he'd never be the life of the party, but she'd been that person and lived with people like that for years. A more mellow vibe appealed to her more than she'd expected. Keith never felt the need to act *on* all the time, and in turn, she could relax and be herself around him. Or at least be the self she was becoming. Someone who appreciated the simpler things in life and woke each morning looking forward to the day ahead.

"Yeah, you're right about all of that," she said as she batted a wayward stalk away from her face. Every so often, their shoulders brushed, and a punch of awareness streaked through her core. She tried to ignore it, but each time it happened, she wanted more. "Now that I'm here, I can't imagine living in a city again. This is just so…peaceful, I guess." She hummed. "I don't even know what I'm trying to say. Just that I like it here."

The slightly narrowed-eyed look he gave her told her he didn't fully believe it, but whatever. She no longer cared whether people approved of her or what they thought of how she lived her second chance at life.

The path tightened again, so she took the lead. One of the stalks grew sideways, directly blocking the path. Mickie pushed it aside, stepped past then heard a *thwack*. "Oh, my God," she said as she spun in time to see Keith swatting the plant out of his face. The thing had hit him square in the nose.

Mickie pressed a hand over her mouth as she tried to muffle her giggle. "I'm so sorry," she said mumbled behind her hand. "I totally didn't mean to do that."

Instead of getting pissed as she'd have expected, Keith's eyes sparkled with mischief. "Yeah, you sound really torn up about it."

After another round of giggles, this time without even pretending to hide her immense amusement, she walked closer to him. Reaching up a hand, she paused before touching his hair. "You have…" —more snickers— "You have some leaves in your hair."

He mock scowled. "Guess you're gonna have to get 'em out then, huh?" His eyes held a challenge that heated her blood and made her want to press her legs together to relieve the sudden ache.

Swallowing, Mickie gave herself a fraction of a second to take him in before she removed the foliage. The tip of his nose had reddened from the rapidly cooling evening air. Her own cheeks tingled and practically begged her to lean in and rub against the neatly trimmed dark beard that gave him such a roguish look. After clearing her throat, she reached a hand up and sifted her fingers through his hair. At the feel of the silky strands sliding along her palm, she nearly groaned.

The urge to curl her fingers into a tight grip and pull his mouth to hers struck her so hard, she staggered back. "All better," she croaked.

Keith caught her hand. Time seemed to stand still though the world kept on spinning. "Thanks," he said, voice rough, as he lifted her hand and pressed a kiss to her fingers. The warmth of his mouth on her frigid digits sent a shiver of delight down her spine. The man was far too sexy for his own good, and if he kept up the gentleman routine, she'd cave and beg for a repeat of the other night.

With a gentle tug, she pried her hand away. "Guess we better keep moving if we want to be out of here by midnight." She peeked at her phone. "Uh, doesn't the maze close at seven?"

"Yeah, why?"

Holding up her phone with a grimace, she said, "It's seven fifteen."

"Well, fuck."

They began navigating their way again. "Do you think they've ever left anyone in here overnight?" she asked.

His tight laughter floated over her shoulder, making her realize she wasn't the only one affected by their nearness. She risked a glance back in time to see him take a deep breath as though in attempt to calm himself.

"Pretty sure they'll send someone through at some point to catch any stragglers." His voice had roughened, and she swore she could almost feel it caressing her skin. "Hopefully we'll get out before then."

"Oh, look. Over there." Swallowing around a thickened throat, she pointed to an opening in the maze. "I think we found the exit! Damn, we're good." She glanced over her shoulder at him with a grin that had to be cheesy, but she didn't care. These kinds of clear-headed experiences were entirely new to her, and she was having a blast.

Mickie picked up her pace and hustled to the break in the corn stalks. As she burst through, she said, "Who knew I'd be so good at—uh oh."

Keith slammed into her back as she stopped dead in her tracks. "Uh, sorry." He grabbed her shoulders to keep her from flying forward. Even that almost dispassionate touch had her nerve endings tingling.

"What's wrong?" After a quick look around, he groaned. "Oh fuck."

Mickie couldn't help it. She began laughing. It grew and grew until she was doubled over with a cramp in her stomach. Somehow it appeared they'd found a random opening in the maze and ended up on the opposite side of where they were supposed to exit. As large, open field stretched dark and as far as the eye could see.

That'd teach her to be brag about her navigation skills.

KEITH WAS COLD, hungry, tired, the sun was setting, and they were lost as fuck. Were he with anyone else, he'd have been grumpy and bordering on hangry. But Mickie's laughter and lighthearted acceptance of their screwed-up situation had him not caring one bit about any of those irritants. In fact, he was having fun.

Having fun with the rich woman who didn't bitch about being cold, was thrilled to tromp through a goddammed cornfield, and who acted like their sleepy little town was a hidden paradise.

Who on earth was this woman, and why did she appeal to him so much when her type typically had him running in the opposite direction? Maybe it was the eager way she soaked up new experiences. Or the way he respected her fight to gain control of her life. Or the bond they shared, both having had their lives negatively affected by the loss of a mother at a young age. Whatever it was, he wanted Mickie for more what was beneath her clothing.

"Okay," she said, straightening after a solid few minutes of hilarity during which he took the time to get his bearings. "I have control of myself now."

He smirked. What a loaded statement considering the way they'd both thrown control out the window the other night.

Her cheeks grew even pinker, and she slapped his shoulder. "You know what I mean. I'm done laughing and ready to head back in there and figure out where we went wrong. Do you think we're directly on the other side of the maze?"

Nodding, he scratched his beard. At least he had the hair to keep his face warm. Mickie had to be freezing. "That's exactly what I think, and we're probably better off just walking the perimeter instead of getting lost in there again."

Mickie pouted. "Oh, come on, party pooper. Where's your sense of adventure?" Her eyes twinkled and lips twitched with delight.

He raised an eyebrow. "Seriously? You want to go back in there and hike around until we collapse from hunger and dehydration or freeze to death?"

With a laugh, she shook her head, sending her hair swirling around her face. "Hell, no. I was just messing with you. Perimeter walk sounds good to me, followed by a greasy cheeseburger and fries. My treat since I dragged you in here. You game?"

He was unable to do anything but stare at her. She had to be even colder than he was and just as hungry, but her good mood remained, and she even appeared to be having fun.

Guess that made two of them.

"Hello, Keith? Did your brain freeze?" She patted his cheeks then let out a little moan. "Oh, your face is warm. How is that even possible?" Now she was practically petting him, rubbing her hands over his beard, which instantly made his cock hard. It'd been halfway there since she removed the leaves from his hair, but now it throbbed. If this went on much longer, the constriction in his jeans would make it impossible to walk.

Before he gave his brain a chance to remind him how stupid this was, he grabbed her upper arms and yanked her close, crushing his mouth to hers.

She let out a surprised little squeak before sinking into the kiss with as much enthusiasm as he did. Her lips were icy cold against his, as was her nose, but her tongue was warm, and the contrast had him delving even deeper into her mouth. She tasted sweet and fresh as though she'd been popping mints, but it was merely the clean air and time outdoors combined with the sugary apple donuts.

In a bold move, Mickie sucked on his tongue, moaned, and then pressed against him. He punched his hips forward, letting her feel his hardness and giving her no doubt as to what he wanted from her.

When she arched into him, he ripped his mouth away. "Get on the ground," he ordered around his labored breath.

She was huffing and puffing as well. A sly smile curled her lips. "Right here? On this dusty farm ground?" she asked, indicating the half-dirty, half-straw ground beneath their feet.

His cock pulsed in time with his rapidly beating heart. "I know you now, Mickie. You can't pretend you don't like it a little dirty."

Though the temperature continued to drop, he yanked his sweatshirt over his head then spread it on the ground. "M'lady,' he said, indicating her makeshift blanket.

"Romantic," she said with a wink, but her voice had thickened with desire. She was right there with him, wanting this as much as he did. Slowly, she lowered herself down to his sweatshirt. With her knees bent, she propped herself up in her elbows and gave him the sexiest come hither look he'd ever seen. Even with layers of clothing and a damn wool hat, the woman was so effortlessly sexy, he couldn't stand it.

After doing one last quick scan of their surroundings, he was satisfied they were alone, and he lowered to his knees between her spread thighs.

"Get those pants off."

With her smoldering gaze on him, she did as asked, taking her sweet time. It was fucking torture and foreplay all at the same time. His cock grew with every wiggle of her hips as she worked the leggings over her ass. He flicked his button open and lowered the fly just to give him some relief.

"Bridge up," he ordered in guttural rasp.

Again, she did as he commanded. He took over, tugging the pants over her curvy hips, taking her panties with them. This wasn't the time to admire what he had no doubt was sexy and expensive lingerie.

That could come next time.

Next time. Jesus, he'd lost his damn mind.

The pants got stuck at her ankles since neither of them thought to remove her boots. Laughing together, she tried to lift a foot.

"Don't bother," he said as he shoved it back down. She cocked an eyebrow that made his cock twitch. He swore every damn thing this woman did revved his engine. "Not sure I can wait until we get out of here. I'm hungry now," he said as he settled on his stomach between her butterflied thighs, lying right overtop her boot-covered feet and bunched leggings.

"Oh fuck," she whispered.

"Once I'm satisfied, we can get going again. That work for you?"

Her head bobbed up and down so fast he'd have laughed if there was enough blood in his body to power anything besides his needy dick.

"Cold?"

"Hell, no," she whispered. "I'm burning up."

Damn, so was he.

She stayed on her elbows, watching him intently as he leaned in and inhaled.

The scent of her mixed with the fresh fall air, going straight to his head. "Christ," he murmured, "even your pussy smells fancy."

Mickie laughed then let out a loud gasp as he licked her inner thigh.

"You're wet for me," he said as her flavor hit his tongue. She was so soaked he hadn't needed direct contact with her sex to taste her. He repeated the move on the other side, and her inner thigh trembled beneath his wandering tongue.

"Keith," she whispered, eyes imploring. "Please."

"Begging already? Someone needs it bad, huh?"

She nodded.

"I was right, wasn't I?"

"W-what?" she asked.

"You like it like this. Outside, where someone might hear us, see us. Spontaneous. Hot as fuck."

"Yes," she rasped. "Yes, I love it like this. Now put your mouth on me."

He didn't bother responding, just nipped her thigh then, before she had time to react, licked a circle around her clit.

She gasped and arched up into his hungry mouth. "Yes."

He did it again and again until her arms shook, then he sucked her clit between his lips. She lost the battle to remain up and flopped back onto the ground with a low moan. Her hand immediately found his hair, fisting the strands with a firm grip. Then she canted her hips, lining her pussy up with his mouth.

The woman was not shy during sex, and he fucking loved it. There was no point in dragging this out by denying her what she wanted, so he rimmed her opening with his tongue a few times then shoved it in her pussy. She shrieked and rocked her hips against his face, still holding him right where she wanted him.

He fucked her with his tongue as she mewled and thrashed on the ground for long minutes.

Every sound she made, every tug to his hair, every pant had his cock leaking and dampening the front of his boxer briefs. He was headed straight for coming in his pants like a honey teenager.

"Shit, Keith, I'm close," she wailed a few seconds later. "Lick my clit. God, please lick my clit."

He did as asked and thrust two fingers inside her at the same time. With a sharp cry, she detonated like tripped mine. Her pussy doused his fingers. Her taste flooded his senses, and her grip on his hair grew punishing, but only served to turn him on even more.

Eventually, she sagged into the ground, limp and sated. Her grip on his hair slackened and she patted the top of his head. "Sorry."

He chuckled. "I'm sure as fuck not."

Her giggle was weak, tired. "Give me a minute, and I will return that favor."

God, he laughed more with her than anyone. As he rose to his knees and off her splayed legs, she straightened her knees. Keith straddled her thighs as he reached in his navy boxer briefs to pulled out his slick cock. Her gaze followed his hand as it wrapped around his length and stroked. "Not necessary." His dick was so hard, it nearly shot off from one pump.

Her sleepy eyes flared, and she cursed. Her sweater had ridden up during her trashing, exposing a creamy white stomach. Keith tilted his head in a silent request for permission.

Mickie nodded. "Do it," she whispered before hiking her sweater up the rest of the way, taking her bra with it. As soon as her gorgeous tits were revealed, he sped up his hand, jerking himself at a furious pace.

"Fuck, Michaela, you're so goddammed stunning." Somehow the hat stayed on her head. He had no idea why, but he fucking loved the sight of her half dressed for the outdoors and half bare to him.

She played with her pointed nipples as she stared at him, working himself over. "Pretty sure I'm the one with the better view right now."

He snorted. "Fuck no. You playing with those tits beats anything." Fuck, he wasn't going to last long. Already, his balls felt heavy and full with the need to come. They grew tighter with each passing second. His stomach muscles coiled in a familiar warning.

Her grin turned positively wicked. "Well, it sure seems to be helping you *beat* it." He threw back his head and laughed as he tugged his cock with rough pulls. Even her jokes made him want to blow his load all over her.

That was all it took.

The split-second mental image of her covered in his cum had him coming in a blinding rush. He emptied all over her stomach, coating her in white. Fuck if it wasn't even sexier than he'd imagined it would be. He wanted her to spread it all around, rubbing every drop into her skin, but it was now cold as fuck, and they needed to get dressed and back to the car before someone discovered them.

"Jesus," he whispered when his body finally settled. He fell forward, catching himself with one hand next to her shoulder. "You are a dangerous woman."

Her smile faltered for such a small wink of time he wasn't even sure he'd seen it. But then she bucked her hips up with a laugh. "Up you go, cowboy. This is getting really cold really fast."

He stood then extended a hand for her, lifting her to her feet when she grabbed on. Once she was up, he snagged his sweatshirt off the ground, used it to clean up her stomach, and righted her pants for her. After she was as covered and warm as possible, he tucked his spent cock back in his underwear, did up his pants, and tucked the come-stained sweatshirt under his arm.

"To answer your question, a burger sounds fucking perfect right about now. I know just the place."

She placed her chilly hand in his with a squeeze. He held it tight to provide as much warmth as possible. Together, they made their way around the exterior of the corn maze, chatting and laughing about random nonsense.

Keith did his best to ignore that this didn't feel anything like an illicit hook-up but a perfect date with a fascinating woman.

Chapter Sixteen

Keith stood third in line at the local coffee shop he'd been frequenting since the first time he'd cashed a paycheck. Somehow, their small town managed to keep the big-name coffee chains from setting up shop, allowing the little café to thrive. They served everything those pricy chain shops did, plus an array of delicious and waist-expanding pastries baked fresh every day. Townsfolk gathered every morning for their daily jolt of caffeine and a chat with their friends.

This morning he was on a java and breakfast run for himself and JP, who'd agreed to lend a hand at the garage again. Maybe someday, the second youngest Benson would get serious about his life and find a real job. For now, he was more than happy bouncing around from family business to family business, lending a hand where necessary. He also worked around town as a handyman. He never seemed short on cash between all the random jobs, and the atypical schedule worked for him. Would a day ever come where JP would be forced to grow up and act his age and find steady employment? Who the hell knew? With that guy's luck, he'd skate by without ever officially being on anyone's payroll.

As he waited for his turn to order, Keith's gaze drifted around the eclectic, hipster-style café. Not more than three seconds into his inspection, his gaze landed on a woman sitting alone at a table with her attention riveted to her laptop.

Michaela.

She wore stylish sweatpants—Ronnie had called them joggers or something—with an oversized sweatshirt that also managed to look chic and stylish instead of sloppy. The woman could make a Mumu look like high fashion. As usual, her short hair was smoothed to perfection, framing her gorgeous face. Then there were those dark-rimmed glasses giving him all kinds of naughty thoughts. His favorite fantasy consisted of her riding him wearing nothing but those glasses.

Christ, if he wasn't careful, he'd be rocking a full-blown stiffy by the time he stepped up to the counter. Good way to give the sixteen-year-old barista a lifetime of nightmares.

Mickie lifted what appeared to be a cinnamon sugar cruller to her un-glossed mouth without tearing her gaze from the screen. She took a giant bite. Of course, the freakin' sugar got stuck to her lips, which she licked in the most unconsciously erotic move Keith had ever seen. Without meaning to, he groaned.

Laughter from behind him had his spine stiffening and his dick deflating. He knew that fucking laugh, half cackle, half smug guffaw.

Fucking Chuck.

Despite knowing better, he glanced over his shoulder. Sure enough, the one person he hated above all stood right behind him in his uniform from where he worked as a manager the logging company.

Keith didn't bother acknowledging Chuck's irritating presence. Instead, he turned back and took a step forward, now one customer closer to much-needed caffeination.

"Oh, this brings back memories," Chuck whispered way too close to Keith's ear.

Giving in would be a mistake, but what the hell. "Oh yeah? You have a lot of good times waiting for coffee?" If he ignored

Chuck, the asshole would likely get louder. They'd have curious customers staring at them in no time.

"Nah, I'm talking about you and me both looking at the same beautiful woman." His crooked front teeth begged for a rearranging.

Keith was more than happy to provide the first to knock them back into place. "Don't know what you're talking about." He went for as bored a tone as he could muster. If the line didn't get moving, Chuck would be in danger of needing a straw to drink his coffee. This barista had to be the slowest employee in the café's history.

"Sure you do. Your rich neighbor over there. Heard she's spending a mint renovating her house," Chuck whispered at Keith's ear.

Goddammed small-town gossip.

"I see you drooling over her the same way you slobbered all over Della. Huh, maybe I'll make a pass as this one. See if she chooses me over you same as Della did."

Twenty years later, Chuck still couldn't let Keith live his humiliating high school heartbreak down. Had he known at the time Della was only with him to punish Chuck, Keith wouldn't have touched her with a ten-foot pole. Chuck had been brutal to him while Keith had been dating Della. Once she dumped him in an embarrassing display, Keith had assumed the taunts would stop, but Chuck loved nothing more than reminding Keith the well-off girl had left him because of his low-class family.

"But maybe she has a thing for white trash. Then you'd be perfect for her. They don't make 'em trashier than you Bensons."

Don't take the bait.

"Bitch like that?" Chuck continued as though Keith had encouraged him. "Bet she's a wild one in the sack. All classy on the outside, total freak once she's near a dick."

Keith gritted his teeth and willed the customer in front of him to stop adding to his enormous order. Though Keith would never describe Mickie in such crude terms, Chuck's words hit a little too close to home considering the nature of their two sexual encounters. She'd been hotter than hell and adventurous once the expensive clothes came off.

Fucking finally, the customer handed over his credit card. Keith let out a sigh of relief until the goddammed card reader beeped with an error message.

For fuck's sake.

"She's got great tits, too. Maybe I'll go have a chat with her. See if she's in the mood for some quality dick. If it turns out she's a white trash freak, I'll pass her your way."

Growing up, Keith's family had been one of the shittiest in town. That wasn't a secret to anyone who'd lived there for more than a few years. But he had worked his ass off to not only lift his siblings out of the poverty in which they grew up but to change the town's perception of the Benson name. For the most part, it'd worked. While none of them would ever own private jets or vacation in penthouses of five-star resorts, they were comfortable enough to enjoy their lives and even indulge in the occasional splurge.

But memories ran deep, and with his father still alive and causing frequent disturbances in town, the Benson name still carried the stigma of junkie, white trash, and loser in some circles.

Chuck made a low-pitched obscene sound. "Bet she takes my monster cock like a fucking pro—"

Okay, fuck it. Just as Keith was about to let his baser instincts take over and grab Chuck by the neck, shaking until his face turned blue and he passed out, Chuck's phone chimed. Keith still refused to turn and give the man any more of his attention than he'd already received.

"Dammit," Chuck cursed, then he stepped out of line. He jammed the phone to his ear and strode out of the shop, barking at whatever poor schmuck was on the other end.

"Hey, Keith. Sorry for the wait. What can I get you today?" the perky barista asked, wrenching Keith's gaze from Chuck's retreating form.

After ordering two vats of coffee and a host of pastries, he stepped aside to wait for the barista to call his name. He tried to keep his gaze from drifting back Michaela's way but failed after about ten seconds.

She was by far the most appealing person in the entire café.

"Keith!" the barista called after a few moments.

A quick and final glance at Mickie revealed she was so in the zone, she hadn't so much as reacted to the shouting of his name in the relatively quiet café.

"Thanks," he said to the barista before shoving a few singles in the tip jar. Then he scooped up his purchases and started for the door to head straight outside to his waiting truck.

His feet had other ideas, though. Before he made it to the door, he found himself standing next to the table occupied by the woman he'd eaten out four days ago and hadn't seen since. Hadn't seen her, but he'd sure as hell thought about her. She'd entered his mind at least once an hour since that night.

"Hey," he said in a stunning display of communicative skills.

Mickie jolted then looked up from her laptop. Immediately her face broke out into a wide smile. "Keith, hi! Sorry, I was totally focused. Hope you weren't standing there long."

"Nope. Not at all."

As though she just recalled what they'd done the last time they were together, her cheeks turned pink.

God, he loved making her face flush.

"Um, want to sit?"

No. He definitely should not sit. He should say goodbye and continue on to work.

"Sure, I have a few minutes." Since when did he not have control over his tongue?

Since a brown-haired beauty popped up in his town and turned everything upside down.

"Great." She motioned to the empty seat across from her.

He slid into the chair as she shut her laptop, making it easier to see each other. "What are you doing out so early?" he asked as he set the coffees and bag of pastries on the table between them as though they'd serve as some kind of barrier.

Rolling her eyes, Mickie sighed. "Ugh, construction on my kitchen is fully underway and very loud. I've been trying to stay away as much as possible the past two days."

"Oh, that's right. Jag mentioned things were moving along nicely."

She beamed. "Yes, they finished demo yesterday, and I think he's called in a few favors to have cabinets and countertops delivered quicker than usual. They'll be in sometime next week as will the appliances. This whole process will be completed way earlier than I expected."

"That's great." Jagger did quality work. Her kitchen would be a masterpiece once the reno finished. He sipped his coffee. God, that was good stuff, though not nearly as good as what he'd had the other night in the cornfield.

Silence fell between them, thick with unspoken words and the usual desire.

Christ, stopping by to chat had been a mistake. What the hell was he supposed to say to her now?

He wanted more. More of what they'd done in his lobby. More of what they'd done at the corn maze. More of her screams, more of her sighs, more of her hands and mouth.

But he didn't want to get tangled up in a woman. Especially not one who seemed to have oodles of money, more class than an entire school, and was a recovering drug addict. As fun as Mickie was, she wasn't for him in the long term. Even fucking Chuck saw the writing on the wall.

So why the hell was he so drawn to her when she couldn't be more wrong for him?

COULD THIS GET any more awkward?

Mickie cleared her throat.

Say something.

Whether the plea was to herself or a mental one to Keith, she wasn't sure.

A few more agonizing seconds passed where they each sipped their coffee to keep their hands and mouths busy.

She'd been wrapping up a text check-in with her therapist when he'd popped up next to her table. Maybe she should get her counselor back and ask for some advice on how to talk to a man she wanted.

As though she were a teenager.

Ugh.

How was it possible for a man to be so attractive in a pair of worn jeans and a charcoal hoodie? Of course, the dark beard, deep blue eyes, and peek-a-boo glimpses of tattoos at his neckline didn't hurt.

And those full lips, those long skilled fingers…

Okay, clearly, she wanted more of the man. The two times they'd been together had only stoked the flame of desire she'd experienced the moment she laid eyes on him on that dark road weeks ago.

But they hadn't spoken in days, and he was one of the hardest people to read. His face never gave away his thoughts, and his mouth stayed firmly shut most of the time.

Though he sure knew when it was time to put it to good use.

Ugh, there she went again, fantasizing about the maddening man as she'd done a million times over the past four days. She'd never admit how many times she'd picked up the phone to call or text him only to chicken out. She didn't know how to do this. In the past, men had flocked to her whenever she blinked. Though she may not be proud of it, it was certainly easier than this messy uncertainty and emotional entanglement.

As she frowned down at her coffee, a thought hit her. Michaela Hudson wasn't a shrinking violet. Hell, she could work a room of celebrities and press blindfolded and gagged. Why the hell was she acting like a shy schoolgirl afraid to ask for what she wanted? They were adults who enjoyed having sex with each other. Why the hell shouldn't she ask for more and dictate the terms? Hell, even if only fuck buddies, it'd be the healthiest relationship she'd had in, well, ever.

"Well, I'd better get going," he said at the same time she blurted, "I want to talk about what happened the other night."

Not the smoothest, but she got her point across.

Keith sighed in that classic way men did when relationship conversations were on the table, as if they'd rather be in a dentist's chair getting drilled without anesthesia. Instead of waiting for whatever mansplaining he was about to engage in, she forged ahead. "I want more of what happened the last two times we were together."

His deer-in-the-headlights expression made her laugh. "For crying out loud, Keith, this is not a profession of love." She glanced at the nearby tables then leaned in as she lowered her voice. "I want us to keep fucking." Best to keep this on strictly physical terms. "You can't tell me we aren't good together," she whispered.

Before her eyes, he visibly relaxed.

"Good? Pretty sure we almost set that cornfield on fire."

Her face heated but not with embarrassment. Pure, hot lust shot through her. "Yeah," she managed as her throat thickened.

"And you want more of it?" He shifted the disposable coffee mug between his hands on the table.

"I do. Look, I'm not in any position to start a relationship. I just moved, I'm working on finding a new career path, I'm renovating my house, and I'm—" She cleared her throat as she averted her eyes. "I'm recovering from some things. All I'm looking for right now is friendship."

"And fucking?" His lips quirked.

"Right." She shrugged. "I mean, a girl has needs. Before you, it'd been a while for me. Batteries can only get you so far, ya know? Sometimes, you just need a real-life man."

"So you want this because I'm a flesh and blood man, and you're sick of BOB?"

A loud laugh bubbled out of her, drawing the attention of patrons at neighboring tables. She slapped a hand over her mouth as she continued to laugh. "First off, I'm impressed that you know about battery-operated boyfriends. Second, no, it's not only because you're a flesh and blood man." She shrugged. "I like you, Keith."

When his eyes narrowed, she held up a hand. "Don't go freaking out. I just mean I like you. That's all. I've done the random hookups in the past, and even though I'm not interested in a relationship, I don't want random. I want someone who I can laugh with and talk to as well as sleep with. I want someone whose company I can enjoy." Okay, maybe that sounded like a bit like a relationship, but she really didn't want one.

Nope.

That was her story, and she was sticking to it.

He seemed to consider her words, remaining silent as he sipped his coffee. "Well, I've got a sister who claims BOB treats her better than any man ever has, so that's how I know about that," he said with an exaggerated shudder. Then he grinned, and her stomach flipped. "And I'm down with this arrangement. Friends and fucking. Sounds like a pretty damn perfect setup to me."

And just to keep the denial of her real feelings going strong, that wasn't disappointment she felt at his easy acceptance of no strings. "One more thing."

He tilted his head as he waited for her condition.

"Just us. No one else."

Those sexy lips of his turned down into a dramatic pout. "Well, that sucks. Guess I'll have to cancel the threesome I had planned. Figured it'd be right up your alley, but—"

Blood rushed in her ears. Her heart pounded so fast the room spun, and she had to grab the edge of the table to keep from tumbling off her chair. Oh fuck. He knew. He knew who she was. Knew she'd been splashed all over social media for having woken up in bed with two men she didn't know or remember on that fateful day all those months ago.

Her stomach clenched. She was going to be sick.

"Mickie?" Keith shot out of his chair and came around to her side of the table. His big hand landed on her back, jolting her out of her trance. "Shit, you okay? I was just joking. Damnit, I'm sorry if I crossed a line."

A joke.

He was joking.

Of course, he was joking. Keith hadn't given any indication that he had any idea who she was, and even if he did, he sure as hell didn't seem to follow entertainment news and probably wouldn't know what happened the day her entire life crashed around her.

The day she had a heart attack that nearly killed her before her thirtieth birthday.

The hot burn of shame rushed to her cheeks as she noticed other customers staring at her with concern. Clearing her throat, she shook her head. "Sorry. I'm fine. Just got dizzy there for a second." Summoning up every ounce of her acting skills, she smiled and forced a laugh. "Too much coffee and not nearly enough sleep, I think."

Though he didn't look convinced, Keith returned to his seat. "If you're sure you're okay."

"I'm great." And she was. Now that she'd asked for what she wanted, fun nights awaited them.

Somehow, she had to learn to stop expecting someone to out her at any time. It was proving a difficult habit to break, but perhaps putting a bit of trust into Keith was the first step. "Uh, so I can't offer to make you dinner since my kitchen is in shambles, but I can certainly order delivery if you're up for dinner tonight."

He smirked. "You asking me to Netflix and chill?"

Now that the momentary panic had passed, Mickie could breathe and fell back into the fun and flirty banter they'd seemed to develop. "That just sounds wrong coming from you. But yes, that's exactly what I'm asking. As friends, of course."

His darkening, lust-filled eyes were all the answer she needed. Rising from his chair, Keith picked up the two coffees and paper bag filled with something that smelled delicious. She had to tilt her chin up to meet his gaze.

"I'll swing by around seven. Order anything. I'm easy."

"Hmm," she said as she admired the ease with which he carried himself. "That bodes well for me."

He snorted out a laugh that almost had him dropping his coffee.

After saying goodbye, Keith walked two steps away from the table. As her gaze fell to his ass, he turned back to her. "Oh, make sure you wear those glasses. I'm kinda obsessed with them." Then he winked and continued to the exit.

Mickie didn't even pretend she wasn't staring at that stellar ass with each step he took. She'd be getting her hands on that for sure tonight, maybe gripping it tightly as he thrust into her. Leaving imprints of her fingernails on his ass suddenly became the number one goal of her day.

Practically giddy with excitement, Mickie polished off her coffee and cruller as she tried to dive back into what she'd been doing before Keith arrived. Turned out, choosing hardware for her cabinets wasn't as captivating as fantasizing about the night to come.

So she gave up and let her mind wander.

This arrangement they'd agreed on would be perfect as long as she kept her heart out of the game, which should be easy enough. It'd never gotten involved before.

And as long as no one discovered who she was, which was the more worrisome task. So troublesome, she spent at least an hour before falling asleep at night replaying each encounter of the day and wondering if someone had discovered her secret.

Chapter Seventeen

"So, I'm a baseball fan, but will I be voted off the island if I admit I've never sat through an entire football game?" Mickie cringed as she awaited their shocked responses.

Ronnie's mouth fell open. "Get the fuck outta here." She wore a Patriots jersey and had her long dark hair in a ponytail high on her head. As usual, her face was makeup-free and flawless.

Seated beside her on the plush couch, Jagger just snorted. "Nah," he said, gently elbowing her side. "But you will get a ton of side-eye if you interrupt every few seconds with questions."

Laughing, she said, "Message received. I'll just cheer when you do so everyone thinks I get it."

Jagger also had a Patriots shirt on, which tickled her to no end. There they were in the comfort of their own home wearing their team's name as though someone on the team would see it. "There ya go." He ruffled her hair like she was his kid sister.

Keith came to her rescue, nudging—okay kicking, Jagger's legs. "Get your puny body away from my woman."

With a grunt, Jagger flipped his brother off, but moved over so Keith could take the spot next to her.

My woman.

The two little words sent a thrill straight to her heart. And between her legs. Mickie did internal backflips at the claiming.

For the past month, their friends with benefits had led to plenty of hot, steamy nights. What she hadn't expected was all the incredible mornings where they woke up together. In recent weeks, they'd spent nearly every minute of their spare time together yet hadn't defined their relationship further than they had that day in the café.

A few times now, she'd tried to broach the subject of what they were without seeming like a cliched needy woman, but either she'd chickened out, or he'd evaded the conversation with surprising skill. She'd meant what she said when they began this…whatever it was. A full-blown relationship wasn't on her radar. But now that they were a month deep and couldn't seem to make a full day without seeing each other, things had changed. They could pretend all they wanted, but the arrangement was more than friends who had naked sleepovers. And she loved it. She loved every second of spending time with Keith and the friendships she'd developed with his siblings.

She was in deep water and terrified to rock to the boat.

Keith dropped down on the couch next to her and handed over the Diet Dr. Pepper now always on hand in their fridge. It'd become her drink of choice since alcohol no longer provided the majority of her hydration. "Here, babe."

Smiling broadly on the outside, which still didn't match the magnitude of her internal smile, she took the offered beverage. "Thanks." Would it be a setback for all womenkind if she admitted she loved when he called her babe?

He twisted the top on his soda then settled back on the couch with his arm around her shoulders. As though she belonged there, Mickie snuggled into his side.

"Keith," she whispered, so hopefully Jagger wouldn't hear. "Please don't feel like you can't have few beers when I'm here." Her face heated. They hadn't spoken about her alcoholism. She couldn't explain it without delving into the rest of her messy past. The thought of sharing everything had stark fear tearing through her every time the notion entered her mind. Which was frequently these days.

Keeping her true identity—for lack of a less dramatic description—secret from the people who'd come to mean the world to her had guilt gnawing at her stomach daily.

Keith cupped the back of her head with his large hand, making it so she couldn't turn away from the heat of his intense gaze. "I know. I'm good with soda."

She traced the Patriots' logo on his T-shirt. "No, I know. I just mean that I don't want you to change your normal behavior because I'm hanging around. Just do what you would do any other time you watched the game."

His lips curled up in the rare smile that made her chest flutter wildly. The man melted her heart and her panties without even trying. "This been stressing you out?" He kept his voice low as well.

If Jagger and Ronnie overheard, they kindly pretended to be oblivious, ragging each other and paying her and Keith no mind.

She shrugged. "A bit. I just noticed you don't ever drink when I'm around, even if your siblings are."

"We all have a few on occasion, but none of us are big drinkers. Result of our upbringing."

Another topic they steered clear of. Nodding, she said, "That makes sense. I just want to make sure you know you don't have to do anything special because I'm here."

He ran a finger down her cheek. Though embarrassed, she couldn't tear herself from the intensity of his gaze. She felt like a schoolgirl, giddy and excited every time she was near him. Totally ensnared in his world.

"Well, you're pretty damn special, so everything I do when you're here falls under that category."

Once in a while, he spoke to her with such sweetness she felt she wasn't the only one who wanted more than their current arrangement. Maybe it was only her imagination, but those moments had her spinning wild fairy tales in her head of happily ever after. But they always died a quick death when she remembered who she was and the secrets she kept. "Thank you," she whispered as her throat constricted.

He kissed her. A deep, passionate kiss typically reserved for private moments. His hand cupped the back of her head, holding it in place as he ravaged her mouth. Within seconds, she almost forgot they weren't alone. The urge to rip off his clothes, straddle him on the couch, and ride him to bliss was nearly impossible to ignore. When his hands and mouth were on her, she never wanted it to end.

"Switch seats with me, Ronnie," Jagger said on a groan. "I'm not sitting next to this shit all game."

With a tiny growl, Keith ended the kiss. Heat rushed to Mickie's face as she settled under his arm once again.

Ronnie snorted from her spot in an overstuffed chair, lounging with her legs dangling over the armrest. "Hell no. I was here first. You snooze, you lose, buddy."

"I wasn't snoozing. I was in the kitchen getting you a drink."

With an unrepentant smirk, Ronnie lifted her beer. "And I thank you for it. This is good stuff."

Jagger flopped back on the couch, grumbling about being stuck next to the horny teenagers.

With a barely repressed laugh, Mickie said, "Sorry, Jagger. We'll behave."

Keith grunted. "Don't apologize to him. If we wanna make out all game, he's gonna hafta deal."

"You know," Jagger said as he kicked his legs up on the coffee table. "I think a man who's getting laid regularly is supposed to be less of an asshole. You sure you know what you're doing, Mickie?"

"Hey!" Keith shouted as he whacked Jagger's chest with the back of his hand. "Show some respect."

Jagger had the good graces to grimace. "Sorry, Mickie. I'm sure you're a rockstar in the sack. Didn't mean to imply otherwise. Keith is just a grumpy butthead no matter what."

The man in question let his head drop back on the couch as he groaned.

Mickie couldn't help it, she burst out laughing. Nothing about what Jagger said came close to offending her. Seven months ago, if anyone had told her she'd be lounging in Vermont watching football with three siblings who ribbed each other constantly, and happier than she'd ever been, she'd have called them crazy.

Glitz, glam, spotlights.

That's what her life had been about and what she'd thought she wanted. Not this slower-paced, simple pleasures living she'd fallen in love with. She didn't miss Hollywood or acting at all. She didn't miss the fame, glamour, or even exhilaration of it. Here, she'd found acceptance and friendship by just being herself.

If only she felt confident enough to let people know who that self was.

"I don't know, Jagger," she said as an impish impulse overtook her. "Maybe you should shield your eyes, and I'll see if I can put a smile on his face for you."

Keith's eyes lit up. "Now there's an idea I can get behind." He turned toward her just as JP burst into the room.

"Did I miss kick-off?" he asked around a mouthful of chips. He had a six-pack of beer tucked under one arm and a bowl full of tortilla chips in the other hand. Eyeing her and Keith, he scowled. "You two aren't planning to be schmoopy all game, are you?"

"I'm not fucking schmoopy," Keith grumbled. "Jesus, you guys are annoying."

"Don't worry," she purred in his ear, not bothering to whisper this time. "There are still plenty of hours for fun after the game is over."

He groaned. "You're as bad as they are. Trying to kill me before the game starts."

A tsking noise came from JP. "Death by blue balls. That's rough, brother." He winked at her. "Not that I would know. Mine get drained on the regular."

"Oh, gag me." Ronnie tossed a pillow at JP.

"Huh, that's what my date said last—"

"La, la, la." Ronnie stuck her fingers in her ears. "Please don't finish that sentence. I'll puke."

Their banter went on for the next few minutes. Keith and Jagger joined in of course, ripping on JP for being a "man-slut." Mickie sat back and observed it with an amused smile.

As the game began, she snuggled next to Keith. The first two quarters passed by much as she'd expected, with the three Bensons verbally sparring back and forth. All of them stuffed their faces with chips, pizza, and wings. Not surprisingly, Mickie had no clue what was happening on the TV, but the three of them kept her so entertained with their banter, it didn't matter. By the time the second quarter came to an end, her stomach ached from laughing, and she was having a blast.

As the halftime show kicked up, Ronnie grabbed the remote control and switched the channel.

"Hey!" JP called, tossing a chip at his sister. "What the hell are you doing?"

"Seriously!" Jagger shifted on the couch. "I don't remember agreeing to watch the fucking news."

Waving her hand, Ronnie made a shushing noise. "Shut up. I'll put the skimpily dressed cheerleaders back on in a second. I had a news alert on my phone I want to check out."

"What was it? A shooting or something?" Jagger asked with his mouth full.

Ronnie shook her head. "No. Someone thinks they spotted Scarlett."

Mickie's blood ran cold. In an instant, her entire world flipped upside down. The soda bottle slipped from her limp fingers to the carpet. "I, oh, shit. I'm so sorry."

Keith squeezed her thigh as he bent to grab the bottle. "It's all right, babe, cap's on." He righted the bottle then stood. "Gotta take a leak. I'll be right back."

But Mickie couldn't speak. Her eyes were glued to the television, where a grainy picture was the topic of discussion. Every cell in her being tuned into what the anchor was saying.

"Who the fuck is Scarlett?" JP asked.

"You know." Ronnie waved a hand in the air. "That hot mess actress who fell of the face of the earth a buncha months back after losing her shit on a director."

"Ohhh yeah," JP said. "She had a banging body. Total headcase, though."

"Had being the opportunities word," Ronnie added. "That woman was so coked out, she looked like absolute shit the last couple years. I heard she had a heart attack, too."

Their conversation pinged around her head, not registering fully. She felt like a small animal, caught in the blinding headlights as they barreled toward her on the highway. She couldn't move, couldn't speak, couldn't do anything but stare at the TV.

Had they found her?

If so, how long before the paparazzi appeared on her doorstep and upended her entire life once again?

"Las Vegas seems like the type of place Scarlett would hide," the female newscaster stated. "She's always been a party girl. Scarlett's people have not confirmed she is in Vegas, but the man who snapped the photo is positive it's her. He said he spotted her in the casino gambling."

What? Casino? Vegas?

Mickie blinked then blew out an unsteady breath as the fog of shock began to clear. The photograph, pixilated as it was, could not be her. The woman in the distorted image had long, platinum blond hair, was skinny as a rail, and tattoo peeked out from the waist of her very short shorts. Mickie should have been relieved. The picture wasn't her, and now the public assumed she was hiding out in Vegas. In reality, this article insulated her from discovery for a little longer.

But instead of a reprieve from the stress, all she felt was a bone-deep sickness. Though the woman in the photo wasn't her, that was how the world saw her—an unhealthy woman who had no respect for her own body or others. The stark realization that despite all the changes she'd fought to make, the world still saw that Scarlett made her soda rise to her throat.

It shouldn't matter what anyone thought.

It *didn't* matter. The days of living life in the public eye were long over. Even knowing and believing it, she couldn't shake the sense of failure. It was as though every hour of therapy, self-reflection, and hard-won victories vanished in the wind.

Her three friends continued their back and forth, unaware they were discussing her right in front of her face. The experience was surreal in a way she'd never thought she'd experience.

"Wait until Keith hears about this one," Ronnie said as she tossed her pizza crust back in the box on the coffee table.

"Ha, he'll probably just grunt and look disgusted." Jagger leaned back, crossing his ankle over a thigh. "I think he threw a party the day she disappeared from the limelight. She's like his least favorite actress."

"Yeah, it's pretty safe to say he hates her," Ronnie continued. They were oblivious to the fact she'd been sitting statue-still lost in her head since they uttered the name Scarlett.

They had her attention now, though.

"He hates her?" Her voice sounded small and terrified.

"No," JP cut in with a laugh. "He doesn't hate her."

"Oh." Thank God.

"What's a stronger word for hate?"

Her stomach dropped out.

"Hmm…" Ronnie tapped her chin. "Despises? Detests? Oh, loathes."

JP snapped, then pointed to his sister. "That's it. That's the one. Keith loathes that woman. She basically embodies everything he hates. Rich, high-maintenance women who want everyone's attention."

Mickie shot to her feet. If she didn't get out of there in the next ten seconds, she'd get sick all over the floor.

"Who do I loathe?" Keith asked as he re-entered the room.

Oh, God, she couldn't hear him say it. It'd squash the last of her self-esteem. "I'm gonna get some air," she said though no one's attention was on her.

"Scarlett," Ronnie announced. "Your favorite actress. Someone spotted her in Vegas."

Then, as though a car wreck she couldn't look away from were occurring right in front of her, she watched Keith's expression morph into one of absolute revulsion. "That woman should do the world a favor and crawl back under whatever rock she's been hiding beneath. She's seriously everything that's wrong with this world."

Ronnie shot her a *see-told-ya* look.

Mickie couldn't respond. She couldn't even breathe. With one change of channel, the entire secure world she'd fought like hell to build collapsed around her. How on earth was she supposed to look the man she'd come to lo—like a lot in the eye now that she knew he hated her?

No, not hated, *loathed*.

Stronger than hatred.

They were still discussing her failures and shortcomings as Keith reached the couch. "Hey, why are you up? You feel okay?" he asked, forehead scrunched. "You look a little pale."

She blinked. A world-famous actress should have been able to sit through the rest of the game with a smile on her face and act as though everything was peachy. But he just couldn't muster the energy to pretend anymore. Not now that she knew Keith hated who she'd been. It didn't matter that she wasn't that woman anymore. All that mattered was the disgusted glint in his eyes when he heard the name Scarlett.

Finally, the urge to flee kicked in. She couldn't tolerate another minute in that house under false pretenses. "I'm fine," she said, sounding robotic. "Actually, I feel a little sick. I'm gonna go."

Keith frowned with genuine concern. Her heart clenched as though it'd been squeezed with a giant fist. "Here, I'll come—"

"No! Stay and watch the game," she cried with far more strength than the situation called for.

And then she ran as though her life depended on it.

Chapter Eighteen

"What just happened?" Keith asked from where he stood in his den, watching Mickie run from his house as though her panties were on fire. He spun to his siblings. "What the hell did you guys do to her?"

"Nothing!" all three shouted at the same time.

"Well, it wasn't me." He ran a hand through his hair, tugging the strands as though it'd pull the frustration out of him. "She was smiling and laughing when I left her with you three." He stalked toward the door where'd he'd left his shoes.

When he came back to the den, sneakers in hand, Ronnie was standing in front of her chair, wringing her hands. "Do you think she's sick?" she asked with genuine concern written on her face. That was Ronnie. Hard shell, soft gooey insides.

"That'd be my guess," JP added with a nod. He raised his hands, beer and all. "Swear we didn't say anything to piss your girl off. You better run over to her house and make sure she's okay. And, maybe I'll stop eating this pizza now."

"What the hell do you think I'm doing?" he murmured as he stuffed his feet in his shoes.

Mickie had been feeling fine all day, and the look on her face as she'd run was more despair than illness. No, not despair.

Shock. Complete and utter shock. What the hell could have happened in the two minutes he'd been gone to put her in such a state?

As he straightened, he caught sight of the empty beer bottles littered across the coffee table. "Oh fuck," he whispered. He'd taken her word that the presence of alcohol didn't bother her.

Jagger rose as well. "What?" He gripped Keith's shoulder.

"The beer. I bet Mickie is struggling with being around us when we're drinking."

Ronnie looked so stricken he moved to pull her in for a hug, but JP got there first. "I don't know, man," he said as he held their sister. "She's hung with us while we were drinking plenty of times and has always been cool with it."

True. But what the hell else could it have been? "I'm gonna go check on her. I'll let you guys know if it's anything serious."

He turned and jogged out of the room. An uneasy feeling settled low in his gut. For some reason, dread clawed at the back of his neck, and his senses went on high alert. Whatever had driven her from his house at full speed was big.

Ronnie caught up with him as he was exiting the house. "Keith," she said as she grabbed his arm. "Please apologize for us if it was anything we did. I really like her, and I don't want to lose her friendship."

"Hon, I'm sure it wasn't anything you did. Okay?"

Mouth turned down, she nodded. "I like her for you, too," she whispered, staring at her feet. They never spoke of relationships, or the emotional aspect of relationships, probably because none of them had been serious about anyone in ages. "You smile so much more now." She met his gaze. "So, whatever it is, remember how much more you smile now, okay?"

He gave his sister a quick hug. "Be back later."

After a quick run across the street, he found Mickie's door open and let himself in.

"Michaela?" he called out as he entered the foyer. When she didn't respond, he started for the newly renovated kitchen. Her phone buzzed from the counter three times, then stopped. Five seconds later, it started up again.

Frowning, Keith picked up the phone. Fifteen missed texts and six calls from someone named Ralph.

He'd spent the majority of nights with her over the past month. He'd been inside her countless times, tasted every inch of her body, and talked with her until the wee hours of morning more than once. Never once had the name Ralph come up.

Who was he?

Friend? Ex? Current lover? Husband? Shit, he knew nothing of her past. Not where she'd moved from, why she'd moved, who'd been in her life. The only information she'd volunteered was that of her sobriety. And even then, he knew the bare minimum.

Not that he'd tried to dig deeper. No, he'd been enjoying the fun, the sex, and the surface-level connection. At least he'd told himself he had been. Now that she might be in some kind of pain or trouble, he wished he had some background knowledge to go on.

"Mickie?" he called again as the phone stopped buzzing.

No answer. Where was she? Upstairs in her room? Out back? In the bathroom?

This time when the phone started buzzing again, curiosity and possibly jealously won out. "Hello?" he answered without an ounce of welcome in his tone.

"Who the hell is this? Where the fuck is Mickie?" The panicked voice had him yanking the phone from his ear and frowning at it. When he returned it, the voice continued shouting questions without waiting for answers. "Is this Keith?"

Well, he might not have any idea who Ralph was, but Ralph knew him.

"Hello? Answer me!"

He cleared his throat. "Yes. It's Keith."

Air rushed from Ralph's lungs. "Oh, thank God." Then as though speaking to himself, he muttered, "Thank God she's not alone." Louder, he said, "How is she? I'm guessing by now she's seen the photo. She must be freaking out. I've spoken with her attorney to see if there is anything we can do to get the picture off social media, but it's already trending." Without taking a breath, he rushed on. "Since it isn't her, we might be out of luck. I'm sure she's totally freaking out. I'm so glad you're with her. This is such a bunch of bullshit. All she wants is to be left alone and not be on the media's radar. It's gonna take time, though. Remind her of that. But I've been thinking this could be a good thing. Throw people off her trail. Or maybe it's time for her to hire someone to lead the media astray, you know?"

Keith's head spun from the rapid-fire verbal onslaught that poured from the man's mouth. The man calling his woman. The one he was still in the dark about beyond a name. Ralph.

"Uh, know what?" Stupid, but the only words he could come up with when he didn't know where to begin dissecting Ralph's one-sided conversation.

"Oh, shit," Ralph breathed. "You still don't know."

Now his hackles began to rise. Enough with the games. "Don't know what?" he asked with force.

"Shit, shit, shit. I thought she'd have told you by now. Especially with the picture of her on the news." He was back to talking to himself.

Picture of her? What the hell did that even mean? The only picture he could think of was the one of Scarlett, the skanky actress he'd never understood the appeal of. She'd disappeared off the face of the planet about seven months ago. Some, like himself, figured she was living large in some exotic location, laughing at everyone who gave a shit about her. Some conspiracy theorist claimed she'd died. Others assumed she'd tried to better herself by going to rehab and…

His blood ran cold.

Rehab.

"Keith? Are you still there?" Ralph asked through the phone, but he ignored it because, at the same moment, Mickie shuffled into the kitchen, wiping a hand across the back of her mouth. In one hand, she carried a bottle of mouthwash.

"Keith? Hello?" Ralph's voice rang out like a shot in the quiet room.

She froze when she caught sight of him.

Without thinking, he lowered the phone to the counter. Ralph could still be heard hollering questions and demanding answers.

Keith and Mickie ignored the shouts echoing into the kitchen. They stared at each other across a distance of ten feet. Mickie's eyes were red, puffy, and full of despair. Her skin had taken on a sickly green hue, and her shoulders drooped in a defeated posture he'd never seen from her before. The bottle of blue liquid dangling from her fingers had his heart sinking.

Christ, was she so desperate for a drink she'd chugged mouthwash?

"S-sorry," she croaked. "I must be getting sick. I threw up." She didn't meet his gaze.

Maybe this was all a misunderstanding. Perhaps Ronnie had been right, and she'd eaten something that didn't agree with her. Maybe whoever the fuck Ralph was, he was dead wrong.

But no, his gut told him the woman standing before him, the woman he'd kissed, held, pleasured, fucked, that woman was none other than Scarlett. One of the most famous and richest actresses in the world. A woman who represented everything he hated.

She'd moved to his town and played him and his family for a band of fools.

He saw it then, in her ravaged eyes.

The truth.

She was Scarlett.

Christ, just thinking it felt like a horse kick to the stomach.

Physically, the changes were remarkable. Before she'd gone dark, Scarlett's face was everywhere: magazines, television, movies, commercials, social medial. You name it, her twig skinny body was there. She'd had long, bleached hair, wore pounds of makeup, Caribbean blue eyes, scandalous outfits, and a raging drug habit. She'd loved the spotlight. Lived for it. And the woman had the ethical code of an unrepentant mob boss.

He couldn't reconcile the classy woman in front of him with the attention-hungry actress who attracted male interest every time she blinked and loved nothing more than to see her name in lights and hear the cheers of her adoring fans.

Her gaze cut to the phone, which was now quiet, then back to him. Her mouth opened and closed a few times before she finally said, "H-he told you? Didn't he?"

As the shock began to ebb, betrayal hit him with the force of a boxer's hook. He took a step back even though plenty of distance already separated them. Mickie's face crumpled even further into misery.

"He told you," she whispered to herself. "I..." She shook her head.

Suddenly the last thing Keith wanted to hear was a bullshit excuse or insincere apology from an Oscar-winning actress. God knows if any time he'd spent with her had been real.

"Yes, Scarlett," he said. The name tasted bitter. "He told me."

She shook her head back and forth. "Don't call me that," she whispered. "Please don't call me that name. I'm not...I'm not her."

"Anymore?"

"Anymore," she agreed in a steady voice that betrayed the tears streaking down her beautiful face.

Were those tears real or a skill she'd perfected over the years?

Would he or his siblings' lives end up dissected on social media once she got bored of this small-town, quiet life game?

Would he find his face splashed across tabloids and his family's ugly history the talk of millions when she returned to the spotlight?

"But you were," he said, voice flat. The sentence conveyed everything rolling through his mind that he couldn't express. "You were the one who did all that shit the media loved. You ruined relationships, fought with colleagues, made a fool of yourself in public, what? Hundreds of times?" She'd been Scarlett. She'd committed countless acts he disapproved of, disagreed with, didn't respect. Scarlett wasn't just someone he rolled his eyes over when discussed. She was a woman he despised…loathed, as Ronnie said. She embodied everything he hated.

"I was," she said. Her shoulders straightened, and she met his gaze.

As much as he hated every second of this encounter, a bit of pride filled him at the small return of backbone.

"I've made a lot of mistakes, Keith, but I've chan—"

He lifted a hand before she could speak the words he'd heard his entire life. Empty words that meant nothing. "It's not my business, Scarlett," he said.

How many times had his father changed through his childhood? Countless. After every ugly fight with his mother, every missed obligation, every beating, he'd promised to change. Over and over, he and his siblings heard promises of extraordinary changes coming from both his parents: more money, better living conditions, sobriety.

It never happened.

People didn't change.

They only pretended for a while. Sometimes not even a day had passed before his father would fall back on dysfunctional and destructive habits.

Change was an illusion. A seed of hope that only drove the knife deeper when it inevitably cut again.

"I can't do this," he said as he set her phone on the shiny new marble countertop she'd chosen.

She merely nodded with slumped shoulders and those damn tears.

He turned and made his way out of the kitchen.

"K-Keith?" she called when he reached the door.

He froze, hand on the knob, but didn't turn. Another look at the agony on her face, and he'd cave. Pull her into his embrace and fall down that rabbit hole.

"P-please don't tell anyone. I mean, outside your siblings."

Unfuckingbelievable. Of course, all she gave a shit about was her own needs. "I wouldn't. Unlike you, I have no desire to destroy anyone else's life."

Her sharp inhale indicated a direct hit, but instead of giving in to the instinct to turn and hurl her into his arms, he yanked the door open and stormed out of the house.

And if he happened to hear a choked sob before the door closed behind him, he ignored it.

It was just another bid for attention from a Hollywood superstar.

Chapter Nineteen

Bang, bang, bang.

Mickie groaned and flopped over for what had to be the thousandth time since she'd fallen into bed. She yanked the covers over her head as the pounding started up again.

What the hell was that?

When it wouldn't let up after another few seconds, she forced herself to sit up. Blinking away the cobwebs in her brain, the noise finally registered.

Someone was at her front door.

Ronnie, probably. Come to grill her on yesterday's embarrassing meltdown and what she'd learned from Keith.

"Ugh," Mickie groaned aloud as she dragged herself from the bed and shuffled toward the stairs. Her head throbbed with each step, and her eyeballs felt as though someone had taken the coarsest sandpaper to them while she slept. A tidal wave of nausea rolled through her gut, and her tongue had adhered to the roof of her mouth. All in all, one of the worst hangovers of her life, and she'd earned it crying, not imbibing.

"I'm coming!" she hollered with a wince as the volume of her voice poked at her tender brain like needles. "Though I might die before I get there." She made her way down the steps. Never had one staircase seemed like such a taxing journey, but her energy was at an all-time low. The sleepless night, hours of crying, and self-recrimination had done a fantastic job of wringing her out.

Bang, bang, bang.

"I said I'm coming. Chill out," she mumbled as she finally reached the ground level. Fifteen steps later, she tugged the door open only to have five-feet-eleven inches of excitable male grab her in a bone-crushing hug. "Ralph," she choked out against his slim chest. She squeezed him back. "Oh, my God."

There shouldn't have been an ounce of liquid left in her body, but the tears came from somewhere. Flowing out of her unchecked, they soaked Ralph's cashmere sweater.

"Oh, sweetie," he crooned as he rocked her back and forth right there in her open doorway with the chilly air flooding her home.

"Are you really here? I can't believe you're here. You shouldn't have come. You're too busy," she said into his slender but firm chest.

He snorted. "My best gal needs me, I'm there. Even if I have to fly across the country all night to be with her."

"Oh, Ralph, I love you." One minute in his presence and already the world had righted a fraction.

"Not as much as I love you, my Mickie."

A throat cleared behind Ralph, which had her wrenching back and peering around his shoulder. Jagger stood there with a puzzled, slightly judgmental frown on his face. "Uh, sorry to interrupt, Mickie. I just needed to drop off some caulking materials for the crew who'll be finishing up the master bathroom this afternoon."

Before she had a chance to reply, Ralph was on it. "Well, hello there, handsome. Mmm, they grow 'em big up here in the northeast, huh?"

She pressed her lips together to keep the laugh inside as Jagger's eyes flared wide. The pale pink cashmere sweater Ralph wore with his designer jeans, five-hundred-dollar Gucci shoes, and Ray-ban aviators perched on his head made for a look not common in rural Vermont. Trendy Ralph would stand out like a rose in a wheat field among the flannel-loving, boot-wearing locals.

Poor Jagger had no idea what to do with Ralph. At least with Ralph blatantly hitting on him, Jagger no longer assumed she'd moved on from his brother less than twenty-four hours after they'd broken up. Or whatever they'd done since there had never been a conversation about officially being together.

"Uh, hey, man, I'm Jagger."

"Ralph," he said as he extended the back of his hand like a princess waiting to be kissed in greeting.

"Nice to meet you." Jagger took Ralph's hand in an awkward grip and gave it a shake.

Michaela had to bit her lip to keep from laughing out loud. "Sorry, Jagger, come on in. It's cold. Ralph is my best friend, and he's visiting from LA. I wasn't expecting him, so it's a wonderful surprise." No point in hiding where she'd lived now.

"Yesss," Ralph said, drawing it out. "Please come in, handsome, and bring your…caulk."

She elbowed her friend's ribs. "Down, boy. Pretty sure he doesn't play for your team."

"They all don't. Until they do," Ralph crooned.

Jagger laughed then stepped into the house. At least he'd lost the deer-in-the-headlights look. "Well, I don't, but who doesn't appreciate being called handsome?"

Ralph pouted. "Well, you are that. Handsome and so big."

Jagger laughed again. "He's a pistol, huh?" he asked her.

The breath she hadn't realized she'd been holding whooshed from her lungs. Back in LA, no one thought twice about being out and proud. She wasn't naïve enough to believe the entire world was as accepting. Small towns were notorious for being more conservative, but she was beyond relieved to learn those closest to her would embrace her best friend with open arms.

Though she may have killed any closeness to the Bensons with yesterday's outing of sorts.

Speaking of…

"Thanks, Jagger." Her face heated, and she'd have dived down the hole if the floor opened up beneath her. "Um, did Keith speak to you yesterday after he left here?"

He set the tubes of caulking on her counter and whirled to face her. Ever her champion, Ralph stood at her side, ready to leap to her defense. His silent yet steely support enabled her to meet Jagger's skeptical gaze without the morbid embarrassment and shame she'd been expecting the next time she ran into any of the Bensons.

With a sigh, he folded his arms across his chest. "He did not. He wasn't exactly in an approachable mood, so we decided to give him until this afternoon before we pounced."

She nodded, absorbing the information. So, Ronnie, JP, and Jagger still weren't aware of her true identity. Part of her, a huge part wished it could stay that way. To beg Keith to keep it under wraps and never speak of it again. But that seemed unfair.

Lying to his family on her behalf would only drive a rift between him and his siblings, as well as eventually tear their friendships apart. She trusted them all to keep her confidence but didn't have the energy to deal with it at the moment. Let Keith bring them up to speed later when they descended on him for details.

"Look." Jagger strode her way. "Keith has a lot of reasons for his gruff exterior and even his bitterness. Doesn't excuse him from being an ass, but…" He shrugged. "Give him some time. Whatever it was yesterday, he'll come around after he processes." Then he winked. "Or after Ronnie kicks his ass back in line."

How was he on her side without even know the details?

"Catch you later, hon." Jagger kissed the top of her head, and she swore Ralph sighed like a swooning damsel.

As Jagger started for the door, she grabbed his arm. "Wait."

He raised an eyebrow. "Yeah?"

"How do you know I don't deserve his scorn?" When Ralph opened his mouth to refute her question, she silenced him with a look. For some reason, Jagger wasn't backing his brother by being angry at her for upsetting him. She needed to know why. Needed to know what he saw in her that led him to give her the benefit of the doubt. After yesterday's kick to her self-esteem, she needed something to prop her back up.

Jagger folded his arms across his chest. The impressive muscles in his forearms popped beneath his long-sleeved Henley.

Ralph squeaked.

"I've gotten to know you, Mickie. Sure, I don't know everything and not much about your past, but I know the woman you are today. The one living in this house, spending time with my family, and making my brother smile more than he has in years. I'm not one to judge people for their pasts. Especially someone who has clearly worked hard to get themselves to a healthier and happier place in life."

She shook her head. "Jagger, you make me sound better than I am. I've done many things I'm not proud of. Hurt people with my words and actions," she whispered.

"Mickie…" Ralph circled an arm around her shoulders.

"You know it's true, Ralph." She turned to her friend. "Supporting me is one thing, but you can't deny I made tons of poor decisions in my life and treated people in ways they didn't deserve."

"Who hasn't?" Ralph said with exasperation as he hugged her to his side. They'd had this conversation countless times over the past months.

"We've all made mistakes, hon," Jagger said. "Big ones, small ones, and some monster-sized ones. I see a woman who recognizes hers, owns them, and is working damn hard to avoid repeating them. Your past is not my business. It's your choice to decide if you want it to be Keith's, but trust me when I tell you we all have a laundry list of regrets."

For a moment, his gaze clouded. Did he have painful memories of his own? What were his mistakes? What stole his sleep at night? Were his demons similar to Keith's?

"Thank you," she said. "For being able to see me without judgment. That might change in the future, but I appreciate it now."

If only his brother could do the same.

"Keith doesn't judge you," Jagger said, reading her mind.

That was just plain untrue. "Jagger—"

He held up a hand. "He doesn't. This is about his own past. Not yours. It's his story to tell, but trust me when I say he has his reasons for being how he is." He nodded at Ralph. "Nice to meet you, man. Enjoy your visit."

"Don't be a stranger," Ralph called out as Jagger opened the door.

"I won't. How could I stay away with my favorite actress living across the street?" He winked over his shoulder then jogged away.

Mickie gasped and grabbed Ralph's arm. "He knows," she said. "He said Keith didn't tell him?"

He knew. And he still said all those incredible things to her. Maybe he said them because he knew. Her heart beat fast, but lighter too.

Ralph shook her shoulders gently. "Maybe he put two and two together after witnessing your reaction to the media clip. Now." He lifted the ends of her hair. "You're gonna get dressed, let me fix this mess, then show me around your new little town. Okay?"

Blinking away the shock of Jagger's little bomb, she nodded. "Yeah. That sounds perfect."

Ninety minutes later, showered, caffeinated, and with fresh highlights in her hair, she and Ralph waited for their late breakfast in a booth at the local diner. Family owned and operated since the early nineteen-fifties—or so the sign boasted —the place appeared to have needed a facelift thirty years or so ago. It was cute and charming, but had faded seats, old-fashioned décor, and cracked flooring tiles. Mickie would have loved to get her hands on the place and bring it into the current century. A modern diner with a retro vibe would draw a massive crowd of tourists who came to the area for ski trips and snowy weekend getaways to nearby mountain resorts.

After taking in her surroundings, she faced Ralph to find him watching her with a half-smile.

"What?" Though she knew her hair was perfect, as he'd been the one to style it, she smoothed it down anyway. "Is there something on my face?" she asked, patting her cheeks.

"Nope."

"Then why are you staring at me?"

He rested his chin on his folded hands. "Because you're so pretty."

With a laugh, Mickie rolled her eyes. God, she'd missed him and the lightness he brought to her days. "Get serious."

"You're happy here," he said, tone taking on a serious note. "I mean, barring yesterday's drama, you're happy here in this itty-bitty town away from the glitz, glam, and spotlight."

She took a sip of her lukewarm coffee then set the ceramic cup down. "I am. Surprised me too."

Silence fell as they watched each other across the table. Only Ralph knew what her time in the hospital then rehab had been like. How much she'd struggled, torn her psyche apart, then worked to build herself back up again. How hard she'd worked to learn to love herself, forgive herself, and how deeply she wanted to begin a fresh chapter of her life. Reporters, influencers, friends, and coworkers spent the first few months of her disappearance from the media speculating on when she'd make her grand return to cinema. The answer was never, but all assumed someone like Scarlett could only go so long without the attention her narcissism demanded.

But Ralph knew better. He knew what lay beneath the exterior.

"It suits you. You look healthy, and there's a peace about you that I've never seen." His grin grew, and he extended a hand to her. "I like it. I'm happy for you."

She reached across the table and squeezed his hand. "Thank you." The words nearly stuck in her thickened throat. She cleared it, then said, "Now if only I could decide what to do with the rest of my days" — and Keith— "it'd be perfect."

Their waitress arrived and deposited Ralph's pancakes and her eggs Benedict. The diner may look like a throwback to another era, but the food was fresh, piping hot, and smelled heavenly. Never would she have ordered something like this back in LA. It was all egg whites and avocado toast, but damn, eating real food was perk enough to keep her from returning to Hollywood.

"Thank you," Ralph said, flashing a grin to the older waitress with a giant pouf of white hair. "You are my new favorite person."

She laughed and swatted his shoulder with her menu pad. "You two kids enjoy. I'll check back in a bit."

"Thank you," Mickie added.

"You are aware you don't have to work, right?" Ralph said with the fork poised at his lips. He took a bite then rolled his eyes upward. "Oh. My. God. I think I just came."

Mickie laughed loud, drawing curious stares from the other customers. "God, I missed you," she said in a much more indoor-appropriate tone. "What am I supposed to do if I don't work? Sit around my house eating Bonbons all day? I'm already starting to feel tired of my own company. I need purpose. I need something that excites me."

"I bet Keith excites you," he said with a wink.

She groaned. "Ugh, can we not talk about him right now? I'm compartmentalizing until later."

His lined eyes narrowed. "Fine." He pointed his fork at her. "I'll give you until tonight, but that's it. Then we're gonna eat ice cream, do face masks, and you're gonna spill the dirty details."

All she'd told him when they'd spoken the previous night was that she'd confessed who she was to Keith, and he'd left in a lingering cloud of shock and disgust.

"Yes, sir," she said, saluting with her fork.

Despite everything that happened over the past day, Michaela found herself smiling. It had been a false alarm. No one knew where she'd disappeared to. Sure, speculation on her whereabouts resumed with a renewed vigor, but not a single person aside from Ralph knew. Not her agent, publicist, business manager. No one. And Ralph would take the information to his grave.

She could push forward and move on because all in all, life hadn't been disrupted by some random fan's false sighting of her.

Except for the collapse of her quasi-relationship. And she didn't have a clue how to begin repairing that destruction.

Once they'd finished their meal, Mickie and Ralph walked arm in arm through the parking lot toward her car.

"Damn," Ralph said with a dramatic shiver. "It's not even winter yet and it's cold as a polar bear's balls out here. How do you stand it?"

With a chuckle, Mickie staid, "I love it, actu—" She stopped short at the sight of Chuck resting against her car with her arms folded across his chest. He wore loose fitting jeans, work boots, and a fleece jacket. A Patriots cap topped off the ensemble. It was the gleam in his eye that had her stomach flip-flopping.

"What's a wrong?" Ralph asked as he followed her gaze. "Oh, who's that?"

"A huge jerk," Mickie grumbled.

"Need me to bitch him out for you?" Ralph asked. "I've been itching to since I haven't gotten a chance to take a run at Keith yet."

Normally she'd have laughed at Ralph's ridiculous comment, but her spine tingled with impending doom. "Don't suppose you'll wait here while I talk to him, will you?"

An inelegant snort was all she got in response.

As she approached her SUV, she straightened her shoulders and prepared for battle the only way she knew how, by channeling what remained of Scarlett. "Something I can help you with, Chuck?" she asked in as snooty a voice as she could muster.

"Get it, girl," Ralph mumbled beside her, bolstering her confidence even more.

Even though things were a disaster with Keith right now, she wouldn't tolerate Chuck speaking poorly of him.

"New boyfriend?" Chuck asked, tilting his head. He stuck an unlit cigarette between his lips.

"That's why you're waiting by my car? To ask if I have a new boyfriend? Wow, Chuck, I didn't realize you cared so much. I'm flattered."

He tossed his head back and let out a laugh that grated on her nerves. Beside her, Ralph stiffened, "Oh I care," he said, "but not about who you're fucking. Though I gotta say if you shook Benson off you made the right choice there. His old man's the town embarrassment. Mom sure was sweet, though. If you know what I mean." He winked. "Of course, the price had to be right to get it from her."

Mickie squeezed her fists together to keep from bitch slapping this asshole across the face. Did he seriously just disrespect Keith's dead mother by calling her a prostitute?

Ralph wrapped a hand around her forearm. "Oooh, boy, there better be a point to all this. I'm the only thing standing between you and my girl clawing your eyes out. So I'd either say what you came to say or move the hell outta the way."

As though he just realized he was in the presence of a gay man and believed it might rub off on him, Chuck tensed and seemed to flatten himself against her car.

"For Christ's sake," Mickie muttered. "Just walk the hell away."

"Uh, yeah," he said, still giving Ralph the side-eye.

Ralph, in all his glory, took a step closer to Chuck. "You okay? Looking a little pale there. Need me to feel your forehead?"

The idea of Ralph touching him snapped him out of whatever homophobic trance he'd fallen into. With a grunt he stepped forward until he was in Mickie's personal space. "You know, I figured out who you look like," he said, standing too close. His breath smelled of breakfast meat. "It's that actress, Scarlett. Think someone saw her in Vegas yesterday."

"Huh," she said affecting a bored tone. "I've heard that a few times."

"I'll bet you have." With that, he strode away, whistling the theme song to one of Scarlett's more famous movies. In seconds, he was in his car, pulling out of the parking lot.

Mickie doubled over. "He knows," she whispered. "He hates Keith, and he knows."

Ralph crouched down beside her. "Hey," he said. "Listen to me. He's an ass. And we don't know anything for sure. Bullies like him aren't smart. If he does know, he'll probably come at you asking for money or he'll post a pic of you to social media. If he does that, you come at him with guns blazing. He won't know what hit him. You're Michaela fucking Hudson and you won't take shit from anyone."

He was right. She had the resources to keep Chuck from doing anything that could out her. Unless he went and sold a picture of her to a tabloid. Then she'd be screwed. But it didn't seem his style. He'd be more the type to demand money from her directly. Either way, she could ruin him and that gave her some measure of comfort.

Like Ralph said, she was Michaela fucking Hudson and it was time she started acting like the badass she was.

"Ralph," she asked as she straightened, "will you marry me?"

Laughing, he threw an arm around her and guided her to the driver's side door. "There's my girl."

Chapter Twenty

Keith walked into his room only to draw up short at the sight of a large man sitting on his bed, reading a mechanic's magazine. Of course, that man was his brother, but still, he let out a curse as he drew his shirt over his head. "How long have you been hanging out in here?" he asked Jagger as he tossed the grease-stained shirt into his hamper.

"Not long. Half hour, maybe." Jagger set the magazine down and speared Keith with a look that had him sighing.

"Guess my reprieve is over, huh?" He picked a black T-shirt out of his drawer and tugged it on.

"Reprieve?" Jagger laughed, then kicked his feet over the side of the bed, bringing himself up to sit. "There was no fucking reprieve. We've been trying to pin you down for three days, but your stubborn ass has managed to evade all of us. What, have you been sleeping at the garage?"

"No," Keith grumbled, suddenly realizing how childish he'd been behaving, avoiding his siblings at all costs. "I just came home late."

"Yeah, as in long after we all fell asleep."

With a shrug, Keith dropped in the comfortable recliner in the corner of his room. It'd been the first piece of new furniture he'd ever purchased for himself nearly twenty years ago. Though worn and not nearly as plush it used to be, he couldn't part with the thing. It was so much more than a relaxing seat. It represented his escape from the shit he'd grown up in.

"Not my fault you all can't make it up past eight," he said.

Jagger smirked, flipping him off.

Silence settled between them. When the weight of Jagger's judgmental glare grew too heavy to ignore, Keith rolled his eyes. "Just say it."

"What the fuck are you doing?" Jagger asked.

"Well, right now, I'm sitting here waiting for you to say whatever the fuck it is you've invaded in my space to say. Then I'm going to hit the gym. Maybe grab dinner after. You want this all in writing?"

Narrowing his eyes, Jagger leaned forward, propping his forearms on his knees. "Fine. You wanna play games? Want me to be more specific in my questions?" His lips curled. "Why are you hiding from Michaela Hudson who, once upon a time, was a very famous actress named Scarlett?"

The bottom dropped out of Keith's stomach as his jaw dropped. "She told you?" He'd known they chatted when Jagger worked at her house, but he hadn't expected her to confide in his brother the way she'd confided in him. Jealously he thought he'd nixed came roaring back to life.

Jagger, damn him, knew it and fucking loved it. His smarmy smirk grew until it was all Keith could see.

"What?" he barked.

"She didn't tell me anything," the smug bastard said. Sitting straight once again, he tapped the side of his head. "I figured it out all on my own."

Keith grunted and refused to admit the relief at knowing Mickie hadn't had a deep heart-to-heart with his brother. Ridiculous as the envy was. Jagger would die before poaching Keith's territory. Not that Michaela belonged to him.

"Well, if you know who she is, you pretty much answered your own question then, didn't you?"

"How's that?" Jagger's patience was maddening. The man could wait until the end of time for something he wanted. And apparently, he wanted Keith to talk.

Sighing, he ran a hand through his hair. "Jag, she represents a world I want nothing to do with. I don't just mean because she's rich," he added when Jagger opened his mouth. "She's famous for being a high-maintenance drama queen. She craves attention, the spotlight, men fawning over her. She's awards shows, galas, and mansions. I'm oil, cars, and small-town. You know she has seven million Instagram followers? I don't even have an account. I live a quiet life, and that's how I like it. I'm not interested in any of that insanity."

"Not to mention her drug and alcohol use are no secret," Jagger added, voice dripping with sarcasm. "As are the very public mistakes she's made in the past."

Keith shrugged. "It's the truth."

"Mm-hmm. Got another question for you."

Keith motioned for him to speak.

"Have you seen any of that since she's been here? Any drama or attention-seeking behavior? Is she high-maintenance? Sure, she has money and likes nice things, but the woman I know is nothing like the one portrayed by the media. The woman we know has worked damn hard to change her life completely. She's left Hollywood, avoided social media like the plague, spent months in rehab, and given up a glamorous existence to live, as you called it, a quiet life. She's made mistakes, some pretty damn big mistakes, and done things she'll forever be ashamed of, but she's different. And she's different because she made the very difficult decision to change her life then put the time and massive amounts of effort toward making that happen."

With a snort, Keith threw up his hands, hopped to his feet, and began pacing. "Come on, Jag. You can't be that naïve. If my, *our*, childhood has taught us anything, it's that people don't change. It just doesn't fucking happen. Yeah, sure, maybe for a hot minute, but not long term. Just you watch, before long, she'll be bored of small-town life. The shiny appeal of Hollywood will be too tempting to resist forever, and she'll leave here to resume her real life as Scarlett." Christ, the name tasted wrong on his tongue. Try as he might, he could not picture the woman who'd spent nights in his arms as the world-famous starlet.

But she was. And she would be again.

And where would he be? Stuck here pining after a woman who'd never intended to make his town her home. Never intended to be with a man like him. He'd made that mistake before. Once was enough. Best to end it all now before broken promises and fake assurances of change ruined him as they'd tried his entire life.

Jagger's sigh spoke to his displeasure in the conversation. He rose, walked to Keith, and clasped him by the shoulders, keeping him from escaping. "You know she isn't Della, right? And she's nothing like Dad."

Keith's stomach turned over. He shook his head. "What?"

"Michaela isn't Della. She's not a teenaged brat with stars in her eyes. She's not going to leave you because she doesn't think you're glittery enough. The woman has had all that and left it on purpose because it almost destroyed her. I don't know why, but she thinks you hung the fucking moon. And she sure as hell doesn't deserve to be lumped in with Dad just because she's in recovery. Or because you're afraid."

Keith scoffed. What the hell had his brother been smoking? "Afraid? What the fuck am I afraid of?"

"You're afraid of being disappointed again. Of having someone promise you better and different and not delivering. Mom always promised Dad would change some day. He always claimed he could quit at any time. And Della offered you a world you'd never experienced. But they all disappointed you, and you're terrified of it happening again because this time, you care more than you ever have before."

He opened his mouth to blast his brother's incorrect opinion, but instead, his shoulders sagged.

Well fuck.

"But she isn't them," Jagger continued. "And it's not fair for you to judge her through their lenses, Keith. If you could get your head out of your ass for two minutes and take a good look at the woman, you'd realize that. Whatever drove her to make such drastic changes in her life affected her on a cellular level. Go see her, Keith. Look at her and *listen* to her when she speaks. You'll see it and hear it. It's not lip service. You'll see someone who worked harder on herself than any of us will even come close to. It takes immense courage, strength, and resilience to face the darkest parts of ourselves. To not only own up to them but atone for them and work to change them. Our parents never even took the first step toward change. Michaela has made it happen." He squeezed Keith's shoulder. "Listen to her, and you'll find a woman who is happy now when she never was before. And you are a big part of that happiness, brother."

With that, Jagger strode out of the room, dragging the door closed behind him, and leaving Keith standing in the middle of the room with his jaw on the floor.

Christ, when had Jagger become so fucking in tune with this kinda shit?

His brother had a point. Multiple points, really. Keith had let his personal past shit get in the way of hearing anything Michaela had to said. As soon as she'd told him her secret, his brain ran with the news to dark places.

He ran a hand down his face.

The least she deserved was a chance to tell her story.

Fuck, it must have taken a ton of courage for her to admit to him who she was. Especially after her near-violent reaction to the news reporting a sighting of her. She'd opened up, shared the most intimate part of herself with him, and he'd fucking bailed on her like an asshole.

He'd be lucky if she didn't slam the door in his face.

Suddenly, the need to see her grew in intensity until he could feel it scratching at his skin. Keith snatched his keys off the dresser, grabbed his jacket then jogged out of his room. As he blew through the kitchen, Jagger, who was nuking leftovers, shouted, "That's my boy. Go get 'em, tiger."

"Go fuck yourself," Keith called back, then rolled his eyes at Jagger's laughter.

Twenty seconds later, he was hustling up Mickie's driveway when her front door opened, and a man walked out.

Keith drew up short. His fists clenched. Who the fuck was this? Had she moved on already? Christ. The man couldn't be more different than himself. Slender, with dark jeans, a dark sweater, and an expensive-looking leather jacket, the guy smirked and folded thin arms over his chest as he leaned on the door frame. His hair was perfect, not a strand out of place. And was he wearing eyeliner?

"Well, you must be Keith," he said, voice letting Keith know his immediate distrust.

Thanks for the heads up, Jagger.

"Yeah. I am."

"Hmm."

"Who are you?"

"Oh, I'm Ralph. Mickie's best friend from LA. I flew out here a few nights ago when my girl called me. Crying." He tilted his head, and his glossy mouth turned down. "You see, it takes quite a lot to make Mickie cry."

Fuck. Keith shifted, allowing his hands to relax. "Is she inside?"

"Are you here to upset her further?"

Keith could take the guy blindfolded and with his hands tied behind his back, but he had to admire the way the smaller man defended Mickie. Clearly, they were close, and Ralph was very protective of his friend.

Keith shifted. He wasn't accustomed to people questioning his actions. The urge to tell Ralph to go fuck himself rose, but he shoved it back down. Last thing he needed to do was piss off someone he could use in his corner. "No. I'm not. I'm hoping to apologize and fix things between us."

Ralph studied him without trying to disguise it. Keith refused to drop his eyes or give Ralph a reason to send him packing. After what felt like an hour, he must have seen something he approved of because he nodded and walked out onto the porch, then down the four steps to meet Keith. "She's upstairs taking a bath. Jagger's team finished up yesterday. I was on my way out to pick up some ice cream. We ran out. I'll keep myself busy for an hour and a half, but that's all I'm giving you. You hear me?"

"Yeah, I got it."

Ralph nodded. "Okay."

"She's lucky to have a friend like you," Keith said as he started around the man.

"Oh, I know my worth, honey," Ralph said, his entire demeanor changing from guard dog to pussy cat. "Oh, and Keith?"

He looked over his shoulder. "Yeah?"

"I've known her for over ten years." He pointed up toward a second-floor window. "That woman up there, the one you know, that is Michaela. The other was a product of a toxic environment and poor self-worth. Please don't hurt my friend. She's an amazing person."

Keith swallowed hard. "I'll try hard not to."

"Guess that's all any of us can really ask for." Ralph grinned. "Say hello to that sexy brother of yours for me," he said before winking and disappearing into Michaela's Audi SUV.

His brother? Which one?

With a snort, Keith took the steps to Michaela's door two at a time. Once inside, it took a surprising amount of effort not to bound up the stairs like a stampeding elephant, but he didn't want to scare her. He walked into her dark room, toed off his shoes, then made his way toward the bathroom, where a line of light flickered below the cracked door.

Without a sound, he nudged the door open and lost his breath. Not because of all the recently completed upgrades. Those he didn't even notice. Mickie captured his attention immediately. She was breathtaking. Absolutely stunning as she lay in the giant tub surrounded by a cloud of bubbles. Her eyes were closed, head tipped back on a small pillow. Around the back rim of the tub, candles flickered, casting a romantic glow around the space. Even without a stitch of makeup, she was magnificent. So much more spectacular in her natural state than with the trappings of Hollywood.

She didn't startle as she opened her eyes and turned his way as though sensing his presence. "Keith," she whispered on an exhale. Her eyes widened, and she seemed to freeze in place, uncertain how to react to his presence.

He took her lack of shouting at him as an invitation to enter and walked closer. When he reached the tub, he sat on the tiled ledge. Mickie's breath quickened as though his nearness made her nervous.

Or maybe…aroused?

Her chest rose and fell, shifting the bubbles. Within seconds he could see the dusky tips of her nipples beneath the water. His throat thickened, forcing a hard swallow. Christ, she was just so damn sexy. He couldn't keep from wanting to touch and taste when she was close.

Their gazes met. She didn't shy away from his obvious perusal of her naked body. Mickie knew she looked good and enjoyed her body. Not in a vain way, but in the way a woman should when she knew her man wanted her. But her eyes held fear for a different reason. She had no idea why he was there or what he'd say.

"Do you miss it?" he finally asked when no other words would come. He had to know to end the clawing worry she'd up and leave at any point.

Clarification wasn't necessary. She understood he meant her extravagant life in California.

"No," she said with conviction. "I thought I would, to be honest. I kept expecting to for the first few months I was away from LA." She pressed her lips together as she shook her head. "But I don't. I hadn't realized how toxic my life had become. How genuinely miserable I was. How much of myself I'd destroyed with drugs, alcohol, and blind ambition."

He trailed his hand in the water, making a pattern in the bubbles. "Living here must feel so small compared to what you had. No one knows you. It's quiet. There's nothing dazzling or exciting about us or the town. It's—"

"Keith?" She captured his hand as she sent him a sweet smile. "This is what I want. I didn't come here on a whim or for a vacation from my real life. I spent long, hard, and sometimes agonizing months in rehab and therapy, working on myself. I don't want the life I had. I wasn't healthy physically or mentally." Her face flushed. "I've learned to love, well, at least like myself, which I never did before. For years, I sought to fill that void with drugs, or love from my fans, or with men." The last part was whispered.

He cared less about her past sexual history than everything else. He certainly hadn't been a monk in his twenties, so what right did he have to judge there?

"And if, down the road, you get bored? If someone finds the perfect script for you and offers you the role of a lifetime?" Would she take his heart, stomp on it and leave it behind? Not that he'd given it over, but if they kept on this road, he might not be able to keep himself from it.

Mickie cleared her throat. "I grew up with a mother who was obsessed with Hollywood, fame, and the dream of seeing her name in lights. It was all she ever talked about. All she ever wanted. Her unrealistic desire to be a star, which, after many therapy sessions I realize was probably an unhealthy obsession, bled into me until I wanted it as well. Before she passed, when she was sick, she thought of nothing but regret at not pursuing her dream. When she died, I vowed to bring her dream to life. To live it out for her. I now realize I internalized her desires and made them my own without ever giving myself a chance to determine my goals and desires. I'm not sure if that makes sense to you, but it's my truth."

Well, shit, if anyone understood the self-induced pressure of living up to a departed parent's wishes, it was him. It may have taken her years, but it sounded as though she'd dealt with her issues in a healthier way than he had. He still harbored a fuck ton of jumbled emotions regarding his screwed-up childhood. "I understand that more than you might think," he said, giving her a tiny smile.

She returned it. "Don't get me wrong. I don't regret everything. My acting career was amazing at times. I've had that role of a lifetime, which was an incredible experience. But that chapter has ended. So, to answer your question, should the industry come for me, I will politely turn them down. I don't want it, Keith. And I won't want it. I've come too far, grown too much, changed in too many ways to risk the happiness and peace I've gained. Moving here wasn't a whim or a fun way to take a break. It was my new hope after hitting rock bottom."

He liked Michaela. Liked her spirit, her wit, her personality. Liked how she fit in well with his family. It went without saying that he liked the way she looked. And their sex?

Fucking off the charts. All the makings of a potentially long-term relationship. If only he could get past this one hurdle.

He did not fully trust her assurances.

His silence must have triggered her curiosity. "You don't believe me?" she asked, sadness filling her eyes.

Keith sighed. "I want to, Mickie. It's not *you* I don't believe." She'd been so open and honest, he owed her a piece of himself in the process even if he hated the memories. "I dated a girl in high school whose family had money. They own a ski resort on the mountain. She'd been Chuck's girlfriend for the first three years of high school, but they broke up the summer before senior year. I started seeing her shortly after." He cleared his throat as he watched his hand in the water. "I fell for her hard. It was amazing and she introduced me to a life I'd never dreamed of. Once school started up again, I heard a rumor that she was just with me to get back at Chuck, who'd always hated me."

"Oh, Keith," Mickie said.

He shrugged as though the memory didn't humiliate him all over again. "It was the truth. She dumped me in a very public way, calling my family trash and letting the entire school know she'd never be with someone low class like me. My past has taught me over and over not to trust and that people can't change. That lesson has fucked with my head and made it hard to trust. Not just you, but in general."

She bit her lower lip, making her look young and innocent. Two things she was not, but he'd never asked for an inexperienced or naïve woman. He wouldn't want one. They'd never survive him.

"Fair enough," she said after a long pause. "I suppose I can't expect you to believe me on my word alone. Not after only a month of knowing me and not after you and the entire world have seen me act in direct contrast to the things I'm claiming. But I'm asking anyway. I'm asking you to put a little bit of trust in me, and I will show you that I deserve more of it. That I deserve all of it. I like you, Keith. In a way I haven't liked anyone in a very long time." She blushed. "I think we're really good together, in and out of bed. So, I'm asking you to try."

Could he do it? Could he ignore his instinct to wait for the other shoe to drop? Would he be able to hear her phone ring and not assume it was Hollywood calling her back? And could he believe she would say no if they did call?

I'm not sure I can.

But she wasn't asking for a guarantee. She hadn't promised him forever. Just a chance at something.

So he said the only thing he could offer her at that moment. "I'll try."

Chapter Twenty-One

Mickie blew out a breath she hadn't realized she'd been holding. Those two simple words meant more to her than the awards she'd won or the money she'd earned. "Really?"

He nodded. "Yes. I'm told I'm less of an asshole when you're around. Something about you making me laugh. I don't know." He winked.

A delighted laugh bubbled out of her. "Ronnie may have mentioned something like that to me as well."

He dipped his fingertips into the warm water, trailing them through the bubbles. Her body reacted immediately as if he'd stroked her skin instead of the lucky bubbles. Despite the heat of the water, her nipples pebbled, and her pussy clenched in need. It'd been too many days since they'd been together. She'd gotten spoiled by his consistent touch and craved it in its absence.

"I like you too, Mickie," he said, joking gone as their gazes met. "I can't promise anything. I've got issues, but I like us together. It's felt wrong the past few days. Not seeing you, eating with you, laughing with you, fucking you."

She inhaled a sharp breath. "I know." God, did she know. "I've been off, too. I've missed you. A lot. Maybe too much," she said as heat rushed to her face.

He nodded. "Me too."

The glow from the candles flickered off his tanned skin, accentuating the dark hair of his beard and giving him a dangerous look. He tilted his head, studying her, and instead of feeling self-conscious, her desire for him intensified. God, one heated look, and she was ready to beg him to ravage her.

"Now what?" she asked, hearing the invitation in her words.

"What do you want?" the rough timbre of his voice stroked over her nerve endings, making her shiver despite the hot bath. That voice was pure sex, promising the dark pleasures she loved, but in a way she'd not only remember in the morning but revel in instead of regret. Maybe it was foolish, especially since he'd told her she didn't have his full trust, but she trusted him. Trusted him to keep her secrets. Keep her identity and body safe while sending her to new heights.

What remained to be discovered was whether she could trust her heart with him. Though part of her wanted to hand it over on a silver platter, she'd be wise to keep it protected for the time being.

"I want you to touch me," she whispered, because the moment seemed to call for quiet words.

A wicked grin curled his lips. He stood, then slowly removed his jacket. After tossing it on the closed toilet lid he seared her with a hot-as-fuck stare. The plain black T-shirt he wore clung to his chest and arms.

Her mouth watered at the thought of running her tongue across his pecs or the ink that decorated them.

"Touch you, huh?" He slid off the ledge of the tub, coming to kneel beside it as he slid his hand deep into the water.

She sucked in a sharp breath as his wide palm splayed over her stomach beneath the surface of the water.

"Any particular place you'd like my hands?"

Her eyes fluttered, wanting to close, but she fought it, unwilling to miss any of the moment. "Y-yes."

She spread her legs and tilted her pelvis, trying to bring his hand closer to where she needed him most.

"Oh," he said, that grin growing even more devilish. "Here?" His hand closed over her upper thigh. He gave a squeeze.

Even as her muscles jumped under his touch, Mickie couldn't help the little growl of frustration. It made Keith laugh.

"No?" He slid down to her bent knee and tickled the sensitive skin behind it, making her squirm. Water sloshed up the sides of the tub. "How about here?" Each time he spoke, he moved his face closer. His lips were mere inches away from hers. A minty puff of air wafted across her face. "Not there either, huh?" he asked when she narrowed her eyes.

The man was having way too much fun torturing her. She grabbed his hand and, with another low rumble, placed it between her legs.

"Ohhhh," he said as though the light bulb had just gone off and he wasn't playing with her. "Here?" With light touches, he teased the opening of her pussy, making her squirm and whimper with need.

It felt so damn good, yet not nearly enough. The teasing touch only made her crave to be filled by him.

"Yeah. That's the spot, huh, baby?" He was so close his lips brushed hers with each word.

"Y-yes," she whispered, trying hard not to beg for more. Flames licked at her skin. How the water wasn't evaporating from the tub faster than a puddle in the desert sun would remain a mystery. "Keith, it's not enough." The whine would have embarrassed her had she not been so damn desperate for relief.

"Mmm, I fucking love that. You begging for my fingers. My cock." He licked her lower lip then drew back when she chased his mouth.

God, his playful, inadequate fingering was driving her out of her mind. If he enjoyed hearing her beg, he was about to be the happiest man in the world. She had no shame. The need to feel him inside her trounced her pride. "Yes, all of that. Please, Keith. I need it. I need you, so bad. It's been too long." She was practically babbling now.

Each time she pushed her hips up into his mischievous hand, he yanked back, denying her. Her breath came in short bursts, and she gripped the edges of the tub so hard her knuckles ached.

"Shhh," he crooned as she whimpered over and over. "I got you, gorgeous. I'll give you what you need." He sank two fingers into her, capturing her sharp gasp with his mouth.

Instead of sating the need, the feel of his lips against hers had her ravenous for more. She grabbed his wrist, holding it against her pussy as she thrust her pelvis against his magical fingers.

"That's it, baby," he said against her lips. "Use me how you want."

She moaned into his mouth. He took advantage of her parted lips to slip his tongue inside. The kiss quickly turned aggressive, with both of them battling for the upper hand. She bit his lower lip, drawing a harsh grunt from him. His fingers worked her over until she was a tingling, panting mess.

Eventually, he tore his mouth away. "Fuck, your pussy's so goddammed hot." His eyes were nearly black, smoldering with need.

His cock must be putting his zipper to the ultimate test.

His lips quirked up into the sexiest smile she'd ever seen, and suddenly, fingers weren't enough anymore. What hung between his legs had her attention now.

Mickie lunged forward, attacking his mouth again. She scrambled to her knees, which dislodged his hand, sent water splashing over the side of the tub. His shirt was the victim of the spray as well.

"Sorry," she muttered into his mouth as she climbed out of the tub and into his arms.

He chuckled as she wrapped her wet body around him, soaking him from shoulders to knees. "Pretty sure you're not." Bubbles clung to her skin and now his clothing as well.

He squeezed her slippery ass, making her gasp. "You're right. I'm not."

Somehow with lots of shifting, awkward bumping of limbs, and water droplets flinging everywhere, they ended up on the bathroom floor. Keith lay on his back atop a fuzzy, plush rug while she straddled his stomach. Water dripped from her hair onto his shirt, but he didn't seem to care in the least. Instead, his attention went to her wet breasts.

"How is it possible you're even sexier when wet?" he asked as he thumbed her nipples.

She jolted as a streak of electricity shot from her breasts to her clit. Her eyes fell shut, and for a moment she reveled in his touch before the need for more took over yet again.

Giving him a sultry smile, she shimmied down until she straddled his thighs. "Shirt off," she commanded.

He winked. "Yes, ma'am." As he curled up, he reached behind his head and pulled the damp shirt up. One by one, he revealed the ridges of his chiseled abs. Her mouth watered, and she could no more resist licking a path up the valley of his stomach than she could stop breathing. Keith sucked in a sharp breath the moment her tongue hit his heated skin.

That gave her wicked ideas of other places she could work her tongue. As though she'd die if she didn't get him naked in the next five seconds, she assaulted the button and zipper of his jeans. He bridged his hips, allowing her to yank them down below his knees.

As he shifted to kick the jeans off his legs, she bent down and took as much of his cock as she could manage into her throat.

"Jesus, fuck," he shouted. His hips shot up, and his cock bumped the back of her throat. She gagged slightly but regained control quickly and sucked him with vigor. The silky skin glided across her tongue, making her hum her enjoyment. Keith smelled as she'd have expected. Masculine and earthy with the hint of motor oil he never could shake.

His heavy sac hung between his bent thighs, beckoning her. She cupped it, giving the lightest of tugs. His reaction was instantaneous and near violent.

"Fuck!" he shouted, slapping his palms against the tile.

Mickie loved this with every fiber of her being. She loved taking this big, strong, sexy man and reducing him to a puddle of need and curses with just her mouth.

His harsh groans and straining muscles only spurned her on until he finally yelled, "Stop! Baby, you gotta stop, or I'm gonna come way too fucking early. Shit, that mouth is a goddammed weapon."

She released him with a final lick and lifted her gaze to meet his. He looked dazed and delirious but nowhere near done. Mickie wiped her slick lower lip, and he groaned like a tortured man.

"I want you like I've never wanted anyone," he said, voice rough as gravel. "It doesn't go away. I can't think of anything but you. All damn day. All damn night."

What woman in her right mind wouldn't want to hear those words from a man like Keith? "I know exactly how you feel," she whispered. Something lodged in her throat, making the words croak out. Must have been fuzz. It couldn't have been emotion or l—or anything else.

As she crawled back up his body, she makes sure to pause and hover her tits over his cock. She brushed her nipples over the dripping tip. His growl was seriously the sexiest sound she'd ever heard. Finally, she was astride his hard length once again, hovering her pussy over him.

"You gonna ride me, baby? Ride that cock until I pump you full of my cum?"

That dirty talk. Shit, the man had a black belt in it.

"That's exactly what I'm going to do," she said as she wrapped her hand around his length and began to lower down on him. She'd been on birth control or years, so they'd ditched the condoms about two weeks ago after getting tested. Thank God for all the squats she'd done over the past months, because watching him fight for control as she took him inside her at a maddeningly slow pace was too good to miss.

His jaw ticked, the veins in his arms bulged, and his nostrils flared with the force of his rapid inhalations. "Michaela," he said, warning clear in his tone. Against the gray tiles, his nails stood out, stark white as they pressed down hard.

She grinned. He wasn't the only one suffering. Her body screamed at her to move faster, but the delicious torture won out, and she kept up the snail's pace.

At least until Keith growled a "fuck it," grabbed her hips, and slammed up into her.

Mickie cried out as the sensation of being stretched and full ripped through her. Nothing felt better in the world. He held her hips with a vice grip, keeping himself buried inside her. They stared at each other, chests heaving. Electricity popped and crackled between them. The powerful connection they shared went far beyond physical. The need for him. To just be near him. Talk to him. See him. It scared her as much as it thrilled her. If he eventually realized he couldn't put his full trust in the changes she'd made to her life, he'd walk.

And she'd shatter, proving him right. That she wasn't a strong as she proclaimed.

She shoved the intrusive thoughts aside. Worry for the future. Right now, they had what they both wanted, and she refused to spoil the magic with pessimism.

She swiveled her hips, loving the way his neck arched and abs tightened. Not to mention how every stroke of his cock inside her had sparks shooting through her.

"Christ, you feel so fucking good," he said as he released her hips and stroked his large hands up and down her burning thighs. "So damn perfect." The words were whispered as though he meant them for himself.

She smiled and began to move over him.

"That's it, baby. Take us to the moon."

With each roll of her hips the pleasure multiplied, and within a minute, she was riding him fast and hard to the finish line.

"Fuck. That's it. Yes." She planted her hands on his thighs and leaned back. The angle had him stroking along the front wall of her pussy, making her shout and nearly collapse from the intense rush. Her head fell back, breasts thrust out, and she shuddered.

"Keith..."

"I know. Never want it to fucking end."

Exactly. She could stay in that moment forever. She could starve, waste away, none of it would matter as long as she felt this good all the time.

Keith drew his knees up, planted his heels on the floor, and thrust up into her. Hard.

Her mouth flew open on a cry as she fell forward. Her hands landed on his chest, stopping her forward momentum. He was so deep she could feel him in her soul. She worked her hip like a mad woman. Every downstroke had him hitting something inside her that lit her up like a damned light shot. "Yes!" she shouted. "Right there. Right there. God, Keith. *Right* there."

He kept powering up into her. The water from the bath had long evaporated, replaced by sweat that had her just as wet and slippery. The edges of her vision blurred at the same time her fingertips started to tingle. Her eyes fluttered shut, and she let the climax rise up.

"Eyes on me," Keith said, sounding like a man on the brink.

Her eyes flew open and locked with his. They both moved faster, harder, more desperate to watch the pleasure take over.

And then it happened. Mickie slammed down on him one final time, cried out so loud her voice cracked, and her fingers curled into his chest. Her entire body shook, pussy clenching over and over again.

Keith screamed out her name, gripped her hips with punishing force and emptied into her. His rhythmic contracting and relaxing caused her to rock over him, prolonging her orgasm. Eventually, she collapsed on his chest. He wrapped his bulky arms around her. Neither moved beyond catching their breath.

"Missed you," he whispered.

She pressed a kiss to his damp pec.

The moment was perfect. Hot, erotic, but also tender and sweet in a way. Something warm and pleasant spread through her chest. It was then she realized she'd never been happier than she was at that moment. Wet, sore, exhausted, lying on her bathroom floor. All the fame, money, possessions, and adoration she'd received in the past didn't come close to reaching the joy of this simple moment.

She wouldn't voice one ounce of complaint if they fell asleep right there, no matter how much her body would hate her in the morning.

Just as she was about to ask if Keith was still awake, a loud bang followed by a screeched, "You bitches better be done making up. If I walk upstairs to find something that makes me pluck my eyeballs out, I'm telling you right now, I'm gonna throw a helluva fit."

"Oh my, God," Michaela said with a gasp as she pushed up. "Ralph! I forgot about Ralph." She scrambled off Keith. "My friend from LA is visiting."

Keith smirked. "I know. Who do you think gave me the time to be ravaged by you?" And ravaged was exactly how he looked, sprawled on his back on her wet bathroom floor. His sated cock rested against a muscular thigh, slick from their combined arousal.

Her jaw dropped. "You met him?"

Keith nodded as he sat up with a wince. "Yeah, ran into him in the driveway. Quite the guard dog you have there."

Mickie ran a hand through her damp hair. "Yeah, sorry about that. He's protective. We've been through a lot together."

"Shit." He stood, rolling his shoulders. "Not as young as I used to be."

"Aww," she said with a giggle as she moved into his body. "I'll rub the sore spots later." Now that they'd worked through things, she didn't want to be more than inches away from him.

He wrapped a bulky arm around her back and drew her in for a dirty kiss.

"That sounds perfect. For Ralph's sake, I hope he bought enough ice cream for three."

She couldn't even try to stop the enormous smile from gracing her face. "You're gonna hang out with us?"

With a snort, he slapped her ass. "If you're gonna be my woman, I'm gonna get some ice cream out of the deal." Then he winked at her and strode into her bedroom, naked as could be. "Give us two minutes," he shouted before shutting her door and flipping the lock.

"Two!" Ralph shouted back. "And unless you're an embarrassment to men everywhere, that's not enough time for you guys to go at it again, so don't be getting any ideas."

Keith laughed as he rummaged through her closet for a pair of jeans he'd left last week.

Mickie stood in her bathroom, grinning like an idiot.

His woman?

He'd called her his woman.

Yeah. If he was going to call her that, she'd buy him every tub of ice cream in the shop.

Chapter Twenty-Two

The next morning Mickie found herself seated at her brand-new kitchen island behind a giant stack of pancakes. When Keith didn't return home the previous night, the rest of the Benson crew assumed he and Mickie had reconciled, which resulted in them inviting themselves over for an epic breakfast. They'd brought all the ingredients, and Jagger did the cooking. How could she refuse?

"Slide the fucking syrup down this way, would ya?" Ronnie asked with her mouth full. She sat there in pink dog pajamas that were the last thing on earth Mickie ever pictured her wearing.

JP snorted as he sent the syrup gliding across the island to his sister. "You're such a lady, Ron. Can't imagine why you don't have a boyfriend."

As though six instead of twenty-six, Ronnie opened her mouth and gave her brother a gross view of her half-chewed pancakes.

"I rest my case," he said.

"Children, let's try to make it through one meal without fighting, okay?" Jagger said as he reached over Ronnie's head to deposit a platter with more bacon than Mickie had ever seen in her life. Beside her, Ralph sighed like a damsel swooning over the prince.

She elbowed her best friend and whispered, "Straight, Ralphie. The man is straight."

"The penis wants what the penis wants, hon."

Mickie burst out laughing, nearly choking on her coffee. From her other side, Keith raised an eyebrow. She shook her head. "Nothing. Ralph is just lusting after Jagger. Again."

"Well," Keith said, "Jag's not having much luck with the ladies these days, so maybe he'd be willing to give you a go, Ralph." He stuffed a forkful of chocolate chip pancakes in his mouth.

The kitchen fell silent except for the sizzling of bacon on the stove.

Really? How much bacon did they need? Mickie glanced at the now empty platter. Apparently, a *lot* of bacon.

"Holy fucking shit," JP burst out as they all gaped at Keith. "Did the grumpiest Benson brother just make a funny about Jagger's sex life? Damn, Mickie, whatever you did to him last night, keep at it. He's a new man."

Her face heated, but before she had a chance to fire back, Keith flipped his brother off.

"Hey!" Jagger said from the stove. "No offense, Ralph, but I do just fine with the ladies, and I'm not jumping ship on pussy anytime soon."

With a dramatic sigh, Ralph said, "A boy can always hope," at the same time JP said, "Tell that to your apron, bro."

Michaela bit her lip to keep from laughing as Jagger flipped JP off, too. The poor guy was going to get a complex at this point. Though with the shit he talked, he probably deserved it and more. Giving the finger in this family was akin to hugging in others.

Jagger pointed his spatula at JP. "Don't knock the apron, man. It's a classic."

A laugh bubbled out of Mickie as Ronnie snorted. The apron in question had cartoon images of a cow, pig, chicken, and deer standing in a row. Beneath the pictures, it read, "I want your meat."

Ralph giggled as well. "Despite the homoerotic apron, if we're getting technical here, Michaela is the one who should really be with Jagger."

Keith stiffened, so she rubbed his back as she rolled her eyes. "Seriously, Ralph?"

"Ohhh, now we're talking." Jagger winked her way, causing Keith to growl.

This possessive side of him gave her a secret thrill, not that she'd admit that to anyone.

"Not that I'm arguing your incredible insight, but why me?" Jagger asked as he added the second round of bacon to the empty platter.

"Uhh, it's so obvious." Ralph paused, seeming to love the way they all hung on his words. "Mick and Jagger, duh!"

There was a five-second pause before JP, Ronnie, and Jagger all burst out laughing.

"Oh, my God," Ronnie said between hoots. "That's perfect. How did we not notice that?"

"I noticed," Keith grumbled. "Just didn't think it needed a fucking discussion." He stabbed a pancake with his fork then plopped it on his plate.

That only set his siblings on another round of hysterics. This time Ralph joined in, nudging her arm. "I love them all," he whispered once he caught his breath.

Her smile grew so big her cheeks ached. As she glanced around her recently renovated kitchen at the faces of her new friends and best friend enjoying each other, she began to well up from the multitude of emotions.

"Hey." Keith stared at her with concern in his gaze. His hand went to her lower back. Warmth radiated through her body at the caring gesture. "You all right?"

"Yeah," she whispered back, though no one seemed to be paying attention to them. They were too busy praising Ralph for his discovery. "It's just…" Her face heated. "This might be the most perfect morning I've ever had." It had started by waking with Keith's strong arms anchored around her in her bed. Never before had she wanted to be touched while sleeping. Now she cuddled up to him like a small kitten in need of warmth. If he was near, she wanted contact, whether awake or not.

Keith's face softened. He captured her chin between his thumb and forefinger then pressed the sweetest kiss she'd ever experienced to her lips. "Makes sense," he said. "A follow-up to the most perfect night."

Yes. The night had been perfect if hours of hot, dirty sex and multiple orgasms defined perfection. And it did. After their bathroom adventure, they'd pigged out on ice cream with Ralph before retiring to her room, where they split the rest of the night between short dozes and intense reconnection.

"Hey, think you two can stop making goo-goo eyes at each other for like one minute?" Ronnie asked.

A balled-up napkin hit Mickie on the side of the head, jerking her out of her lov—uh, lust bubble. Not love. Lust and a lot of like, but not love. That'd be insane.

And foolish.

Reckless.

Just plain stupid.

Giving the gang a sheepish smile, she broke the connection with Keith. "Sorry. He's just so hot."

"Oh, God, it never gets less disgusting," Ronnie said, adding gagging sound effects and gestures. "Anyway, what you don't realize and what makes this extra great is that we are all named after British rock stars. So the fact that you're Mick, means you truly belong with us."

If only.

Beside her, Keith shifted away. The movement was subtle, hell, maybe he didn't even realize it himself, but she caught it.

Shaking off the disappointment, she pinged her gaze between Ronnie and JP. "You were?"

JP nodded, swallowed his mouthful, then said, "Yep. Our mom was obsessed with British rock bands. Mostly Led Zeppelin and The Stones. Jagger is obvious, Keith is for Keith Richards. I'm JP for John Paul Jones. Ian is Ian Steward. Jimmy for Jimmy Paige. And last but not least, Veronica for Ronnie Woods."

"Lucky me," Ronnie mumbled.

Mickie's eyes widened. "Wow, I had no idea. That's pretty cool. It's something fun that binds you all but isn't completely obvious, like having all your first names begin with the same letter."

"Yep," JP said. He winked. "And now you're part of it."

Ugh, why did Keith flinch every time someone lumped her in with the lot of them? Was it because he didn't want to include her in his family or because he worried she wouldn't view herself as one of them? He'd flat out admitted he expected her to get bored and run back to Hollywood in the near future.

She'd forced herself to purge that from her mind the previous night, but now it hit her with a vengeance. What if he couldn't get past the fear? What if she spent months, years, growing closer to him and his family only to find he woke up each morning waiting for her to hand him a movie script and a plane ticket? Could their relationship—could any relationship for that matter—withstand such doubts and distrust?

But on the flipside, maybe all he needed was to more time to get to know her. To learn her inside and out. If he did, perhaps he'd discover she meant it when she said she no longer wanted that life. Nothing could or would entice her back to Hollywood because leaving hadn't been a decision to improve her life. It had been a necessity to save her life.

"Hey," Ralph whispered, bringing her back to the present. The Bensons were all chatting, laughing, and ribbing each other as usual.

"What?"

"Have you told him?"

She wrinkled her nose. "Told him what?"

He rolled his eyes. "All that sex is making you forgetful. Told him about the guy from the diner."

Oh, crap, impossible as it might seem, she had forgotten about Chuck after Keith came over. "No. Not yet. But I will. I don't want to ruin the moment."

His perfectly shaped eyebrows drew down. "Okay, but don't put it off for too long. He needs to know."

With a nod, she whispered, "So what do you think of the crew?"

A smile transformed Ralph's face from serious to playful. "I think they are perfect for you and you are perfect for them."

So did she. It was what she'd been missing all those years in Hollywood. A deep connection to other people. She hadn't had a group, a family, and it'd nearly destroyed her. Now that she'd found it, she wanted to protect the precious gift with all she had.

"So don't blow it," he added, tossing in a wink to soften the statement.

I'll try my very best.

CHRIST, HE THOUGHT his family would never fucking leave.

Yeah, breakfast had been enjoyable and all, but after watching Mickie laugh, have fun, and fit like a glove with the most important people in his life, he was hard as a fucking diamond once again. This need he'd developed for her was insane and bound to be a major distraction, but right then, he didn't give a fuck. They were alone, and it'd been too many hours since he'd had his hands on her.

Or in her.

"Ugh, why did I tell them I'd take care of the clean-up?" she asked with a groan as she hiked up her sleeves. With her back to him, she stood by the island, surveying the mess. Those damn jeans that probably cost as much as he made in a week hugged her round ass, calling to him like a beacon in a raging storm. He'd say it was money well spent, except he'd been all over that ass without the jeans, and it was even more stellar in the nude. The woman could wear a cloth sack and that ass would still turn heads. "You realize JP ate more than all of us combined? He should be on clean-up duty. And P.S., where the hell does he put it all? That shit's just not fair," she grumbled as she whirled to face him.

The smile on her makeup-free face, the playful spark in her eyes, and the slightly rumpled hair all made for an irresistible picture of a happy woman. If simple days like this made her shine so bright, maybe Mickie could live in Vermont long term. Perhaps she really had changed her life in a permanent way.

He nearly snorted out loud. That was the trap right there. Get comfortable. Start hoping. Start believing.

Then the ax would fall, and he'd be left bleeding inside.

Again.

Fuck that. He had an impenetrable cage around his heart for a reason and no plans to locate the key. No matter how gorgeous the woman. Or how well she got along with his family. Or how many times she made him smile and laugh. Or how hot it was to bury himself inside her…

Shit, he needed to stop his mind from spiraling.

"What's wrong?" Mickie tilted her head at him. "What's that look fo—oh!"

He snagged her around the waist and yanked her flush against him, cutting her off with his mouth. She tasted of vanilla from that fancy coffee shit she made with her ridiculous machine.

As if he possessed everything she'd ever need, Mickie melted against him, moaning into his mouth. He filled his hands with her ass and held her close as he ground his erection against her.

"Fuck the dishes," she whispered, breathless right before kissing him again.

Some sound in the distance almost halted him, but with the way his ears were rushing from the surge of arousal, drowning it out was too easy.

"Sorry, honey, just me. I forgot my pho—oh well, *hello* there." Ralph's amused voice had Mickie jumping back with a squeak.

Her face turned beet red and she pressed the back of her hand to her shiny lips—the lips he'd ravaged and made swollen with his own.

"Puh-lease," Ralph said as Keith turned around. "Do not stop on my account." He propped his hip against the kitchen island. "I'll just, you know, watch." He winked and smirked. On a typical day, the smug gleam in Ralph's eye would have driven Keith up a wall, but he was feeling pretty chill and only snorted.

Mickie started laughing. "You'll need to find someone else to perv over today. Get your phone and go."

Ralph's eyebrows winged up. "So you can go back to *kissing*?" he sing-songed.

Now it was Keith's turn to laugh. "No wonder you get along with my family. Ballbusters, all of you."

Ralph opened his mouth, no doubt to shoot off some snarky comment about balls, but Mickie beat him to it, winging a potholder at his head.

He dodged the flying missile with a bark of laughter. "Okay, all right, I'm going." He snatched his phone off the counter with a flourish before blowing a kiss Mickie's way. *"Caio!"*

The second he left the room, Keith tugged Mickie close again. Just the feel of her fully clothed against him in a non-sexual hold had him fired up more than any woman had in years. "I believe —"

"I'm assuming you told him, right, Mickie?" Ralph yelled right before the door slammed shut.

Mickie's shoulders slumped, and she groaned.

Told him? "Told me what?" Dread crawled up his spine with icy fingers.

Her face screwed up, and she mumbled. "Freakin' Ralph."

Fuck, it happened already. She'd been offered a script she couldn't turn away from. He took a step back as his insides froze.

She reached for him. "It's nothing. We can talk about it later. Ralph is just being his usual dramatic self."

"Tell me," he barked, then winced as her eyes flared and her hand dropped to her side. "Sorry. That came out rougher than I meant." He took another step away. Being close to her muddled his thinking. All he wanted to do was sink into her sweetness, and if she was about to crush him with another secret, he needed his shields in place.

Mickie sighed. "Fine. I really didn't want to do this now and ruin this amazing morning." With a small smile, she grabbed his hand, keeping him from putting even more distance between them. Even the small touch spread through him, making him crave skin when he should have been focusing on her words instead of the heat between them.

With more mental strength than he'd thought possible, he blocked out the desire and focused on what she was about to say.

Here it comes.

Steeling his heart as much as possible, he clenched his teeth and tried not to break the bones in her hand with the force of his grip.

"Ralph and I had breakfast at the diner the morning he got here and when we were leaving," —she shifted her eyes away then back to his— "that guy from the day I was in your shop—Chuck? —was waiting at my car."

"Look, I expected this to—wait, what?" What the hell did she just say? Chuck? This wasn't a warning of one final obligation that would take her back to LA?

Chuck hassled her. Oh, fuck no. He grabbed her shoulders. "Did that fucker hurt you?"

"No! Of course not." She shook her head so fast her hair flew in her face. "Ralph was with me," she said as though her sassy friend could take down Chuck. "He just...said a bunch of bullshit."

Yeah, that was Chuck. One hundred percent bully. All talk, and no action, but talk could do as much or more damage than fists. Keith had learned the hard way.

"Did he come on to you? Or say a bunch of homophobic garbage to Ralph? He's an out and proud bigot. So's his douchebag cousin, Bud."

"No." She squirmed, clearly uncomfortable with what she was going to say next. "He led me to believe he knows that I'm Scarlett, though."

Fuck me.

"Shit, babe, he's just the type of asshole to use that for his own benefit. Wait, why aren't you panicking?" As soon as he left here, he'd be paying Chuck a visit. Maybe he'd bring his trusty shotgun along.

"No," Mickie said, wagging a finger in front of his face. "Whatever murderous idea just went through your head, you're not doing it. I did freak out, but Ralph talked me off the ledge. He reminded me that I'm fierce and I don't take shit. So if Chuck is stupid enough to come after me—which he probably is since he seems to have been blessed with only a few brain cells—then I'll deal with it like the badass bitch I am."

He smiled. God, she was something when she got all fierce. "I'm proud of you," he whispered before pressing a kiss to her mouth. When he pulled back, she tried to chase for more, but he wasn't finished talking. "It's good to see you ready to fight instead of running like you did the other night."

Nodding, she slipped her arms around his neck. Her cheeks turned an adorable shade of pink. "I think that was more about us, and your reaction to Scarlett than anything."

"I'm sorry," he whispered. And damn he was. Even if he still worried she wouldn't want to stay in Vermont forever, he hated the idea of hurting her.

"Shh, we already talked about it. It's done." Then she bit her lower lip and averted her eyes.

"What? Is there something else?" He wanted to demand she tell him what had her eyebrows drawing down.

"Chuck, he said stuff about your mom." The words were practically whispered as though the low tone would buffer the blow.

His blood had been ice a moment ago, but now it shot to an instant boil. He started to pull away, but she grabbed his other hand and held him in front of her.

"I didn't believe a word he said," she rushed on. "I *don't* believe it. None of it is my business, so you don't have to explain anything now or ever. I just thought you needed to know that he's insinuating things about your mother."

With a grunt, Keith shook his head. Mickie quieted, letting him sort through his thoughts while watching him with those curious eyes. Christ, she was good for him. In such a short time, she'd learned to navigate him and his moods. After a few seconds, he lifted one of her hands and pressed a kiss to her palm. "Let me guess. He said she was a prostitute."

"Not in those exact words, but the meaning was clear. Yes. But like I said, I didn't believe him. He's an asshole, Keith." She tightened her arms around his neck, pulling him into a tight hug.

It's not a lie," he whispered against her ear. Physical pain erupted in his chest.

She released him and gripped his hands in hers squeezing gently. "Keith, you don't need to—"

"I want to." He needed to show her same level of trust as she'd done with him if he wanted this to work. "I'm trying, remember?" He gave as much of a smile as he could muster.

Her eyes softened. "Yeah. Come on, let's sit somewhere more comfortable." Still holding his hand, she guided him upstairs and into her bedroom, where she sat on the edge of the bed. One little tug had him next to her. She turned, draping her legs over his thighs. "Anything you tell me stays here, Keith. My life is not an open book anymore, and I'd never, *never* do anything to betray your trust, or jeopardize your family's privacy. That includes suing the pants off Chuck if I need to."

She must have been referring to her very active presence on social medial in the past. Basically, every moment of her life had been tweeted, photographed, and chatted about. Since meeting her, he'd yet to see her so much as scroll through Facebook, but still, opening up was a risk as her vacation from social media was probably just that, a short stint. Habits were hard to break.

But as he'd told her, he'd try. And bailing at the first opportunity to trust didn't count as trying.

Her soft weight resting against him helped ground the tumultuous feelings. She gazed at him with compassion and care. It was…nice. Comforting without feeling smothering. He'd been with many women over the years. Hell, he was a thirty-eight-year-old man who'd never had a relationship last more than a year. And he liked to fuck. That meant a fair number of bed partners, but this was the first time he could recall feeling better about himself because a woman merely sat with him.

Clearing his throat, he set his hands on her thighs and forced himself to begin. "We've talked a little about my mom, but she was amazing. Sweet, hardworking, always trying to make the best out of life. She got pregnant with me at seventeen before she'd finished high school. Her parents didn't care much about her, and she ended up dropping out of school and marrying my dad, who you know is a raging, abusive alcoholic." He met her somber gaze. "I'm sorry. Is this too much?"

A soft smile greeted him. "No, Keith. If there's one thing I learned in my months of rehab and therapy, it's that I cannot hide from myself or my actions. I abused alcohol and drugs. It's my reality. Hearing what I could have become I not dug myself out of the pit only strengthens my resolve. Besides, this isn't about me. I'd want to hear your story regardless of whether it was difficult for me."

He cupped her smooth face between his beat-up hands and kissed her long, slow, and sweet. It wasn't the type of kiss he usually shared with women as it didn't lead anywhere but to a smile and a flip of his stomach. But in some ways, it was even better than a dirty, sloppy, lead-to-sex kiss. When it ended, she rubbed her nose against his before straightening as though to urge him to continue.

Fuck, he hated tearing the sutures off these old wounds.

"Both my parents grew up in shit—they themselves were products of teenage parents with no education, money, or love for their kids. My mom tried so hard to be different and to give us a different life even though we were dirt poor. It was hard for her to work with so many kids and without a high school degree. My dad worked odd jobs but spent the majority of his earnings on booze. When she could, my mom cleaned houses and always made sure every penny of her earnings went to us, even if it pissed off my father."

Revealing the parts of his past he never let himself relive felt like taking a paring knife to his skin. The agony almost had him swallowing the words back down. But Michaela sat without an ounce of judgment in her gaze, patiently waiting for him to be ready to continue.

He ran a hand down his face, pausing to scratch a non-existent itch in his beard. Anything to prolong the morbid story of his life.

"Mom was always promising Dad would change. That one day, he'd turn over a new leaf. Always swearing things would be different—better. She constantly swore we'd have more soon. The money would roll in soon. God, I grew to hate the word soon. The old man never bothered with the lip service. He was and is content being a miserable fucker. I think for her it was more of a wish for us than a promise. But as a kid, I couldn't help but hope every time she said the word soon."

Hope was the most agonizing memory of all. The countless times when he'd been young and naïve enough to believe things would change. Once, when he'd been eleven and old enough to take care of his younger siblings by himself, she'd been able to get a steady job cleaning rooms at a local motel. She'd promised to take them to Disney with the money she'd be able to save. At the time, he'd been too young to understand the financial mountain of such a promise. Regardless, he'd spent the following week on cloud nine, imagining his entire family laughing and smiling in the happiest place on earth. Ten days later, he returned home from school to find his mom sitting at the table with a black eye while his dad stuffed his pockets with the money she'd been keeping in a coffee jar.

The trip never happened. To this day, he'd never been to Disney World.

"Keith?" Mickie prodded in a gentle voice.

He blinked. "Sorry. Lost in the past."

She cupped his cheek. The subtle stroking of her fingers through his beard had him wanting to purr like a spoiled cat. Who knew that would be a sweet spot?

"Take your time, baby. I'm not going anywhere."

Promises. Hope. There they were again. Back in his life, only this time, he failed to resist the temptation was beginning to believe in them again.

Keith sighed and pushed the present aside to continue dredging up the past.

"Anyway, around the time I was fifteen, shit got really bad money-wise. Ronnie was only three at the time. One night she woke up crying. When she didn't stop after a few minutes, I went in to check on her. She'd wet the bed. After I'd changed the sheets and gotten her new pajamas, I went to peek in on my mom. But she wasn't in her room. She wasn't in the house. Neither was Dad, but that was nothing new. He spent most nights at the bar. The next night I set my alarm and woke up to find the same thing. She wasn't there."

He took a breath to keep his breakfast down. All the while, Mickie's soft hand roamed over his back providing a comfort he'd never allowed himself before.

"The third night, I tailed my mom when she left the house around eleven at night. She walked about a mile to the shitty motel she cleaned. I thought maybe she was cleaning rooms at night, which was weird, but what the fuck did I know. She walked to one of rooms. Room seven. I'll never forget it. Then she took out a keycard and let herself in. I followed and stood outside the door with my ear pressed against it."

His stomach lurched. He'd never forget what happened next, but he never allowed himself to think about it either. It destroyed him, filled him with guilt, and made his hatred for his father grow exponentially.

"Sorry, I just need a minute."

"Baby, take all the time you need. There's nowhere I'd rather be than by your side."

His eyes fell shut as he absorbed her sweet words. God, he wanted this. Wanted her so much more than was wise.

"I'm okay. Uh, so I was outside the door and I could hear… things. Men's voices, grunting, a yelp from my mom. I thought maybe she was selling drugs. That my dad had put her up to it. I was so pissed, I rammed the door in. Even then, I was over six feet and the lock was practically made of toothpicks and chewing gum. When the door crashed open…" He shuddered at the visceral memory of the odor, the smoky fog throughout the room, and the sounds of bodies slapping together.

"It stunk so bad, I held my breath until I was dizzy to avoid breathing in whatever crap floated in the air. There were too guys in the room and my mom was on the bed. N-naked."

Mickie sucked in a breath.

He was almost in a trance now, seeing it as though it were in real-time. The words fell from his lips without thought, just rote memory. "A hundred-dollar bill lay on the dingy comforter next to her. One of guys was between her legs, fucking her. She was staring off into space like she wasn't even aware of what was happening. Like she'd gone somewhere else in her head, but there were tears on her cheeks."

Keith swallowed a painful lump.

"What about the other man?" she whispered in a voice full of dread.

"Not a man. Chuck. A fifteen-year-old boy like me. Sitting in the corner jerking off as he filmed the piece of shit doing my mother." His stomach clenched at the nauseating memory. "Found out later, it was his older cousin."

"Oh, my God. What did you do?"

"I had the element of surprise, and I was way bigger than both of them. I ripped the first guy away from my mom, grabbed her clothes and threw them at her. While she was getting dressed, I laid out the guy who'd been fucking her with one punch. Then I moved on to Chuck. I hit him once, then again. I was about to nail him a third time when the room was suddenly flooded with cops. Turned out the motel owner suspected what my mom was using the room for and called the police."

Mickie's hand stilled on his back. "Oh, my God, Keith. What did they do?"

"They arrested all of us. But, uh, Chuck's old man is the Chief of Police. Back then he was just a captain, but still, he had a lot of clout. Chuck and his cousin were out within the hour. I was brought into an interrogation room and told that if I didn't want my mother brought up on prostitution charges, I was to forget Chuck was ever there. If I made a thing of it or ever brought up the fact that Chuck had been filming it, they'd throw the book at my mom."

"Keith..." she murmured as she stroked her hands up and down his chest in a soothing pattern. "That is so fucked up."

He shrugged. "Yep. But my mom had kids to take care of. Chuck's father destroyed the video and we never spoke of it again. I wasn't charged with assault. But Chuck has hated me ever since. It was only compounded by the mess with Della.

Anyway, my mom promised she'd never hook again, and we all moved on with our lives."

"Don't do that." She continued petting him as though calming an agitated animal. He'd be lying if he didn't admit he leaned heavily into her touch.

"Don't do what?"

"Minimize how you felt. How you still feel about it. Keith, I can't even imagine…you were fifteen."

He snorted. "Yeah. It fucked me up, that's for sure. When I got home my dad beat my ass for being out late. Mom tried to stop him but he just screamed at her about losing a source of income." He let out a harsh laugh. "God, it was so fucked up."

"Your siblings—do they—"

"No!" he barked. "And they never will. They don't need that information tainting their memories of our mother." He'd die before letting a soul know what happened in that house that night. He owed his mother and his siblings that much. He'd go to his grave knowing he hadn't destroyed the only positivity in their childhood.

"Keith, you need to learn to share the burden. Your siblings aren't kids who need you to take care of them anymore. This won't ruin their memories of your mother. It'll make them sad, sure, but it won't destroy who she was to them. And it sounds to me like she was a woman who would do literally anything to make sure her children had what they needed. There's no shame in that."

He should have known Mickie wouldn't cast an ounce of judgment on him or his mother. Her easy acceptance of him and his demons was just another reason he couldn't stay away from her.

Chapter Twenty-Three

Michaela's heart fractured and bled for the mistreated boy who'd been forced into adulthood way before his time. To shoulder such a heavy burden alone and for the protection of his mother and younger siblings was precisely what she'd expect from this honorable man. Words failed her, but the desire to ease the pain that still haunted him became a living need.

"Keith," she whispered as she climbed off his lap. With her knee, she nudged his legs apart. Standing between the strong thighs, she stared down at the somber man who gave so much. Without another word, she lifted the hem of his T-shirt and worked it up his abs. When she reached his armpits and cocked an eyebrow, he kept his arms at his sides.

"Babe…"

"Shhh," she soothed. "Let me take care of you, Keith. Please. Let me show you what I think of you, how much I want you, how much I admire you." She swallowed a lump. "And how much you mean to me."

His intense gaze bore into hers for long seconds before he finally raised his arms. Once she'd freed the tee from his delicious body, she pressed a hand to the left side of his chest. The strong, steady beat of his heart thrummed against her palm. "Do you feel that?" she asked, soaking in the warmth of the firm pectoral muscle beneath her fingertips. "You have a tough exterior that's so hard to pierce, but beneath it, this heart holds so much love. It's extraordinary. *You're* extraordinary, Keith. You are such a good man. Thank you for sharing a piece of this powerful heart with me. I promise to be worthy of the gift."

His eyes flashed at the word promise, but he didn't balk against her claim. Instead, he covered her hand with his much larger one. Together, they cradled the organ Keith sought so desperately to protect.

Mickie vowed to keep that heart safe no matter the cost. Even if he couldn't give her the entire thing, she'd guard every piece he shared with all her strength. And as she'd recently learned, she was tougher than she'd ever given herself credit for.

He helped her see that.

With her hand still beneath his, she lowered to her knees. Tearing her gaze away from the intensity of Keith's wasn't an option. As she descended, he followed her with his eyes. They grew more fiery with each passing second.

"Lift up," she whispered from her spot on the floor.

The muscles in his throat worked up and down with his hard swallow. "I want you naked too," he rasped. "Let me see all of you."

She nodded as he released her hand and went to work on lowering his sweatpants. She shoved her yoga pants down, wiggled around, then tossed them aside. Her shirt followed, leaving her in a lacy bra.

When she reached for the clasp behind her back, he said, "Leave it. I love how it pushes your tits up like that." He sounded like a man close to the edge. The emotional upheaval combined with physical need had his voice gravelly and the veins in his arms popping as he gripped the sides of the bed.

A sly smile curled her lips. Shouldn't take much to nudge him into oblivion.

She shifted her attention from his face to the erect cock jutting up at her. Her mouth watered at the knowledge she was going to drive him insane just by tasting him. The head was nearly purple, and he was so hard, it had to be uncomfortable. This whole scene excited something deep and primal in her. She'd been out of control of her entire life, including encounters with men. Now, as she rested on her knees in front of a heavily muscled man, she'd never felt more powerful. He had no choice but to wait for her to deliver the pleasure. To sit at the edge of the bed with an aching cock. To beg her, if it came to that. Mickie licked her lips. She wouldn't make him beg. She wanted him with too powerful a force.

"Fuck, you look hungry for it."

"Oh, I am." With a light touch, she traced the vein running up the underside of his length. He hissed when she drew a circle around the head.

She did it again. This time, she captured the drop of precum welling at the tip. Then she brought it to her lips and licked the salty digit clean.

Keith groaned, which brought a smile to her lips. She made eye contact, loving the way his eyes swirled with heat and his nostrils flared. Keeping her gaze locked with his, she sucked the tip of his dick between her lips.

"Jesus Christ," he whispered, as though it really was a prayer.

She sucked the head and he grunted, fisting the comforter with a white-knuckled grip. She kept her focus on the silky tip, tonguing the underside as she sucked hard. The increased force of his breathing and the rumbly noises coming from his chest spurred her on. She wanted, craved, to hear those low sounds become harsh shouts of pleasure. Without warning, she slid his cock to the back of her throat, holding him there as she added extra suction. He barked out a curse, and his hips lifted off the bed involuntarily.

She gagged, and saliva slipped from her mouth, running down his shaft.

"Fuck. Sorry," he panted.

When his hand started to push her head back, she batted him away. Would he think her a freak if he knew this was how she liked it? A little rough, maybe a little extra rough? To show him, she descended even further, once again hitting the back of her throat.

"Oh, fuck," he ground out. His hand landed on her head, moving with her but not forcing anything. "You love it, don't you? You love choking on that big cock."

"Hmmm," she hummed with him still lodged at the back of her throat.

"Fucking perfect." It was said reverently, as though he couldn't believe she was real.

Eventually, the need for air won out, and she let him slip from her lips. The second, she'd reoxygenated, she was back on him, licking up and down the sides of his shaft. The smooth skin felt heavenly against her tongue, and his curses were music to her ears. She went to town, licking, sucking, playing with his balls—that drove him absolutely wild.

She loved that she knew that about him. That she'd been with him enough times and knew him well enough to give him the pleasure he desired.

Fisting his shaft, she slowly pumped while lifting it up to give her access to the heavy sac. When she dragged her tongue across it, he bucked his hips, and when she sucked one ball into her mouth, he shouted so loud the entire block must have heard.

Mickie was so wet her thighs slipped against each other as she tried desperately to ease the ache in her pussy. She needed him to touch her, fill her, fuck her, but the urge to make him come overshadowed her own raging need.

"Michaela," he said on a groan.

She was back on his dick now, sucking hard and bobbing her head like she'd been an actress in a different sort of movie.

"Enough," Keith barked after a few more minutes of sexy groans and cries.

Before Michaela had a chance to react, his hands gripped under her armpits. With impressive strength, he hauled her off the floor. The next thing she knew, she was descending onto his lap. She had just enough brainpower to think to grab his cock and position him seconds before he thrust into her—hard.

"Oh, my God," she cried as she went from empty to full in a flash. She locked her ankles behind his lower back and wrapped her arms around his shoulders, clutching him as close as possible.

They stayed like that, glued together for long moments.

She loved every second of it and could have stayed just like that all day. As close as could be with his hard cock so deep she swore it nudged her soul. Their cheeks rested against each other. Every time he breathed, she felt it. Every beat of his heart reverberated through her body. Eventually, he gripped her hair and tugged her head back, fusing their mouths in a hot, sloppy, downright filthy kiss.

Time disappeared. Morning? Night? Who the hell knew? It could have been anywhere in between, and they could have been anywhere on earth. It wouldn't have mattered. All that existed was the pleasure they were giving and absorbing from each other.

They continued to kiss as though trying to steal every ounce of each other's breath as Keith began to rock his hips. Together, they moved in a slow, sensual way she'd never experienced. Getting off would happen for both of them, but it wasn't the primary goal right now.

Connection, intimacy, reverence—that's where the focus lie, whether or not they could admit their terrifying and breathtaking emotions out loud. Every inch of her skin tingled, and shivers ran up and down her spine, chasing his fingertips as they stroked her heated skin.

The kiss turned slow, languid, and exploratory but no less intense. They moved as a unit without breaking contact once. Neither seemed to bear the thought of separating enough for a whiff of air to pass between them. After a time, their mouths stilled, and they rested with foreheads pressed together. Mickie opened her eyes to find Keith watching her and couldn't have closed them again if she wanted to. The raw, naked longing in his gaze touched the very center of her chest and filled her with hope for a happiness she'd long ago given up achieving.

Suddenly, everything she was experiencing came to the surface, and keeping it in seemed impossible. "Keith," she whispered. "I—" She swallowed. She'd be a fool to say it, but the words couldn't be contained.

"Thank you," he murmured against her lips, stealing her chance to blurt the impulsive claim.

This couldn't be love. It was only lust, potent affection, and two kindred souls finding peace.

Then he moved his mouth to her ear. "Every second I'm with you, I want a thousand more. I think I need you more than air."

Her breath hitched. The words, spoken with so much sincerity, made her heart soar. But they also struck fear into her core. Her life had fallen apart once, and it'd taken months of grueling, humiliating work to get herself on the right track. She'd lost nearly everything and left her entire world behind to find herself. Yet that punishing and the arduous journey seemed fun in comparison to what it would be like to scrape herself off the cement if Keith eventually decided she wasn't worth the risk to his own world.

Shit, she couldn't start down that tunnel of dark thoughts, or she'd end up searching out a bottle. To keep herself in the moment, she kissed him again. Desire flared when he groaned into her mouth. They moved with purpose now, rocking, thrusting, and grinding their hips. Her nipples dragged across his chest. The sparse hair tickled, adding a new level of sensation to the already out-of-control riot of electricity shooting from her nerve endings.

"Come for me, baby," he whispered against her mouth. His hand found its way between their sweat-plastered bodies and went straight for her clit. "Let me feel that pussy squeezing me. Show me how much you love this cock filling you."

"Yes," she said as the tingling increased and her mind fuzzed. "I love it."

I love you.

She ground her clit against his seeking thumb just as he sank his teeth into the side of her neck. The light bite sent her over the edge into an orgasm unlike any she'd ever experienced. The mind-blowing explosion she usually chased didn't happen. Instead, intense pleasure rolled through her in a wave, starting at her toes and claiming each muscle in her body one by one. By the time it ceased, she was limp, exhausted, and more satisfied than she'd ever been in her life.

Keith came at the same time. His arms banded around her in a vice-like embrace. He buried his face in her neck and let out a long, low moan as he shuddered in her arms.

They stayed that way, naked, clinging to each other for endless minutes. She wished it could have persisted forever. Eventually, Keith finally lifted his head and met her gaze. Then he kissed her with the lazy hunger of a man who came moments ago yet wanted more.

His hips moved again in a slow roll, setting off a course of aftershocks. Still inside her, he began to harden all over again.

She gasped into his mouth.

Keith chuckled. "What can I say?" he whispered as he drew his head back enough for her to see his face. "Can't get enough of you." Then he winked and flipped her to her back with a smooth and skillful move.

He gripped her hands, pinned them above her head, and began to fuck her in earnest this time.

It didn't take long for him to drive her up all over again, and this time as she came apart beneath him, she saw it clear as day.

She'd well and truly fallen for the man.

Fallen in love with him.

And she'd splinter into a million broken pieces if he didn't feel the same.

Chapter Twenty-Four

Days turned to weeks, fall transitioned to winter, and before Mickie knew it, two months had breezed by. Two months of evenings spent eating and laughing with the Benson crew, sweaty nights of Keith in her bed or her in his, and mornings spent waking up next to the man she'd fallen head over heels for.

Keith was still holding back. Sure, he was affectionate, fun, and attentive and curled her toes in bed, but he cleverly redirected any discussion of the future, feelings, or their relationship in general. Mickie worked to keep from getting frustrated, at least in front of Keith. Ralph, on the other hand, got an earful during their weekly FaceTime dates. The poor guy was probably going to block her number if things continued.

Nothing ever came of Chuck's comment in the parking lot of the diner. After a few weeks, she'd begun to relax again. While she hated the man on Keith's behalf and avoided running into him at all costs, she decided his comment about her looking like Scarlett was merely that. A throwaway comment made by an idiot.

Along with the bliss of a new relationship and new friendships, Mickie had made great strides on filling up the non-Benson hours of her day. Actually, that wasn't entirely true as Jagger was the main reason her days were now busy as well.

He'd shown her kitchen and bathroom remodel photos to some of his customers, and they'd raved not only over his craftsmanship but her decorating style as well. He'd been only too happy to point any interested parties in her direction, and before she knew it, she'd been hired on to style three homes. Not having any formal training as a designer, Mickie spent countless hours researching design philosophies, techniques, and working toward an online certification.

She was in the process of signing up for a class on creating functional spaces when a knock on her door nearly had her computer slipping off her lap. She'd been so in the zone the noise jolted her as though it'd been an explosion.

"Coming!" she yelled as she set the laptop aside and rose to her feet. Glasses on, hair in a half ponytail, and wearing sweats, she wasn't quite company-ready, but more than likely, it was just a delivery driver with her most recent purchase of design books. "Hey—oh, Ronnie! Hi."

"Hey, Mickie," Ronnie said. She stood huddled in on herself, clutching a thick binder to her heavy coat. A bright blue wool hat sat askew on her head.

For the first time since Mickie met her, Ronnie didn't make eye contact. Her gaze darted everywhere but never landed on Mickie, and she projected an air of insecurity Mickie wouldn't have thought possible for her outgoing friend.

"Come in, come in. It's freezing," she said, waving Ronnie in. "I've got a fire going. Feel free to dump your coat anywhere and come sit to warm up. Want some coffee or anything? I need a refresh anyway."

"Uh, sure." Ronnie stood on the small rug in the foyer, still clutching the binder tight to her chest.

"Okay, I'll be right back. Make yourself at home, which you better already know to do." She smiled at her friend and jetted into the kitchen for the coffee and to provide Ronnie with a minute to settle her nerves.

As she puttered around preparing the coffee the way she'd learned Ronnie liked it, Mickie tried to sort through reasons her friend would be nervous or uncomfortable.

Boyfriend trouble? Maybe, but as far as she knew, Ronnie wasn't seeing anyone.

Job trouble? Nah, the sports bar couldn't function without her.

Family problem? Again, she rejected the idea as she'd seen Keith and Jagger not an hour before, and everything was status quo.

That left the one thing Mickie was afraid, no terrified, to think about. Someone outside the Benson family knew who she was. It was bound to happen eventually. Never had she thought Scarlett would be able to remain hidden for the rest of her life, but even though she'd tried to prepare herself for this moment over the past few months, the thought of losing her anonymity still sent panic skittering across her nerve endings.

Now nervous as fuck, Mickie returned to the den to find Ronnie curled up on the couch near the roaring fire. The binder she'd brought sat on her lap, and she stared off into space, lost in thought. "Here you go," Mickie said in a soft voice so she wouldn't startle her friend.

"Thanks."

She sat next to Ronnie. "Okay, girl, you're freaking me out a little, so just tell me what's up, and we can deal with it." Then before poor Ronnie had a chance to speak, she continued, "Someone knows who I am, right? That's what it is? Someone took a picture of me, and they're going to post it? Or somebody talked to the media?" The idea had her gut roiling. She pressed a fist to her stomach. "I'm not ready for this yet."

Ronnie's eyes popped wide. She grabbed Mickie's free hand as she shook her head briskly. "What? No! Oh, my God, no. I am so sorry. I didn't mean to freak you out. There isn't anything wrong at all, and no one knows anything about you as far as I know."

Air left Mickie in a whoosh. "Oh, thank God. Phew." She stared at the ceiling and exhaled as she shook out her tingling hands. "No matter how many times I tell myself I'm prepared for it, it's a huge freakin' lie. Not sure I'll ever be ready."

Ronnie grimaced. "Shit, I'm really sorry." Her shoulders slumped, and she mumbled, "This is not off to a good start."

Waving her concern away, Mickie said, "Seriously, don't worry. I pretty much jump to that conclusion anytime I see an unknown number pop up on my phone, so I should be used to it. Let's pretend I didn't say anything, and you can tell me what's really on your mind."

"Sure, um…" Ronnie stared at the binder on her lap while she traced the edge with an unpolished finger. "So, I have an idea. It's a proposition, really. Well, more like an opportunity. A business idea for us." She cleared her throat. "Uh, I mean me, or well, I guess an investment for you, if you're interested." The rambling stopped, and Ronnie's eyes widened as she finally glanced up. "Oh, God, I'm not just here to ask you for money. I know it seems like that, but I have an idea I think you'll be interested in. I know mixing business and friendship can be a terrible idea. I'm not using you for money or just being your friend because I know you have money. Our friendship has become so important to me and I'd never want to take advantage of it." She hopped to her feet. "I'm sorry, this was a terrible idea." Her glassy eyes indicated impending tears. "Forget it."

As she took a step away from the couch, Mickie caught her arm and tugged her back to the couch. "Hey," she said with a smile. Hopefully it set Ronnie at ease. It took guts to put yourself out there, even in front of friends. "Please sit, Ronnie. I've never thought you or any of your family were only friends with me because of my money. You've never once given me that impression, and you still aren't now."

With a bitter laugh, Ronnie said, "I'm literally about to ask you for money."

Mickie shrugged. "I know." She pointed to the binder. "But whatever it's for, it seems important to you. You're not frivolous or flighty. Plus you said you think I'll like the idea. So let's hear it."

Blowing out a break, Ronnie nodded. "Okay. You know that campsite over near Mount Mansfield?"

Nodding, Mickie set her coffee down on the table in front of her couch. "Yeah, the one that's for sale, right? I've driven by it a bunch of times but haven't been on the property."

"Yes, that's the one. I know the owner. He comes to the bar at least twice a week. He's been talking about putting it on the market for the past two years now but only did about a month ago." As she spoke, color returned to her cheeks, and her eyes began to sparkle. Whatever she was about to propose, she was passionate about the idea.

"I'd like to purchase the property and turn it into luxury rental cabins. And I mean *luxury*." She opened the binder and pulled out a map of the campground.

Interesting.

Mickie scooted closer.

"Right now, there are fifteen log cabins and one lodge on the site. They're in great condition but rustic. Each cabin has electricity and plumbing, but it's all very basic. My plan is to turn ten of the cabins into ten luxury rentals. Then use one as a gym, one a spa, one a gift shop of sorts with locally sourced products, and one as a movie room. The lodge I'd like to transform into a breakfast spot and recreation area. My vision is a very upscale, high-end bed and breakfast."

Now that she was into it, Ronnie plowed on without missing a beat.

"Through the research I've done, I've discovered this area is becoming a hotspot for winter travel among the extremely wealthy. There are great resorts and ski lodges, but nothing that specifically caters to that level of clientele."

She pulled what looked like some kind of market analysis from a sleeve in the binder. Mickie couldn't help but be impressed. This idea hadn't come to Ronnie yesterday. It was something she'd been thinking about and investigating for quite a while.

"I've run numbers and projections for booking fees. It can be good. Profitable. Very profitable if done right."

A seed of excitement began to bloom in Mickie's stomach. Whether it was Ronnie's contagious enthusiasm or her own desire to find her niche, she loved the feeling. Passion for something career-related had been missing since she left Hollywood. Hell, it'd been missing for years.

"Clearly, I can't fund this on my own. I'd like to offer my siblings the opportunity to buy in so it's a family project. But even if they all do, with the plans I'm projecting, we won't have enough. I've also spoken with a few banks about getting a loan, which is the route I'll choose if you aren't interested. So yes, I'm asking for an investor, but I'm hoping for more than that. I'm hoping for an active business partner. And I'd like it to be you."

"Oh, really?" Mickie's jaw dropped. "Seriously?"

Ronnie grabbed her hands. "Mickie, you know luxury. You know wealth. You know, high-end style. You know what the ultra-rich want." She waved her hand around. "You've done an incredible job with this place. I want you to help me design and run it. You could make it beautiful and lavish without being gaudy or ostentatious. I want to go all out for each and every holiday in a big way without being tacky or cheesy. You could do that. My dream is to draw people for the ambiance and gourmet food as much as for the skiing. I want the place to stand on its own and be draw for the area during the tourist season."

The idea was remarkable, to say the least. As Mickie sifted through the well-organized pages of Ronnie's detailed binder, her heart raced. She loved this. More than loved it. A chance to make things beautiful, elegant, expensive, and enticing to others. The ability to change it up and continuously utilize her creative side. She'd want to be involved in all of it. The day-to-day management as well as the design elements. She and Ronnie could be full-fledged partners.

Her silence must have made Ronnie apprehensive because her friend fiddled with the sleeves of her oversized sweatshirt. "I know the start-up cost would be huge. But there are ways to keep it manageable. Jagger would do all the construction work, Ian and Jimmy will be getting out of the military soon and looking for work. They can be involved. I'd love for this to be a family business where we—"

"Ronnie," she said, placing a hand on her friend's arm.

The chatter stopped. Ronnie chewed her bottom lip. "Yeah?"

Mickie couldn't contain her grin. "This idea is…I can't even think of a word to tell you how much I love it."

"Really?" Ronnie asked on an exhale. "You think it's good?"

Mickie shook her head. "No, I think it's phenomenal. And I want in. In every way possible."

Ronnie let out the most un-Ronnie squeal, which had Mickie laughing and doing a bit of squealing herself.

"Oh, my God!" Ronnie said. She launched herself at Mickie, and they hugged while laughing and rocking and back and forth. "This is the best thing that's ever happened to me. Do you really mean it?" She pulled back, a hint of vulnerability back in her gaze.

"I mean it, Ronnie. Look at what you've done here." She lifted the binder. "You're going to be a fantastic business owner, and this is going to be the best place to stay in the entire nation by the time we're done with it."

With a hand on her chest, Ronnie beamed. "My heart is beating so fast I think I'm going into cardiac arrest. I was so nervous. Seriously, I've been planning this for over a year and a half. It's…" Her voice cracked. "It's become my dream. And my best friend is going to help me make it come true."

The tip of Mickie's nose tingled. "Ronnie, stop. You're gonna make me cry."

"Too late," Ronnie warned as she sniffed. "So much for being a girl boss. Shit, good thing the guys aren't here. They'd never let me hear the end of it." Wiping under her eyes, she let out a watery laugh.

"Have you mentioned any of this to them?"

"Nope. None of it. I wanted to secure funding so they wouldn't roll their eyes and pat my head."

"Damn, you're a good secret keeper, girl."

Ronnie winked. "Tell me about it. I'm a vault. Lucky for you, right?"

With a laugh, Mickie nodded. "Seriously." At first, she'd been itchy and uncomfortable with the fact that people knew who she was. Even the friends she trusted. Now, with the passage of time, she'd relaxed and even enjoyed the occasional joke about her identity. None of the Bensons would ever blab, and they were a group who ribbed each other about everything. She'd grown to realize teasing was the way they expressed love for each other, odd as it was.

"I think the next thing to do is set a meeting with Jagger and start ironing out construction plans."

"Well, I think we need to put an offer on the place first." Mickie raised an eyebrow.

Ronnie's cheeks pinked. "Oh, yeah, that might be important. What—"

A loud crash from outside had both of them jumping to their feet. "What the?" Ronnie asked as she darted toward the door. Before Mickie had the chance to shout a warning of caution, Ronnie swung the door open and peered outside. "Oh, hell."

Mickie hurried over and joined Ronnie in the door. Her stomach bottomed out at the sight of Earl Benson lurching out of a car that had slammed into her brick mailbox. He mumbled something under his breath and staggered away from the wrecked vehicle.

"Why don't you go back inside," Ronnie said as she stepped onto the porch. "I'll deal with him."

Mickie held her back. "No way. He's trashed, and I'm not risking you getting hurt. We'll deal with him together."

"Strength in numbers?" Ronnie asked with a raised eyebrow.

"Exactly."

Their conversation must have alerted Earl to their presence. His head jerked up, and his glassy gaze landed on them. The force of the movement caused him to stumble backward. Six in the evening and the man was blitzed out of his mind.

It looked like he hadn't shaved since she'd last seen him months ago. Hell, it looked like he hadn't showered since then, either. A long-sleeved T-shirt and jeans hung off his body, at least two sizes too big. It couldn't have been more than thirty degrees out, but the alcohol seemed to have made him impervious to the cold—or at least given him the illusion of being warm. His hair was longer and grayer than last time. Sunken eyes and yellow skin completed the sickly look of a man with a severe alcohol addiction. Her heart squeezed for Ronnie but especially for Keith, who'd dealt with this man's abuse for so long.

A light snow began to fall, and she shivered. The urge to invite the improperly dressed man into her warm home hit hard, but she fought it. His toxicity would poison everything he touched.

"What the hell do you want?" Ronnie called.

He snorted. "Ahh, my wayward daughter. Can't make time for her old man but has plenty of it for the rich bitch."

"Shit," Ronnie muttered as Mickie thought the same thing.

Ronnie took a step onto the porch. "Let me drive you home, Dad. Mickie was just on her way out."

"Ronnie," Mickie growled under her breath as she reached for her friend. No way was she letting her get in a car with him. Not that they could leave him out there. The car might still be drivable, and he'd kill someone for sure if he got back behind the wheel. As much as she hated the man, he was still Keith and Ronnie's father, and she'd never forgive herself if harm came to him because she turned him away.

Ronnie only shrugged.

"Is there something you need, Mr. Benson?" Mickie called out.

"Money. Overheard Chuck complaining about the new rich bitch in town who won't even give him the time of day."

Okay, maybe she hadn't managed to completely avoid Chuck and the few times she'd crossed his path, she'd gone out of her way to give him the cold shoulder.

"It got me thinking that my stupid son finally did something right, shaking up with money. But he's too fucking selfish to share. So, I'm here to get mine."

"I'm sorry, sir, I really can't help you out," Mickie said.

"Now listen here, bitch," he started as he wobbled up her lawn. Straight through the snow without anything more than threadbare sneakers. "I—"

The shine of headlights had them all turning toward the Benson's house where Keith's truck rolled to a stop. The driver's side door flew open, and Keith burst from the pickup, practically steaming with fury. Jagger chased a few feet behind as Keith stormed his way toward their father. "What did I tell you would happen if you came anywhere near my woman?" he snarled as he grabbed his father and slammed him against the ruined car.

"Keith!" Jagger yelled.

Ronnie and Mickie exchanged worried glances.

So much for their good news.

Fuck.

Chapter Twenty-Five

"So, things seem to be going well with you and Mickie," Jagger said as Keith drove them home from the garage. Jagger had built some shelves for tools, which Keith could kiss him for. It freed up so much space. Enough for an additional car to fit in the garage. Not that he had time for extra work, but if business kept trending upward, he'd be in the position to hire another mechanic before too long.

"Yeah, it's good," he said, giving Jagger a sideways glance. His brother wore a shit-eating grin.

Here it comes.

"So do you *love* her?" Jagger sing-songed.

He rolled his eyes. "For real? What are you twelve?"

"Nah, man, just seems like this could be it for you. You two are rarely seen apart anymore."

With the earlier snowfall, the ground had slickened, so Keith kept his gaze fixed on the road as he said, "It?"

"Yeah, you know. The one. Your life partner. Soulmate. Wife."

Keith grunted and nearly jerked the wheel. "Wife? Are you for real? It's been a few months. Can't imagine it'll be too many more before she's itchin' to get back to her real life."

Jagger didn't respond.

Keith risked a glance and found his brother scowling. "What?"

"The fuck is wrong with you?" Jagger asked with more heat than Keith would have expected. He slammed his clenched fist on the dash. "God, you're an idiot."

"What the hell? Why are you getting all worked up about my relationship?"

Jagger scoffed. "Because you're an idiot. Because you have an incredible woman who's crazy about you, and you're too much of a pussy to admit you feel the same. You still think she's like Della and she's gonna trade you in for someone shinier."

He pulled up to a red light and faced a fuming Jagger. "Look, Jag, I know you're fond of her and have worked with her a lot, but you don't know her like I do."

Jagger tilted his head. "You saying she talks about missing her old life? Mentions that she wants to go back to LA? She's antsy here and unhappy? That what you're saying?"

Guilt twisted in Keith's gut. Damn, nosey family. "Well, no. Not exactly." The complete opposite, actually. Mickie took every opportunity to reassure him about how happy she was with her life in Vermont and with their relationship.

"Look, brother, don't pin your head shit on her. All us Benson kids have our own issues. You can't grow up with parents like ours and be without baggage. But that's on you. Not her. She hasn't given you a single reason to think she regrets her decision to move here and change her career. Shit, man, she's fucking loving her life right now and you are the main reason for it. Gotta start trusting it some time, man."

Keith let the words sink in. Jagger was right. Mickie hadn't done anything to deserve his continued skepticism, but he just couldn't shake it. No matter how much he wanted to and no matter how much she deserved his trust and faith, he couldn't hand it over yet. Not all of it anyway.

"I don't get it at all," Jagger said with a smirk. "What she sees in you, I mean."

"Fuck you." Keith said, flipping him off. The light turned green, and he continued toward their house. Thankfully Jagger ceased the inquisition, but that only gave Keith quiet to think. He was pretty sure he loved Michaela Hudson. It had hit him like a ton of bricks the night she sat on his lap and listened to him pour out his screwed-up past. But, two months later, he couldn't give her the words. Every time he tried, his jaw locked up and his tongue seemed to swell.

But Jagger was right. Somehow he had to unfuck his head, or he'd lose her and have no one to blame but himself and his own stupidity.

With a sigh, he turned onto their street. "Thanks, Jag," he said. And he meant it. He loved to spar with his brothers and sister verbally, but they all knew he loved them and had their backs one hundred percent.

"Don't mention it. I'm happy to impart my wisdom anytime."

Keith snorted as Jagger said, "Who is that?"

A car parked crookedly outside Mickie's house drew their attention. "Keith strained to make out the vehicle. "Does it look like it hit her mailbox?"

"Yeah, hope the driver's okay—oh, fuck me."

"What?" Keith canted the steering wheel to shine his headlights toward Mickie's house. There on her snowy lawn stood, or rather swayed, their drunk-off-his-ass father. "Goddammit," he bit out as he hit the gas. They shot down the street and screeched to a stop when he slammed the brakes in front of their house.

Keith shoved his door open.

"Keith, buddy," Jagger called, but Keith was already charging out of the truck. "Keep your head. He's not worth a night in jail."

When Keith didn't respond or alter his course, Jagger cursed, and Keith heard his door slam. The sound of his brother's footsteps pounding the pavement as he chased him faded into the rush of blood in his ears. He kept his gaze fixed on the man who'd caused so much pain and suffering throughout their lives. Now the old man was harassing his woman?

Fuck. No.

Keith grabbed his father from behind, spun him, and slammed him against the car.

Someone shouted for him to back off, but he ignored them. "I warned you to stay away from her," he snarled in his father's face.

Glassy eyes and a smirk met his ire. "Just want to talk to the bitch. See what all the fuss is about."

The rumble that erupted from Keith's chest resembled that of a junkyard dog, ravenous, violent, and eager for blood.

Just as he cocked his fist, ready for the satisfaction of ramming it in his father's face, a hand landed on his shoulder. "Not worth it, brother." Jagger's steady voice spoke at his ear.

"Jagger, my boy," their father slurred.

"Shut the fuck up, old man," Jagger spat out. "Just because I'm holding him back doesn't mean I wouldn't love to see him tear you apart." He lowered his voice. "Too much of an audience, Keith."

The softly spoken words snapped him out of the fog of rage that had clouded his judgment the second he saw his father on Mickie's lawn.

He felt her gaze boring into the back of his head, pleading with him to come to her instead of spilling his father's blood throughout her snowy yard. Across the street, a lighted window revealed a parted curtain and the curious eyes of their prying neighbors.

"This bastard's not worth a night in jail," Jagger whispered. "I got him. You go to your woman. Make sure she's good."

"He's my resp—"

"No, he's not." Ronnie's voice appeared behind him. "Let us do this for you, Keith. For you and Mickie."

Their father laughed loud and drunkenly. "Isn't this cute. My kids coming together to disrespect their father."

"Shut the fuck up," Ronnie and Jagger said at the same time.

Keith's lips twitched.

Jagger squeezed his shoulder. "Come on, brother."

"Keith," Mickie called from the porch.

His spine lost its starch. For so long he'd carried the weight of managing their burden of a father on his own. The instinct to keep his siblings from his poison ran deep. But it was time to let that go.

"All right," he said as he turned his back on their father's continued laughter. "Any way I can talk you out of going with him?" he asked Ronnie.

She set her jaw and shook her head. "No. He's my father, too. My burden to share."

With a resigned nod, he met Jagger's gaze. "Keep her safe."

"Goes without saying." Jagger patted his shoulder then Ronnie gave him a quick hug. "Be good to her and let her be good to you," she whispered before releasing him.

They may have come from trash, but his siblings had grown into damn good people.

After kissing Ronnie's cheek, he drowned out all happenings behind him and focused his full attention on Michaela. She stood without a jacket, waiting for him on the porch with a concerned furrow between her eyes. As he approached, she held out her hand. The moment he took it, she clutched her cold fingers tight around his and guided him into the house.

"I've gotta go get the tow truck to haul his car outta there," Keith said when they reached her couch.

Mickie placed an icy finger over his lips. "Shh, that can wait until later. Or you can text JP to do it. In fact, I bet Jagger gets him to take care of it. It's okay to rely on your siblings. They want to be there for you as much as you are for them, you know."

With a grunt, he grabbed her hand and nipped the end of her finger. Her yelp turned into a groan as he soothed the sting with his tongue.

"Lie down with me," he urged, tugging her to the couch. He stretched out on his back and pulled her down on top of him. Her softness immediately conformed to all the hard planes of his body. Tension left him in an instant. This was where he belonged.

Christ, how he hoped she felt the same. He was exactly where he'd promised himself he wouldn't end up. Fucking in love with a woman who might not stick around. Hoping for a future that may never happen.

What a fucking fool he'd become.

"You just tensed." Mickie lifted her head, resting her chin on his chest.

"What did he want?" he played with the ends of her chocolaty hair.

She gave him a lopsided grin. "Money. You showed right after he did, so he didn't have time to say much beyond feeling like he was owed some money."

"Good. I don't want him bringing his filth anywhere near you."

"I'm tougher than you think." She flexed a small but toned bicep, probably trying to get a laugh out of him, but he didn't have one for her.

"No." He grabbed her hand and kissed her knuckles. "I know exactly how tough you are because I'm in awe of it."

"Keith…you…I mean I…thank you," she whispered. "I'm so glad I found you."

"You mean you're so glad I found you on the side of the road."

That had her giggling and lightened the heavy emotions of seconds before. He wasn't ready for it, cowardly as it made him.

They stayed there on the couch in silence, just being with each other. Eventually, the air thickened, and the feeling changed from comforting to arousing. Beneath her hips, his cock filled and hardened. She squirmed against him before lifting her lust-filled gaze to his.

Christ, she was so fucking beautiful in her natural state. No makeup, fancy clothes, or styled hair. Just one hundred percent Michaela Hudson.

Perfection.

"Thank you," she whispered as she scooted up his body, aligning her mouth with his. Either he'd say the word out loud, or his eyes conveyed his thoughts. Either way, he accepted her kiss eagerly.

Never shy, she slid her tongue against his, causing his dick to jerk against her leg. She hummed her approval and ground against him. The need to fuck her spiked through his system. He grabbed the back of her head, no longer content with leisurely kisses, and plundered her mouth.

Mickie kissed him back with as much urgency. She straddled him, placing a knee on either side of his hips. The new position gave her control of the incendiary kiss.

"Oh, God, my eyes!" Ronnie's shout had them jerking apart as though on fire.

Wide-eyed and panting, Mickie stared at her door.

"Is it over yet?"

Keith wrenched his head back to see Jagger standing in the open door with one hand over his eyes and one straight out as though trying to feel his way through the house.

"Mickie, don't move. If you get up and I have to see a tent in my brother's jeans, I just might vomit." Ronnie waltzed in as though she owned the place, heading straight for the kitchen with a plastic shopping bag hanging off her arm. Gone was the bashful woman who'd showed up only a few hours before.

JP was last through the door. "Oh, sexy times! Need me to tap in, bro? I'm about due for a good romp. Think it's been about twenty-seven hours since I got laid."

Mickie groaned and dropped her head to Keith's chest. Her shoulders shook, and a bolt of fear shot down his spine. Was she crying?

A bubble of laughter burst from her.

Nope. It took a lot to kill his woman's spirit. She was laughing, of course.

Keith flipped his brother off. He seemed to be doing that a lot lately. All of his siblings wore smiles and teased as though they hadn't just had to deal with their embarrassment of a father. He opened his mouth to ask how everything had gone but then decided against it. The mood was high, and they'd have said if they'd had an issue. Why ruin the good vibes? Instead, he asked, "Why the fuck are you losers here perving on us?"

Ronnie appeared from the kitchen with a frightening smile stretching her cheeks.

"I had nothing to do with this," Jagger said, lifting his hands in surrender.

"Uh oh, what'd you do, Ronnie?" Mickie climbed off him, allowing him to sit and swing his legs off the couch. When she plopped down next to him, he pulled her flush against his side and draped his arm across her shoulders. She beamed at him, happiness radiating from her like rays of light.

"I got ice cream for us to pig out on and..."

Keith narrowed his eyes and she fished around inside her shopping bag. With a shout of victory, Ronnie pulled a DVD out and held it up for all to see. "Tada!"

"Nothing to do with it," Jagger repeated.

Beside him, Mickie shook her head. "Oh no. No way. Absolutely not."

Keith's spine stiffened as he turned back to the movie. "Mars Alien Massacre?" he read from the cover.

Mickie covered her face and groaned. "I can't believe you guys found that." With a resigned sigh, she lifted her head. "It's the first movie I had the lead in. A really, really, really awful slasher film. I think I was twenty. Oh, God, it's so bad."

Ice filled his veins, and he turned a scathing look Ronnie's way. What the fuck was she thinking? Mickie had spent months trying to shake the reach of Hollywood, and now Ronnie was going to throw it in her face. "Ronnie, what the hell?" he barked.

"Seriously," Mickie said. "We are not watching this." She was laughing instead of freaking out, but his mind was stuck on the day he'd learned who she was.

"Oh, hell yes we are," JP said. He snatched the DVD from Ronnie and ran for the television.

A buzzing in Keith's ears drowned out the rest of the argument, and before he knew it, a young Michaela—young Scarlett, rather—appeared on the eighty-five-inch television screen mounted above her stone fireplace.

Keith began to stand, ready to lambast his family for their insensitivity, when Mickie gripped his thigh.

"Hey, Keith, it's okay," she whispered for only his ears.

When he studied her face, he saw only sincerity and peace.

"Seriously, I'm okay with this. Your siblings have become my best friends. Because of all of you, I'm happy and can look at my past with new eyes. I'm okay to watch one of my movies with them. With you. Even the stupidest one."

"Jesus, you're amazing," he said before kissing her silly.

"Hey!" A pillow hit the side of his face. "This is a no-smooching zone. You'll have plenty of hours to be gross after we leave. For now, we want to make fun of Mickie for agreeing to do this movie, and we can't do that if she's halfway down your throat." Ronnie picked up another pillow and prepared to hurl it at him.

"Okay, okay! Hold your fire." Mickie laughed and reached for a bowl of ice cream that someone must have delivered during his little freak out. With a happy hum, she settled against him then lifted the spoon to his mouth.

Keith relaxed into the couch cushions. Protective instincts aside, this could be a fun idea. With a playful growl, he grabbed the spoon and devoured the chilly bite.

The next ninety or so minutes were spent with massive amounts of laughter from his siblings, groans of embarrassment from Mickie, and silence from him. The movie was terrible no matter how you looked at it. But it had put Mickie on some pretty prominent director's radar.

Throughout the film, his siblings asked a million questions about her co-star, filming, memorizing lines, and anything Hollywood-related they could think of. Mickie answered each question with a smile and didn't outwardly seem bothered by their inquiries.

But with each additional explanation of the way the filming industry worked, Keith tensed further. Every time she laughed, recalling a memory of her acting days, or spoke fondly of someone she'd connect with, his stomach twisted with ugly darkness. Mickie's sparkled as she regaled them with a story of almost missing the Oscars because Ralph was a perfectionist who'd started her hairstyle over at least four times.

It was clear in her tone and body language that'd she'd loved it. And talk of the Oscars reminded him that not only had she loved her career, she'd excelled at it. She'd been honored time and time again for her stellar work. Only in recent years had the toll of the lifestyle become too great for her to endure. There had been many wonderful years for her, and those were the times that would inevitably call her back to her life.

Suddenly, the air in the room vanished. Keith sprang to his feet, making Mickie topple over on the couch. "Excuse me," he croaked. "Just remembered I forgot to return a customer's call. I'll be right back." He escaped up the stairs, aware of three sets of confused eyes trailing him.

But he didn't care about them. It was the fourth pair, full of concern, that would be the ones to destroy him eventually.

He lay down on Mickie's bed, flinging his arm across his eyes as he fought to keep from hyperventilating. After a few seconds, a soft weight shifted the bed beside him. Mortification slammed into him. Of course Mickie saw through his lie. She was in tune with him in a way no one else ever had been.

"Hey, baby," he said. "I'm good. You didn't have to check on me."

"Keith, I had some great years in my career as an actress. Years I loved and will always remember with great fondness."

He let his forearm slide off his face. She spoke with authority in no-nonsense tone he rarely heard from her. "I'm glad." And he was. He wasn't a monster who wished she'd spent every minute of the past ten years in misery.

"But what I do not have is one single twitch of desire to return to it. Not one, Keith. I am happy here in Vermont. I have friends. I have some exciting career prospects which I haven't even had a chance to talk to you about yet. And I have you. I'm most happy with you. Leaving is not on my radar. And it won't ever be. What can I do to convince you of that?"

"Don't give up on me," he whispered, even though it made him sound needy and weak. When it came to her, he was needy. "I'm trying to believe it, Mickie. My head does. It trusts you. But here." He grabbed her hand and placed it over his heart much as she'd done the night he confessed his deepest sorrow to her. "It's so battered, I'm afraid it will never fully heal."

"It will," she said. "I know it. But for now, to help the process along, I will promise you this." She looked straight in his eyes and spoke with one hundred percent certainty. "I promise you that I will not return to my life in Hollywood. There is nothing now or ever that will make me change my mind. I promise."

He pulled her down for a sweet kiss then wrapped her in his arms. His siblings would know to leave once they'd finished their movie. Like him, they'd become as comfortable in Mickie's house as they were in their own.

They fell asleep light that, fully clothed, on top of the mattress, and when he woke around three a.m. to a soft body shifting on top of him, Keith felt a confidence in his life and relationship he'd yet to experience.

Gently as he could muster, he maneuvered her off of him and onto her side. Then he gathered her close and watched the peace on her face as she slept.

He'd fallen asleep with many women over the years, sometimes waking in the middle of the night only to scurry out before they woke, occasionally waking them or round two, and once in a rare while rolling over to catch a few extra hours sleep if it was more of a friends-with-benefits type of relationship.

Never before had he felt this perfect contentment while merely lying next to a woman. Sure, there wasn't much he loved more than fucking Mickie, but at that moment, though he felt desire for her, it was different than usual. They'd have plenty of time to sate their physical urges. Tomorrow, the next day, the day after that. Hell, they could spend the entire weekend in bed, gorging themselves on each other.

Right then, he wanted nothing more than to be next to her as he drifted back to sleep. To know his body provided her warmth when she snuggled close. That his presence made her feel safe, as she'd told him on more than one occasion. And that the first thing he'd see when he woke was the smile on her face.

The writing had been on the wall for weeks, he'd only been ignoring the print. He was in love with her. Head over fucking heels in love with Michaela Hudson.

For the first time since he'd met her, the clawing fear of losing her didn't catch him in its iron grasp. He believed her reassurances tonight when she said she loved Vermont and had no plans to return to Hollywood.

Now he only had to find a way to tell her because she deserved so much more than him shouting it out while inside her or blurting it at breakfast.

She deserved the world.

Chapter Twenty-Six

Mickie inhaled the crisp, frosty air as she tugged a fluffy scarf tighter around her neck. Her lungs burned with an icy fire as they filled with the frigid, thirty-six-degree air. It'd been more than a decade since she'd been in the presence of snow or such a cold winter. The knee-length down jacket she'd purchased last month had quickly become her new best friend, along with the wool beanie, thick gloves, scarf, and UGG snow boots.

Mickie strolled through the freshly fallen snow on a walking trail she could barely make out. Aside from her and one snowshoer trudging his way through the trees, the park was blessedly deserted. A small plow must have come through at some point because only a few inches dusted the walking path. At least eight inches of undisturbed, sparkling white snow blanketed the rest of the park closest to her house.

The tip of her nose stung and her cheeks burned, wind-chapped from the hour she'd been wandering outside. Soon, she'd need to return to her car and the luxurious heated seats, but for now, she adored the way her body shivered and her eyes watered from the cold.

Most would probably think her nuts, but she'd have stayed out there all day if she could. Something about the pristine, untouched, shimmering snow spoke to her soul. It was clean and fresh. A blank canvas. Maybe that's what resonated with her. She felt a kinship to Mother Nature's efforts to cover up the fallen leaves and dormant grass of autumn with something pure and fresh.

Beyond soaking up nature's beauty, the peace and quiet of being alone had given her time to think. Over the past week, her relationship with Keith had shifted. He'd been less reluctant to speak of the future, more open to making plans down the line, and less hesitant to mention her life in Hollywood. Hopefully, it meant her time and patience had paid off, and he'd finally begun to believe she wouldn't steal away in the middle of the night.

Holding back from telling him she loved with him had become near impossible. If she bit her tongue any harder in his presence, she was going to draw blood.

Maybe it was time to stop playing it safe. Perhaps if she told Keith she loved him, it would kill the last of his apprehension.

The appearance of another bundled individual walking her way had her smiling. Were they another wounded soul seeking mental clarity in the splendor of nature? She lifted her hand, ready to greet the newcomer with a friendly wave.

As she opened her fingers, the smile slipped right off her face. If she thought she'd been cold before, she'd been dead wrong. Ice slithered through her veins and down her spine, making her freeze in place.

She blinked. It couldn't be. She had to be hallucinating.

Mark Degrasse, Scarlett's manager of six years, strode straight toward her. The man had lost his shit when she'd walked away from her career, threatening her with lawsuits, tabloid exposés, and promising he'd track her down. It seemed he'd made good on that threat. Over the years, the man had made many millions of dollars off her hard work, and he hadn't handled the loss of his golden goose well.

"Scarlett!" he said, holding out his arms to her as though the last words he'd spoken to her hadn't been, "Without me, you're nothing but a worthless junkie. I give you five months before you're crawling back to me on your knees."

Well, it'd been about ten, and she still had no need for the man. In fact, the sight of him turned her stomach.

The sound of her stage name from his lips did nothing to help his cause, whatever it was. "Mark," she said, putting years of acting skill to use.

"God, it's good to see you, beautiful." He hugged her and she returned the embrace, trying hard not to stiffen in his arms. "Love this new look. It's so mountain chic."

Lord, she barely resisted rolling her eyes.

"You're looking well, Mark." She stepped back, putting a few feet between them as soon as he released her.

He laughed. "Banal platitudes, Scarlett? Is that where we are now? After everything?" He tilted his head. The wool peacoat he wore along with his Burberry scarf gave him a sophisticated, polished appearance, as always. His clean-shaven face had a rosy hue to it, no doubt from the cold, and his short blond hair hid beneath a black winter hat. That had to be grating on him like nothing else. The man was a psycho when it came to his hair. He also despised the cold. Anything under seventy degrees, and he was ready to fly further south.

Mickie had come a long way in her metamorphosis but wasn't a good enough person to not take some pleasure in his discomfort.

"Well, I asked to be left alone, and you did not respect my wishes." She shrugged. "I'm not sure what kind of greeting you expected."

He laughed again. This time his head fell back, and the haughty sound carried through the quiet park. "Fuck, I've missed you, Scarlett."

She ground her teeth. "I'd prefer you call me Michaela." Not Mickie. The nickname was reserved for friends and friends alone.

He scoffed. "I can't do that. Michaela is nobody special. Scarlett is a star. My star."

She raised an eyebrow in a classic Scarlett stare down. "How did you find me?"

The grin that curved his mouth didn't help her unease a single bit. "I didn't. I was contacted by a man named Chuck. Guess my name is still listed on your official website as your manager."

Her website. Hell, she hadn't looked at that in a year. Who knew it was still active? "How much did you pay him for information on me?"

"Not a dime." He stepped closer and gripped her upper arms. Eyes sparkling with greed, his grin grew. "I have it. The role of your life. Oscar-worthy for sure. Scarlett, they're offering fifty million right out the gate."

"I'm not interested," she said in a flat voice, as his fingertips abraded her skin through the layers of warm clothing.

He shook his head. "You say that now, but once you hear what it is, I promise you, you will not be able to turn it down. I'd bet my life on it."

As she tilted her head, she studied him for a moment, then said, "I don't care what it is. I'm not interested. This isn't a game, Mark. I'm happy here."

The automatic response popped out, but she realized how much she meant it. She had no interest in anything this man had to say. He'd pushed her for so many years. One film after another, shoving drugs her way when she'd been tired, stressed, overworked. Thinking her manager would have had her best interest at heart, she'd indulged again and again. Before long, she'd fallen down a rabbit hole so deep, it'd taken a full escape from that life to climb out. Not that she blamed him for her addiction. That responsibility lay squarely on her shoulders, but he certainly hadn't done anything to help her as she'd spiraled out of control. As long as the money kept rolling in, he didn't give a shit how unhappy she was.

"You only say that because you know you won't be able to resist. Come on, Scarlett. You know you're curious."

If she were a different person, she'd knock the self-satisfied smirk right off his surgically enhanced face.

"Fine," she said with a huff. "Tell me what it is. But take your hands off me and three steps back first." Anything to get him to leave faster.

With a nod, he lifted his arms and stepped away. "So prudish now," he said with a wink. "Would never have expected that from you."

She didn't bother to take the bait. Instead, she folded her arms, tapped a foot, and waited in silence.

With a snort, Mark adjusted his hat. "It's *Princess Carmella.*"

His smug expression grew as he dropped his little bomb then fell silent. No doubt, he assumed she'd jump for joy and hop on the first plane back to Hollywood.

To his everlasting disappointment, all she said was, "Not interested. I think this is the third time I've said it. Now do you believe me?"

Though she kept a mask of disinterest on her face, inside, she was performing mental backflips. She'd done it. Passed the test. If there was any role to draw her back to the limelight, it'd be Princess Carmella and she could say with complete certainty she didn't want it. God, she felt giddy with excitement and a sudden burning need to see Keith.

Mark's smile morphed into a sneer. "Not interested? You've got to be shitting me. Scarlett, it's Princess Carmella. When we first started working together, you told me there was no role you wanted to play more than Princess Carmella. You went on and on about that fucking book and how you wouldn't be able to die happy without being cast as Princess-fucking-Carmella. It's your fucking dream come true."

It was true. As a child, her mother would read her the book *A Princess Lives* all the time. It was the story of a girl born into poverty who found out in her early twenties that she was, in fact, the daughter of a king. She'd risen from the gutter to lead her country with grace, elegance, beauty. She'd been beloved by all, but especially the handsome prince from a neighboring country. It was a fairy tale. *The* fairy tale in Mickie's mind and she'd always hope it'd be made into a feature film. True, she'd wished for it for many years, but not now.

Her dreams had changed. Now she envisions a future full of evenings by the fireplace with Keith and his siblings, nights in Keith's arms, and days building an exciting business with her new best friend.

"Mark, I'm sorry." Maybe sincerity and truth were the way to play it. She lifted her hands in a gesture of surrender. "I'm not bullshitting you. I'm just not interested anymore. I have a good thing here. Friends, work, a home." She left out mention of Keith. Mark was the type to exploit what he could for personal gain. "I'm happy and healthier than I've been my entire life."

"You can't be serious. I saw your house. It's nothing! Nothing compared to what you had just a year ago. The Scarlett I know could never be satisfied with…" Holding his arms out, he gazed around the sparkling park with a grimace as if it was a garbage dump instead of a winter wonderland. "With this."

Tossing her hands in the air, she almost shouted, "The Scarlett you *knew* couldn't be satisfied with anything because she wasn't satisfied with herself. She was a character in a world that chewed her up and spat her out. I'm Michaela." She thumped her chest. "I don't play anyone but myself anymore. And I am satisfied with everything in my life."

The strength of her conviction grew with each word out of her mouth. Damn, it felt amazing. When she'd left, the few people who knew she was leaving called her insane. They'd railed at her for deserting them and swore she'd be back in no time. Everyone said she wouldn't survive without the glitz, the glam, without her name in lights and hordes of fans slobbering over her. They'd thought of her as nothing more than a narcissistic diva.

Proving them wrong was the sweetest revenge.

"I'm sorry you wasted your time, Mark, but you need to go now. I'm due at a meeting soon." A meeting might have been a bit of a stretch. She and Ronnie were finalizing their pitch to the rest of her family for the bed and breakfast idea. But she was due at the coffee shop in fifteen minutes. "Have a safe trip back to California."

With a nod, she turned and began to walk back the way from which she'd come.

"Scarlett," he called out in a voice far less affable than it had been seconds ago.

"We're done, Mark." She didn't bother to turn.

"Do you think I would have come here without a backup plan? Without doing my research and developing a strategy to ensure your cooperation? If so, you underestimated me. I thought you knew me better than that."

Her steps slowed. Shit. She did know him better than that and had been a fool to think he wouldn't try to strong-arm her. Turning once again, she pierced him with her most hateful look. "What are you gonna do? Tell the media where to find me? Disrupt my peace with crowds of paparazzi and press? Do your worst, Mark. I've been prepared for it for months."

For the first time, she didn't feel the familiar stab of fear at being discovered. She was strong now and had a badass support system to stand behind her.

"Hmm, nah, I figured that wouldn't be enough to sway you. They'd come here and get bored of you within minutes. No, I have a much more powerful weapon." He held up his phone. "Video is always best."

Now it was her turn to scoff. "What? Do you have video of me high? Fucking someone random?" She advanced on him. "I. Don't. Care. Newsflash, it's all been said about me before. Like you said, I'm boring now. No one will care about a dated story of the same old shit from Scarlett. Especially once they realize I'm a nobody now."

"Well, I agree with you there. That you've become a nobody, but the world hasn't forgotten about you yet, so it won't take much to make you somebody again." He swiped on his phone a few times. "Here, watch it." He held up a hand as she opened her mouth to refuse. "I promise, your boyfriend will be glad you did."

The bottom dropped out of Michaela's stomach as she snatched the phone from his hand. Though dark, the video was clear enough to make out what was happening. On the screen, a woman with dark hair lay naked on a bed with a pale man rutting between her legs. She faced the camera, blank stare seeing nothing. A tear rolled down her cheek just as Keith had described.

Michaela's heart dropped to the ground and shattered into a million pieces.

Without ever having seen the video or the people in it, she knew precisely was she was witnessing.

"What did you do?" she whispered, throat tight. Only sheer force of will kept her from collapsing to her knees in the snow. He'd won. Mark found her weakness. She'd do anything to spare Keith the horror of this video.

"Well, old Chuck told me you've been avoiding him, so he called me. Offered this baby to me for a hefty sum to keep it off his Facebook page. By the way, you owe fifty thousand dollars. I'll be transferring it to him in a few days."

Tears filled Michaela's eyes as she watched the camera pivot to a devastated young Keith as he entered the motel room. Rage, hatred, disgust, and a myriad of other emotions crossed his face in the blink of an eye. The video cut out as he charged forward. Not that it mattered. She knew what happened next and how it had altered the rest of Keith's life.

He'd die if this got out. This horrifying video of the worst moment of his childhood, which he'd been promised, had been destroyed.

"Be a shame if this baby ended up on TMZ, wouldn't it? I imagine that'd be embarrassing as fuck for your boyfriend. But here's the thing. I'm thinking you can keep the money and I'll take twenty-five percent commission on the money you make from your next movie. I hear the role of Princess Carmella is up for grabs."

If only embarrassment was the worst of what Keith would suffer. No, he'd be less concerned about himself and more worried about his siblings and the reputation of his deceased mother whom he loved with all his heart and was never able to save.

The release of this video, even the knowledge of its continued existence, would break him in a way she'd do anything to prevent. Even return to the life that had nearly ruined her.

"There's a way to make this all disappear," Mark continued. "You start shooting in three days. I've already emailed the script."

She could contact her attorney but filing injunctions and going after both Mark and Chuck would take time. By then, the video would hit the media and how would she ever prove it came from Mark?

The first tear fell, plopping onto the phone screen. Mickie lifted her head and, with as much strength as she could muster, said, "I'll fly out in the morning."

With nod, she dropped his phone in the snow and walked away from the man who'd just wrecked every good thing in her life.

By this time tomorrow, she'd be halfway across the country, but as far as Keith was concerned, she might as well be traveling to the moon.

A sadness like she'd never known washed over her as she made her way to her car. She'd do what she had to do to protect Keith and his family. Even if it killed her.

Even if it destroyed *them*.

Chapter Tenty-Seven

Everything was set—the candles, the blanket, the food. Ronnie had been the one to create the ambiance, or so she called it, and thank God for that because he could barely say the word, let alone make it happen.

His siblings agreed to make themselves scarce for the evening so he could have this romantic picnic without their meddling eyes peeking around the corner. If all went according to plan, he and Mickie would start their night in front of a roaring fire but end it in his bed, sweaty and writhing for hours.

He peered out the window just as Mickie's car pulled into her driveway. She was an hour or so earlier than he'd expected her but fine by him. Even better, actually. Now he didn't have to sit around nervous as fuck for the next sixty minutes. Sad as it might be, he'd never put effort into a woman in this way. Never cared what they thought about a date beyond generally having a good time. But this, this had to go off without a hitch. He wanted Mickie to understand he was all in and loved her. That he wouldn't hold back anymore and would stop waiting for her to leave at any time.

That he trusted her.

All he had to do now was collect his woman and wow her. He didn't bother with a jacket, just shoved his feet in his boots and jogged across the street. As he reached her porch, his phone pinged with a text.

Ronnie: You seen Mickie? She was supposed to meet me 10 mins ago & she's not answering her phone.

He frowned. She'd probably just forgotten, but that wasn't like her. She and Ronnie had been thick as thieves lately, up to something for sure, but she'd told him they'd reveal their secret when they were ready, so he'd let it slide.

Keith: She just got home. Heading over. I'll have her call you.

Ronnie: Don't worry about it. Enjoy your afternoon ;) I'll catch-up with her tmrw.

As he stuffed the phone in his back pocket, Keith let himself into Mickie's house "Babe?" he called out as he went straight for the staircase.

She didn't answer, which made him grin. Maybe she was in the shower. He could certainly get behind that idea. Getting a show of her little wet and slippery before he enticed her across the street would only enhance the excitement and make the semi he'd been sporting for half the day stand at full attention.

Rubbing his hands together, he speed-walked to Michaela's room only to draw up short at the sight of her stuffing clothes into an open suitcase on her bed.

What the hell?

Don't panic.

Her movements were stilted, with hunched shoulders and mumblings under her breath. "Mickie?" he asked as his heart sank. None of what he saw had him thinking positively.

She squeaked and jolted as if he'd zapped her with a cattle prod. How had she not heard him calling her and clomping his size thirteens down the hallway? "Shit." She whirled around, hand on her chest. "You scared me."

Though he wanted to grab her and pull her close, he stayed five feet away.

"What are you doing?" he asked in a tone so flat it made her cringe.

But she recovered fast, brightening and giving him her world-class smile. The one drew millions of fans and melted heart everywhere, but it did nothing to calm the raging storm in his gut. That wasn't *her* smile. It was Scarlett's. The movie star smile.

Made of plastic and PR coaching and meant to fool the world, which it did.

Everyone but him.

"I have to go to California for a little bit." She took a step closer, still sporting the tooth-paste ad grin. "But I'll be back. This is not a permanent thing." Her tone held an overly cheerful pitch.

"Is it for the sale of your house?" He thought that had been finalized through Ralph.

She swallowed as her smile wavered but didn't fade. "Uh, no. It's not that." Then she turned her back on him and began rearranging the perfectly organized suitcase. "It's for a movie." She said the words so low, he couldn't be sure he heard accurately.

At least he hoped he'd misheard. Because, Christ, she couldn't have said what he thought she'd said. She'd promised just last week she wouldn't return to film. That she had no desire to revisit that chapter of her life.

And he'd believed her.

Fuck, his chest felt tight. Too tight. Heart attack tight.

"I'm sorry?" he said with a sharp bark of laughter. "Did you say you're doing a movie?"

Her shoulders slumped as she kept her back to him. "Y—" She cleared her throat. "Yes. I did."

Keith's laugh turned ugly. "You have got to be kidding me."

She turned around without the phony smile this time. Instead, her eyes and flattened mouth held the bleak truth. Exactly seven days after she'd vowed to remain in Vermont and listened to him express his belief in her and commitment to their relationship, she threw it all in the trash.

With an almost urgent desperation, she reached for him. "Keith, it's—"

He lifted a hand. Christ, if she touched him, it'd be all over. He'd break down like a child and sob on the floor. Without the softness of her hands on him or her body pressed against him, he could keep anger as the prevalent emotion. "Don't bother." God, how could he have been so fucking stupid? How many times did he have to learn the same lessons?

People couldn't be trusted.

Promises weren't worth shit.

Hope was a cruel illusion.

This was Della all over again only she wasn't leaving him for a man she considered better, but a more glamorous life. Except this time, it hurt a million times worse because he was an adult who'd fallen instead of a stupid teenager.

"I don't want to hear whatever bullshit excuse you've come up with to justify this."

"It's not what you think," she rushed on as though he hadn't spoken. "I'm not leaving for good. It's temporary. I'll be back after the movie and on breaks. This is just a job."

Was she for real? "Do you seriously think I buy that horseshit?"

"W-what?"

"Seven days. Seven fucking days, *Scarlett*."

She flinched when he spat the name as though it tasted spoiled on his tongue. That was exactly how it felt as it left his mouth.

Her head shook back and forth rapidly. "Wha—I don't...what do you mean, seven d-days?" Her voice cracked and wobbled as if she were near tears.

The work of a skilled actress, no doubt. No how many tears came out of those lying eyes, he wouldn't be swayed. He wouldn't fall for her deceit again.

He was finished.

"You lasted a whole seven days after promising, fucking *promising* nothing could tempt you back to Hollywood." He stepped closer, letting the fury flow through him. She didn't recoil as his menacing height loomed over her, only tipped her head back and stared at him with a devastated gaze.

Another trick of the trade, no doubt.

"You laid right here, next to me in this godforsaken bed, and listened to me tell you I fucking believed you. And then seven days later, the spotlight called you back, and you went running like a whipped fucking dog."

"No," she choked out, reaching for him. Tears poured freely down her face now. Damn, the woman really had earned those Oscars she'd won. She was hands down the best actress he'd ever seen.

"No, Keith. That's not true." The words came out around a choked sob as he stepped away from her extended arms.

"No?" Christ, he sounded so bitter and hateful. Yet it was only a fraction of how vile he felt inside. "You know what, Scarlett? How about you quit lying to me? How about you look me in the eye and tell me the fucking truth?"

"Please…" she whispered. Her lip trembled.

"Do they teach that little trick in acting class or it is raw talent?" he asked as he flicked a finger over the quivering lip.

Unbelievable.

"Keith, it's just me. I'm just me. Your Mickie."

He scoffed. "Come on, tell me again how you don't care about the spotlight anymore. How Hollywood burned you out until there was almost nothing left. How you'll never, *never* be tempted to return? How you love it here in Vermont with my family and me. Tell me you've already had the role of a lifetime, and no movie part could ever lure you back."

"Keith…" She reached for him.

"Tell me!" he shouted as he stepped back.

She wilted before his eyes, but he steeled his spine and fortified the fucking cage around his heart. No matter what it took, he'd keep her away from that damn organ.

"I-it's the one role I've always wanted," she whispered in a broken voice as she stared at the floor. "I can't…I cannot let this one pass me by. I'm sorry."

"That's what I thought," he said as he backed away.

"Keith, please!" she called out, sounding frantic now. "I'm not leaving for good. This is my home now. This movie is just a job, and I'll be back when it's over. This is where I live, where my life is. Where you are. Keith I lo—"

"Fuck, don't." His eyes fell closed as the jagged knife entered his heart with a slow stroke, twisting and gouging as it sank deep. So much for the cage. She managed to slide that shiv right between the steel bars. "Just don't."

She sagged as though crumbling under the weight of the world and even broken, his heart pulsed with the need to comfort her. She'd done something to him. Changed something deep within, and now he was nothing but collateral damage in her rise to the top.

"I'm sorry. I never meant—"

"I hope you have the decency to keep my siblings and I off your social media posts. I was prepared for someone to discover where and who you were at some point. I've been ready for headlines and to tell off nosy reporters, but that was when I stupidly thought we were in this together. The last thing we want is media vultures descending on us for no reason."

She gasped then shook her head. "I would never. Keith, after everything, how can you think so little of me?" The pain in her voice mirrored that in his chest, but he shoved it aside. She didn't get to be sad right now. She didn't deserve his sympathy.

She'd done this.

She'd broken them.

Broken him.

And he wasn't sure he could put the pieces back together the way they were before Michaela Hudson got a flat tire in the night.

He raised his palms as he walked backward. "I think that question answers itself. Goodbye, Scarlett. Hope Hollywood is worth it."

With that, he turned and strode out of the room, down the stairs, and straight across the street, closing his ears to the sound of Mickie's hysterical sobs. They'd come back to him later, in the dead of night while he slept in his bed all alone.

He stormed into his house, shoving the door open. JP stood in the living room with a chocolate covered strawberry hanging from his lips. "Shit! Sorry, I'm leaving. I'm checking them for poison. It's a favor, really. Don't kill me. You're early. Wait. What's wrong? Where's Mickie?"

"Packing for her flight to California," he said as he stomped past his brother.

"Wha—"

"Eat whatever the fuck you want." He stomped into the kitchen, grabbed a bottle of vodka from the freezer then started for his room.

"Keith!" JP called as Keith walked past his shell-shocked brother a second time. "Keith, wait. Talk to me. You hate vodka!"

He ignored JP's shouts and trudged into his room, slamming the door behind him.

JP's mumbled, "What the fuck?" came through the door, followed by a light knock.

Keith didn't bother to respond. He yanked the cap off the vodka then took a long, burning drink of an alcohol he despised. The taste didn't matter right now. All that mattered was forgetting this fucking day and numbing the excruciating pain.

After a few minutes, the sound of footsteps in the hall indicated JP's departure.

Good. He wasn't fit company for anyone but the frosty bottle in his hands.

Over the next few hours, his sibling's voices appeared at his door, mostly whispering to each other but occasionally calling out to him.

He ignored it all. Besides lifting the bottle to his lips, all the had the energy for was staring at the white ceiling above his head and berating himself for falling in love.

And hours later, when his eyes finally blurred and he fell into a fitful sleep, his dreams were just as tortured with visions of Mickie as his waking hours had been.

Chapter Twenty-Eight

"Excuse me, sir," Mickie said as she sidled up to Ralph where he stood waiting for her outside the airport. As usual, his outfit was styled to perfection. Black jeans, a hot pink polo, and his favorite Gucci shoes. The warmth of California felt foreign after enduring the cold Vermont winter.

"Yes? Holy shit!" His eyes bugged and he covered his mouth as he laughed. Then he glanced around at the other people busting by. "I'm sorry, have we just traveled back to nineteen-eighty-five?"

"Shut up," she muttered as she adjusted the straight-up eighties wig. "It was all I could find on short notice. No one recognized me in rural Vermont, but here I'm not willing to take the chance."

The wig came from the costume section at a party store about an hour outside of where she lived. It was a penny copper color, had puffy bangs, and frizzy crimped hair. Paired with giant dark sunglasses and baggy clothes, no one would ever recognize her.

"Well, I don't want you walking next to me because people know me here and I can't have anyone thinking I did that to your hair," he said with a horrified expression as he refused he hug.

"Missed your face," she said grabbing him into a monster embrace despite his protests.

Squirming out of her arms, he gently shoved her away. "Oh, my God, get in the car before someone sees you like this."

With a roll of her eyes, she handed him her suitcase and slipped into the passenger's seat. "Happy?" she asked when he joined her.

Ralph snorted. "Hell, no. I'll be happy when we get to my place and I can burn that furry animal on your head."

Once they pulled onto the highway, Mickie removed her sunglasses and the wig, letting out a huge sigh. "Ahh, that feels so much better."

"Looks better too." Navigating the traffic with the ease of years of LA driving experience, Ralph gave her a side glance. "So, I kind of expected you'd be a weepy mess when I picked you up," he said. "Are you faking this chill vibe?"

"A little bit," Mickie said. She looked out the window at the familiar scenery she hadn't seen in many months. "I'm compartmentalizing. If I think about what happened with Keith, I'll turn into a blubbering idiot, so I've stuck that in the corner of my mind until I deal with the other matter first."

Ralph looked at her like he didn't believe a word of what she said. Smart man. His smartness came shining through again when he didn't call her out on the lie. "The video?" he said as he took the exit to his condo. She'd explained the situation to him on the phone the previous night. Actually, she'd been in freak out mode and had sniveled and sobbed out the entire blackmail then break-up story.

Now, that the initial emotional reaction had passed and she had a few—very few—hours of sleep in her, she was able to process the entire situation with more of a rational head. "I used the flight to come up with a plan," she said as she pulled out her phone. "Wanna hear what I'm thinking?"

The background image on her phone was one of her and Keith taken by Ronnie a few weeks ago. She'd fallen asleep with her head on his lap while watching a movie. He'd remained awake, playing with her hair. Unbeknownst to them, Ronnie had snapped the candid shot and later texted it. They both looked so happy and at peace with each other, Mickie had set it as her background. Now, looking at it brought fresh tears of sorrow to her eyes.

"Of course, sweetie. I'm here for whatever you need," Ralph said, cutting into her sadness. "Speaking of." He stuck his hand in the center console of his Beemer. "Twizzler?"

She blinked way the tears. It hurt just to look at how happy they'd been such a short time ago. If her plan worked, she'd be on a plane back to Vermont in just a few days. She had no idea what she'd do when she got there, but somehow, she'd get Keith back. After experiencing true happiness, she wasn't willing to walk away from it without a fight.

Sober and fully in control of herself, Mickie realized how lucky she was to have Keith and his family in her life, and she wanted to keep them there. She loved him. Plain and simple… okay fine, extremely complicated, but still, she loved him.

Michaela knew how to throw down for what she wanted. She just needed to remove a few very large and potential life-destroying obstacles.

So much for compartmentalizing.

"Mickie?" Ralph said. "I asked if you want a Twizzler."

"Oh, yes, thank you." Time to focus. As she chomped on the strawberry treat, she opened her email app. "I emailed Angelica and filled her in on the entire story."

"Angelica French?" he asked of her long-time attorney and once close friend.

"Yeah."

"Huh," he said. "What does she think?" Another turn had him pulling into the parking garage under his ritzy building. He maneuvered to his assigned spot, killed the engine, then rested back against his seat.

"She said I have a number of options if I decide to take action against both Mark and Chuck, as well as keep Keith's father from getting his hands on this video." Mickie scanned the last communication from the lawyer.

The email from Angelica had been professional and detailed a few routes Mickie could choose to pursue. When she'd asked her attorney what she'd do if in this predicament, Angelica chose the same plan Mickie had been leaning toward. Now, after reading through it again, she was filled with confidence and even excitement. The scheme would ensure Chuck couldn't become a problem for Keith in the future and would hit Mark where it hurt: in his fat wallet.

"So what's the plan?"

"Well, she said, settling against the comfortable leather seat. "Chuck offered to hand the video over to Mark for fifty thousand dollars. After doing some digging, Angelica was able to find out that the money hasn't changed hands yet. Mark will be wiring the money the day after tomorrow."

"Okay…" He pursed his perfectly shaped lips.

Mickie smiled. "She's setting up a meeting with Mark and Chuck at her office tomorrow under the guise of facilitating the money transfer."

"Oohh, that slightly evil." Ralph's eyes lit up. "I like it. Will Chuck be able to get here?"

"Yep." Mickie stowed her phone in her purse after one last longing look at the background screen. She'd resisted scrolling through the hundreds of pictures she'd take of her and Keith over the past few months, but tonight she'd probably give into that urge as she gorged on chocolate fudge brownie ice cream.

"Angelica purchased a ticket for him, and he'll be here in the early afternoon tomorrow. We have a meeting set for four p.m. And that's when we'll blow up a few lives."

"Oh, man, can I be there? Please?" Ralph bounced in his seat. "Pretty please!"

Laughing, Mickie nodded. "I'd be offended if you didn't want to be there."

"Yay." He clapped his hands. "So what I didn't tell you when we talked is that I actually have a flight out to New York tonight for an early morning job tomorrow. But I'll switch my return ticket so I'm here in time to catch the meeting.

"So I'll have your posh apartment all to myself tonight?"

"Is that all right? I hate to leave you when I know you're just going to eat my ice cream and cry."

"You don't know that."

Ralph shot her an I-know-you-better-than-you-know-yourself glare.

"Okay, fine. That was the plan."

With a grin, he pushed his door open. "Lucky for you, the freezer is stocked."

A few hours later, after Mickie had settled into Ralph's guest room, she sat on the bed with her ice cream and a box of tissues as she scrolled thorough pictures from Thanksgiving. It'd been the best one she'd ever had, full of food, fun, and family nonsense.

Had she gone about this the entirely wrong way? Should she have told Keith Chuck still had the video and was selling it to her smarmy manager who might put it out in the world if she didn't act in the movie he'd chosen?

Despite the misery of being alone and heartbroken, she just couldn't imagine doing that to Keith. She loved him and would do what she had to ensure the most horrifying moment in his life wouldn't resurface and cause any more trauma than it already had.

Even if it meant she lost him.

Sparing him that immense pain meant more to her than her own happiness. She'd rather spend the rest of her life with this ache in her chest than have to witness Keith relive the moment he learned his mother had been prostituting herself to support her children.

Chapter Twenty-Nine

"You hear the news?" Jagger's voice rang out in the garage, somewhere nearby.

"Yep." Keith didn't bother to roll himself out from under the car he'd been tinkering with for the past hour.

"And?"

"And what?" He felt around on the ground for the wrench he'd set next to the creeper. Where the fuck was it? Finally, his fingers grazed the cool metal.

"And are you gonna see him? Bail him out? Discuss it with the rest of us? I heard from a friend on the force that the old man's facing serious time this go around. It's his third arrest this year, and with it being a home invasion, he's looking at a whole new category of charges."

With a snort, Keith kept working. "Fuck no, I'm not bailing his ass out. He made his bed. Told you guys I was done, and I'm done." Really, the final decision had been made the moment he confronted Mickie at the garage. Earl only added an extra nail to his own coffin when he showed up at Mickie's home.

Somehow, despite quite a few arrests through his adult life, their slimy father consistently managed to weasel himself out of long prison sentences. The longest he'd served was sixty consecutive days in county lock-up a year or so back. If the courts wanted to put him away for a few years this time, more power to 'em. That'd be a few years of one less headache for Keith.

"So how long are we gonna do this, Keith?"

"Got a bit to do on this car then two oil changes with tire rotations before I'm done. Why? You need help with something?"

"Not what I'm talking about," Jagger said.

"Then what?"

"How long are you gonna keep up this shit mood?"

Gritting his teeth, Keith cranked the wrench as hard as he could. Fucking bolt didn't move. "It's been less than two days. And no one's forcing you to be in my company." He tried again, this time groaning as the wrench dug a divot into his palm. Fucking finally, the goddammed thing loosened a smidge.

"You really are a miserable fuck."

"Tends to happen when the woman you love shits all over your heart."

Jagger grunted. Keith could imagine his brother standing near the hood of the car, legs spread, arms crossed, and a disapproving frown directed his way. "You know Ronnie's been texting her?"

Of course, she was. Those two were thick as thieves. Shit, before Jagger came in, he'd managed an entire six minutes of not thinking about Michaela Hudson. Now he had to start the clock all over again. "There something you need, Jag? Or you just here to bust my balls?"

"Christ. Fine, I'm going. Enjoy your day, asshole."

As Jagger's footsteps retreated, Keith grumbled under his breath, but it didn't take more than a minute for the guilt to set it. With a sigh, he let his arms flop off the sides of the creeper. It wasn't Jagger's fault that Mickie carved his heart out with a rusted knife. Nor was it his fault their father had been arrested the previous night on robbery charges. It just took less effort to be a dick than to make nice when he felt so low, and he didn't have the energy to play the part of happy Keith.

Not when he hadn't slept the past two nights. Obsessing for hours only to finally crash but then wake with a raging hard-on from erotic dreams would curdle any man's brain.

Still, Jagger didn't deserve the sharp edge of his tongue yet again, especially since he'd come to discuss the very real issue of their incarcerated father.

"Shit," he grumbled, wiping his greasy hands on a rag from his pocket. "Jag, wait!" As he shouted, he rolled himself from under the car. He sat straight up. "Hold up, brother, I'm sor— Ralph."

"You just missed him." Mickie's best friend stood at the open windows of the garage bay leaning on the frame wearing a long, trendy black coat, black pants and boots, as well as a black hat. If Keith hadn't known better, he'd assume the man was heading to a funeral.

Still wiping at his oily hands, Keith strode closer. "Uh, thanks. Look, I hope you didn't come here to plead Mickie's case for her because I'm really not in the mood."

Ralph tilted his head and raked his eyes up and down Keith. "You look like shit."

"Yeah, well..." He had nothing to finish off that statement. Clearly, Ralph was aware of what had gone down between him and Mickie. "There something I can do for you?"

"Mm-hmm." Ralph pushed off the wall and strode Keith's way. His shoulders were straight, and a cocky gleam shone in his eye despite the fact Keith had six inches and at least fifty pounds of muscle on him. "You can pull your head out of your ass."

"You been talking to Ronnie?" he mumbled.

"What?" Ralph's perfectly shaped eyebrows scrunched.

"Nothing. Look, Ralph, Mickie is lucky to have you in her corner, ready to jump in for her at any time, but this visit was a waste of your time. She made her choice. She's back in

Hollywood and playing the role of her life. Sucks for me, but what are you gonna do?"

"I don't know. Maybe you should ask the bags under your eyes?" There was a decidedly bitchy tone to Ralph's voice now.

Keith rolled his eyes and fought to keep his temper in check. "Look—"

Ralph held up a hand. "No, you look. I came here because my best friend is hurting just as badly as you are. Trust me. She's eaten a startling amount of ice cream in the last twenty-four hours."

As pissed as he was, the thought of Mickie in pain twisted him up inside.

"I need you to do something for me," Ralph said in that bitchy tone Keith had come to recognize indicated he meant business.

With a sigh, he tossed the rag on the ground near a toolbox. "What?"

"I need you to pack a bag and meet me at the airport in three hours."

Keith's eyebrows must have his hairline. "Are you crazy?"

"No. I'm not. It's for your own good. And for Mickie's."

"Why—"

"Ralph held up a hand. It's not my story to tell. But trust me when I tell you you'll want to be there. It's important."

With a sigh, Keith stared past Ralph into the parking lot. His siblings didn't know, but he'd actually gone back to Mickie's house a few hours after their blow up. She'd already gone. Probably for the best since he'd been drunk as a skunk and might have only made the situation worse, but he'd become so accustomed to sleeping with her, he'd just wanted one more night.

Now, the thought of seeing her again, well it was too good to resist.

There was one thing he knew for certain after two days of soul searching and berating himself for reacting like a caveman.

He was head over heels in love with Michaela Hudson. It wasn't the acting job that had caused him to act like a complete idiot, it'd been the intense fear of losing the perfection he'd found with her. But instead of acting like a grown up, and communicating his anxieties, he'd thrown a tantrum and ended up losing her anyway.

Now with her closest friend standing before him indicating there may still be a chance to redeem himself, he couldn't pass up the opportunity to try. Hell, at this point he'd get on his knees and grovel if that's what she wanted from him.

"Three hours?"

Ralph's lips curved into a smile as he nodded. "I'll text you the flight information."

"Okay. There's something I have to do first, but I'll be there." He held out a hand to Ralph.

The smaller man nodded, expression grave as he took Keith's hand. "You better be worth all this trouble, Keith Benson. I don't like seeing my best friend cry."

He'd bet his year's salary he hated hearing of her cry more than Ralph despised witnessing it. Keith cleared his throat. "I will be."

"And if you manage to fix this shit, you better fuck her so good that she forgets I lied and told her I was working a job in New York this morning so I could come here."

Barking out a laugh, Keith released Ralph's hand. "Consider it done." For the first time since he walked out of Mickie's house two weeks ago, the crushing pain in his chest dissipated. He'd get Mickie back, no matter what he had to do.

"See you soon," Ralph said before he headed toward his rental.

As he reached the car, Keith called out. "Ralph?"

"Yes?"

"Thank you."

"My pleasure. It'll be glad to see Mickie smile again."

As he packed a bag and prepared to spend a few days in LA, Keith's mind spun through all the possible reasons Ralph wanted him there. Was something wrong on the set of the movie? Was Mickie regretting her decision? Was she struggling? Was her sobriety at risk? Or was she happy and thriving in a profession she'd been gifted at? Maybe that's what Ralph wanted him to see. Perhaps he wanted Keith to have a chance to witness Mickie, or Scarlett, in action.

All of a sudden, it hit him like a ton of bricks, just how stupid he was. He claimed to love her, but he hadn't given her his trust. Wasn't giving his trust a critical part of loving someone? If he loved her, which he did, one hundred percent, then he should have listened to her explanation for leaving. He should have known deep down there was a solid reason she went back on her word not to return to Hollywood. Why the fuck hadn't he listened?

Because he'd been so overcome with the shock of her supposed betrayal. He'd let his emotions rule his thinking and fucked up the best thing in his life.

He owed her a million apologies and would give them to her the moment he landed in LA.

But before that, he had one critical stop to make.

Twenty minutes later, Keith strode into the police station, where the young receptionist cast him a pitying look. Certainly wasn't the first time he'd been there, usually to drag his father home after a night in the drunk tank. Today, however, he'd be leaving without a second passenger in his car.

"Hey, Keith," she said as she pulled out the paperwork he'd need to pay the five-thousand dollars in bail. "Fill these out for me, and I'll have someone get your dad's personal effects for him."

"Not necessary, Lisa. I'm just here to talk with him for a few minutes."

Her mouth formed an *O*, but no sound came out. As she blinked at him, the police chief strode out of his office. Chuck's father glared at him with a smug grin, pulling his pants higher up the gut that had grown exponentially since Keith had last seen him. "Thought about bringing you some donuts, but it seems you already get enough of them."

The slightly hostile repartee wasn't uncommon on the rare instances they ran across each other as there was no love lost between them. But Lisa wasn't used to it, and she snorted out a poorly disguised laugh. "Um, Keith would like to speak to his father, Chief," she said, face turning pink.

"If not paying bail is a matter of money, there are plenty of places that will loan you the cash to bail him out."

Keith grunted. Christ, how he wanted his fist to meet the police chief's face. "Nope. Not the money. Doin' just fine for myself, *sir*. I'm through bailing his lousy ass out. He's your problem now. Just need two minutes to tell him so."

The chief scowled but waved Keith to follow him through the station to the jail cells. The halls were quiet, as was typical for the small station. As they walked side by side, Keith couldn't keep himself from letting some of his frustration and anger slip out and land on the chief.

"How's Chucky?" he asked.

Though the chief had and would always excuse his son's asshole behavior, they had a contentious relationship. How could they not? Chuck would be an embarrassment to any parent, but even worse for the Chief of Police, who'd had to bend the rules more times than he could count for his piece-of-shit son.

"None of your goddammed business," the chief barked just as they reached the cell. "You've got five minutes."

"Only need two."

With a grunt, the chief moved out of sight but not out of earshot. Fine by Keith, he had no problem with that. It saved him from having to repeat himself.

"Fucking finally," his father barked, rising from the concrete bench along the back wall of the cell. His hair stood on end, and his all-black outfit came straight out of a crime drama. Stereotypical burglar attire. "Took your sweet ass time bailing me out of here. I'm your fucking father. Let's go, Chief, open the door."

Keith's mouth spread into a wide grin as he cocked his head, studying his aged father. "Sorry, old man. I'm not here to bail you out."

"What?" Earl gripped the bars of the cell and shook them as though they'd actually part.

"Yep." Keith popped the p sound as he rocked back on his heels. "Turns out I'm all out of fucks to give when it comes to you."

"Get one of your siblings down here now! They'll get me the fuck outta here." His father's face turned a deeply satisfying shade of purple as he continued to shake the bars. Every foul word he could drum up flew from his mouth along with spit as he raged. Keith waited until he ran out of steam, which was only about thirty seconds. Then he moved in for the kill.

"Nah, you burned all your bridges with them, too."

"This would kill your mother all over again," he said, throwing out a line that had worked on Keith numerous times in the past. "She's rolling in her fucking grave right now."

For the first time, that guilt trip didn't hit the mark. His mother would have loved Mickie and been thrilled to see her son happy and in love. She wouldn't have wanted him wasting his life on a man who was pure poison, no matter what she'd said before her death. He'd known his mother and what made her happy. She was a true romantic who believed in love.

"Actually, I'm pretty sure she'd be damn proud of me for finally manning up and doing what needs to be done to protect my loved ones from you."

Watching his father's face go from purple to deathly pale in an instant might have been one of the most satisfying moments of Keith's adult life. After every second spent with Mickie, of course.

"Have a good life, old man," Keith said as he turned and strode away, lighter than he'd felt in ages. Fuck, it was good to have that albatross off his neck.

As he emerged from the police station into the cold, crisp evening, he inhaled a deep breath to cleanse himself of his father's filth.

One hurdle down. One to go.

The thought of begging Mickie to take him back terrified him.

There was a chance, maybe a high one, she'd tell him to shove his apologies straight up his ass.

What the hell would he do then?

Chapter Thirty

Michaela smoothed down the front of her professional black dress as she stared through the two-way mirror.

"Nervous?" her attorney asked.

Apparently, the two-way mirror gave the law firm's staff the advantage of observing clients for a few moments prior to meeting with them. Also provided victims of crime a chance to see their accuser without having to be face to face.

"More like anxious. I want this over with more than you can imagine." She fiddled with the simple silver bracelet on her right wrist. In a few moments, she'd pull it together and act in the most important role of her life, portraying cool, calm, and collected, but for now, she allowed herself to fidget as jittery energy coursed through her blood stream.

Once upon a time Scarlett and Angelica French had been friends as well attorney and client. Their social relationship ended after Angelica told her she could no longer keep up with Scarlett's heavy partying lifestyle. The friendship breakup came after a particularly embarrassing night where Michaela ended up passing out in the bathroom of a club.

"It's nice to have you back, Scarlett," Angelica said with a genuine smile.

"Oh, I'm not here to stay. I'm heading home as soon as this is done." She had some serious groveling to do. That and she missed Vermont a hundred times more than she'd ever missed LA.

"No, I mean it's nice to have *you* back."

Mickie met her lawyer's accepting expression with a smile of her own. "Well then, please call me Mickie. I shed Scarlett almost a year ago. And I can't tell you how nice it is to be back. Thank you for being willing to do this on such short notice."

With a snort, Angelic said, "Please, sticking it to assholes like these two is one of my favorite pastimes. Ready to go?"

Mickie took one last look at the conference room table where Mark and Chuck waited, awkwardly not speaking. They'd been brought in under the false guise of facilitating the money transfer to Chuck in exchange for the video. "Let's do this."

Dressed in a cobalt power suit with four-inch nude heels, Angelica strode into the room ahead of Mickie. "Good afternoon, gentlemen," she said with all the authority she commanded.

"'Bout fucking time," Chuck muttered right before noticing Mickie walk into the room well. "Wait! What the fuck is she doing here?" His head swiveled to Mark, whose face paled.

Angelica pulled out the chair at the head of the mahogany oval table. "Please, Ms. Hudson, have a seat."

"Thank you," Mickie said, biting her lip to keep from smirking.

Once Mickie was settled, Angelica click-clacked to the other end of the table. "Let's not waste any time. Don't know about you gentlemen, but Michaela and I are busy women." She laid out three stacks of paper.

"I asked what the fuck she is doing here?" Chuck snapped. He hopped to his feet, pointing at Mickie as though he needed to identify who the *she* was.

"I'll get to that in a minute, Mr. Pierce. Please sit so we may begin." Angelica indicated the chair Chuck had been in a moment ago. Her long honey-colored hair had been sleeked straight and hung halfway down her back. Minimal makeup and jewelry complemented her professional and authoritative presence.

Grumbling, he sat back down but refused to look Mickie's way.

Her lawyer remained standing. "As I was about to say, I am Angelica French, attorney for Michaela Hudson who used to go by the stage name Scarlett. You gentlemen have been called here today to sort out a manner involving a video taken of Ms. Benson's boyfriend's mother, used in attempt to blackmail Ms. Hudson."

"What?" Chuck burst out. "I didn't blackmail nobody."

Mark turned green. He knew he was fucked.

Holding up her hand, Angelica said, "Mr. Pierce, please try to refrain from any more outbursts."

Damn, she was cool as could be while Mickie's insides popped and fizzled with nerves, though she kept them well hidden from the rest of the room.

"Now, Mr. Pierce, I understand the agreed upon price for the video was fifty thousand dollars, is that correct?"

Chuck flicked his eyes Mickie's way before giving Angelica his attention again. He seemed to consider the question as though wondering if it was a trap before saying, "Yes."

"Excellent," Angelica picked up a piece of paper and slide it to Chuck. "Since no money has changed hands as of yet and there is no bill of sale, Ms. Hudson would like to offer you double that amount to sell the video to her instead."

Chuck's eyes nearly bugged out of his head. "Fuck yes, where do I sign?" he asked with a greedy grin.

"Just a moment, I'm not finished."

Narrowing his eyes, Chuck said, "You're not?"

Angelica smiled a shark's grin. "Nope. As part of this deal, you agree to relinquish any and all copies of the video in both the digital and hard copies. Should this video ever appear again, in any form, say on social media or in the news, you will be prosecuted to the fullest extent of the law. That includes ten years of jail time for violating this agreement."

"What? There's no way in hell I'm agreeing to that."

"I'm not finished yet," Angelica barked. "A similar but much less lucrative offer has been made to Mr. Earl Benson who couldn't be here today because he is currently incarcerated."

Michaela's eyes widened. She hadn't heard that tidbit. Did Keith know? And how was he taking it? How about the rest of the Bensons? God, she wished she was back in Vermont with them instead of sitting in this room negotiating with scumbags. But this was necessary and would protect Keith from every having to worry about that video again.

"Please feel free to have your attorney look over the document. There are no loopholes. We've covered every possible contingency. Believe me when I say that once you sign this, if you so much as reference this video, you'll be prosecuted and spend time in jail."

"I'm not signing this." Chuck said, shoving the papers away.

Angelica continued as though he wasn't throwing a mild hissy fit. "The deal expires in twenty-four hours. In case you don't understand what that means, let me spell it out for you. If these documents aren't signed by," she checked her watch, "Four thirty-five tomorrow, the deal is null and void. You will not receive a penny from my client."

When Chuck's gaze slid to a scowling Mark as though expecting him to up his offer, Angelica chuckled. "We haven't gotten to Mr. Degrasse yet, but trust me, you won't be receiving anything from him, either. Once the timer runs up, this deal is gone, and you can do whatever the hell you please with the video. If you approach Ms. Hudson in the future she will not pay. We have already prepared injunctions to keep this from hitting the tabloids, so you won't find any money there. Sure, you could post it to your Facebook page, but you won't be making a hundred thousand dollars off your fifty Facebook friends."

This part was a bit of a bluff. Okay, it was a full-on bluff. Mickie would pay any amount necessary to keep this video from harming Keith or his siblings. And there were other avenues Chuck could go to make money off the video if he didn't sign the agreement, but Angelica had warned her to keep that to herself. Greedy men like Chuck, she'd said, would never walk away from a guaranteed offer of cash like this.

"So, Mr. Pierce, would you like some time to have a lawyer review the documents?" Angelica asked knowing full well Chuck didn't have an attorney on standby to perform such a task.

Michaela held her breath as she watched the man swallow. His face had turned a deep radish red and damn, was it satisfying. Sure, she'd be out a hundred thousand dollars, but it was well, well worth it to ensure Keith's happiness and safety. She'd have paid the money just to see this sour look on Chuck's face.

He cleared his throat. "No," he said sounding close to tears. "I'll sign. Can I have a pen?"

Angelica winked at Mickie as she handed a pen to Chuck.

As she watched him scrawl his name across the pages as instructed by Angelica, she wanted to jump out of her chair and shout for joy.

They were almost there. This was almost done. One hurdle down, and one to go. Then she'd be on a plane, heading back to Keith and hoping with all her might that he understood why she'd had to do this.

"Thank you very much," Angelica said as she gathered the papers. "My paralegal will be providing you with copies before you leave here today. You have forty-eight hours to provide any and all copies of the video to Michaela and will be given instructions on how to do so. Do you understand?"

"Yes," Chuck grumbled with a hangdog expression Mickie couldn't help but derive immense pleasure from.

"Is there anything you wanted to add, Mickie?" Angelica raised an eyebrow in her direction.

Mickie grinned. "I think you covered everything. Chin up, Chuck," she said with false sweetness. "You're going home one hundred thousand dollars richer."

There wasn't a doubt in her mind or Angelica's that the man would have used this video to extort money from Mickie and torture Keith for years to come had they not taken legal action. Sure, a hundred thousand dollars was a lot to give such a disgusting human being, but not nearly as much as he could have gotten if she'd been stupid enough to fall for his game. And in the grand scheme of things, if it kept him away from the Bensons, the money was more than worth it.

Chuck opened his mouth, no doubt to cuss her out, when Angelica cleared her throat. "Now," she said as she turned her attention to the other man in the room. "Your turn, Mr. Degrasse."

Mickie smiled. This one would be even more fun.

Chapter Thirty-One

"Ralph, I've been patient, but I'm at the end of my rope. Why the fuck and I in California standing in the lobby of an attorney's office?" Christ, the last twenty-four hours had been a whirlwind. He'd flown to LA at Ralph's insistence—first class for the first time ever he might add—but a man could only take so much secrecy.

"Look, Keith, it's not my story to tell. I got you here, which is already gonna get my ass kicked by Mickie. You're just going to have to see the rest for yourself. Okay?"

"Ralph, hello!" A perky blonde holding a clipboard emerged from behind a desk. Was every woman out here in LA a size two blonde? Sure seemed like any female he'd come across since the airport was a semi clone of all the others. "Please follow me. They've already begun."

"Thank you, Joslyn," Ralph said, holding his hand out for Keith to precede him.

Keith tried to keep his jaw from hitting the floor as they made their way through the enormous and extremely swanky law office. Hell, it just might be the fanciest place he'd ever been, and it was a goddamned office building. He sure looked out of place with his jeans and Nirvana T-shirt.

Joslyn stopped outside a closed door. "You'll be able to observe from in here," she said with an animated smile. "It's a two-way mirror so they won't be able to see you. The room is also soundproof so feel free to talk. If you need anything push that silver button there on the wall and I'll come running." She pointed to the button.

What the… Had he stepped into an episode of the *Twilight Zone*? More like *Lifestyles of the Rich and Famous*.

"Thank you, Joslyn. We'll be just fine. Come on, Keith." Ralph ushered him in.

He probably seemed like a complete country bumpkin gawking at the fancy splendor of the place and not speaking, but he was admittedly extremely overwhelmed by his surroundings and the fact he still didn't know why he was there to begin with. All he knew was it had something to do with Mickie.

Ralph stood there holding the door open. "Keith?"

"Oh, yeah sorry." He walked into the room and immediately his eyes were drawn to Mickie behind the window.

His heart started to pound. Had it really only been four days since he'd last seen her? Fuck, he missed her with a force so strong it hurt. Rubbing the ache in his chest, he drank in the sight of her seated at the head of an oval table. His beautiful woman wore a smile that lit her eyes behind those sexy glasses. As usual, her hair was sleek and shiny in its stylish bob, but she had a fitted black outfit he assumed was a dress. Since meeting her, he'd only seen her in jeans, leggings, or sweats. Or, well, naked. Lots of naked.

Today she looked sexy, polished, and powerful.

"Ms. Hudson, I believe you wanted to be the one to speak to Mark."

For the first time, Keith realized Mickie wasn't alone in the room. A woman stood at the other end of the table wearing a blue suit. Next to her sat a very elegant man who looked like he might vomit. And across from him sat—

"What the fuck is Chuck doing here?" Keith's heartrate skyrocketed as he spun to face Ralph.

"Shhh." Ralph pointed to the window. "You don't want to miss your girl in action. She's something to watch."

Michaela stood, smoothing down what was in fact a simple fitted black dress. Though no sparkles, ruffles, or whatever else women like on their dresses, she looked like a million freakin' bucks. "Thank you, Angelica, yes."

She straightened her shoulders and glared at the man called Mark. Keith had the distinct impression he was in the presence of Scarlett, movie star extraordinaire, about to act in the most vital performance of her life.

Pointing to a stack of papers in front of the attorney, she said, "Mark, that is the non-disclosure agreement you signed when you began working for me six years ago." She cocked her head. "You do remember that, right? *You* worked for *me*. Not the other way around. And I made you a very rich man over the years. In fact, like me, you were a nobody before I came into your life. You don't need me anymore. You have plenty of high-profile clients thanks to the name you made for yourself because of your affiliation with me."

Whoa boy, his woman was steamed. Keith smiled. Damn, she was something.

"Told ya," Ralph said with a laugh. "And I believe she's just getting warmed up."

"And how do you thank me for the many millions of dollars I've made you? By blackmailing me."

Keith sucked in a breath. "What?" he whispered, pressing his hands to the glass.

"How dare you?" she sneered, with so much hatred Keith wondered if she might hop across the table and strangle the man. "You were willing to buy a video of my boyfriend's mother off this piece of shit here," she said pointing at Chuck, "all so I would make another goddammed movie."

A video. Keith frowned as his gaze shifted from Mickie to Chuck.

"Oh fuck."

He covered his mouth as he gagged.

"Need the trash can?" Ralph rushed across the little room to grab the small can.

"No, I'm good," Keith said, though he sounded wrecked. He couldn't tear his gaze away from what was happening in that room. Christ, Chuck still had the video and he'd tried to sell it to Mickie's manager.

"You know what this life did to me, Mark. Who it turned me into. Who you helped turn me into."

Mark snorted. "You always were a drama queen, Scarlett."

"Don't fucking call her that," Keith growled.

Behind him, Ralph chuckled. "Down boy. She's got this."

"Now," Mickie continued. "This little stunt has violated your NDA in about ten different ways. After a thorough review with Angelica, we've devised a very solid lawsuit that would ruin you." She gave him the most sugar-sweet smile Keith had ever seen from her and he couldn't keep from laughing.

She was truly a marvel to watch in action.

"Mickie, wait. We can work this out." Mark held up his hands. A bead of sweat ran from his forehead down the side of his face. "Please."

Mickie held up her hand. "Mark, don't beg. It's pitiful. I've decided not to pursue the lawsuit."

Her manager breathed a sigh of relief.

She did? Why the hell wouldn't she go after the asshole with everything she had?

"Would you care to guess why?"

"Um, because you know I made a mistake, and it won't happen again?" There was a pitiful note of pleading in her manager's voice.

Laughing, Mickie shook her head. "Oh no, that's not it. It's because it would take up too much of my time. Once I walk out that door today, I plan to never think of you again and a lawsuit would make that impossible. So as long as you forget you've ever met me, I'll leave you alone to run your business as usual. Are we good?"

Though Keith felt Mark was getting off much easier than he deserved, he was fucking proud of her. Head held high, she turned to her attorney. "I think we're done here, Angelica."

"I believe we are."

Mickie strode toward the exit like a queen walking to her throne. Just before she reached the door that would open to the room he and Ralph occupied, she stopped and turned. "Oh," she said, slapping a palm to her forehead. "I almost forgot. I was angry after you showed up in Vermont to blackmail me. And in my emotional state, I may have emailed a few of your clients to let them know of the gross violations of the NDA and to warn them to be wary of working with you. So…" She grimaced as though regretting her actions but everyone in the damn room knew differently. "I apologize if you lose quite a few clients over it. My bad."

Then with a victorious laugh, she yanked the door open and came face to face with him.

"Keith." she whispered on a gasp as she stopped dead in her tracks.

"Well, my work here is done," Ralph said. "I'll be downstairs waiting to chauffer your asses out of here when you're ready." He sashayed over to Mickie and smacked a kiss on her cheek. Then he did the same to Keith.

"Sorry," he said, not sounding a bit remorseful. "You'll have to get used to that if you're going to be part of the family."

But Keith barely paid him any mind. He couldn't tear his eyes away from Mickie.

"Geez, I'd be offended if you weren't taken," Ralph muttered as he snuck out of the room.

"Um, how much of that did you see?" She stepped in the room, letting the door close behind her.

"A little. Some. Enough to know I'm an asshole."

She shook her head. "No. I misled you and let you believe I was doing the one thing I promised I wouldn't do. I panicked. Mark told me if I didn't do the movie, he'd send the video to TMZ." Her voice cracked. "All I could think about was what that would do to you."

"Mickie, why didn't—" She could have told him.

"I didn't want you to know the video was still out there until I was certain it could never hurt you or the rest of your family. Paying off Chuck is nothing to me."

Paying off Chuck?

"Wait!" He lifted hand. "You paid off Chuck?"

Biting her lower lip, she nodded. "Yes. He was given money for the copies of the video. And he signed a very extensive document stating he would end up in prison if the video ever surfaced again. Hell, he's not even allowed to talk about it."

Fuck, she'd gone so far above and beyond.

It was then he realized that video no longer held the power over him it once had. The thought of losing Michaela struck fear into his heart release of the video couldn't touch. She was the most essential thing in his life, not what happened one fateful night over twenty years ago. He'd come to terms with the world seeing that video. What he couldn't do was let Mickie destroy her life to protect him. What happened in the present was more important than what happened in the past. Hell, Mickie had taught him that lesson with her bravery and resilience. She'd owned up to a tumultuous history full of questionable choices that had been analyzed and judged by the world a hundred times over, yet she'd moved on and become stronger, more grounded, and happier.

What a fool he'd been to put her in this position. To cling to events of the past he had no control over even back then and certainly not now.

"You shouldn't have." He shook his head. He could have handled Chuck his own way without her losing money. "I'll pay you back. However long it takes."

"Of course I should have, Keith. It's only money. And it's legal and takes care of the problem forever. Now we know for certain we never have to worry about it. And you'll do no such thing. It was my decision and my money."

"We?" he asked tilting his head. He barely heard anything after that incredible two-lettered word.

He could barely breath, so terrified she didn't mean it.

"Yes, we, Keith. I—"

He grabbed her face. "I love you Michaela Hudson. I fucking love you so much." Then he kissed her and kissed her and kissed her until she sagged against him with a whimper. "I'm so sorry for how I acted the other day," he said between kisses. "I was a goddammed idiot."

"I'm sorry too. I freaked and rushed out of Vermont without thinking. I was just in a panic. Once I got on the plane and had hours to sit, I was able to formulate this plan. I was heading back to you tonight to beg you to forgive me."

"Baby, there's nothing to forgive. Thank you for wanting to protect me. Thank you for caring about my family enough to protect all of them."

"Keith, there's nothing to thank me for. I love you. And I will always protect you and your family. I know this might be presumptuous, but I feel like they're my family now, too."

She loved him. God, she fucking loved him. "Not presumptuous at all. Trust me when I tell you they'd pick you for the family over me."

She laughed and kissed him, making his heart soar like a hero in a cheesy movie.

"There's one other thing," he said as he drew his head back.

Her forehead scrunched. "Okay?"

"I just want you to know that if you ever decide you want to do another movie, I won't stand in your way."

"Keith, I—"

"Wait. I know you don't want to. This isn't about me not believing you want to be in Vermont. It's about me telling you I love you and I trust you. So if it ever did happen, I won't freak out and I won't be scared that you'll leave me. Because I trust you. And I love you."

Her smile lit his fucking world. "I don't want to. And I won't want to. But I understand what you are saying, and your trust is the best gift you could ever give me. Thank you," she whispered, choked up.

He wrapped his arms around her and held her tight against him. Hell, he might never let her go at this point. "Can we go home now?" she whispered after a minute.

"Yes. I'm more ready to go home." The big city was not the place for him.

"Good," she said, beaming. "Because I'm ready to start the rest of our lives." Then she linked their fingers, and they left the law office hand in hand.

He didn't release her hand the entire flight back to Vermont. Just the feel of her palm against his provided the reassurance that she was really there with him. They'd almost lost this and now that he had her back, he was loath to let her go.

Epilogue

Five months later

THE SUN WAS shining, and the air was a warm and dry sixty-eight degrees. Maybe too chilly for a barbecue in some parts of the country, but Vermonters were quite used to throwing on a jacket during their Memorial Day barbecues.

"Thanks," Keith said to his brother as Jagger handed him a beer. He took a sip then let out a contented sigh. "Damn, that's good stuff."

With a nod, Jagger took a seat next to him. "It's from that new microbrewery a few miles from here."

"We'll have to hit it up soon." As he and Jagger sipped their beer and JP manned the grill, Mickie and Ronnie sat at the outdoor table, poring over a thick binder.

"What the hell is up with those two?" Jagger asked. "They've been thick as thieves since Mickie got back from LA. Always meeting in secret and whispering about shit."

Keith grunted in agreement. "Your guess is as good as mine."

"Oh, come on, you're telling me your woman didn't let something slip during a little pillow talk?" Jagger raised an eyebrow.

With a laugh, Keith shook his head. "Nope. Her lips have been sealed."

"Sucks for you," Jagger said with a grunt.

"Not what I meant, perv. All I know is that they have something to talk to all of us about today. They even wanted us to get Jimmy and Ian on Zoom so they could hear it too."

"Think it has to do with the lawsuit or anything?"

"Nah, that's pretty much a done deal." After Keith surprised Mickie in California, they'd immediately flown home together where they'd spent the next few days holed up in her house. To be honest, they hadn't left the bed much, but he wouldn't have had it any other way. After talking through everything that had happened, their reactions, and their hopes moving forward, they finally emerged from her home to spend time with his siblings.

There were no guarantees Chuck had destroyed all files or copies of the video, but Keith was confident Mickie's lawyer had thoroughly seen to all potential concerns. And if someday the video hit the media, they'd send Chuck to jail, then they'd find a way to get through it. As they'd done with the hordes of paparazzi and press who'd descended on their sleepy town in the weeks following Scarlett's trip to California. As hard as she'd tried to stay anonymous, it hadn't been possible. A coffee shop employee had recognized her and that had been that.

By now, most of the media attention had died down, allowing his family to return to a semi-normal life. There'd always be someone lurking around hoping to snap a shot or sound bite of Mickie, but not enough to fuck with their daily lives anymore.

"Oh, they're waving us over." Jagger stood and extended a hand to Keith. "Need help getting up, old man?"

With a snort, Keith batted his brother's hand away. "Fuck off. I'm only two years older than you."

"Yeah, but you got four years on me," JP piped up as he strode to the table with a tray piled high with cheeseburgers. "You guys ready to dig in?"

"Yes, I'm starved." Mickie's eyes lit as she eyed the platter.

Keith went straight to her. When he reached her, he snagged her around the waist and pulled her in for a deep, dirty kiss. As usual, she melted against him and gave as good as she got. His cock hardened and he groaned into her mouth. "That was a bad idea," he whispered against her lips.

Mickie laughed as she took a step back. "Better sit quick before they notice. You'll never hear the end of it."

Again he grumbled as he gingerly sat down, careful not to damage the merchandise.

"You okay there, buddy?" JP asked with a knowing smirk. Keith flipped him off which had the whole group laughing. Clearly, they'd caught on to his predicament.

Once they'd all loaded their plates with burgers, potato salad, chips, dip, and the grilled veggies Mickie had demanded, Ronnie pulled the missing family members up on a Zoom call on her laptop.

"Hey, guys!" JP said around a mouthful of meat as he waved.

"Oh, fuck you all," Ian said, groaning. "You wanna know what I had for my last meal?"

"Nope." JP took a huge bite of his burger. "Mmmm, this is soo good."

"Careful, bro," Jimmy said from the computer with a laugh. "Pretty sure they don't have burgers in hell."

"Worth it." JP's eyes closed as he exaggerated a moan.

"Maybe you should just eat it and not fuck it," Jagger said. "None of us wanna see that shit."

"All right," Keith broke in. "I think Ronnie and Mickie have something they want to talk to us about, so let's listen up."

Mickie shot him a dopey eyed, grateful smile as Ronnie said, "Thank you. At least one of my brothers isn't a complete moron."

"Hey!" JP said, mouth still full as though he wasn't the worst offender.

"Anyway..." Ronnie rolled her eyes. "Mickie and I have an idea to run by you. It's something we're very serious about so try to act your ages for a few moments, okay?"

Keith gave his woman a curious look as she winked at him. Though he'd tried every trick in his book to get her to blab, she'd been unusually secretive about her time spent with Ronnie.

"You have our compete attention," he said.

"Thank you," Mickie said. "Okay, guys, here it is. Ronnie and I recently purchased the old campground at the base of the mountain. We plan to turn it into luxury cabin rentals, and we'd like your help. Our hope is for this to become a family business that we can maintain for generations."

Silence met her words. The rest of his brothers looked at Mickie and Ronnie as if they'd lost their minds, but Keith could only hear one phrase repeating in his mind.

Family business.

Though he'd long ago put aside his fears of Mickie leaving, hearing her include herself in business with his family made his heart soar.

"Fuck, I love you," he whispered to her. "More each day. I'm in," he announced.

She turned to him with a playful smile. "You haven't even heard a single detail yet."

With a shrug he said, "Doesn't matter. If you're in, I'm in."

Her answering smile said it all. They'd be looking at each other like that for the rest of their lives.

"WELL, HOW NICE for you, bro, but I'm gonna need a little more info here," Jagger said. "I mean, what the hell do you know about luxury anything, Ron? Your idea of glamour and luxury is using the Chapstick that costs three dollars instead of ninety-five cents."

Mickie hid her chuckle as Ronnie stuck her tongue out at her brother. Doing business with his crew would be an experience like no other, but she had no doubts it would not only be a profitable and satisfying operation, but an extremely fun adventure as well.

"That's where I come in," Mickie said before the conversation could devolve into a full-on sibling war. "I do know luxury. And I've been working toward a design certification." She handed each person at the table a stack of papers. "Jimmy and Ian, I've emailed these documents to you. It lays out our business plan in great detail. Basically, we want to use Jagger to renovate all of the cabins."

She gave them all a minute to sift through the papers and get an idea of what she and Ronnie had laid out.

"If you look at page five," Ronnie said, "You'll see a market trend for this area. It's been drawing a huge crowd of extremely wealthy individuals during the ski months. The resorts and hotels in this area are basic. We think we could capitalize on this and create a resort experience far above what the area offers."

"Huh," Jagger said as he turned the page. "You two have really done your work here, haven't you?"

"We have," Mickie said. "It'll be a lot of work. A ton, really. We aren't under any illusions that this will be easy, or cheap. But I have the money and there isn't anything I'd rather invest in than a business with this family."

Keith squeezed her hand, which had her glancing down at him. He stared up at her with so much love in his gaze, she couldn't help but feel all warm and squishy inside.

"Jimmy and Ian, I know you guys will have to make decisions soon about whether you're going to re-up or not, so we thought this would be a good time to let you know you have an option here if you decide to go the civilian route." Ronnie spoke to the computer. She'd make a terrible actress. The poor girl didn't stand a chance at hiding the nerves or hopeful look on her face.

Mickie on the other hand, steeled her expression though her insides rivaled Ronnie's outside anxiety. "We don't expect an answer from anyone today. We want you to look over what we've proposed then decide what if any role you'd like to play.

How about you guys take the week, and we'll do this again next Saturday?"

"Pfft," JP said as he tossed his papers down on the table. "Hey, you know me. I'm game for anything. I'm in."

No surprise there. JP's endorsement was never in question. The guy would literally jump off the roof if they asked him to. Nothing got him riled and the word serious didn't exist in his vocabulary.

After a few minutes of chatting about what Ian and Jimmy have been up to overseas, they bid goodbye.

"Let me run inside and get the dessert," Ronnie said, practically bouncing out of her seat. There was a rare giddiness to her. "I made strawberry shortcake."

As she ran inside, Jagger and JP started ragging on each other about who knew what.

Keith grabbed her hand and gave a squeeze. She turned to face him.

"You'll tell me more about this tonight?" He asked as he tucked her hair behind her ear. She leaned into the touch as she admired his handsome face. The first face she saw each morning and the last one she saw each night.

"Of course."

"Naked?"

Resisting a snort, the let out an exaggerated sigh. "I suppose if that's what you require."

"Oh, it's what I require," he said, wagging his eyebrows as he leaned in for a kiss.

"Thank you," she whispered against his mouth.

He tilted his head. "For what?"

The list was endless, but she smiled and said, "For my life. I love it. And I love you."

"Baby, I'm the one who should be thanking you. I had no life until you blew out that tire."

They kissed until JP groaned. "Seriously, you guys are like watching a Lifetime movie. It's disgusting. I think we would all prefer it if you moved onto porn."

"Um, excuse me?"

All heads whipped in the direction of the unfamiliar voice. Standing near the gate from the front yard was a woman probably in her mid to upper twenties. She had a mop of curly jet-black hair that fell down her back. Chewing on her lower lip, she wrung her hands at her waist.

"I'm so sorry to interrupt, but I'm looking for someone named John Paul."

JP sprung from his chair with a shit-eating grin. "Well, gorgeous, that would be me. What can I do for you? Do you need directions? Maybe to my bedroom?"

Jagger groaned. "Maybe try not to be arrested for harassment before you know what she really wants."

JP laughed. "I'm just fucking with you." He walked around the table and started toward the woman who now looked seconds from bolting.

She took a few steps to the side and grabbed a stroller which none of them had seemed to notice when she first spoke.

"Um, this is—"

Mickie gasped and Keith squeezed her hand so hard, the bones crunched.

"Whoa," JP said with humor in his voice. "Maybe someone else should help you out, here. I'm allergic to anything baby. Jag?"

Jagger rose to his feet with a solemn look on his face. "JP, I think she's trying to tell you something important."

"Oh, okay. Sorry, what's up?" He turned back to the woman who now chewed her bottom lip.

She cleared her throat. "This is your daughter. Her name is Kayla."

"Oh, my God," Mickie whispered. She turned to look at Keith, who wore a stunned expression.

JP laughed. "Okay, guys, very funny." He turned toward where they all sat at the table. "You got me. Who is this, Mickie, a friend of yours?"

Words wouldn't come so Mickie just shook her head.

"I'm serious," the woman said so low she could barely be heard. "She's your daughter. Her mother, Mary Anne met you at a concert about a year and a half ago. She was my best friend."

"Was?" JP croaked. His voice didn't sound like him at all.

"Sh-she's no longer living," the woman said as she swiped at a tear. "There's a letter for you in the diaper bag."

"I'm sorry," JP said, shaking his head as he started to back away. "This can't be right. I can't…I've never even held…" He lifted his hands in a helpless gesture that broke Mickie's heart.

She stood. "We'll help you, JP. We're all here to help you with your daughter."

"Holy shit!" A loud clatter followed the expletive. Everyone turned to see Ronnie standing at halfway between the French doors and the outdoor table. She'd dropped the plate with the strawberry shortcake, shattering it. "JP has a kid?"

Mickie met Keith's gaze again. He'd be going into full big brother mode for sure, wanting to protect everyone.

"Hey," she whispered. "We'll get him through it."

He nodded and mouthed, "I love you."

"Love you, too."

And they would get JP through it. She was part of the family now and as long as they stuck together, they'd get through anything.

Thank you so much for reading **FIRST COMES LOATHE**. If you enjoyed it, please consider leaving a review on Amazon or Goodreads.

Other books by Lilly Atlas

* * *

No Prisoners MC

Hook: A No Prisoners Novella
Striker
Jester
Acer
Lucky
Snake

Trident Ink

Escapades

Hell's Handlers MC

Zach
Maverick
Jigsaw
Copper
Rocket
Little Jack
Joy
Screw
Viper
Thunder

Audiobooks

Audio

Join Lilly's mailing list for a **FREE** No Prisoners short story.

www.lillyatlas.com

Facebook

Instagram
TikTok
Twitter

Join my Facebook group, **Lilly's Ladies** for book previews, early cover reveals, contests and more!

Keep reading for a preview of Zach, Book One of the Hell's Handlers MC Series

About the Author

Lilly Atlas is an award-winning contemporary romance author. She's a proud Navy wife and mother of three spunky girls. Every time Lilly downloads a new eBook she expects her Kindle App to tell her it's exhausted and overworked, and to beg for some rest. Thankfully that hasn't happened yet so she can often be found absorbed in a good book.

Zach Preview

Tennessee 2008

It was finally fucking over.

Or maybe it was just beginning.

Either way, years, *years* of busting his ass, taking shit, and being treated like a worthless maggot were finished.

The vote was unanimous.

He was finally a brother.

Well, he was ninety-nine-point-nine percent of the way in. They couldn't just vote him in and chuck him the patch he'd been salivating over for the past two years. No, they had to throw him one last challenge, and a bitch of a test it was.

A branding. The Hell's Handlers Motorcycle Club emblem. On the left forearm. It was as important as the patches on the leather cut each brother wore. So important, if a man was tatted on his left forearm he couldn't even prospect. No, the emblem had to be seared into clean skin, so anyone and everyone would know who belonged to the motorcycle club.

And if being branded wasn't bad enough, there were rules that went along with the barbaric ceremony.

Every brother had to be in attendance. Heckling, ribbing, waiting to see just how much the new member wanted to be a part of the life. Waiting for them to crack.

No screaming.

No tears.

No passing out.

A grunt of pain was allowed, but beyond that, any outward show of weakness would null and void the unanimous vote to end the prospecting period and make him a fully-patched member of the Hell's Handlers MC.

He wouldn't make a peep. They could cut his fucking arm off and beat him with it and Zach still wouldn't utter a sound. That patch was his, and the only way he'd give it up was if some lucky motherfucker managed to pry it from his cold, dead hands. Even then, he'd haunt the bastard and wear the thing as a spirit.

A shrill whistle cut through the raucous laughter and drunken male partying around a huge bonfire. The fire was necessary because the night air was barely butting up against forty degrees. And, of course, the guys made him stand around shirtless while he waited for his fate.

Usually, the sound of fucking made up much of the party's noise, but not tonight. This was just for the men, brothers in all but blood. At least this early part of the night. After Zach got his patch, they'd bring in the club pussy and he'd have his pick of the litter. One, two, hell even three women if he wanted. He'd earned it, watching brother after brother partake in the sweet privilege that was not bestowed on prospects. Club pussy was for patched members only.

And now he was one.

His dick twitched in his pants but died the moment his president spoke. "Okay, fuckers, listen up."

All around him, his soon to be new brothers lowered their drinks and gave their leader, Copper, their full attention. At twenty-nine, Copper was young to be in the role of club president, and since he'd been at it for almost four years, he was officially the youngest leader in the club's near fifty-year history.

"We're just minutes away from welcoming another brother into the club. Shit, Zach's been one of the best prospects we've ever had. Tough as fuckin' nails, pulls more than his own weight, never runs his mouth, loyal." A puff of steam drifted from Copper's mouth as he spoke to the group.

The prez wasn't one to be fucked with. A good few inches over six feet, with a beard the color of a dirty penny, and plenty of hair to match, he was mean as a starving pit-bull. But Copper had the respect of every man in the club. Not just because he held the title of president, but because he'd earned it, dragging the club from the brink of disaster and making it a thriving brotherhood once again.

Zach blew on his hands, trying to infuse some warmth into the frozen digits. Damn, it was colder than a witch's titty and standing around shirtless for the past half hour hadn't helped anything.

"Just one more test of this asshole's strength before he gets to be one of us. Ready, boys?" Copper waved Zach over to the mountain of wood crackling and spitting sparks. Sticking out of the bonfire, a long branding iron roasted away, just waiting to scorch some of Zach's skin.

Shouts of encouragement and a few hecklers betting on how much of a pussy he was and what octave his scream would hit reached him as he made his way to the fire and his waiting president. Careful to keep his expression neutral, Zach drew up next to his prez and paused. Wasn't that the whole point? Act like he wasn't scared. Wasn't about to shit his pants in anticipation of what would probably be the worst physical pain he'd ever experienced.

Fuckin' Copper's facial hair split and his teeth gleamed in the flickering fire. Prez lived for this bull. And if he didn't, he sure acted like he did with that shitty grin of anticipation. "Anything you want to say first?"

Zach shook his head while he bounced on the balls of his feet, hitting his pecs as hard as he could. Maybe if he could get some pain going somewhere else, the burn of the iron wouldn't be so bad.

"Won't work," Copper said, as though reading his mind. "Tried the same thing when I was in your spot. Ain't nothing gonna make this shit any better." He bent and retrieved a bottle from next to his foot. Zach had no idea what was in it, moonshine probably. "You know the drill. Bottle in your left hand. Ten seconds to drink as much as you can. Hold your arm out straight. I'll mark ya. No dropping the bottle. No spilling. No screaming. No puking. Stay on your feet for two whole minutes. Then you're a fuckin' brother."

Zach nodded. His chest rose and fell in a rapid rhythm as his breathing increased and the blood raced through his veins. After blowing out a breath, he grabbed the bottle and brought it to his lips, tilting his head back and opening his throat as much as he could.

Some of the nastiest hooch he'd ever tasted flooded his mouth and streamed down his throat, burning a path to his stomach. Fitting really, since he was about to be burned all to a crisp anyway. Somewhere in the distance, he could hear his soon to be brothers whooping like a horde of wild baboons, but he managed to drown out most of the noise. All but the sound of Copper counting down from ten.

"Three…two…one…arm!"

Zach tore the bottle from his lips and extended his arm. Unable to look away, he stared in fascinated horror as the glowing end of the iron made contact with the thin skin of his forearm. There was a fraction of a second where his eyes registered the flesh-to-iron connection, but the pain hadn't yet reached his brain.

And then it did.

All-consuming, searing pain like he'd never experienced fired through his nerve endings. Though the spot being branded was no bigger than a silver dollar, agony seemed to encompass his entire being until he couldn't recognize where it originated from. Then there was the audible singe accompanied by the stench of melting flesh. He wasn't expecting that.

Blinding pain was a phrase he'd heard before, but in that moment, he lived it. Darkness clouded his vision, and he slammed his knees back, determined not to succumb to the blissful oblivion that hovered just out of reach.

All around him, men screamed and hollered, but he couldn't make out their cries over the rushing in his ears. Nostrils flaring with each forceful inhalation and exhalation, he mashed his teeth together, probably pulverizing the enamel, as he fought to remain conscious.

Then, the nausea hit. Instead of helping to lessen the pain, the damn moonshine sloshed in his gut and started a trip back up his esophagus, just as disgusting the second time around.

His eyes locked with Copper's. The grinning bastard was definitely enjoying it. All the more motivation to remain standing, quiet, and avoid vomiting the moonshine all over.

Copper pulled the iron away and tossed it to the ground, but it did nothing to diminish the agony. After what seemed like an eternity, Copper pulled his gaze away and checked his watch. Seconds ticked by slower than the thickest motor oil dripping from an engine. Finally, he looked at Zach again and this time his smile was genuine, welcoming. "Two minutes, brother."

Brother. Sweeter fucking words had never been spoken.

Copper grabbed him by the elbow and lifted his throbbing arm. The pain was still there, but now the rush of excitement at achieving his two-year long goal overrode the worst of it. That, and the moonshine was kicking in.

With a loud cry of triumph, Copper held up Zach's branded arm. "Say hello to your newest brother, men." Cheers rose up all around.

Zach swayed on his feet as pain and nausea still warred for victory over his consciousness.

Copper whistled, reigning in the crazy. "He's now to be shown the same respect any other brother receives. He's going to make a damn fine addition to the club."

Zach's chest constricted as pride surged.

"Proud of you, brother," Copper said, for Zach's ears only. "You were one hell of a prospect, and you'll be one hell of an addition to the club."

"Thanks, Prez."

Raising his voice again, Copper turned to the rowdy crowd. "Now someone get Zach a beer and some pussy. The man's waited long enough."

They wouldn't be giving him any pain medication for the burn, but losing his dick in a club girl should take care of the last of the discomfort.

Brothers converged on him from all angles, slapping his back and welcoming him. Not only would the moment be burned into his skin forever, but it was seared into his brain as well.

Best night of his life.

He was in.

Now it was time to set his sights on an executive position.

Enforcer would do quite nicely.

Made in the USA
Middletown, DE
14 July 2021